IT IS TWO HUNDRED MILES
FROM MEXICO TO THE COWDEN RANGE.
TWO HUNDRED MILES OF WAR AND BLOOD.

BEN COWDEN: The tall, young, dark-headed horseman let his heart carry him away—right into a war engineered by Duncan Vincent and his hired guns.

EILEEN COWDEN: She was the workhorse of the Cowden women. What the Cowden men couldn't see was how beautiful she really was, and how her heart was aching.

A. B. COWDEN: The patriarch of the Cowdens was still recovering from a beating one of Vincent's men gave him in the fall. But the man who did the beating was dead—by a blast from A.B.'s shotgun.

JACK ODOMS: The tall, silver-haired former Texas Ranger craved the respectability of money and power. Getting it meant making war, and making war would be a pleasure.

COLONEL GABRIEL KOSTERLINKSKY: He was in business with the Duncan Vincent faction and liked the money Vincent gave him—liked it enough to kill again and again.

Bantam Books by J.P.S. Brown
Ask your bookseller for the books you have missed

THE ARIZONA SAGA:
Book One—The Blooded Stock
Book Two—The Horseman
Book Three—Ladino

THE OUTFIT

THE ARIZONA SAGA, BOOK III

LADINO

J. P. S. Brown

BANTAM BOOKS

NEW YORK · TORONTO · LONDON · SYDNEY · AUCKLAND

LADINO

A Bantam Domain Book / May 1991

DOMAIN and the portrayal of a boxed "d" are trademarks of Bantam Books, a
division of Bantam Doubleday Dell Publishing Group, Inc.

ISBN 0-553-28979-9

Published simultaneously in the United States and Canada

Bantam Books are published by Bantam Books, a division of Bantam Doubleday
Dell Publishing Group, Inc. Its trademark, consisting of the words "Bantam
Books" and the portrayal of a rooster, is Registered in U.S. Patent and
Trademark Office and in other countries. Marca Registrada. Bantam Books, 666
Fifth Avenue, New York, New York 10103.

For Viv,

maestro of good style, good horses, and good times.

CHAPTER 1

In southern Arizona mountain country lived a wild man named Ben Cowden. Everybody wanted to tame him. Even his sisters wanted him tamed, and they were almost as wild as he. He was wild, but good people loved him because he was a gentle man from gentle people.

He had been pushed to wildness. People were trying to take away his father's land and livestock. The Cowdens were husbandmen in a range war.

Ben Cowden's two brothers were like him. They wanted to be gentlemen, but this did not work well. A syndicate of New York oil, railroad, and mining interests was trying to eliminate them.

Ben was twenty-one, the oldest of the three brothers; Les a year and a half younger; Mark two years younger than Les. On a day in early December 1885 they were moving cattle across a range called the Buena Vista on the Santa Cruz River near the Mexican border. The country was in a drouth, and their cattle and the cattle of other ranchers who shared that range were dying. The brothers worked the country a quarter mile apart, gathering the weak cattle and driving them south toward the headquarters of the María Macarena ranch in Sonora, all the cattle

of the outfits who shared that range with the Cowdens—
the Vincents, Romeros, Salazars, and Eliases.

Mark was behind the drive, leading a packhorse and
letting the cattle drift, Ben and Les throwing cattle to him
from the flanks. The pace was slow, for the cattle were
weak and had a long way to go. The brothers hoped to
reach a camp called La Acequia before dark, and the sun
was just coming up.

Ben was riding a stocky floppy-eared sorrel he called
Topo, Gopher. On a steep slope, he rode onto a two-year-
old maverick bull. The animal was lying so still in a cedar
thicket that Ben almost rode by without seeing him.
Cattle did not jump and run away at the sight of a rider or
move much at all that December. When they found
something to eat, they tried to stay until it was all gone.
The brown-and-white maverick reverted to his calfhood
and lay as still and flat as he could, his chin on the ground,
his tail tucked alongside him. He did not twitch an ear or
blink an eye.

Ben took stock of him. His backbone did not stick out.
His hair was bright and slick. He was doing better than
the other cattle. He must have found a high lonesome
place with enough feed to keep himself healthy, then got
lonesome and decided to come down and look for company.

The bull's head was turned away from Ben. Ben rode
across his front, and he lowered his long white eyelashes
as Ben rode past. His horns were long, black at the tips.
He was a *granizo*, his dark brown and merle coat studded
with small white spots like hailstones. He had clean brown
lines under each eye and a rich merle cape over his
shoulders. His sides were white with dark studs, and he
had a wide, solid dark stripe down his backbone.

Ben was recovering from being shot in the back, and
he could not throw any kind of an overhand loop to catch
the bull. He acted as though he did not see the bull, rode
on by, then dropped a loop across his chest to the near
side of his horse and caught the bull cleanly around the
horns. The bull bawled and jumped straight into the air,

his tail winding, and when the reata took hold of him, he bucked and bellered as though a lion were riding him.

Ben laughed and let the reata burn on his horn so the bull would not jerk and tire his horse. He was fifty feet away before Ben tightened the reata and stopped him.

The bull was too fine an animal to be left a maverick. If Ben took him to the María Macarena, someone else might claim him.

He gave Ben his full attention now—backed on the end of the reata, shook his horns and glared at Ben, blew strings of slobbers in the air, and armed himself for a fight.

These cattle fought when they were cornered or caught. The man did not have a great advantage being tied to the bull. His reata would not stand a sudden jerk by a five-hundred-pound animal. He rode toward the bull and invited him to charge. The bull blew out a rush of wind and came on with his head up, looking straight into Ben's eyes. Ben quartered around his side and stayed close to him, not enough to make him whirl in place but enough to keep him running in a close circle, to tire him.

The bull stopped, rested a moment, and charged again. Ben quartered him again, kept him one-quarter off-center all the time so he could not bracket Ben's horse evenly with his horns or reach him with his hooking horn. The bull could not drive his weight toward Ben evenly behind his horns, could not do anything but stretch and reach and hook the air with the horn nearest the horse.

The bull kept resting and charging. After his eighth charge Ben said, "Dammit, ain't you ever going to stop?" but he charged three more times before he finally pulled up and was still, so mad the pupils of his eyes had turned red. When the bull was finally fixed in place and refused to untrack, Ben quartered him again, letting his reata trail along his side and riding around behind him. He held the reata above the bull's hocks and rode around in front of him, wound the reata below the bull's knees, and drove off. The reata tripped under the bull's front legs and looped around the hocks. Down he went with his head trussed to his hind legs. He was so winded, he did not even grunt.

Ben coiled his reata as he rode back to him, tied off when he was close to him, stepped off, and let Topo hold him down. He tied the bull's bottom front and hind legs together, then built a fire to heat his running iron. He carved bullet holes in both ears to earmark him. He whacked off the bottom half of the scrotum and took hold of the first nut. The bull did not stir or make a sound. His eyes were half closed. He was either resting or dying, but Ben did not think he was dying because his breathing was subsiding and he was calm. Ben sliced down through the outer skin on the nut until the organ popped out, separated the outer skin from the nut, pushed it high up the cord, and cut the cord where it was thinnest. Granizo bled about forty drops. After all, they were in a drouth.

Ben searched for the other nut. It had run for cover way up in Granizo's belly. Ben pushed gently on his belly to get it down, but he couldn't find it. He knew better than to carve or fumble for it. The nut might have been injured in calfhood and turned into scar tissue, but he saw no sign of that. The nut was hiding, and Ben would not find it that day. Lucky Granizo would remain a bull.

Ben branded him with his own brand, 7X, on the left hip. He went to the cut-off boot-top on the back of his saddle and took out his screw-worm dope, a mixture of chloroform, mescal, and pine tar, and smeared it on the brand and scrotum to keep off the blowflies and their progeny, the screw worm.

He took his reata off the bull, rolled him on his back, and untied him, but held on to the crossed legs. A small dribble of blood, about as much as a double shot, dropped freely out of the scrotum. Good—he probably wouldn't swell, and he was strong enough to fight off the blowflies while the wound dried.

Granizo's tail was still, his eyes closed. He acted dead as a carcass. Ben grabbed a horn and turned his head over so both horns were stuck in the ground and his clean white throat and a mole on his jaw were bare to the whole world, and he still did did not resist.

"Are you alive, Granizo?" Ben asked. He knew from long, long experience that he better not believe this bull was dead after eleven charges and a good rest. He let go of the legs and stepped up on Topo almost before they settled to the ground. Granizo's horns were still stuck in the ground, his head upside down, his body on its side.

"Well, you might as well get up. I'm going to leave you here anyway," Ben said. "I'm not going to take you into a roundup so my neighbors can see you fresh-branded. You're strong enough to stay out here until next year."

Ben rode Topo close to the bull and whacked the root of his tail with the reata.

No response.

Ben snagged Granizo's nose in the loop of his reata and rolled his horns out of the dirt so he could raise his head. The head flopped on the ground as though it had been cut off and dropped on a slaughterhouse floor.

Ben started to ride away. All of a sudden the bull's eyes glared open, and the horns raised up. The bull speared toward Topo quick as a lizard. He scraped Topo's butt with the tips of both horns before Ben could spur the horse away. Topo bucked and kicked at the bull and stampeded off the hill.

Ben stopped Topo at the bottom and looked back. Granizo was silhouetted on top of the hill with his head high and the sun at his back. He tossed his horns as if to say "You hurt me. Don't come back here again because I'll be ready for you."

Ben dismounted and looked at the scrapes on Topo's butt. Topo rolled an eye at him as if to ask "Is it very bad?"

Ben laughed. "We've damn well been put to flight, Topito, but you'll be all right. That's the cheapest lesson you'll ever learn. Now for the rest of your life you'll know what a bull's horns can do, and I bet you never let them get that close again."

Ben mounted and admired Granizo a moment longer. He thought, Now you've done it, Cowden. That gentleman'll be a lot harder to catch next time. He's smart as a jaguar, and now he's been turned loose after being trussed up, knifed, and hurt. From now on, he'll be hard to see, let alone catch. Sure as hell, he'll become another famous *ladino* and give us cowboys lots of trouble. Before his horns ever get stuck in the dirt again, he'll be called El Ladino Granizo and be known to every *vaquero* in this country. I'll bet a new hat on that. Now, he'll be a ladino just like me, running from the law and getting smarter about it every day.

The brothers penned the cattle at La Acequia at twilight and left them with vaqueros who had worked the roundup from other sides. When they reached the headquarters of the María Macarena ranch long after dark, they could see no light in the main house. They rode behind the house and were heartened by the sight of a fire in front of Chapito Cano's house. Chapito was the ranch's *mayordomo.* They sat their horses in the firelight. Everyone on the place had already gone to bed.

"Chapito-o-o," Ben growled in a low voice.

"*Et,*" shouted Chapito as he awakened. After a while he came to the door, pulling on his pants, and recognized the three horsemen. "*Dios mío,* the fire, the plague, and the flood have arrived, and the drouth is already with us. Get down from there, horsemen." He turned back over his shoulder. "Luz, send the boy to wake up the main house. The horsemen are here."

People began to stir, and a lamp was lit in Chapito's house. A sleepy-headed boy came out barefoot, skirted the fire and the horsemen, and headed for the main house. Ben recognized Pepe, Don Juan Pedro Elias's grandson. The boy had seen his father and uncle killed by Apaches in June of that year at La Acequia.

The brothers followed Chapito to a shed row where they unsaddled, fed, and stabled their horses. They unsheathed their rifles, took blanket rolls off their saddles, and followed him toward the main house. They met Pepe as he was returning.

"*Que hubole, Pepito?*" Ben said. "How's my friend?"

The boy stopped and shook Ben's hand, then Les's and Mark's, and looked them in the eye.

"You must be working full-time as a vaquero now," Ben said. "Is that why you're living with Chapo?"

"Yes," the boy said.

"Are you making a hand?"

"*Sa-a-abe?* Who knows?"

"He's making a top hand," Chapito said.

"I better go sleep now," the boy said.

"Correct."

"*Buena noche.*"

"*Buena noche,*" the brothers said.

The boy hurried on.

"He's young to wean, but I know he's a good vaquero," Les said. "Can you imagine us weaning our little sister Paula Mary and putting her to work at that age?"

"That is absolutely beyond my imagination," Mark said.

"That's not it," Chapito said as he led the way toward the back door of the main house. "He's not living with me by choice."

"How could that be?" Les said. "You mean he's been run out of the house?"

"You'll see."

The brothers followed Chapito through the back door and a long, narrow passageway to the open patio in the center of the house. The house was built like a fort. The front and back doors were its most vulnerable places. The back door was reinforced by iron straps and studs. The front entrance was wide enough to accommodate a wagon and team, but two iron gates and an iron-reinforced door were locked across it at night or when the hacienda was under siege.

Margarita, the person Ben most wanted to see, crossed the patio to meet them. She was a good friend of Ben's, but when he stepped forward to see it in her eyes, she turned her cheek to him and went on to shake hands with his brothers. Ben thought Margarita was the most beautiful woman he had ever seen, but that night she looked old and dry. Her hair had been cut short, and she looked used and sad.

Margarita was Pepe's mother. She had been in mourning since June, but Ben had seen her enjoy a visit to Tombstone on the sixteenth of September. Though still wearing her widow's weeds, she had been vibrant, pretty, and coquettish. Later, when Ben was laid up at home with his wound, she and her father, Don Juan Pedro, came to see him, and she, by god, flirted with Ben. He could not understand why she looked so mournful now.

"Please take your *mochilas* to the room you always use and then seat yourselves in the dining room. I'll bring you supper," she said and went away to the kitchen. The brothers did as they were told, ducking their heads when they passed through the door to their room. A lamp was already lit there, and they laid their blanket rolls down and drank water from clay pitchers and cups.

Chapito excused himself and went home. The brothers washed at a basin on the patio and trooped into the dining room. Ben went into the kitchen, but Margarita kept her back to him.

"Margarita, what happened to your hair?" Ben asked.

"I had a fever and it fell out."

"When were you sick? I didn't know."

"Last month." She turned with a trace of the fresh smile Ben remembered. "I think it's coming back. Do you think so? Please say you do."

"Of course it is. It is only curious-looking, not unattractive."

"Thank you for that."

"You must have been very sick."

"I almost died."

"Is that why Pepito is living with the Canos?"

"Oh, yes."

"What caused your fever?"

"I got married."

"You got *married*? Who did you marry, an ogre?"

"He's not so bad. Yes he is. He's old, stern, and cruel, and believes the touch of a woman is evil."

Ben decided he might as well believe what he heard, but it sure was not any of his business. He straightened in the doorway and saw a tall figure standing in the shadows of the patio. The figure stepped forward into the light, a long, bony white man in trousers and undershirt. His hands were huge and brown on thick-boned wrists. His big feet were bare under his trouser cuffs. His long forehead was white, his big nose burned red, his small close-set blue eyes round and staring. Ben stared back.

Margarita flinched as though popped by a whip.

"What is this man here for?" Odoms demanded.

"For his supper. For the roundup. Why would anyone visit here these days except to work?" Margarita said.

Odoms looked into the dining room at Les and Mark, then looked closely into Ben's face. "You're Ben Cowden?"

"*A sus ordenes, señor*. At your service."

"Yeah, you'll think 'at my service.'" The man was a giant, mostly bone, very little flesh and blood.

Ben could see Margarita was afraid of him. She kept her mouth so tightly closed that the corners turned down. She owned the darkest brown eyes Ben had ever seen, so dark the pupils could not be seen unless she was out in the sun. They were wide open with fear now.

"I'm Jack Odoms of the Texas Rangers," the man said.

"Never heard of you," Ben said.

"Well, so you'll know, I've been hired by the Vincents and the Pima County Livestock Association to police this area against cowthieves. That's my wife there, fixing your supper. Keep in mind, she's mine, and I want her back as soon as you've been fed." Odoms turned and walked hugely and soundlessly away, his big hands swinging with their palms toward Ben, the soles of his big feet showing white in the kitchen light.

Margarita sat at the table while the brothers ate supper. Les and Mark had not heard what she said about her marriage. She did not talk about Odoms again, and the longer she sat with the brothers, the more she brightened up. By the time the meal was over, she was their friend Margarita again. The last time Ben had seen her, she had given him a long, wet, warm kiss and then wiggled her hips when she left the room to make him feel good.

When his brothers went on to bed, Ben stayed to help Margarita clear the dishes off the table. As he stood up from his chair, he bumped her accidentally with his hip. Then he reached for a dish and accidentally grabbed her hand. "*Ah, perdón,*" he said when she recoiled.

She turned and found something to do away from him and seemed not to appreciate being touched.

"Sorry, I almost knocked you down," he said.

With a serious face and at arm's length, Margarita handed him a stack of dishes.

"Excuse me, Margarita. I'm too accustomed to my sisters. We're always bumping and grabbing each other."

"Don't worry."

"You sure have changed."

"In what way?"

"You remember how we used to dance at the fiestas, how close we used to get when we were having fun?"

"I'm married now."

"You were married to Pepe's father, the musician, then."

"Ah, but Pepe's father was not a Texas Ranger. Pepe's father handled a woman on a featherweight rein."

"And this one?"

"*A golpes.* By blows. *A puñaladas.* With his fists. And sometimes at the point of a pistol, and sometimes even with the blows of a pistol.

"He pistol-whips you?"

"Sometimes, but only after he has come to the fresh conclusion that I am a whore and a slut."

Ben had never in his life heard a woman say those words, not even the Campana girls in Santa Cruz who entertained men in their home. *He* never said those words. He could not imagine anyone deserving to be called that. He suddenly realized he was in the wrong place at the wrong time, not a situation to which any cowpuncher aspired.

"How nice it would be to be touched again," Margarita said. "I want to be touched and rubbed and kissed again. Let me tell you, Ben, if a woman can't look forward to that, her life is over."

"Ah, Margarita." Ben sighed. He had no idea how the woman could resolve her problem.

"You, Ben. Will you be my lover? I've always loved you."

"But you're married, Margarita, and I'm engaged to Maudy Jane Pendleton. What would you do with Maudy and your husband?"

"I told you, I need to be touched. Don't you?"

"Everybody needs that."

"Just think about it, won't you?"

In all truth, what answer could a gentleman give? "Yes, I will," he said.

"That's all I'm asking you to do."

Ben looked up and saw that Les and Mark had turned back to wait for him. Their faces were stern and angry. He knew they could not have heard what he and Margarita said, but they could guess the nature of it and were giving him identically disapproving looks.

CHAPTER 2

The people who occupied the main house of the María Macarena ranch usually slept late when they did not have pressing work to do. The cattle the Cowden brothers had brought to the roundup were the last remnants of stock on the Buena Vista range. The work was over. Ben's brothers were slumbering when he got up, washed his face and combed his hair, dressed, and walked out onto the patio. He heard someone at work in the kitchen and went to see if the coffee was hot.

Margarita was in the kitchen. Her face was soft again, almost happy when she looked up at Ben and invited him to sit at the table. Their eyes met pleasurably. He did not want to give her a chance to start up about wanting to be touched, so he excused himself and went back out to the patio.

He walked out the back door and squatted against the east wall to warm himself as the December sun came up. An old game rooster was already there with four young hens. The rooster's body was covered by a shiny blue-and-white armor with a copper glint over the blue that showed his mettle. His head and cape still showed some blond feathers, but most of them had turned gray. His tail feathers curved up behind him, heavy and smooth as blue tempered steel. He was in fine condition and was absolutely satisfied with himself.

One of the hens decided she needed the rooster's attention, so she fluttered up and pecked him softly on the face. He did not pay attention. Impatiently, she rubbed her bill against his. He turned away and pecked at the ground without touching it, feigning disinterest. She pecked him lightly in the middle of the back, and he turned to face her. She liked that, so she pecked him there again and began teasing him and making him pirouette. Each time he pivoted, though, he did so with great care in setting down his spurs and for the dignity of his carriage.

All this time he kept an eye on Ben. Suddenly he growled and chuckled, and shouldered the little hen roughly aside, then again gently. She leaned against him. He fixed her in place with his beak, stepped upon her, crushed her under his rough feet so that her beak doubled over against the ground, and quickly bred her.

The rooster slowly stepped away, accommodating his spurs as he did. He raised his wings, fanned the dust away, threw back his head, and gave voice to all the power in his heart. The little hen gathered herself lightly and strolled over to join her sisters.

Ben thought, That's the question between me and Margarita, I guess. It's a question of responsibility. Should a rooster live up to his responsibilities with dignity, or should he be weak and deny them? He laughed at himself.

Margarita came around the corner of the house, smiling, and their eyes met again. "Ah, I've found you. Come for your *desayuno*, your breakfast, Ben."

He rose and waited for her to start back ahead of him, but she stopped and held out her hand. "Come on," she said. He took the tip of her little finger. She let him have it until she rounded the corner of the house, then took it away.

He fell in step with Les and Mark as they came out of the room. Odoms nodded vaguely at them from the head of the table when they said good morning. The brothers were laughing when they walked in the room, but seeing

Odoms in the light of day subdued them, and they took their places in silence. Odoms's white hair was neatly combed, and he was freshly shaved. He wore a spotless white shirt, a black tie adorning his long neck. His big workman's hands looked clean and soft, as though they did not know hard work. His cuffs were long enough to cover his wrists and fastened by golden links.

Odoms cleared his throat. "Before you boys take another meal in this house, I want to tell you something," he said. "I've been hired and have been empowered to put an end to you three and all the rest of the cowthieves in this region. Make no mistake about me. I'll do it because I'm good at it.

"I cleaned all the renegades and cowthieves out of three Texas counties. Every man went to trial, so that should tell you I'm not a killer. I am a just man. You will go through so much humiliation at your trials that before I'm through with you, you'll wish I'd killed you when I caught you.

"I brought with me five Texans who are not as just as I. Woe to the young man they catch doing wrong when I'm not with them. They, like me, hate Meskins, half-breed Meskins, Indians, half-breed Indians, Negroes, bandits, cowthieves, harlots, burros, pigs, cowboys, vaqueros, and dogs. We are all from sheep and goat country, and we have no use for cows either. We will kill cattle we catch trespassing on Duncan Vincent's VO range.

"I'm not telling you to mend your ways. You will not escape going to jail and the gallows in retribution for the laws you've broken. You've already committed the sins that will condemn you. I won't arrest you now and take you to Prescott for trial because you enjoy my father-in-law's hospitality. I've married into this family and must abide by its rules.

"I'm going to be kind enough to warn you, however, that five cowards are waiting for you to leave this ranch so they can kill you. They are wolves. They camp out of sight every night. Most of the time *I* can't even find them, so I can't be with them *all* the time, and they are as liable to snipe you from behind a rock as knife you at a waterhole. They're too awful for me to control, but I couldn't get any gentlemen to take this job, and didn't look for any.

"Another thing. The American side of the Buena Vista belongs to Duncan Vincent now. He is in Hermosillo with Juan Pedro Elias, my wife's father, drawing up the papers. I don't know how you're going to do it if you're dead or in jail, but you will remove all your livestock from the Buena Vista and María Macarena ranges. Maybe you can get the Salazars and Romeros to move them for you before my Texans kill them all.

"Now, you're free to go. Nobody will bother you until you cross the U.S. border. You're safe here, but you can't stay. We don't allow cattle thieves on this ranch."

Margarita came in with a pot of coffee, a plate of hot tortillas wrapped in a clean dishcloth, and a bowl of butter.

Les poured coffee for his brothers, generously sugared his own, uncovered a steamy tortilla, buttered it, and offered it to Odoms. "Want a hot torte, Mr. Odoms?"

"It's *Captain* Odoms. I asked you to leave."

"No? Tortillas too 'Meskin' for you?"

Margarita came back with two plates of beefsteak, beans, potatoes, and scrambled eggs. She placed one in front of Odoms and looked up to see where to put the other. Les waved his table knife. "Me," he said.

Odoms stood up and left the table. Mark reached over and took his plate. Margarita brought a plate for Ben and one for herself, sat down with them, and asked about their father, mother, and sisters in turn.

"And you, Mark, how is your *novia*, your fiancée, and when are you getting married?"

Mark did not blush or act embarrassed. He looked deeply into Margarita's eyes because they invited him there. "She's not my fiancée, and I don't have any plans to marry anybody."

"Why do you wait? How can you stand to live without a woman, a young handsome man like you? Are you going to grow old like your brothers before you start looking for a woman to hold? Look at Les, your brother. All he wants to do is fight. Look at your brother Ben. He drives himself protecting his cows so much he has no time for *el amor*. Are you going to be that way too?"

"I don't want to get married, yet. I haven't had any fun hardly at all. I want to play some fiddle music and dance a little first."

"Yeah, Margarita, why didn't you invite us to your wedding?" Les asked.

"It was a sad thing. We were married in the civil offices in Santa Cruz by Kosterlinsky, then we sneaked out of town escorted by his *Rurales*. We came right back here, and Odoms went off with Kosterlinsky to track Yaquis, or something."

"You're not really married, then."

"Oh, he came back and made sure no one could say we were not married. He stepped on me at the point of a knife, took a grip on my head, and exercised his rights."

"That's awful," Les said, embarrassed.

"And you, Les, how do you treat your women?"

"Good. Why wouldn't I? I like women."

"I know two or three in Santa Cruz who like you."

"Yeah? Who?"

"Josefa and Cloty Campana are two."

Les blushed. "They were my friends. Just friends. I don't know how they would receive me now."

"You mean after you shot up their customers?"

"No. Well . . . yeah."

"Les, handsome as you are, enjoying the reputation you do, you would be very well received anywhere in Sonora, as well received as you are by me."

"What day are we going to Hermosillo, Margarita?" Ben asked. "I promised Don Juan Pedro I'd be there before the Feast of Guadalupe to pay him and get the deed to the Cibuta ranch."

"Vibora, the rattlesnake, and I will board the train for Hermosillo at Cibuta the day after tomorrow. Please, please, please be on that train with me, Ben. I don't want to ride all that way alone with him."

"Vibora? Who's Vibora?" Les asked.

"Jack Odoms, who else?" Margarita laughed. "Doesn't he remind you of a rattlesnake, one of those great big ones whose rattles have turned black? The rattles are the soul of the snake, are they not?"

The brothers smiled. He did look like one. He moved like one too.

"Did you name him that?" Mark asked.

"No-o-o. He brought that name from Texas."

"We've never heard of him. How could he woo and marry the prettiest girl in Sonora in less than a month?" Ben asked.

At the beginning of the meal, Mark and Les had also been given a nice taste of the look in Margarita's eyes. Her dark approving gaze drew at each brother's heart and made him believe she would never give it to anyone else. Now they wanted more, but they were not getting it because Ben was being given it all. Les and Mark were privately disappointed. Each thought he had seen the look of his first passion. Now they were amazed at the intensity of the looks that passed between Ben and Margarita.

"My marriage to Jack Odoms is the result of my own weakness and a bargain made between Kosterlinsky and my father."

"Explain," Ben said.

"I just did. A bargain is a bargain, is it not? Who cares? The world won't come to an end." Margarita began gathering the dishes. "Now get going, so I can take care of my house, but don't leave without saying good-bye."

The brothers gathered their mochilas and went out to the stables. Odoms was standing in the center of a corral holding a hardwood *vara*, a yard-long stick carved from a *guasima* tree. The tree grew mostly in more southern climates, and a guasima vara was the favorite whip of some horsemen. Ben could tell the vara was a favorite tool of Odoms's by the way he held and handled it. He had polished it smooth and shiny with his hands. And at no time since the arrival of the brothers had English been spoken. Odoms spoke flawless Spanish. To Ben all this

was good evidence that Odoms knew his way around
Mexico and Mexicans, as a lot of Texans did.

The brothers stopped in an alley adjoining the corral
and leaned against the fence to watch Odoms at work.
Chapito Cano was gypping an Arabian studhorse in the
center of the corral. The stud frisked and bucked, loath to
line out and begin his exercise. Chapito was trying to
make him circle on a reata, the coils of the reata looped
over his arm.

"Make him line out and circle you, you *pinchi mayor-
domo*," Odoms boomed, emphasizing the title to belittle
Chapito. "MAYORDOOOMO. What a fine, capable
MAYORDOOOMO you are."

Chapito did not look at him. He sweated with stress.
He reached down and threw a pebble at the stud to make
him go, but he did it in such a halfhearted manner that his
aim went bad and the pebble bounced off the stud's
forehead.

"Idiot!" Odoms growled. "Are you trying to put his eye
out? Don't you know better than to throw rocks at a
valuable animal? How long have you been MAYOR-
DOOOMO on this ranch? No wonder Elias has to sell his
land. One more year of management by a *pelado* like you
and we'll all have to find work as bean pickers. *This* is the
way to make a horse line out."

As the stud pranced by, Odoms raised the vara over
his head, took two long steps to get in range, and brought
it whizzing down. "*Toma, cabrón,* take that!" he said, and
the vara loosed hair off the stud's backside in a tuft that
floated to the ground as he bolted away.

Odoms threw his head back with laughter. Chapito
was in trouble, though. The reata half-hitched on his
wrist, and he was jerked off his feet. The stud hurtled into
the gate and knocked it open, turned down the fence, and
sold out down the alley past the brothers. Chapito was
dragged headfirst toward the gatepost. As the stud stampeded by, Les's knife appeared in his hand. He threw his
left arm over the rope and cut the reata as it burned across
the breast of his jacket. The stud kept running across a flat

toward the Santa Cruz River and plunged out of sight in a willow thicket.

Les helped Chapito to his feet. The horse had dragged him on his face. Dirt was ingrained in his face, and his mouth was full of dirty blood.

Odoms walked past Les into the alley and whipped his leg with the vara. He looked down the alley after the stud, shook his head, and turned back to Chapito. "Go get him," he ordered.

Chapito forgot about himself and snapped to attention. Les rolled up Chapito's shirtsleeve and examined the reata burn. Chapito tried to free his arm so he could hurry and do Odoms's bidding, but Les would not relinquish it.

Odoms stepped up and tapped Les's back with the tip of the vara. "Let him go," he said.

Les paid no attention.

Odoms stepped closer, leaned over so his face was close to Les's, and said, "I said, let him go." Then he whacked Les's cracker butt. Les did not have any butt at all, and his trousers were loose enough to pad him with air and material, but he reacted as though it was big and fat and tender. *Splat* went his fist against Odoms's big nose. Then, *splat, splat, splat* on the same end of the big nose before Odoms spread himself on the ground on his back. Anyone might have thought Les would stop at that and have mercy, but he stomped the nose twice with his boot-heel before Ben and Mark could drag him away, throw him down, and sit on him.

Chapito spat on his neckerchief, wiped dirt out of one eye, looked down into Odoms's face with the other eye, and said, "He looks dead."

"What makes you think so?" Mark said.

"The blood is flooding his face, and he's not even quivering. No, I'm sure of it. He's dead. See, his eyes are open and glazed. Every dead man I ever saw had eyes like that."

"He'd goddam better be dead if he knows what's good for him," Les shouted. "I'm not through with him."

"To avoid trouble, I think we better say the stud

kicked him. He bent over to examine the development of the balls the stud has been cultivating. The stud took offence, and kicked off his nose."

People who had come out to watch the horse run away hurried toward the corral. Odoms's leg jerked, and his body trembled. He sighed.

"*Ah, vida bonita*, pretty life, returns. Welcome, little quiver, the first and last sure sign of life," Chapito said. He knelt beside Odoms and wiped the blood away from his nose and mouth so he could breathe.

The brothers released Les. Odoms's nose was split down the middle and flattened against his face. "Maybe he'll be better-looking now," Les said.

Doña Luz, Chapito's wife, came up and surveyed the damaged Texan. "*Ai, pobrecito*," she said, and went back to her house.

Other people gathered in the narrow alley, and Doña Luz had to push her way through when she came back with a pan of warm water and clean rags. Another woman stood by with the water while she knelt and cleaned the blood off Odoms's face. Chapito handed her his jacket, and she put it under Odoms's head. Chapito picked up Odoms's hat.

The Cowden brothers went to the stable to saddle their horses. Margarita hurried past them without saying anything to them or glancing their way.

After all, he's her husband, Ben thought. She's a coquette with all men, but her life is with her husband. That's only right. It's their business how they live, how they get along when they're alone, and they don't have to explain themselves to anybody when they help each other.

Ben was ready to leave first. He watched the people trying to help Odoms. They ought to cut his throat, he thought. Odoms would make a mess of the María Macarena. Don Juan Pedro couldn't sell any part of the American side of the Buena Vista to Duncan Vincent. He'd lost title to it in the Gadsden Purchase. The legal papers he needed to sell it could never be finalized in

Hermosillo. None of the people who used the Buena Vista could claim it. Vincent had been using ten times more land than he had a right to. He justified it by presenting bogus papers to the courts and tying up the titles with litigation.

The brothers mounted and left the Macarena. They were a half a mile out when Pepe caught up with them, riding bareback on a bony little filly. "Don Benjamin, my mother says for you to come back," he said.

"What for?" Ben said.

"Who knows?"

"Is the vibora dead?"

Pepe smiled. "No-o-o, he's wobbling, but he got up and went to the house."

"What does your mother want?"

"She wants to talk to you."

"We'll wait for you at La Acequia," Les said.

Ben rode back with Pepe. The people were all back at work. As Ben dismounted at the stable, Chapito and two other vaqueros drove the stud back into the corral. He pranced around the corral twice with his head up, his tail in a plume. He stopped and snorted his breath in a rush, as though relieved that his lungs had finally been given their fill of air.

Ben put Topo in a stall, hung his bridle outside the gate, and walked toward the house. Margarita came out and met him in a pretty blue dress. Her hair was shining, wet, and curly from being washed, and she was wearing golden earrings.

"No, we're not going to the house," she said. "Come and see my filly."

Ben followed her to another shed row where the stalls were boarded solid, where brood mares and studs were kept in their season. The animals in the stalls could not be seen from outside. Margarita opened a stall door, and Ben followed her inside. Margarita closed the door. The stall was empty, the floor covered with clean wheat straw.

"Where's the filly?" Ben asked.

"This is where I'm going to keep her when you give

her to me," Margarita said. "Odoms likes those Arabs. I want you to give me, or sell me, one of your nice thoroughbred fillies so I can show him the kind of horse we need."

"The first thing Odoms will do is breed her to that Arab stud. He'll keep her bred so you'll never be able to use her."

"Sell me a mare that's already bred, then."

"That will only put you in the horse business. Is that what you want?"

"I want to start my own business so I can cut loose from Odoms and my father. I did not know what it was to be humiliated before Odoms came. He began criticizing me before we even left the civil office as man and wife. For two years I've been running my father's house and much of his business. Odoms comes, and suddenly I'm accused of being stupid, inefficient, and incapable."

Margarita's eyes did not give Ben their usual invitation. Her mouth was turned down. The glimmer of joy that had revived in her face was not there now. Her face was clear, soft, and pretty because she was young and beautiful, but it seemed lifeless, like a mask.

All right, rooster, see what you can do, he told himself, and put his arms around her. She was stiff as a railroad tie, and her lips were cold and bloodless when he kissed her. He hugged her in close and kissed her lips again. They were stiff and unyielding, but she tried to kiss him back, and he felt her warmth through their clothes.

"Thank you," Margarita said. "I had made up my mind, if you did not kiss me, I was through."

The invitation in her eyes had still not returned.

"When can we be together?" Ben asked.

"In Hermosillo, if you want. If you can arrange it to happen."

"I'll make it happen."

"And you'll look after me, protect me?"

"Yes."

"You'll stay by me and won't die, or get killed, or abandon me in any other way?"

"Yes."

"You'll always be my friend?"

"We've been friends always, and that won't change. I'll never quit you, no matter what happens."

"Let's do it, then. We'll be together in Hermosillo?"

"Yes."

CHAPTER 3

The Cowden brothers helped the vaqueros work the cattle at La Acequia. The old culled bulls and cows would be shipped by rail for slaughter to Hermosillo. The weaned calves were to be kept for a while in a fenced pasture at La Acequia. The pasture stretched into the San Bernardino Mountains. The breeding stock would be driven back across the border to the foothills of the Patagonia Mountains and put on the last remnant of good feed.

The brothers worked hard all afternoon and knew they were being watched by Odoms's Livestock Association rangers. They did not spare their horses because they wanted the rangers to think they would have to turn them out and rest at La Acequia that night. They watched the high ground of the San Bernardinos and saw movement on a high rock by a place called Lopez Springs. In the late afternoon they saw the sun's reflection off the watchers' spyglass, sometimes for several seconds at a time.

Mark helped hold the herd while cattle were being culled and vented. The vaquero on his left was Tomás Romero, the patriarch of the Romero clan of Santa Cruz. On his right, was Edmundo Romero, Tomás's son. The Romeros hated Duncan Vincent. Vincent's henchmen had murdered Edmundo's brother Hector only a few months ago.

During a lull in the work when the herd was quiet, Mark rode over to speak with Don Tomás. "Who is up at Lopez Springs, Don Tomás? Have you seen him?"

"Yes, Marcos, I see his glass. He shows it so often, he must be trying to signal us, no?" Don Tomás laughed gruffly. "He's one of your friend Vincent's *gendarmería*."

"You know about Vincent's Texans?"

"Sure I do. They loafed around Santa Cruz for weeks waiting for Kosterlinsky to fix their *poder*, the papers that allow them to act as livestock constables in Mexico."

"How can they work as police in Mexico?"

"Kosterlinsky obtained a special edict from Don Porfirio Díaz giving that long gringo they call Vibora the power to regulate the movement of cattle this side of the border."

"What do you know about Odoms, the one they call Vibora?"

"*Es muy presumido*. He presumes himself to be important, and he keeps presuming until weaklings believe it and bow to him."

"How did you get to know him?"

"When I heard he was partnering with Kosterlinsky, I had my family watch him and his thugs while they were quartered in the cavalry *cuartel* in Santa Cruz. Edmundo and his oldest son worked with the crew building the garrison. Two weeks ago, Duncan Vincent came to visit the Texans. Then, last week, Edmundo and I rode the fence on this pasture to make sure it would hold the weaner calves. We stumbled onto their camp on the other side of the mountain."

"Did you talk to them?"

"Yes. They ride good horses, and they did not offer us coffee. They're pure Texan and don't like Mexicans."

"Did anyone else in Santa Cruz find out anything about them—the bartenders, the grocers, the girls?"

"They speak Spanish perfectly, but they don't like Mexicans."

"Vincent is supposed to be in New York."

"He and his wife returned to the VO ranch almost three weeks ago, and now he's in Hermosillo with Don Juan Pedro Elias. You know, my daughter Jesusita is Mrs. Vincent's maid. She loves Mrs. Vincent, but tells us a lot about old Vincent."

When the work was done, the brothers unsaddled their horses, fed them, and turned them into the weaner pasture with the roundup's *remuda*, horse herd. Sundown was not seen at La Acequia that day. A west wind brought a ceiling of clouds. As the light waned, the wind hooked around and came back from the east, a good sign of rain. Lightning began to play on the San Bernardinos.

The brothers went to their packhorse's load and put on their Saltillo blankets, their yellow oilskin slickers over the blankets. The wool Saltillos had collars in the middle that fit over their heads, wide enough to cover their arms and long enough to cover half their legs front and back. Ben took the saddlebags he had packed for his trip to Hermosillo and rolled his town clothes inside his blanket tarp.

The brothers stopped to say good-bye to the three Salazar brothers as they mounted to go home to Nogales. These three were the same age as the Cowden brothers, lifetime friends. The Cowdens kept looking after them when they rode away. Nowadays, they saw them only during spring and fall roundups. Now they would not even have a chance to visit with them at the cook's fire.

The roundup cook prepared supper at a fire under a *ramada*, arbor, beside the one-room adobe building of the camp. The building was spacious. It had been the headquarters of the María Macarena ranch when Don Juan Pedro Elias's great-grandfather first ran cattle on the Buena Vista. The ramada had been burned at least ten times by Apaches, but the building was stout and in good repair.

The crew settled around the fire under the ramada for supper as a steady drizzle began to fall.

"Marcos, your friends the little viboras will come down now that the darkness and rain obscures them," Don

Tomás said. "They might even get close enough to hear what you say."

"I know it," Mark said. "I'm not worried. I sleep well since we killed the old Yawner."

"*Apache.*" Edmundo Romero spat. "Thank God the butcher is dead."

"Maybe he's not dead," Don Tomás said. Everybody had been looking straight into the fire. Now everybody looked up and felt as though they were too near the fire, too much in the light, too close together, easy targets. Don Tomás laughed at them.

"I hope to tell you, he's dead," Les said. "Ben was there when Ben Tom, the scout, administered the coup, weren't you, Ben?"

"I was as close as I am to you."

"Well, you saw him die, didn't you, brother?"

"I've thought a lot about that. I saw the Yawner crawl out of the brush as though his back was broken, and I saw Ben Tom raise his rifle and aim at his head. I turned away then because I didn't want to see what the bullet did. I heard the report of the rifle and thought I heard the sound of the bullet striking the Yawner's skull."

"What's to think about, then? The Yawner's dead. You looked back after he was shot and saw that he was dead, didn't you?"

"No. We had the Apaches on the run, and I was close behind the only one that was getting away. What has worried me since then is that I don't remember seeing the Yawner's body when I came back."

"Did you come back the same way?"

"I came back the exact same way, and I know I passed the spot where I last saw the old devil, but I don't remember seeing his body."

"The soldiers had moved it by then. Don't you remember, they piled them all together?"

"Yes, but I never looked for the Yawner in that pile, did you?"

Les thought a moment. "No, I didn't. That's the real

truth. After you told us the Yawner was dead, everybody believed it."

"We were busy and in a hurry. I did not have time to think about it until I got shot and was laid up at home. I have to admit, I never saw the Yawner's dead body. The last time I saw him, he was alive."

"You suppose he gave us the slip?"

"*Sa-a-abe?* Who knows? If he did, he must be all by himself like an old *solitario,* an old coatamundi who wanders around alone looking for food and shelter without a friend in the world.

"Now, my friends, if everybody will look at the fire a moment, I'll tell you what we're going to do to get away from the Texans," Ben said. "We'll take a whole hour to do it, but after a while I'll go in the house. In a few minutes I would like Edmundo Romero to go and wash his face as though on his way to bed and follow me into the house. He'll put on my hat and slicker, and come back out, smoking my pipe. Mark, wait about twenty minutes, and then you come on, and Tomás Junior can take your place and come out smoking. After Les comes in, old Tomás can take his place. The Romeros are the tallest men here, so they can become the Cowdens and take our places by the fire while we *pelar,* peel away, out the back.

"Ah, I always wondered when you would to try to make a gringo out of me," Don Tomás said.

"While we're leaving out the back, I'd like the three Romeros to go down to the corral and rummage in our pack outfit. We left it down there so we could use it as a diversion. Take your time and speak softly, so the Texans will strain to hear you. There are two quarts of my father's whiskey in our outfit, and you're welcome to it.

"I hope the spies' mouths water when they see you pass the bottle. I want them to forget the house has a back door."

"How are you going to get away without catching your horses?" Don Tomás asked.

"The Salazar brothers are waiting for us on the river."

"If you give us your *permeables*, slickers, you're going to get wet."

"We have our Saltillos. I'll go first."

Ben went in the house. Edmundo waited awhile, then washed his face and hands at a basin in the corner of the ramada and followed. Ben gave him his pipe, hat, and slicker.

Edmundo handed him his old hat that was made of a double layer of woven palm fronds. "I'm sorry, I don't have a better hat, Benjamin," he said.

The hat was heavy and damp with sweat and rain. "It's just right," Ben said.

"I'll take care of your hat."

"You ought to take care of it—it's yours now."

"Only if it fits." Edmundo placed the hat carefully on his head, backwards. Ben turned it around and it fit down over his brow perfectly. "Does it look all right?"

"Perfect."

"Then, thank you,"

"Thank *you*, my friend. Don't make a target of yourself in that slicker. Stay away from the fire."

When the brothers were together in the house, they picked up their gear and went out the back door. Ben took the lead on the trail, his brothers lined out behind him. The Salazars were sitting their horses quietly, away from the river, and the noise of the wind and rain in the big cottonwood, ash, and sycamore trees. In that country people who could not hear footsteps coming did not live long.

Raul Salazar, the oldest, grunted to let the Cowdens know where he was. The Salazars dismounted and held their horses while the Cowdens tied on their blanket rolls.

Raul was a tall gaunt young man. "I don't know about this," he joked softly. "This is my top horse, my best dancer for the fiestas. He dances 'Dos Arbolitos' like a ballerina. When will I get him back?"

"Hah, five minutes after you start out on Topito, you'll hope I never bring him back," Ben said quietly.

"I don't know, all this *running* you'll be doing. My

father told me, 'Never loan your horse, your pistol, or your woman.' You realize what I'm doing for you? My father would say I might as well loan you my woman.'

"I'll make you a promise, Raul," Ben said, mounting. "Since you're being so generous with your horse, I'll never ask for the loan of your woman or your pistol. How's that?"

"*Hecho!* Done!"

As the Cowdens rode away, Raul's youngest brother said, "Maybe we aren't doing right by loaning them our horses. They'll be running a lot with the Texans after them, won't they?"

"Don't ever worry about loaning your horse to those horsemen," Raul said softly. "We're giving them skinnies for healthies now, and when they come back for their horses, we'll be giving them their skinny horses for our healthy horses. They're the horsemen, Paco."

The Cowden brothers hit a high trot on the wide trail used for cattle drives to the railroad pens at Cibuta. The night was dark, but they could see enough to stay on the trail they knew so well. The Salazar horses were small but smooth and comfortable to ride. Ben thought, I've never ridden a Mexican horse that was rough-gaited. They're narrow between a man's legs, too, and that's more comfortable. The Cowdens bred thoroughbred and steeldust horses. Every now and then, the steeldusts produced a short, stocky, muscular, powerful, but short-coupled colt like El Topo. Topito's trot would grind a man's teeth to nubs on the way to a Saturday-night dance or leave him for dead in camp after a full day's work.

The brothers reached Cibuta in a cloudburst an hour before sunup. They stood their horses under a shed by the cattle pens, unsaddled them and rubbed them down, resaddled, then folded their legs under their Saltillos and slept with their chins on their chests.

Late in the morning, the rain subsided to a light drizzle. Les and Mark loaded all three horses on a cattle car bound for Nogales and climbed on the caboose. In Nogales they would try to get a car on the American train that went through Patagonia, close to Harshaw, their home. If they were lucky, they would not be seen until they reached Patagonia. Once they were there, they would be under the protection of their father, A. B. Cowden, who was undersheriff for that region.

"Say hello to Valvanera for us," Les said, grinning. "We know you'll go over there for breakfast."

Les and Mark waved to Ben from the caboose as the train pulled away. He had two hours to wait before the passenger train arrived from Nogales. The storm subsided, and the sun came out, so he took off his spurs and leggings and put them in his blanket roll, shaved and washed at the water trough in the pens, and changed his clothes.

He picked up his saddlebags and blanket roll, and crossed the tracks to eat breakfast at a place that served regular meals to the railroad section hands. The young woman who cooked the meals and served them was a friend of the Cowden brothers named Valvanera Cañez. She gave him barely a glance and did not recognize him when he walked in. The palm hat was so heavy with rain that it weighed down his ears. No one else was in the place.

Ben sat down at a table and poured himself a drink of water in a clay cup. "*Café*?" she asked, good-humoredly.

"Coffee with milk, if you please."

"*Muy bien.*"

Valvanera made *café con leche* almost ritualistically in the best tradition of Sonora. She poured a small cup half full of thick, black, syrupy coffee that was like dark taffy coiling into the cup. Next, she took a lid off the stove and exposed the flame. She dipped a half cup of milk out of a pan warming on the back of the range and held the dipper over the flame. The ritual demanded that she never pour cold milk into a cup of hot coffee and never, never allow the milk on the range to get hot.

Now she was careful to hold the dipper above the flame so the milk did not get too hot and form a *nata*, or scum, on its surface that would turn flaky in the coffee.

Next, she thinned the coffee with the milk so that it turned into a light coffee cream, not so hot it burned the lips, not so cool it could be swallowed without being tasted.

The young woman's brew probably put at least ten men to work every morning. She prepared a cup for herself, carried Ben's to him, and sat down with him at the table. "Hello, Benjamin," she said.

"*Ah, caray!* I thought I had you fooled."

"You did until you spoke. I know your voice as well as your face."

The room was small, and Valvanera's cookstove was large. The front door was propped open with a conch shell. Valvanera's clear skin, glowing with warm perspiration, was the same color as her café con leche. The flame in the stove made her *chapeteada*, put a scarlet tinge on her cheekbones. Her neck was bare to the top of her bosom, her arms bare. She was barefoot and showing half her calves.

"What's going to happen here now, Benjamin?" Valvanera asked. "Lately, bad things happen wherever you go."

"You'll probably catch pneumonia, or rheumatism from going barefoot on the cold floor in the winter."

"Too hot in here. No, Benjamin, you know what I mean. Are the sheriffs chasing you again? Is that why you show up here alone and afoot in the early morning?"

"I want to catch the train to Hermosillo. I sure would like to do *that* before something bad happens."

"Good, you won't be here very long, then."

"Not very long, Valvanera."

"I saw you before your brothers boarded the train. Whose horses were you riding? Those weren't your horses, were they?"

"They belong to some friends."

"They just didn't look right to be your horses."

Ben watched the trail on the hill behind the cattle pens through the open door. He knew that as soon as the Texans discovered the Cowden brothers were gone from the roundup, they would circle and cut for their tracks. Ben did not want to be overtaken while he sat and talked to Valvanera.

"Has the train to Hermosillo been arriving on time?"

"Usually."

A rider appeared on top of the hill behind the pens, then stopped and backed until only his head was visible while he examined Cibuta. After a while he came down to the pens. He dismounted with his rifle and followed the Cowden's tracks to the shed and then back into another corral.

The rain had wiped out all tracks that did not pertain to him, and the Cowdens' tracks were deep and fresh and muddy. The man followed them inside the corral to the end of the loading chute. He looked as if he had been left behind by his mama when he stood on the loading dock with no more tracks to follow.

Ben could tell by his dress that he was a Texan. He turned and spoke to his horse, and made him back down the chute. The horse was a well-built chestnut sorrel with a blaze face and two stockinged legs. That horse had not been raised in Ben's country. He must be Texan.

Valvanera turned to see what Ben was looking at. "Who is that?"

"Fulano Tejano, or something like that, I believe."

The man strolled around the corral, reading tracks. He stopped at the trough and read Ben's boot-tracks. He straightened, looked around at Cibuta, and found Valvanera's.

"Who's he looking for, Ben, you?" Valvanera asked.

"I think he's looking for his friend, my boot-track," Ben said.

"Didn't I tell you? Benjamin Cowden's here, so something's going to happen."

"Can I have some more café con leche?"

"Are you going to shoot that man, Ben?"

"No. Just don't get excited, and everything will be all right. I'll be just another Sonoran with this hat and

Saltillo. He's a Texan and probably hates Mexicans, so he probably won't even look at me."

"If you promise not to shoot him, I'll divert him. Leave him to me."

Ben watched the Texan lead his horse outside the corral, pick up Ben's tracks, and follow them toward Valvanera's. Ben was sitting in a patch of sunlight, and every once in a while the man would look up from the tracks and through the door at Ben. Ben sat back, lounged in his chair, and stretched his legs under the table so his muddy boots were in plain sight. Valvanera hurried in with a pair of muddy *huaraches*, sandals.

"Here, take off your boots, Ben," she said. "I hope these fit you."

"It's no use trying to hide or disguise me, and I won't run from one man." Ben drew his pistol and held it across his belt buckle under the Saltillo. "He's known my track since he first saw it in the mud outside the back door at La Acequia."

"Shoot him, then, if you're going to, before he comes inside."

Ben laughed. "Why? He might cause no trouble at all. There has to be some reason why he thinks he can track a jaguar into his den without drawing a weapon. Anyway, maybe you better go visit your mother or something, in case there's a fight."

"Ah, no. I want to watch."

Ben looked at her quickly, and she smiled.

The Texan ducked his head and stepped through the door. He was tall, baby-faced, and fair. He stopped and leaned his rifle by the door. He wore a beaded buckskin shirt that reeked of woodsmoke and sweat. As a sidearm he carried a heavy hunting knife in a sheath on his right. "Are you Ben Cowden?" he asked, looking Ben in the eye.

"Yes."

The man stepped toward Ben and held out his hand. Softly, in a relaxed tone, Ben said, "Stand back."

The man backed up, showing the palms of his hands. "Listen, I'm not here to fight you."

"Why did you track me, then?"

"It's my new job, tracking you. I work for Captain Jack Odoms. I'm one of the five Rangers he brought with him from Texas. My name is Bud Hawkins, and I'd like to shake your hand."

"Just stand fast and forget about shaking my hand."

"Got your pistol drawn under that Saltillo, do ye? I'm betting you do."

"You're smart."

"You know, the captain's bosses have promised a five-thousand-dollar reward to the ranger who brings them your head."

"So you ditched your partners when you found my tracks."

"That's right. I want your head and the reward all to myself. For a minute or two after I tracked your horses up the loading chute, I thought you'd got on the train with your brothers, but then I saw where you did your toilet by the water trough, and I knew you'd stayed to do what you set out to do."

"What was that?"

"You stayed to board the train for Hermosillo. Everybody knows you were going to Hermosillo to pay Elias for a ranch, and here you showed up, by God."

"I *am* going to Hermosillo."

"Well, not unless you can go without your head, because I'm taking it back to Captain Odoms."

"Why did you come in here to get it? Why didn't you snipe me with that rifle from the top of the hill?"

"I'm in a hurry. When I was up on the hill, I didn't know where you were. Anyway, it's no fun that way. I tracked you fair, and I want to take you by the hair and cut off your head with you looking at me. I'm like the Comanch that way."

That made Ben nervous. Anybody who bragged like that must be able to back it up. He did not feel formidable at all, even with his pistol in his hand. It wasn't even cocked. He didn't wait another second. He cocked it and pointed it underneath the Saltillo. Hawkins moved smoothly toward the door, profiled his left side to Ben, drew his heavy knife, and threw it at Ben's eyes with all his weight behind it. Ben had time only to duck and pull the trigger. The knife shaved Edmundo's heavy hat off his head without touching him. He raised his eyes, and Hawkins was gone. The blast of Ben's pistol had cleared the doorway, and Hawkins's rifle was still leaning by the door.

Ben went outside. Hawkins was on his belly, crawling toward the corner of the house, shot through the ribs. The smell of burned hair was strong in Ben's nostrils as he walked up beside the man and kicked him between the eyes. He saw he was still conscious and kicked him again. The train was coming.

Ben dragged Hawkins around the back of the house so people on the train wouldn't see him, stomped him on the back of the neck for good measure, and went back into the house. He pulled the big knife out of his hat and told Valvanera to put it away somewhere. He kept smelling burned hair.

Valvanera was standing wide-eyed by her stove. She extended her soft hand and took the knife. Ben leaned down to pick up his gear, and smoke billowed into his face. He straightened.

"Ben, you're on fire," Valvanera said.

He looked down. The bullet hole in the Saltillo was smoldering. He jerked the blanket over his head. His belt buckle was red hot. He went to the water *olla*, doused the hot places with a cup of water, and put the Saltillo back on. He picked up his gear and Hawkins's rifle, and went out the door. He swung the rifle at the trunk of the nearest mesquite and bent the barrel about three degrees. He switched ends and knocked the handle and the hammer off. He picked up his gear and ran and boarded the platform on the last car of the train.

CHAPTER 4

Hermosillo, Sonora, during the week of the feast of the Virgin of Guadalupe was dusty. The rain in that town had only wet down the top of the ground. When the train reached Hermosillo the next afternoon, the moisture had turned to powder. The sun glared off the white dust, and the wind blew it through the open windows of the train.

Now as the train slowed in the heat, Ben's Saltillo was uncomfortably warm. He did not take it off though. The garment with the burned hole in the front and Edmundo's palm hat down on his ears made him appear so disreputable that people did not want to look at him.

He took off the hat, stuck his head and shoulders out the window, strained to see the landing where the passengers would unload, and saw what he expected to see—Colonel Gabriel Kosterlinsky's white horse, Bucefalo. The horse stood out like a thundercloud in a clear sky. Kosterlinsky, head of the Rurales, the Rural Police, was Ben's friendliest enemy. Ben was sure the man had been notified by telegraph that Ben had savaged the Texan, and there he was, meeting the train.

Kosterlinsky was charged with eliminating banditry and cattle theft in Sonora. President Díaz and the Sonoran government preferred that all bandits, cattle thieves, and

Apaches be shot on sight or hanged after questioning. If they deserved respect, they were granted *ley de fuga*, a chance to flee mounted troops, or a firing squad in an open field. The government did not want bandits, cattle thieves, or Apaches in its jails. They deserved no trial.

A policy of genocide was also being carried out against the Yaquis, not because they were criminal but because they were in the way. The government was becoming so murderous, it killed Yaquis as a farmer would clear brush before plowing and planting new ground. The government did not want a tribe of brutes farming the rich Yaqui River land when reasonable people could use it to get rich.

Kosterlinsky was in business with Duncan Vincent and liked the money Vincent gave him. If he caught Ben, he would jail him to please Vincent. After a while, maybe a year, maybe two, he might relent and release Ben. Ben, of course, did not want one day in Kosterlinsky's jail.

He thought Kosterlinsky might be a gentle man at heart, but authority had taught him how to profit by being a bully. He could bully anyone except someone who did not let him do it. He was not dangerous. The people President Porfirio Díaz made him hire were dangerous. A Díaz edict required that he recruit convicts out of the penitentiaries. His key men were murderers. One or two of these men were in every troop of Rurales. They wore black hats that set them apart from the uniform gray. When a bandit, or any fugitive from the government, saw the Rurales coming, the black hats reminded him that the soul and conscience of the unit was murder.

Ben picked up his gear and stepped off the train at the door of a cantina. The bartender watched the whole maneuver. "A swallow of the strong, please," Ben said, and laid a coin on the bar.

The bartender examined him a moment longer, then poured him a drink from a two-gallon demijohn. Ben swallowed the mescal, and its spirit was so strong it was barely wet. The stuff warmed him clear to his toes, over to his heart, and then turned and headed deep into his spirit.

He thanked the man and walked across the tracks toward the center of town.

The train stopped at the station. Kosterlinsky's police rode down both sides of the train, their horses shying at bursts of steam from the locomotive. Some of them dismounted, boarded, and searched inside.

Ben kept walking under the palm hat and the Saltillo, and joined a procession that formed in the street by the public market. The procession would be the first of the eight days of *peregrinación*, pilgrimage, through the streets of Hermosillo to the shrine of the Virgin of Guadalupe. Her feast was to be celebrated the following week, December 12.

The street was choked with wagons, teams, carts, and saddlehorses. Side streets along the route of the pilgrimage were guarded by army cavalry. Soldiers looked closely into the faces of the people. The government had many enemies, and the army figured they would be drawn out to watch the procession.

The procession began near the *Hacienda Federal*, the tax offices near the Governor's Palace. Ben fell in step with other grown-ups behind an oxcart. The cart was a crude float that carried young people in costume who depicted the Virgin of Guadalupe, the Indian Juan Diego to whom she had appeared, and attendant angels. The old people and the very young accompanied it in carts, wagons, and carriages.

To celebrate the procession, to announce it and awaken piety, men launched hand-held skyrockets that exploded above the street, the kind used by farmers to scare blackbirds away from their grain crops. A paper cylinder full of black powder was tied to one end of a long, pliant sliver of bamboo. The other end served as a handle. The fusileer scratched the bottom end of the cylinder with a thumbnail to loosen the powder, then lighted it with a *tizón*, a pitch firebrand. Upon ignition, the rocket was tossed underhanded into the air, the powder took over as propellant, and the rocket rushed into the sky. When the fire reached the front end of the rocket, the powder exploded.

The little girl who posed as the Virgin of Guadalupe was having trouble keeping her balance. She faced backwards, her eyes downcast, her hands joined in prayer beneath her face. The boy who played Juan Diego knelt in front of her, his knees rolling painfully on the deck of the cart. Tinier girls who played angels stood in attitudes of prayer dangerously close to the edge of the cart. Ben figured everyone must believe the tots' guardian angels would keep them from falling, for no one walked close to the cart to catch them.

The oxen ambled along at their own pace, their horns pulling rhythmically on the cart. A band of musicians rode a flatbed wagon behind Ben's gang of walking pilgrims. They played hymns, and Ben's companions sang.

Most of the pilgrims in Ben's group were women. Ben's crowd was the most devout. The only people on horseback were the soldiers, but they were on duty and not paying devotion to the Virgin. Then Kosterlinsky's men rode up behind the procession, split, and came up both sides of the street, searching the faces of the spectators who watched the procession. They paid no attention to Ben or the others in the procession.

Kosterlinsky rode by Ben with a black-hatted bodyguard close behind him. Their uniforms were of elegant gray whipcord. Kosterlinsky's trouser legs were striped by silver metal braid. His henchman wore black braid. Their hats were adorned by silver Mexican eagles and snakes. They carried .45 caliber revolvers, repeater carbines, and bandoliers laden with ammunition. Kosterlinsky stopped by an army cavalryman and questioned him. The soldier kept shaking his head while he spoke to Kosterlinsky, but he faced the procession and absentmindedly studied the faces of the pilgrims.

He caught Ben's face in the open. Ben put his head down and moved his lips as though singing the hymn, giving the watcher part of his face to see but not his blue eyes.

To keep from panicking, he concentrated on the pilgrims ahead of him. In front of the oxcart, a teenage boy dressed as the Christ in a white robe and crown of thorns dragged himself along on bare feet, the cross he carried as tall as he. He was a *guero*, sandy-haired, and blue-eyed. He was sweating, probably because of the pain in his feet. He did not look like the popular image of Christ, but to Ben he was probably as much like Christ as any man.

The women in the procession wore long thick winter *rebozos*, shawls, or lace mantillas that covered their heads and most of their faces. He tried to guess which were the beautiful ones. He watched for a glimpse of their profiles. The shod hooves of the mounts of the cavalry and the Rurales streamed by and went ahead.

A half hour later, Ben reached the home of Don Juan Pedro Elias, a house that faced the street. Cuca, the cook, and the *gatitas de casa*, her young housemaids, were standing in the open door watching the procession. Ben stepped out of the crowd and raised the brim of his hat so Cuca would recognize him. She smiled.

"Is Don Juan Pedro home?" he asked.

"Sí. Benjamin, where did you come from? Look at you."

"I'll tell you later. Where is he?" He went by her into the house.

"In his study, I think."

The two-story house was big and airy with a large backyard surrounded by a twelve-foot-high *tapia* wall. Even in December the shrubbery in the backyard was green and dense. Several *noche buena*, Christmas cactus, and poinsettia plants, were in bloom. Ben pulled off the old hat and the burnt Saltillo as he walked through the house.

Don Juan Pedro was sitting at his rolltop desk under a picture of his great-grandfather that had been scarred by an arrow hole. He wore eyeglasses on the end of his nose and was pecking at a typewriter. He looked up when Ben stopped in the door.

"You know, Ben, I've been thinking of you all morning

while I typed the agreement we made over the purchase of the Cibuta ranch," Don Juan Pedro said. He stood, and he and Ben gave each other the Mexican *abrazo* with its arm's-length pats on the shoulders.

"Look at you, Don Juan Pedro, the old Indian fighter with magnifiers on his nose, at peace with his writing machine."

"The thing is miraculous, and it will be a miracle if I ever master it." Don Juan Pedro kept looking into Ben's face. "A swallow, *un trago*? Will that do you good?"

"That's all right. Go on with your chore. I want to watch you work that machine."

"No, I know you want a trago, because I want one."

This is Margarita's father, Ben thought. And why is that so important right now?

Don Juan Pedro went to a cabinet and poured two large glasses half full of brandy. "French brandy, Ben. Not as potent as mescal nor as stimulating as your father's whiskey, but easier on the liver." He handed Ben a glass, raised his in a quick salute, and sipped at it. "Sit, Benjamin."

"I bet you thought I was going to be here sooner," Ben said.

"Of course. I thought we agreed on that."

"My sister Eileen decided she wanted to come down here and see a doctor, so I said I'd wait for her. Then, after I met your son-in-law and he had differences with my brother Les, I came on."

"Where is she? Is she here? Let's make her comfortable before we talk."

"No, she's not here. I wanted us to ride the train with Margarita, so Eileen would have another woman to talk to, but I had to come on without her. She'll probably come with Margarita."

"What's the matter with Eileen?"

"She thinks she has malaria."

"*Bah!* This is the last place we should allow our families to visit. *La fievre amarilla*, yellow fever, claimed two hundred souls here in Hermosillo last summer."

"That's why she's coming here. She says these doctors will be able to tell her if she has a fever. The weather's cooled off, so she doesn't think there's danger of catching anything now."

"Well, she might have malaria, but not yellow fever. She wouldn't be taking train trips if she had the yellow fever."

"If she doesn't have a sickness, the trip might be all she needs to get well. She's been feeling low."

"We'll see what's the matter with her. Did you cross swords with Odoms? I'm sorry if he chose my home as a battleground. Did he insult you in my house?"

"No, he declared war. He tried to be polite, but the effort was too much for him. Les was forced to school him about his manners. How in the world did that man get Margarita to marry him?"

"Those politics do not concern you. I'll tell you this—their union will not produce children."

"Thank God for that."

"After a while we'll go down to the Federal Hacienda and sign the papers so you can take ownership of the Cibuta ranch."

"All right."

"Now, what's this about you killing a man in Cibuta yesterday? Kosterlinsky came here early this morning to tell me about it. He knew you were coming. He wants to put you in jail to please Duncan Vincent."

"So does Odoms. I guess they can do it in Mexico, but Odoms can't get a warrant in Arizona because I haven't done anything there."

"Listen, no one will arrest you in Sonora as long as you enjoy my sanctuary and protection, but I have to know what you did. Who was your victim this time? What happened?"

"Odoms's men were waiting for us at La Acequia so they could follow us across the border and shoot us. They can't arrest us in Arizona, so they must have been planning to shoot us when we left the hospitality of the María Macarena.

We rode to Cibuta under cover of the storm, and one of them tracked us and caught up to me there.

"Vincent has promised to pay five thousand dollars to the man who kills me. One of them was greedier than the rest and came after me alone."

"And?"

"And, well, he made his move and almost dehorned me with a knife big enough to split a log. He threw the thing right at my eye. I ducked and my pistol went off and sent a round through his carcass."

"You didn't kill him, then."

"That didn't kill him, no."

"Was he alive when you left him?"

"He might have been."

"What do you mean? What else did you do to him?"

"I was still mad, and I didn't want him coming after me, so I put the boots to him."

"How heavily?"

"The one I gave him for good measure might have been too heavy."

"*Valgame!*"

"It was him or me."

"How do you know? How do you even know he was one of Odoms's men?"

"He told me he was taking my head back to Duncan Vincent. I believed it when he threw that big knife at me to remove it."

"That would make anyone believe him."

Cuca came in and told Don Juan Pedro that Colonel Kosterlinsky was at the door. Don Juan Pedro looked at Ben.

"Benjamin, you can hide from him, but the law of sanctuary protects you while you're in my house."

"Let him come on. I'd never hide from Kosterlinsky."

They heard Kosterlinsky's spurs drag across the hardwood floor to the study. He came in with his big hat in his hands, the foretop of his black hair pressed flat with sweat against his forehead. He had grown a Prussian military mustache since Ben last saw him, its ends twisted into

spikes. He strode across the room and shook hands with
Ben and Don Juan Pedro.

"We know why you're here, Gabriel," Don Juan Pedro
said. "You can't arrest Ben, so save all rehearsed protes-
tations."

"But I'm not here to arrest my friend, or to counter
your wishes, Don Juan Pedro." Kosterlinsky raised his
hands with the palms out as though he was being held up.
"I only wanted to be sure Ben was here."

"Here I am, Gabriel," Ben said.

"You look well, Benjamin. The bullet that excavated
your back in Nogales was destined only for an ordinary
man."

"I'm well."

"You must be. I tracked you as far as the procession
and gave up. How did you escape me, Ben?"

"Ah, Gabriel, I better not tell you. I want to keep on
escaping you."

"I'm not your *enemy*, Ben. I'm charged with protecting
everyone who comes under my jurisdiction. That's why
I've come here—to protect you."

"You're so nice, Gabriel."

"You understand, you have to remain in Don Juan
Pedro's custody at all times."

"Yes."

"We'll be going to Hacienda later this afternoon to sign
papers and pay taxes," Don Juan Pedro said. "I assume
Ben will be allowed safe conduct."

"Of course, and I hope sanctuary will be observed by
both sides. We want the state of Sonora to be safe from
Ben Cowden as well. If Ben conducts himself in an
honorable fashion, and I know he will, you can take him
anywhere you like."

"Correct. Ben will accompany me home to the María
Macarena also."

"Fine. We trust him to stay with you. Sooner or later,
however, he will have to answer for killing the man named
Hawkins in Cibuta."

"That was self-defense, and I have witnesses." Ben

told that lie to protect his only witness, Valvanera Cañez. If Kosterlinsky knew she was the only witness, he might send a black hat to eliminate her.

"I don't know any details," Kosterlinsky said. "The constable at Cibuta did his duty and notified me that you killed the man before you boarded the train for Hermosillo. His telegram gave no other details."

"We have an appointment at the Hacienda now, Gabriel," Don Juan Pedro said. "Our business is extremely important, and we do not want to keep Señor Bouvet, the tax collector, waiting."

"Of course. I'll give you an escort. I'll even provide you saddlehorses if you wish."

"No need of that, Gabriel. We'll walk. But first, Ben needs a hat. Our chief tax collector is a formal man and would never attend to Ben unless he wore a nice hat. I have a New York hat I bought when I took my wife for a visit there last year."

Don Juan Pedro went to a closet, brought a hatbox down off a shelf, and produced a stiff black hat with a flat top and a narrow curved brim bound with satin. "Now, *there's* a New York hat."

Ben put it on.

"Does it fit? Of course, it does."

The hat fit perfectly.

"We can go, then."

Ben and Don Juan Pedro left Kosterlinsky at the door and walked on to the palace of the governor, passed through the airy lower floor and up the iron stairs to the office of the *jefe de Hacienda Federal*. Don Juan Pedro's son Pancho was waiting for them outside the door. A short young man, stocky, and sturdily built, he greeted Ben in an extremely formal manner but showed he was pleased to see him again. He was Ben's age, but Ben had not seen him for many years because he was reading for the law the year-round in Hermosillo.

Inside, Ben was introduced to a tall officious man wearing a dark suit and a Vandyke beard. He was Martín Bouvet, the chief federal tax collector. He gave Ben a

long, slender-fingered soft white hand, almost as though
he expected it to be kissed, then turned his back and
walked around the desk to his chair. He shuffled papers a
moment and sat down on a high-backed throne of carved
wood. The cushions in the throne were red velvet, the
wood dark and polished. The desk was big and heavy, and
would have taken five men to move. It would probably not
be moved for at least a hundred years unless an earth-
quake, fire, or revolution moved it.

Bouvet's title was *Jefe*, Chief, and his office was called
the *Jefatura*, Chief's Place. He examined documents on
his desk while Ben and the Eliases stood and waited.
There were no chairs for them.

Finally, the chief looked up and said, "Now, how may
I serve you, Elias?"

Don Juan Pedro looked to his son because his son was
supposed to have arranged the appointment.

"As I told you, Don Martín," Pancho said patiently,
"we're here to search for possible outstanding taxes on the
Cibuta ranch so my father can transfer its title to this
man."

"Ah, but the taxes are of little import," Bouvet said.
He stared at Ben. "You are the buyer?"

"I am," Ben said.

"How much are you paying for this ranch, and where
is Cibuta?"

"Near Nogales."

"Ah, yes. How much are you paying this man?"

Ben unbuckled his money belt, stacked $3,000 in
alazanas, the sorrel gold coin of Porfirio Díaz, on the
desk.

Don Juan Pedro stepped forward, separated a stack of
ten of the coins of $50 value, and covered them with a
sheet of paper for Bouvet. The chief selected the necessary documents and set them on the front of the desk with
an inkwell and quill. Don Juan Pedro signed them.
Bouvet took a knife out of his vest, sharpened the quill,
and handed it to Ben. Ben signed the documents, the

chief signed them, and the Cibuta ranch was Ben's. He stepped back, prepared to leave.

Bouvet said, "Señor Cowden, do you understand that certain factions in this state do not approve of the selling of Mexican land to foreigners?"

"I had no idea that was true," Ben said.

"Oh, yes, certain factions in Mexico do not wish to see the infringement of foreign capital in this country."

"But Ben Cowden is not a foreigner, he is an Arizonan," Don Juan Pedro said. "His people owned their ranches when they were still part of Sonora. He makes his living more in Sonora than he does in Arizona. He and his father and grandfather have always been good neighbors to me. I don't see how anyone can call him a foreigner."

"Do not misunderstand me. Don Porfirio Díaz, our illustrious president, encourages foreign capital. Not one dollar of American money invested in this country escapes his attention."

"I am sure of that," Don Juan Pedro said. "But the five hundred dollars I, a Mexican, just gave you *will*." He laughed.

Bouvet answered with a venomous smile. "This five hundred dollars will defray my expenses in my own campaign to bring more capital into Mexico. I also encourage the traffic of foreign money for ships, cattle, and the development of our forests and farms, et cetera, et cetera."

"Of course," Don Juan Pedro said. "Anyone can see you need a lot of money to oversee the collection of our taxes. I bet the barber who trims your beard costs you more each month than beans for my vaqueros cost me in a year."

"How is that? I don't understand what you are saying."

"We are always happy to contribute to the progress of our country as fostered by our President Porfirio Díaz and his illustrious and bountiful chiefs." Don Juan Pedro put his $2,500 in gold in a leather pouch and hid it away under his jacket.

"Yes, well, I'm sure you are," Bouvet said. "But we are very busy here today, so if there is nothing else . . ."

"We have nothing else. Thank you for receiving us."

Bouvet stood up, smoothed the front of his coat and vest, and bowed curtly as the three men walked out. Outside the palace, Ben reached inside his shirt, counted another $2,000 in alazanas and handed them to Don Juan Pedro. Don Juan Pedro counted them and handed a portion to Pancho. Pancho handed the bill of sale to Ben.

"Ah, and thanks to Don Porfirio for the minting of the alazana, because it is good as legal tender anywhere in the world," Don Juan Pedro said. "Not only is it sound, but it is pretty as a sorrel filly. Eh, Benjamin, is there any better way to settle business than by a transaction in gold? It can be exchanged anywhere, and even the most ignorant know its value."

"Your chief of hacienda sure made it disappear. I bet his pockets never bulge."

"No, he's practiced at taking his bribes. He already has it spent. I pay my taxes every year, but in order to effect this transaction, Bouvet had to be paid his *mordida*, his bite out of my fanny. When he heard we were in town, he sent for Pancho and told him that he would not be able to finalize these papers without investigating my tax records for the last twenty years. He wanted to be sure I was not delinquent. In order to keep him from delaying us, we consented to grease him with twenty percent."

"I didn't know you would have to do that," Ben said. "I can assume half the mordida as my contribution for avoiding the delay."

"I'll get even with you some other way," Don Juan Pedro said. "Now that you own land in Mexico, you'll have to pay mordida every time you sell anything. Don't get started paying people who don't ask for it. I wish you had not been forced to meet him. Now he knows what you look like. He saw the gold in your money belt. He feels entitled to your gold by divine right. He considers himself an aristocrat sent by God to bleed us, even though Benito

Juárez was supposed to have put an end to Frenchmen like him.

"He needs to keep up his expenses in order that people believe he is of the ruling class. He spends like a millionaire, and he bites deep. You need to be more ladino, Benjamin. Haven't you ever been bitten that deep by a *mordelón?*"

"I'm plenty ladino in my own country, Don Juan Pedro. Arizona's bureaucrats make Bouvet look like my guardian angel. I relax when I do business in Mexico. At least I can be sure I'll always be able to get what I want from him with a bribe. In my country, Duncan Vincent's bureaucrats want my life."

"Well, you're in your own country now. By owning land here, you are Sonoran again like your antecedents. But let me ask you, how long have you been carrying that gold around your waist like that?"

"Since I left El Durazno."

"Are you in the habit of doing the work of a vaquero with thousands of dollars worth of gold on your person?"

"I had to bring it, and it's safest when I carry it with me."

"Isn't it heavy?"

"Not if carrying it makes me sure I'll have it when I need it."

"Wouldn't a draft book be a safer way to pay your accounts?"

"If I carried a draft book, I would have to pay a damned banker to know my business. I would have to pay a banker to use my own money. I'll do that when I'm too weak and cowardly to defend my money, or I lose my balls to a banker."

CHAPTER 5

Ben was deep in his bed in Don Juan Pedro Elias's home in Hermosillo, sleeping. He dreamed he, his whole family, and his sweetheart, Maudy Jane Pendleton, were together driving a bunch of mother cows with newborn spotted calves onto a range abundant with sweet grass. Everybody was horseback and happy. His little brother Freddie Lee, who had been dragged to death by a burro a few months ago, was alive again on his palomino horse. Les was riding Sorrel Top, the horse that had been shot out from under him and killed in the range war. The two Soto brothers who had been killed in the war were driving the chuck and hooligan wagons. Ben's sisters, Paula Mary, Betty, and Eileen, were riding out on the flanks of the herd with big ribbons in their hair.

Ben slept on contentedly. Seeing his oldest sister, Eileen, in his dream almost reminded him of a duty he was supposed to carry out, and then he became aware somebody was knocking on his door. He awoke and remembered Eileen was coming on the train to see the doctor. He dragged his bones out of bed, pulled on his trousers, and opened the door for Don Juan Pedro.

"My God, Benjamin, it's almost time to go to the train. We thought you were dead," Don Juan Pedro said.

"Only dreaming," Ben said.

"Ah, pardon me for waking you."

"No, no. I want to go with you."

"It's time. You slept all night and all day. The train is late, so we let you sleep. Come for coffee."

Ben shaved and dressed and went down to the kitchen. He drank coffee with Pancho and Don Juan Pedro, and went out with them to mount horses for the ride with the carriage to the depot. Ben's mount was a bay so light on his feet that he never seemed to touch the ground. His saddle was a big-horned *charro* saddle with a flap over the naked tree to sit on. The saddle was decorated with buttons and piping embroidered in red, and equipped with a three-foot machete in its carved sheath under the near stirrup. Pancho rode ahead of the carriage, and Ben and Don Juan Pedro rode side by side behind it as they made way down the dark narrow streets.

The sky was clear. Winter cold was seldom felt in Hermosillo in the daytime, but the desert nights could be cold. This night was almost balmy.

The Sonora Railway train that hauled both passengers and freight was late arriving in Hermosillo that evening. The army had made it wait in Magdalena for a company of soldiers returning from a campaign against Apaches. Ben and his companions kept their saddle and carriage horses away from the noise and confusion near the tracks as the train arrived. Small bonfires were lighted along the tracks where the train stopped, so the passengers could see to get off.

The train was stuffed with soldiers who unloaded and crowded the landing with their kit and weapons. Ben knew the young captain in command. He ordered the company into ranks quickly while the horses were unloaded. The horses came off the cars gaunt and jaded. Some of them fell at the doors of the cars when they crouched to jump to the ground. The men were gaunt, dirty, and ragged, pieces of their uniforms replaced with remnants of civilian clothing.

Ben rode down the length of the train looking for

Eileen and Margarita. He had been hoping Odoms was too sore to make the trip, but there he was, in a seat across from the ladies. He stared out the window at Ben, his bandaged face a mask that shone white from the shadows in the car. Margarita was near the window, but she did not look at Ben. Eileen, sitting on the aisle, leaned over and lifted a gloved hand to wave, but Margarita still did not turn to him.

Ben was surprised to see Walter Jarboe come off the train. Jarboe was a cattleman from Kansas who had once bought cattle from Kosterlinsky but never received them. After waiting a year to be paid back, Jarboe arranged to have himself commissioned a U.S. marshal, came to Arizona, and enlisted Ben to help him recover the money. Ben found that Kosterlinsky had sold Jarboe's cattle to Duncan Vincent. Vincent then sold them but never paid Kosterlinsky for them. Jarboe was still trying to get his money out of Vincent and Kosterlinsky.

Ben waited to offer Jarboe a ride in Don Juan Pedro's carriage, but Duncan Vincent rode up in another carriage, loaded Jarboe, and left. Ben knew Jarboe to be a shrewd, cold-blooded businessman, but he would never in a hundred years have thought he would throw in with Vincent, even for a ride into town.

Don Juan Pedro and Colorado, the carriage driver, boarded the train to help the ladies. Ben stood his horse by the team to keep it quiet, and Pancho climbed on the carriage to hold the lines.

Odoms came off the train ahead of the women, carrying nothing. He nodded to Pancho and stopped in front of Ben's horse. Both eyes were black all the way down his cheeks. He wore a white handkerchief tied over his nose. He was so angry, the lower part of his face went into a spasm when he started talking. "You better thank your Lord, or whatever god you worship, that you are still under the protection of this Meskin, Cowden."

Ben looked over his head and watched for Eileen and Margarita.

"Enjoy the Meskin's hospitality, because sooner or

later I'm gonna be on you like a catamount. I promise you, your ass will rot in a Meskin dungeon."

Ben dismounted and handed his reins to Pancho. Odoms must have thought he was going to get hit in the nose again, for he scurried quickly to the other side of the carriage. Ben went to help his sister off the train.

Eileen came off ahead of Margarita. She had never in her life been frail or sickly, but lately she had complained of not having any spunk. She always looked so sturdy and did so much of the work around the Cowden home at El Durazno that no one paid attention to her when she said she did not feel well. She was too active and too good-looking to be sick. Even now, her color was good, and her movements were strong enough to belie her fever.

Ben helped her down the steps from the train, kissed her, and relieved her of a leather satchel. Colorado handed him four heavy valises from the platform. Margarita stepped onto the platform and looked for Ben's eyes, and he saw that she still felt the same toward him as she had when he kissed her at the María Macarena.

Eileen saw the look, said, "My gosh," and gave a little laugh.

Ben helped Margarita and Eileen to their seats in the carriage and helped Colorado and Pancho load and tie the luggage. Colorado started the team toward a camp on the Sonora River called El Merendero Dina where the party was to have supper. Odoms sat by the driver, and Margarita sat behind him facing Eileen. Ben rode alongside the carriage so he could look at Margarita's face and the back of Odoms's head.

He thought he was good at hiding the new wonder he felt for Margarita, but after a while Eileen turned to him and said, "Now just quit that, Ben. Are you crazy? Just quit it."

Margarita laughed.

"Quit what?" Ben said.

Being his sister, Eileen was able to speak almost in a whisper to him and be perfectly understood. "You *know* what. If I ever saw a man smitten, it's you."

That embarrassed Ben. He was not used to being caught when acting the ladino. He kept his eyes to himself for the remainder of the journey to the river.

The Merendero Dina was more a cow camp than a restaurant and served *carne asada* under a great nacapul tree. The camp closed early in the afternoon before siesta, but Don Juan Pedro had arranged for the cook to come back and prepare supper for the travelers. The only food served was beef sirloin strips and *tripitas de leche*, marrow gut broiled on open mesquite coals. The meat was accompanied by bowls of *frijoles de la olla*, whole pinto beans in their clear soup, and keg beer made in Hermosillo by a Yugoslav brewer.

Ben picked up the meat with sheets of hot flour tortilla, covered it with *salsa picante*, a sauce made of whole peeled green chiles, whole tomato, onion, and ground garlic, wrapped the meat in the tortilla, and ate it with sips of beer.

No one took the seat at the head of the table. Don Juan Pedro sat between Margarita and Eileen. Pancho and Ben sat opposite them.

Odoms kept to himself on the outside, beside Margarita. He hunched over his food and did not look at anyone or say a word, but his split and flattened nose snuffed through the meal like an old bulldog's. Ben felt sorry for him because his new relatives were jolly people and he would probably never be able to enjoy them. They all should have been able to laugh at the way his poor nose grappled for air when he took a bite of food. He disapproved of his companions and the meal so much, it made him miserable. He refused the beer and tripitas that were brought, as though he were being invited to partake of poison. When Margarita offered him the salsa, he refused it without even glancing at it, or thanking her. He ate his beans and meat though. Ben did not know a Texan or an Arizonan in the world who would have refused that supper.

The party drove back to Don Juan Pedro's house at midnight. Ben's room was large and airy with a tall window and doors that opened onto a balcony over the street. He and Eileen were on the second floor in adjoining rooms. He walked out onto the balcony to look. The streets were empty and dark. Returning inside, he undressed, pushed the pillows aside, lay down flat on the bed, and was instantly asleep.

Ben knew Margarita would be in the kitchen early, so he got up as soon as he awakened to be alone with her. The smile she gave him in the lamplight of her kitchen that morning was handsome, happy, and tender, exactly as he hoped it would be, a new wonder to him. So as not to hold him a slave to her gaze and to keep everything decent, she brought him café con leche, stood beside him, and buttered a hot roll for him.

All of a sudden, Ben realized the range war was so far away, he could be happy for a while. Odoms's enmity was only a threat, no trouble compared to the constant fight Ben and his brothers waged in Arizona. Being alone with Margarita and watching her butter another roll for him was a good reason to be happy.

He sipped Margarita's thick warm coffee and relaxed because he could look at her and did not have to watch for his enemies. He made peace for a while.

"So, Benjamin, have you decided to become my lover?" Margarita asked.

"I want to, but you're married, and I've promised to marry Maudy Jane Pendleton because we love each other."

"Don't worry about Odoms. I won't be giving you anything he wants, or needs, or can even use."

"I can't say that about Maudy."

"I know you love Maudy and will marry her. But when? You act as though she is already your wife. I will never be your wife, but starting now, today, I can be your lover. I know you are a good man and are bound to need a woman. How can a handsome, active, vital man like you be content without a woman?"

"I have women friends."

"Oh, yes, I know all about your women friends.

Everybody in Sonora knows about the women you and your brothers have befriended, but you have no lover."

"No, I don't, and I haven't missed her, whoever she is."

"I, as your lover, will keep you calm, keep you from disease, make you happy. By doing that, I'll be Maudy Jane Pendleton's, your wife's, best friend."

"That would be fine until she found out and quit me."

"She will never find out. No one but you and I must ever know about it. Our love could become mean and bad if we made a scandal of it. As long as we never admit it, our families will defend us, and no one can truly be sure that we are lovers."

"Unless we get caught."

"How exciting that will be, to have a secret intimacy between us and never show it on our faces, never be off guard. Because if we get caught, we will either have to turn our backs on each other or abandon our lives and go away together."

"It's already getting too complicated for me."

"That can only mean you have decided to become my lover. You have decided to do it, haven't you? Tell me you have. Otherwise, I'll have to learn to love someone else. I already love you, Ben, but I have so much love in my heart, I have to give it to you now. If I don't, it will waste me."

Ben knew he would have to do it. The sound of Don Juan Pedro's door closing made him jump. He thought, If I do this, I'll get so wild, I'll be hiding what I do every minute of the day. I'll even have to hide what I think and feel from my family. That will really make me a ladino.

"*Buenos días, Benjamin,*" Don Juan Pedro said. "Ah, you're with café con leche. How beautiful my daughter is in the morning, no?"

Margarita set her father's coffee on the table for him and began buttering his roll.

Don Juan Pedro searched Ben's face. "What do you think, Benjamin, have I not sired the most beautiful woman in Sonora?"

"Only in Sonora?" Margarita laughed.

Ben held his peace.

"The women of Sonora are the most beautiful in the world."

"Ah, your world is only a small place, Papá." Margarita walked away to the stove again, and the sway of her hips was for Ben alone.

"*Ai*," he said, grinning into his cup.

Later, Pancho drove Ben and Eileen in the carriage to the office of Dr. José Inukai, a Japanese fisherman's son who had come to live in Sonora. Dr. Inukai's twenty-year practice had been spent in Hermosillo. He had treated every desert fever and malaise. He was of more than average height, heavy, with wide streaks of silver in his jet-black hair.

When Ben saw that his sister eagerly left his side for the examining room, as though anxious for a cure, he realized for the first time she might be seriously ill. She was anxious to do as she was told, even though it separated her from Ben, as though she could no longer endure her discomfort.

Eileen knew Ben was sensitive to the way she had turned her back on him and hurried away with the doctor. She could not help it. Something was dying inside her. When Dr. Inukai asked her to strip to her underwear and lie on a cot, she did so quickly and unselfconsciously because she wanted to get well.

She had been feeling well with the change of scenery since she had left her parents' home, but she knew the fever could come over her again anytime. Well, it was not exactly a fever; it was more like a surge of white heat that swept over the length of her body from time to time. It was a blush, the shock of heat a person felt when she realized she had done something shameful or very wrong. The "fever" happened too often now. She explained these symptoms to Dr. Inukai.

Dr. Inukai began by gently touching her spine, vertebra by vertebra, from the base of her skull all the way down to the tip of her tailbone. He found out everything he could about every inch of bone that he could distinguish. He felt every inch of her skull, neck, and throat. He questioned her about her breasts and her private functions, sat across the room from her, and watched her, his black eyes showing only as glinting specks. Finally, he sighed to himself and motioned for his nurse to put a pillow under Eileen's head so she could look at him. He sat down in a chair at the foot of the cot.

"Have you ever felt pain with this sickness?" he asked softly.

"I don't think so," Eileen murmured.

"Does your heart ever hurt?"

Eileen thought a moment. "Sometimes."

"Do you get tired after your heart has been hurting?"

"Yes, but the tiredness goes away if I forget about it and do some work."

"When does your heart hurt?"

"I don't think my heart has anything to do with it. It's the flashes of fever that bother me."

"When does your heart hurt?"

"When I'm alone. That's usually only when I'm in bed."

"Does it hurt a lot?"

"Quite a bit, but not a lot. It's an ache."

"And that goes away when you do your work?"

"Yes."

"Do you get the fever flashes when you're working?"

"Not while I'm doing something, but the minute I stop, I might get one."

"Are you married?"

"No."

"Are you engaged?"

"Yes."

"For how long have you been engaged?"

Eileen sighed. "Forever."

"How long?"

"I don't know exactly. At least two years."

"How often do you see your fiancé?"

"He rides over from Benson to see me on the third Thursday of every month, and he goes home Sunday."

"He's been doing that for two years or more?"

"Faithfully."

Dr. Inukai sat so still for so long that Eileen looked for the glint of his eyes to make sure he was awake. Finally, he said she could dress. When she was ready, he asked the nurse to send in her brother.

Ben sat in a chair by the cot. "Is my sister very sick, Doctor?"

"She is gravely ill," Dr. Inukai said.

"What's she got?"

"Young man, I think your lovely sister is ill with a sadness, a *tresteza*."

"She always seems happy."

"Nevertheless, she is hiding a sadness that threatens her life."

"What kind of sadness?"

"A young woman's sorrow for a life she longs for but might never attain."

"Is that true? Are you sad about your life, Eileen?" Ben asked.

Eileen's lip crumpled, and she began to cry. "I guess so."

"Well, by God, we can do something about that," Ben said. "Are you sure about this, Doctor?"

"I can't be sure about anything, except the girl seems to be in fine health and ready to start a life of her own. She's a perfectly normal woman. The only fever that is bothering her is caused by a healthy passion for life that she is being forced to squelch. She needs some fun. If you can't help her find a way to have fun, you'll probably always be looking for doctors' cures."

Eileen was a different girl when she walked out of the doctor's office. Pancho had gone back home and picked up Margarita, and she was smiling in the backseat of the carriage. Eileen gave Ben a look and climbed up beside Pancho with unladylike quickness and agility. The carriage top was down, and Ben jumped in and kissed Margarita as Pancho drove off.

When Pancho came back, he and Eileen looked at each other and laughed. He headed the team toward the Sonora River, and Eileen's smile became more healthy and earthy with every step the horses took. The two couples sat beside the river in the shade of giant gnarled alamo trees, ate cheese, and talked and laughed with the wine until the sun went down.

In the early evening they drove to the shops so Eileen and Margarita could attend to their *compras*, their shopping. Margarita helped Eileen bargain for gold earrings for her mother, sisters, and Maudy Jane Pendleton. Margarita bought a gross of leather *huaraches* for the men and women who worked at Macarena. They parked the carriage by the front door of the ironworker Grijalva's shop, paid a boy to stand at the head of the team, and went in so Ben could buy a pair of spurs and a spade bit he needed for his horse Toots.

When they were ready to leave, Gabriel Kosterlinsky passed by at the head of two ten-man squads of Rural Police, Odoms bringing up the rear. Kosterlinsky was on his dancing, prancing white Bucefalo. Ben smiled to himself. Kosterlinsky did as he pleased in Hermosillo. He enjoyed parading his troop back and forth through town when it was not dangerous for him. Up in the Santa Cruz valley, his parading would make his enemies think he wanted to give them a large target. Kosterlinsky and Odoms rode by Don Juan Pedro's carriage, turned the corner by Grijalva's, and headed toward the center of town.

"Oh, oh," said Ben, "Odoms knows I left Don Juan Pedro's house, and he's got Kosterlinsky out looking for me."

"Hurry, Benjamin," Pancho said. "Go out the back door before they cut you off."

"No. I'm no good afoot. I can bluff Kosterlinsky." He was in no danger. Odoms and Kosterlinsky did not look back.

Then, a half block away, three drunken men rolled arm in arm out the door of a cantina and almost collided with Kosterlinsky's horse. Too late, they realized Rurales filled the narrow street. The effect of the mescal they were drinking made them sway and hold on to one another. They were dressed shabbily, wearing huaraches.

Kosterlinsky drew his pistol, threw up his hand, shouted a command, and halted the troop. He shouted more commands, and two of his Rurales left the ranks, blocking both ends of the street. Two more troopers rode their horses into the cantina. A black-hatted Rural pushed the drunkards up against the wall of the cantina with his horse. The Rurales who had ridden inside herded five customers and the *cantinero* out into the street.

Kosterlinsky rode up and held his prancing horse in front of the three drunkards who stood against the wall. "Worms!" he shouted, waving his pistol at them. "Drunken, mutinous, insurrectionist, bandit worms! Did you think you could come here and get drunk without my knowledge?"

"My chief . . ." began one of the drunkards, removing his hat and taking one step forward.

Kosterlinsky shot him dead. "Don't answer me. I don't want answers from you."

The other two ran. Kosterlinsky shot one in the back before he took five steps. The Rural at the end of the street charged the third with his horse and ran him back to Kosterlinsky. Kosterlinsky ran Bucefelo into him and knocked him to his knees. The drunkard raised his hands above his head in supplication.

"*Levantate, Jodido*. Get up, cuckold," Kosterlinsky ordered, drawing his saber. "I don't want to hear one prayer out of your mouth, not to your God and not to me. You're going straight to hell!" With that, he rode up and hacked at the man's head with the saber. The man deflected it with his forearm and ran past Odoms and down the middle of the street between the two ranks of Rurales.

The Rurales closed ranks across the end of the street.

and drew their sabers. The man ran back through the gauntlet of sabers, and Kosterlinsky headed him into the wall. The Rurales who had driven the drunkards out of the cantina herded them over to join the gauntlet runner against the wall.

Kosterlinsky rode in front of them and pointed his saber at another man. "Leave that one, and put the rest back where you got them."

"No-o-o!" screamed the unlucky man. The cantinero hurried back into his bar with the customers who had been spared. Eileen and Margarita began to cry. After watching Kosterlinsky shoot down two men in cold blood, Ben no longer felt like trying to bluff him. He turned the women around and pushed them gently past Grijalva and his helpers into the shop.

Kosterlinsky barked a command, and his twenty Rurales lined up facing the drunkards. He barked another, and they drew their carbines.

"AAAPUNTEN, AIM! . . . FUEGO, FIRE!"

The volley rattled unevenly up and down the street. Kosterlinsky formed the Rurales in two columns again and rode on without looking back. Odoms left the column at a side street.

"Who were those men he killed, Benjamin?" Pancho asked.

"Part of the remnant of army mutineers who turned against him at Gabilondo's hacienda a few months ago," Ben said. "That third man who ran up and down the street was a brother to Jacinto Lopez, the leader of the mutineers."

"You knew him?"

"All my life. Kosterlinsky caught Jacinto once in Arizona and put him in the same jail where I was being held. He granted him ley de fugo and let him get away because, they say, he got softhearted. Later, Jacinto attacked Kosterlinsky's private stage on its way to Santa Cruz and killed a four-man guard of Rurales and the stage driver, so I don't think Kosterlinsky's heart is soft anymore. I didn't know he was that good with a pistol, either."

The two couples boarded the carriage and drove home past the dead men lying in pools of blood. They were frontier born and bred, and this was not the first time they had been close to violent death. They went on without speaking and without weeping anymore but with sorrow for the men who had been killed. They did not stop in Don Juan Pedro's parlor for a glass of wine and small talk as they had hoped to do.

Ben went in to his room and pulled down the bedspread. A note was pinned to his pillow: *Sleep well until I come to you. Margarita.*

Ben did not sleep well. After several hours of waiting, he figured she would not come, and he did not blame her. She had written the note before she watched the murder of the mutineers. He finally slept.

He first became aware of her when he heard the brush of her bare foot by the bed. A second later she was in his arms.

CHAPTER 6

The evening before Ben, Eileen, and the Eliases were to return home, they went to a *tardeada*, an afternoon social gathering, at the Merendero Dina. The people who attended considered themselves high class, dressed in fine clothes, drove to the function in light carriages, or rode their best horses. Nobody walked.

The women sipped tea, or beer; the men, beer or brandy. A band of *mariachis* accompanied a strong-voiced young girl with trumpet, violin, bass, guitar, and *guitarrón*. The young marriageable men and women searched each other's faces to find someone to walk with in the alamo forest. Some of the bold young stags circled the gathering on horseback, showing off their outfits, horses, and profiles. The shy virgin does packed into carriages with their chaperones and circled the opposite way, peeking out from behind their parasols when they wanted someone to see their faces.

Eileen had been Johnny Bonner's fiancée a long, long time, and she was happier dancing with Pancho Elias. Johnny braved a fifty-mile ride between Benson and Harshaw along the Apache wartrail every month to come and see her. He had killed two horses escaping Apaches, but Pancho's attention made Eileen's color run high.

Ben was glad his sister was having a good time. Johnny Bonner was always worn-out when he reached El Durazno. He barely had time to rest for his return home. About the best he could do for her, besides the marathon rides he made to see her, was to say, "You sure look good, Eileen. Yes, you do, you sure do." He was one hundred percent cowboy and suffered from the worst of all cowboy maladies: He could not look a decent woman in the eye. He could not take hold of Eileen and give her a fine, moving kiss, not even after two years of courtship.

Eileen was the workhorse of the Cowden women. Her hands were the busiest at extending the love of the family with deeds, but she did not get many hugs. She deserved to be admired and caressed for her goodness and beauty. Ben thought she was beautiful, but she kept her head down with work so much that nobody thought about what she wanted. Now, every young stag at the tardeada was trying to take her away from Pancho, and she liked it.

Ben was enjoying being smitten. Odoms had left town with Kosterlinsky, and Ben moved his kit to room 11 of the Garrett Hotel a half block away. One of the doors opened on a narrow alley. All his days and nights of that week had been filled with the company or the thought of Margarita. He had always felt more akin to her than Maudy Jane as far as the pleasures of touching and talking were concerned. He was still resolved to marry Maudy Jane, but he was better acquainted with Margarita now and loved her too.

People came to a tardeada to court and have fun, and looked for the best in everyone else. The music, drinks, and food made everyone feel good, and the view of good-looking women was the best in the world. During his term as emperor of Mexico, before the Mexicans stood him up against the wall and shot him, Maximilian had spread the fame of the beauty of Sonora women abroad. Ben was certain no women in the world could be more beautiful.

Margarita was the best-looking woman of all, and the intimacy he enjoyed with her made him feel he was the most privileged man there. He kept thinking of the Mexican saying "The history of every love begins with a look." There were plenty of those kind of looks at the tardeada but none as lovely as the looks Margarita gave Ben.

The snobbishness of the high society at the gathering bothered him; he did not like too much of any kind of society. He usually worked between four and six every day, including Saturdays, Sundays, and holidays. He had always believed this kind of afternoon gathering kept too many able-bodied people busy looking at one another and making empty talk when they could be working. Now he found he did not mind drinking, dancing, laughing, admiring the girls, and being admired. He did not mind it that Margarita was not the only one who was giving him soulful looks.

Ben was not used to being counted high class though. His family enjoyed good status in the community of southern Arizona, but it did not entertain illusions that it was part of an aristocracy as these Mexicans did. He had always called this fake aristocracy *la alta suciedad*. *La alta sociedad* was the high society. *La alta suciedad* was the "high dirt," self-appointed and worthless as hell. Everybody Ben associated with worked at their jobs during the last two hours before sundown. The hours between four and six were for doing chores on a ranch before going to supper and bed. The time for talking and playing was after the sun went down, when work was not easy to see. The tardeada, the afternooning, with the promenade, seemed like a waste, but he enjoyed watching Margarita and Eileen have fun.

Pancho Elias's manners were perfect, and he was not jealous of Eileen. He introduced her to every handsome horseman and every happy girl at the tardeada. He showed Ben that his sister was a black-curly-haired, fair-skinned, gracious, graceful beauty, not just a good hand who worked for her family.

Ben felt sorry for Johnny Bonner. The fifty-mile ride he made to Harshaw and back through an Apache war zone was a great feat. Pancho would never make that ride. In Johnny's place he would have taken the train from Benson to Patagonia, like a gentleman. The gentleman made Eileen realize that Johnny Bonner had gone home once too often without having laughed and danced with her.

Pancho learned that Eileen's favorite song was the waltz "Cuatro Milpas," so he ordered the mariachis to play it and led her out on the floor to dance. Margarita led Ben out too. She was a modest, graceful, and cheerful dancer. She moved carefully at first, gauging Ben's performance, rating him, and then she matched his pace with her own.

When the set was over, Margarita led Ben up to the leader of the mariachis. "May I sing 'Dos Arbolitos,' Don Ramón?" she asked.

"*Como que no*, we've been hoping you would, señora," the leader said.

"Then I'll launch a good song on the wind for my friend Ben." She left Ben and moved to the center of the line of mariachis as they played the introduction. Then, in a strong, clear voice, she sang:

Han nacido en mi rancho, dos arbolitos,
Two little trees have been born on my ranch,
Que parecen gemelos.
That are like twins.
Si de mi casita los veo solitos
When I look at them from my house
Bajo el amparo santo y la luz del cielo.
I see them as a gift of God in the light of heaven.
Nunca estan separados uno del otro,
They are never separated one from the other,
Porque asi quizo Dios los dos nacieran.
Because God made them that way.
Si con sus mismas ramas se hacen caricias
They caress each other with their branches
Como si fueran novios que se quisieran.
As though they are sweethearts in love.

Arbolito, arbolito, bajo tu sombra,
Little tree, little tree, beneath your shade,
Voy a esperar el dia cansado muera.
I'll wait for the day I tire and die.
Y cuando estoy solito mirando al cielo
And when I'm alone gazing at the sky
Pido para que me manda una compañera.
I ask that I also be sent a companion.
Cuando me voy a mi siembra a los maizales,
When I go to the tilled earth of my cornfield,
Entre los zurcos riego todo mi llanto.
I water the rows with my cry.
Solo tengo de amigo mis animales,
The only friends I have are my animals,
A los que con tristeza siempre les canto.
To whom I cry, always with sadness.

Arbolito, arbolito . . .

As Ben and Margarita walked back to their table, people smiled and clapped for her, happy she was officially out of mourning. Nobody seemed to miss Odoms, but Ben knew the alta suciedad. If Margarita had one enemy there, the gossip would begin, a scandal in the making.

"What a handsome man you are," Margarita whispered to Ben when they reached their table.

"You'd make anybody look good."

"I like to dance with you."

"Let's do it some more, then."

"Oh, no, that's enough. Think of Odoms and Maudy Jane, and stop looking at me like that when everybody is watching."

"Do I show my feelings?"

"Very much. Do I?"

"It's awful."

"Don't look at me, then. Talk to Pancho, and I'll talk to your sister. Let's not cause a scandal."

"You have a right to enjoy yourself."

"No, I'm a woman who was recently widowed and a widow recently remarried. I'm a rehashed woman. I have no rights."

"What a custom."

"It's the end of two lives when a husband dies. If I didn't have you, my life would be over. I've been given away for politics."

"It doesn't have to be that way."

"Then steal me away—hide me and protect me." Margarita laughed.

"That's a good idea."

"Ah, well." Margarita turned to Eileen.

Ben would have done anything to keep Margarita close. He felt deprived because she was talking to Eileen. He tried to talk to Pancho, but he missed Margarita so much, he could not enjoy himself.

Then Captain Carbo, the young officer who had been in command of the soldiers that came off the train, asked Margarita to dance. She smiled at him, took his hand, rose, and walked out on the floor with him. As Ben watched her play the coquette and absently caress the captain's shoulder with a shapely hand, he knew extreme and abjectly miserable jealousy for the first time in his life.

He did not like the way she gave herself to everyone. He did not like her little public laugh either—a soft, common, mirthless laugh she used when people came by to welcome her back from her period of mourning. She flirted and joked with all the men, and she cooed and ah'ed with all the women, using that little laugh to show the side of herself that was common to them all.

Bouvet came and sat beside her. Immediately, without a glance at Ben, she told Bouvet she planned to go into the horse business. She would venture abroad to look for good thoroughbred mares and breed them to her husband's new stallion. She practically invited Bouvet to go with her. Ben and Margarita had already agreed they would go into the horse venture together so they would have secret times together.

"But, young lady, I understand that Meestair Cowden here, raises good horses. Have you asked him to help you pick your mares?"

Margarita gave Ben a polite glance but turned back to Bouvet. "Yes, but I want to travel and see other horses and ranches. For example, I've been wanting to ask you, didn't Maximilian leave some good thoroughbreds in Cuernavaca? Your home is in Cuernavaca, is it not? Are those horses still there?"

"Ah, I don't know much about horses, but I'll look into it," Bouvet said. He rose and took Margarita out to dance, began speaking close into her ear. She quieted and seemed enraptured.

Ben watched for a look or a sign that would tell him she was only performing a duty, but she was completely taken by Bouvet. Ben looked away from her when the dance was over so she would not see how jealous he was. When Bouvet sat down by him, Margarita was not with him.

"Where did Margarita go?" he asked.

"Ah, who knows," Bouvet said. He had a way of lowering his eyelids, making his gaze dull, when he looked at Ben that made Ben want to close them with his fists. "That young woman is one who can speak to one man, think of another, and look at another, all at the same time. Every moment, every encounter, is an adventure for her, now that she has come out of mourning."

Ben searched the crowd. She had vanished.

"I hear you are in trouble over the killing of a constable in Cibuta last week, Meestair," Bouvet said.

"I'm not in trouble. It was self-defense."

"Ah, but you *are* in trouble. In serious trouble. With me."

"How is that? You have a tax on self-defense?"

"I cannot, will not, process the title on the Cibuta ranch until you are cleared of that bloodshed in a Mexican court. If you are not exonerated, it will be my duty to confiscate the ranch and put it up for public sale."

"How can you do that? How can my property be held for ransom?"

"That is Mexican law. You kill a man on your property—the property is subject to seizure. I will invoke the tax laws and take it away from you."

"Try it. You can't bluff me. I own legal title to it, and I'm innocent of wrongdoing."

"That statement offends me. It shows little regard for me, or my power, or the laws of this land. I can condemn that land this minute if I want to."

"Go ahead. You'll have to deal with Don Juan Pedro Elias, and I doubt you're a match for him."

"Don Juan Pedro will not figure in this litigation. The Cibuta ranch will be offered to him when it comes up for sale. He can enjoy the money you paid him. You know, he grossly overcharged you. He'll be able to buy it back from the government for a pittance compared to the amount you paid."

Ben felt it was time to get out of sight. How safe was Eileen with Pancho? He had not seen Don Juan Pedro all day. Was he about to let Kosterlinsky have Ben? Being with Pancho and Margarita did not constitute sanctuary for Ben. He was supposed to be with Don Juan Pedro, or inside his house.

Ben watched for Margarita and saw Kosterlinsky, Duncan Vincent, and Walter Jarboe drive up and dismount from a carriage. Vincent and Jarboe were identically stiff and ponderous. Both were fat in the middle and florid of complexion from spending too much time making deals. Vincent's deals were crooked, but Ben believed Jarboe was honest. He hoped Jarboe was spending time with Vincent only so he could get his money back. Ben felt his enemies were at hand. He was sure they had not come to the tardeada to look at the girls.

Kosterlinsky and Vincent stopped to talk to Captain Carbo. Carbo shook his head at something they said. Jarboe searched the crowd, saw Ben, and made a beeline toward him without saying anything to his companions. Ben rose and introduced him to Bouvet. Bouvet gave him the lily-petal hand to kiss, a poisonous smile, and walked away.

"Well, Ben, you're not as hard to find in Mexico as you are in the States," Jarboe said. "Can we talk business here, or should we go somewhere more private?"

"Anywhere you like," Ben said. This little man wanted Ben to perform for him every time he saw him. "I wanted to get through one afternoon without doing any business, but I'll talk if you want to."

"Let's go somewhere else, then."

Ben walked away into the alamo grove and sat down on the roots of a big tree out of sight of the gathering.

"It's come to my attention that you intercepted some money Duncan Vincent and Kosterlinsky were transporting by stage from Tombstone to Santa Cruz. Is that correct?"

"It is."

"How much was that shipment of gold coin?"

"To tell the truth, I don't know. I never counted it."

"Well, I'm glad you got hold of it. Part of it is mine."

"How do you figure that, Mr. Jarboe?"

"As you know, Duncan Vincent and Kosterlinsky owe me for a thousand steers. At forty dollars a head, that's forty thousand dollars, and it seems to me this is my chance to get my money and go home."

"It might be, but I was hoping to keep it until our war with Vincent is over. How can I tally the cattle that die or are stolen until the war is over? Odoms says he's going to start shooting our cattle."

"You know that Kosterlinsky and Vincent owe me that money, don't you? You were the first man I asked to help me when I came out here looking for my cattle."

"I do know that, yes."

"Well, take me to it and count it out so I can go home."

"I'm not sure what to do next, but I think I've worn out my welcome here. Kosterlinsky wants me in jail. Vincent and Odoms want me dead, and I think I've lost my sanctuary."

"When do you want to go home?"

"Tomorrow."

"Kosterlinsky and Vincent will let you leave Sonora safely if you'll pay me what I'm owed out of that gold you took from them. They would rather see me paid what I'm owed than let you keep it."

"You mean they won't try to jail me down here?"

"I can save you that hardship if you take me to the gold."

"Listen, they don't have men enough to put me in jail again, so I don't need you."

"I'll tell you what I'll do. I'll just split it with you. If my half is less than forty thousand dollars, I'll call it even and not cry over the loss, how's that?"

"No, Mr. Jarboe. You can have your forty thousand dollars if it's there. It's your money. I have to admit that."

"Good. When can we go?"

"Tomorrow."

"Where can I pick you up at train time?"

"At the Garrett."

"Fine. I'm staying there too."

Ben sighed and stood up. "Is there anything else, Mr. Jarboe?"

"No, I knew you would tell me the truth, and I thank you for it. I'll be in front of the hotel with a rig an hour before train time."

"You'll keep Vincent and Kosterlinsky off me?"

"I guarantee it. Oh, and Ben, another thing . . ."

"What?"

"Get back to your room in the hotel and stay there. Don't go to the Elias's. Odoms is waiting for you with a gun."

"What's he on the prod about?"

"He claims you're bedding his wife."

There it is, Ben thought. He has the right to shoot me, no matter how I look at it.

Kosterlinsky and Vincent came around the tree. "Ah, there you are, Benjamin," Kosterlinsky said. "Have you made arrangements to return that money to Mr. Jarboe?"

"Yes, he has," Jarboe said.

"I knew Ben would come to terms. He can always be trusted." Kosterlinsky turned to Vincent. "Didn't I tell you he would uncover that gold when he came down here to pay for the Cibuta ranch?"

Vincent's face was red with anger. "There was a lot more than forty thousand dollars in that shipment. I want the remainder of that gold returned to me. I think we ought to hold him until it's all paid. Why let him go? We've got him where we want him now. He can tell us where the money is or go to the firing squad for murdering those boys at the Nogales cow pens and that other boy in Cibuta."

"No, we made a deal," Jarboe said. "He goes back with me, or I'll prosecute both of you for fraud."

"Don't worry so much, Mr. Vincent," Ben said. "The fight isn't over. My family and I will never forget the beatings you gave my father and me, the deaths of our friends and family, or the financial ruin you tried to deal us. Don't look so sad. You'll get another chance to backshoot me."

"It's probably best this way," Vincent said. "You're too dumb and stubborn to give back that gold any other way. I know we can't make you tell where it is. If we tried to beat it out of you, we'd end up killing you, and then we'd *never* get it back."

"You have a good memory, Mr. Vincent. You tried to beat me to death and couldn't get it done. Could not, by God, get it done. I'll be happy to give your money to Mr. Jarboe."

"Let me tell you something, Cowden. Jack Odoms won't waste time beating on you. He'll escort you unharmed straight up the stairs to the gallows."

Ben went back to the table, took Eileen's hand, and stood her out of her chair. Margarita had not returned.

Pancho smiled at him. "Have you ever danced with your sister, Benjamin? Dance with her. She's like a butterfly."

"I'm taking her to the hotel, Pancho. We'll send someone for her clothes."

"But why, Benjamin? I don't understand."

"Ask Don Juan Pedro. Ask Margarita and your new brother-in-law."

Jarboe gave the Cowdens a ride to the hotel in his rented rig. Eileen cried with anger. "You and your goddammed war," she said.

Ben's heart hurt when he was alone in his room. He felt Margarita's attention and Don Juan Pedro's protection had been a betrayal. Vincent, Kosterlinsky, and Odoms must have forced Don Juan Pedro to lure Ben to Hermosillo to buy the Cibuta ranch so they could capture him and make him give back the gold. He bet the Cibuta gold would find its way back to Vincent and Don Juan Pedro would get his ranch back. Don Juan Pedro must be in a hell of a mess to betray a friend like that. Margarita had petted him into docility.

He undressed and lay in misery for several hours, his body in a state of withdrawal. He had been drinking brandy, morning and night. He had not been sober for a week. His body began to clamor for alcohol.

At midnight he dressed and left his room, the need for alcohol jerking at his limbs. He did not want to be seen, so he did not go into the cantinas. He wandered back to the Elias home. A bottle of mescal was kept in a cabinet by the bed in the room he had used. He was confident he could get in and out of the house without being seen.

Maybe he could see Margarita. He needed the drink, but he needed her even more. He was more addicted to her than he was to the alcohol. Coming down from the drink was not nearly as hard as coming down from the woman. He had been as high on her as a man could be.

He slipped through a gate on the tapia, crossed the patio, and went into the house. He listened at the door to Margarita's room a moment and went on to his room. He found the mescal, sat on the edge of the bed, and drank seven big swallows. He lay down to wait until he felt better.

The walls of the house were thick adobe and nearly soundproof, but the house was so quiet, he could hear a drone of voices. He opened a window. The voices were coming from Don Juan Pedro's study across the corner of the patio downstairs. The curtain was drawn on the window of the study, so he could not see the people inside. He took the bottle and went back to Margarita's room. He needed her so much, his hand shook when he reached for the doorknob.

He stepped inside the room, went to the bed, and struck a match. She was not in the room. He sat on the bed, his heart thumping. He took another drink for his heart and went back down the hall, down the stairs, across the vestibule inside the front door, and down another hall to the study. He was not afraid of being caught. He pitied the poor son-of-a-bitch who was unlucky enough to discover him.

Inside the study Don Juan Pedro asked, "How many this time, Gabriel?"

"Twelve head," Kosterlinsky said.

"Where are they landing?"

"At Puerto Libertad, the same as last time."

"Where will they cross into Arizona?"

"You know where. Don't act stupid."

"Ah, no. I told you, no more Chinos cross the border at my ranch."

"Then we call in your note, Elias. If you want to participate in the profits, you have to furnish a safe route for the traffic. Why else would we need you?"

"There must be some other way for me to pay you what I owe."

Duncan Vincent spoke up. "As I told you, the only other way is for you to give me the title to the Cibuta ranch and let me see what I can do with your old Spanish title to the Buena Vista."

"I don't owe you that much, and I don't own the Cibuta ranch anymore. My friend Ben Cowden owns it," Don Juan Pedro said.

"You're getting it back." Ben recognized Bouvet's

voice. "I will see to that as a favor to my friend Vincent."

"Turn those two titles and a deed to the María Macarena over to us, and we'll liquidate your debt," Kosterlinsky said. "If you don't want to do that, you'll have to help us get those Chinamen to Tucson."

The floor creaked under Ben's feet, and the men in the study fell silent. When they started talking again, Ben slipped away.

He went back to his room in the hotel and found the door unlocked, Margarita sitting on the bed. He could not keep himself from smiling as he went to her and kissed her. Her eyes showed as much addiction as his.

"Where did you go?" she asked.

"I went out to find a drink. Where did you go when you left me at the tardeada?"

"Bouvet made me cry. I didn't want to go back to the table with him, so I went to find my father."

"Why couldn't you come back to the table?"

"You would have seen me crying and started a row with Bouvet."

"What makes you think that?"

"I saw your eyes watching me. It was all you could do to keep from coming out on the floor and knocking him down so you could take me back. I left there with Bouvet's insults in my ears and your eyes devouring me. I'd had enough."

"Where did you go?"

"Colorado drove me out to look for my father."

Ben decided not to tell her that he knew her father was helping Vincent, Kosterlinsky, and Bouvet smuggle Chinese into Arizona. He wanted to see if she would tell him about it.

"What did Bouvet say to you?"

"Ben, let's forget about it."

"All right."

"Just know that by leaving the tardeada, I kept you from trouble."

"Thank you."

"I'm your angel, you know. God sent me to look after you."

"Is that right?"

"Yes, God is worried about you, and I have to put myself between you and the men who want to harm you. It's hard work, but I can do it because I'm an angel."

"Can't the bad men harm you too?"

"Only my body, not my soul."

"Then your flesh is a woman's, but your spirit is an angel's."

"Yes, that's so you can kiss me."

"God must love me a lot. Other men don't get to kiss their angels."

"Nor do their angels fall in love with them."

In the night he awoke, and she was lying still and warm in his arms, giving out contented little snores. He thought, How can anyone sleep like that and ever come back to life? He was lying against her back feeling every live inch of her, even inside the arch of her foot. He moved, and her skin clung to his as though trying to hold him. Her warmth was so moist against him, it almost scalded, but she slept on, seeming dead to the world.

CHAPTER 7

Undersheriff A. B. Cowden was not fully recovered from a beating Duncan Vincent's hired thugs had given him in the fall. He was able to perform his official duties for the county and able to oversee his freight business, but he tired easily. He never thought about the beating though. The man who manacled and bludgeoned him in his own jail had paid his debt by taking a blast in the face from A.B.'s shotgun. Duncan Vincent was still in arrears, though, and his account was mounting.

The soreness of A.B.'s healing ribs constricted his breathing as he drove into Harshaw behind a team of black horses. He circled the Harshaw pond, drove past the hotel to Saloon Row, tied up in front of Vince Farley's saloon, and went in. A.B. was a tall slender man, and he wore a three-piece suit with his badge on the vest.

Vince Farley, who was married to one of A.B.'s wife, Viney's, sisters, had sent word that he would like to see him as soon as he came in town. Vince was carrying a full bucket and sprinkling water on the clean sawdust of the saloon floor to settle the dust. The water brought out the sawdust's fresh pine smell. A.B. observed that the smell of pine mixed with the smell of whiskey could distract the best of men, even an undersheriff.

"Here's someone who wants to meet you, A.B.," Vince said. "His name is Joe Coyle." A wiry young man stepped away from the bar and shook A.B.'s hand.

"I've heard a lot about you, Mr. Cowden," Coyle said. "Lately I've been employed by a man who often speaks of you and your sons."

"Yes, and who might that be?" A. B. Cowden tried to live his life so no man could find a reason to run him down.

"Duncan Vincent, owner of the VO ranch."

"I would not be surprised at anything that man thought or said about me, so that gives you an advantage over me, young man."

"No, sir, it doesn't. Mr. Vincent also made an extremely disagreeable impression on me."

A.B. waited.

"However, that is not the reason I wanted to meet you, sir," Coyle said. "I heard you needed a blacksmith. I'm a good one. I smithed and rode twelve years for the Texas Rangers."

"Why did you leave the Rangers, Mr. Coyle?"

"I lost my wife, and I had a small son to raise."

Vince Farley brought out A.B.'s personal bottle of J.P.S. Brown whiskey and filled half a glass for him. "Mr. Coyle, will you join me?" A.B. said.

"I believe I will."

Vince poured Coyle the same measure of the stuff. A.B. sipped his whiskey, and Coyle did the same. "This whiskey is kind to a man," said Coyle.

"Kind to the man who doesn't fight it," A.B. said.

"It will be nice to me, then, for I don't fight my small pleasures."

"What brought you to Arizona, Mr. Coyle?"

"My son and I owned a small ranch and cattle in Texas and went three years without a rain. After my last good cow died and the remnant of my herd lost its value, Captain Jack Odoms recruited me to come to Arizona with him. He said he'd been hired to form a cadre of Rangers that would campaign against cowthieves for the Pima

County Live Stock Association. He said our cadre would be the foundation of the Arizona Rangers. I liked the idea, for I enjoy being of service to people. I sold my ranch and remaining stock, and rode out here with Odoms and the other men he hired."

"Why did you quit Odoms?"

"I served in the Texas Rangers with three of those men. Two of them were capable fighters with bad reputations. They were always hired provisionally for special jobs and then released. The other was fired from the Rangers after he was suspected of murdering a prisoner. I did not like serving with them while the Rangers tolerated them, and by the time we reached Arizona, I liked them even less. I had never met the other two before we started for Arizona, and I still did not know them when we reached Arizona. I did not want my little son to grown up near those men. I shod their horses while they were waiting in Santa Cruz for authorization to act as provisional police in Sonora, drew my first pay, and quit."

"I take it you don't consider Odoms a bad influence on your boy."

"Captain Odoms is a strict man who claims to be a just and righteous man, but that's all he is. He always treated me with respect, but he's so righteous, he's damnable. His righteousness leaves no room for compassion or mercy. Any man or woman who has been accused of a crime is dirt under his feet, even after they've been proven innocent, and so are their families and friends. He has no more qualms about throwing an accused man in a cage and making sure he is executed than he has for a rabid dog."

"Why did he leave the Texas Rangers?"

"I don't know. He served them honorably, but his service was always a crusade. Maybe he figures this job is another one. As far as I know, that's all he really cares about—his crusades."

"You dislike the man, then."

"I never liked him. I stayed in his service because of his honesty and truthfulness. I liked his judgment in dangerous situations. He is capable, and he never gives up on the trail of a lawbreaker. He has never failed to bring in a fugitive he set out to catch, and he's not a killer."

"How do you explain his hiring bad men?"

"I think he felt the Rangers hampered his crusade in Texas. I think he believes it takes a thug to catch and punish a thug. I quit him because he expected me to ride with his thugs and do their kind of work. He doesn't care if they execute prisoners as long he's not told about it."

"What did he say to you when you quit?"

"He warned me against joining you. Anybody who quits Jack Odoms becomes his enemy. He was sure I quit him so I could join you."

"If he's a just man, we're not his enemies. If he is the arm of Duncan Vincent, he has joined the wrong side in a war."

"I don't want to be in your war either, Mr. Cowden. I only want to make an honest living so I can raise and educate my son."

"That's good enough for me, but I can't guarantee you won't have to defend yourself against the VO. They have carried the fight right into my home and attacked my women. We can use you, and you can come home with me this evening, but you have to know, the VO won't leave you alone if you work for us."

"I'll take the job. My son is in school, though, and won't be let out until this evening."

"Oh, he's already in school with Mrs. Chance?"

"The first thing I did when I came to Harshaw was put him to work at his schooling."

"How old is he?"

"He's twelve."

"Ah, my little daughter Paula Mary's twelve. She's in Mrs. Chance's school too."

Paula Mary Cowden made friends with Jimmy Coyle during the first recess the day he enrolled in school. She was with him so much that her best friend and cousin, Myrtle Farley, complained she never got to play with Paula Mary anymore.

The trouble was, Paula Mary seldom got to be with Jimmy. He had a job after school and would not talk about it. This intrigued Paula Mary. Jimmy was very grown-up and did not play games with the rest of the children. He carried a purse for the money he earned, and in that way he reminded Paula Mary of Guilo Soto, another good friend of hers. Guilo had been murdered for the stakes he was holding in a horse race that fall.

Jimmy and Paula Mary had won first prize in the waltz contest at the Thanksgiving Day dance. He was taking Paula Mary to lunch at Frank Wong's restaurant that day to celebrate. This was the day the school held its entertainment program, and the children had been released for the afternoon. Paula Mary saw Jimmy come out of the schoolroom and worried how she would get rid of Myrtle so she could be alone with him.

Jimmy was small for his age and wiry. He had brown hair, blue eyes, and freckles. His smile was careful and warm, and Paula Mary thought he was as handsome as he could be.

"Well, Paula Mary, if you're ready, we better go," Jimmy said.

"Where you going?" Myrtle asked.

"Jimmy's invited me for lunch," Paula Mary said.

"Well, good. I'll just walk along with you," Myrtle said.

"Good," Jimmy said.

When they stopped in front of Wong's, Myrtle stopped too. Paula Mary turned to see her off, but she said, "You know, I think I'll just have lunch with you. You need a chaperone, don't you? What if your mama and papa find out you went on a date without a chaperone?" She knew Paula Mary better than any other human, and when Paula Mary's mouth clamped shut instead of protesting, Myrtle knew her folks had not been told about the date with Jimmy. She said, "That way, you can tell your mama you went to lunch with your cousin Myrtle, and it won't be a lie."

Jimmy quickly turned his back on the girls and took

out his purse to count his money to see if he could afford Myrtle. "Yes, that will be all right, Myrtle," he said, and put the purse away.

This was a party day at school, and the three of them wore their best clothes. Paula Mary and Myrtle wore hats and gloves. Jimmy was not dressed up, but his clothes were clean, and he had scrubbed himself and wet down his hair. Garbie Burr, Mark Cowden's girlfriend, showed them to a cozy private cubicle and unfolded their napkins for them. Paula Mary sat on the inside next to Jimmy, and Myrtle sat across from them.

"I see you brought an extra guest, Jimmy," Garbie said.

"Yes, Myrtle will be having dinner too," he said.

"You're right on time, and I have it all ready." Garbie went away to her other customers.

"You didn't say you were going to eat here," Myrtle said. "My mama better not find out."

"What's wrong with eating here?" Paula Mary said.

Myrtle said loudly, "Everybody knows chop suey is chopped-up cats and dogs."

Jimmy blushed and looked around to see if anyone was offended.

"It probably is." Paula Mary grinned at Myrtle. "I wonder how much different cats taste from dogs and dogs taste from beef?"

"Paula Mary, we can't eat cat- and dogmeat."

"Huh! I sure can." She couldn't, but she had Myrtle on the run.

Myrtle stood up to leave.

"Where you going?" Paula Mary asked.

"Home. I won't eat dogmeat. You'll just have to do without a chaperone."

"Don't you even want to taste it? Come on, Myrtle, it'll be fun."

"Oh, no. I dressed up like a boy with you at Guilo's funeral, and I stood guard at the back door when you went in the saloon, but I draw the line when it comes to eating cats and dogs."

"You might like it."

Myrtle headed for the door mumbling to herself.

"Come on, Myrtle. You wanted to be with us, you better stay." Paula Mary's tone rubbed it in too deep.

Myrtle stopped and turned back. "This just goes to prove what everybody's been saying about you Cowdens."

"Who's been saying things about us?" Paula Mary gave Myrtle a mocking smile.

"Everybody. All the kids at school got it from their mothers and fathers."

"Got what?"

"That you're a bunch of outlaws and murderers. And you especially are the Cowdens' murdering baby cow-thief."

"*Myrtle.*"

The door was heavy for Myrtle, but she got through it quickly. Paula Mary couldn't tell if she hurried away in anger or in fear. She heard a man in the restaurant say, "Hey, that must be the Cowden girl I heard killed Frank Marshall."

Paula Mary felt she'd been slapped. She said, "How could Myrtle say that? It's not true."

Jimmy looked around at two miners, who grinned and waved at him from a cubicle across the room. When he turned back, his face was red. He got up and moved to Myrtle's place opposite Paula Mary.

"Why'd you do that, Jimmy?"

"To give you more room and watch for our food."

"Have you heard stories about my family too?"

"I never carry tales."

"But I'm asking you to tell me. Have you heard anyone call me a . . . baby cowthief?"

"Nothing like that means anything to me."

"But you have heard it?"

"A thing or two, yes."

"Oh."

"I don't pay attention to talk. Anyone who says things like that means to do wrong, so it doesn't mean anything to me. I'm your friend."

"So I'm the Cowdens' murdering baby cowthief. A rat who worked for Duncan Vincent accused my brother Ben of being a cowthief, beat him up, then beat up my papa, then came to our home and tied up my mother and big sister, and was coming after me and my sister Betty, intending to kill us all, when my papa stopped him with his shotgun. Is that why they're calling me the Cowdens' murdering baby cowthief?"

"I don't know, Paula Mary. I don't care." Jimmy's attention was on the miners, and his face was still red.

Paula Mary looked around the corner at the grinning miners and turned quickly back to Jimmy. "Yes, you do. I can see it in your face."

"No, I don't, Paula Mary."

"Yes you do, and you moved over there because you don't want to sit next to me."

"I didn't move because of that. I told you why I moved."

"Well, you sure don't have to be seen with me if you don't want to, mister."

Garbie came to the table with their lunch and fortune cookies on a tray. "Where's Myrtle?" she asked.

Paula Mary was so angry that she made a face at the food and kicked her legs out of the booth.

"Where are you going?" Jimmy asked.

"Away, so I won't embarrass you."

"Aw, Paula Mary."

"Don't bother to follow me. I'm going home." Paula Mary hurried out of the place. She saw her papa's buggy on the street and climbed on without looking back. Jimmy Coyle and Myrtle were the two best friends she had in the world, but she didn't care if she ever saw them again. She felt a terrible loss, and she started to tremble. Those miners would be tickled to death a Cowden had lost her best friends. Not a speck of love was lost between the Harshaw cattlemen and the miners.

Duncan Vincent had stolen as many mining claims as ranchers' homesteads, but the miners still resented the Cowdens. The Cowdens were the only people in the region fighting the VO. Vincent grabbed the land and water of anybody who was not strong enough to keep it. People figured it was easier to let him have it than to fight his cold-blooded, powerful, influential syndicate.

Paula Mary was becoming aware the range war might ruin her life. She was losing her friends now, and by gosh the war had to stop. She climbed down from the buggy and went to the door of Farley's saloon, looking for her papa. She was about to push open the swinging doors when a miner came out. One look and the smell of him told her he was drunk.

"Little girl, what do you want in a saloon?" he said.

"I want to see if my papa's in there," Paula Mary said.

"No, no, no. No little girls allowed in there."

"This is my uncle Vince's saloon. Could you ask if my papa's in there?"

"What's your name?"

"Paula Mary Cowden."

"Oh, so that's who you are, the baby of that outfit I've heard so much about." He looked up and down the street. "Your daddy's Undersheriff Cowden?"

Paula Mary nodded.

"Your brother's Ben Cowden?"

She nodded again.

"You're the one who pinned Frank Marshall against the ground with a pitchfork so your daddy could blow his head off with a shotgun."

"I did not. My sister Betty stuck a pitchfork in him when he—"

"Oh, your sister Betty did that. Is she littler'n you? I heard the little'un did that."

"No, I'm the littlest one, but—"

"Now you're headed into a saloon, are ye? Well, go right ahead. You belong in there."

"I just want to see if my papa is in there."

"Go right on in. Here, let me hold the door open for you. I'll do anything you want. Where's your pitchfork? Please don't stick me." The man held both swinging doors wide open.

"I wasn't going in," Paula Mary said.

A.B. took the doors away from the man and stepped outside. "Paula Mary, what are you doing here?" he said.

"I was looking for you, Papa. Are you going home now?"

The man turned away and laughed as he walked down the street toward the next saloon.

"I thought your entertainment program was on this afternoon, daughter," A.B. said.

"I don't feel good, Papa. I want to go home."

A.B. looked at his watch. "Well, we have a little while before the doings start at the school. Let's go see if your mother can find out what's wrong with you."

The blacks were at a brisk trot toward home when A.B. said, "Daughter, I thought you knew better than to go in a saloon."

"I do, Papa, but I had to see if you were in there. It was an emergency. I don't feel good."

"You could have gone to the Farleys'. Your aunt Edna knows how to deal with your emergencies. You'll find no comfort in a saloon, whether I'm there or not."

"I couldn't go to the Farleys'."

"Why not?"

"Me and Myrtle fell out, Papa."

A.B. smiled.

"She said everyone in town was calling me a murdering baby Cowden cowthief."

"People are saying that about my little girl?"

"They're saying things like that about all of us, Papa." Paula Mary began to cry.

A.B. remained silent until she subsided, as he knew she would. She never cried long or loud. "That's what's making you feel bad, daughter?"

"Yes. I'll never be able to go back to school now, or face my friends."

"Listen. Myrtle doesn't believe that, and neither do the rest of your friends. But, daughter, you have to watch your deportment and stay away from places like saloons, or everybody will think you're bad. A reputation is hard enough to keep clean when you are good and your family has no enemies. It's nearly impossible to keep clean when your family's in a fight."

At home, Paula Mary climbed into her mother's lap. "I don't know how I can go back to school, now, Mama. Everybody's talking about us."

Viney was small, with glossy black hair, a button nose, and a soft pillowy bosom. She laughed softly. "I wondered how long it would be before you found out you were a baby cowthief."

"A *murdering* baby Cowden cowthief. It's not funny, Mama."

"I know it's not supposed to be funny, daughter, but the way you say it is funny."

"Mama . . ." Paula Mary cried softly.

"Daughter, for every person who says bad things about us, there's another who will defend us and say good things. Everybody in your school who has been your friend is probably still your friend. Terrible things happened to us this past year. People will always entertain themselves with talk. Stories about us are bound to circulate, and they'll get out of shape in the telling. That's life. The way to stop them is to accomplish something new and grand."

"I thought we did something grand when we put Frank Marshall in his grave, Mama."

"We did, but we're the only ones who saw the evil in him, and we're the only ones who really know how he died. Our enemies are bound to make up stories to try and ruin us. That's a way they have of besting us without facing us. You can't let them do it. You have to stand up for yourself, look people in the eye, and set them straight."

"I don't want enemies. The next one who calls me a murdering baby Cowden cowthief is going to get shot."

"Darling, that way of thinking will only find you more enemies. You can't do yourself any good by hurting people. That would only make us all feel worse. We have to stay together, be good, and harm no one. Now, I think you ought to take off your dress and lie down awhile.

Maybe you'll feel more like going to your Thanksgiving Day program after you've rested."

Paula Mary climbed down from her mother's lap and went to the bedroom she shared with her sisters. Viney Cowden said, "I don't want to be sinful, but I sure wish the Lord would do right and strike that Duncan Vincent dead in his tracks."

Paula Mary took off her dress and lay down, but she couldn't rest. After a while she got up, put on her everyday clothes, and went down to the barn. Her brother Mark was shoeing a big gelding named Colonel. Paula Mary sat down on a sack of feed by the door.

"When are you going to let me ride Colonel again, Mark?" she asked.

Mark was underneath Colonel, his mouth full of nails, tacking on a hind shoe.

"Mark?"

"Mmm-mmm," Mark said as he nailed on the shoe. He twisted the sharp points off when they came out the side of the hoof, tapped down the ends so he could form them into buttons, and let the hoof down.

"Mark?"

"Yes, little sister."

"When are you going to let me ride Colonel again?"

"Not until you grow a lot bigger and he grows a lot nicer."

"Why not? I can get on him by myself, walk him away from home, lope him, stop him, and turn him around. What else do I have to be able to do?"

"You have to be big enough to hold him so he won't run away with you and almost kill you and scare this family to death like he did the first time you rode him, that's what."

"That wasn't my fault. I told you why he ran away with me. That old Yaqui Indian scared us both half to death. He'd have run away with anybody when that ugly smelly old thing stepped out and grabbed him."

"Is that your excuse, Paula Mary? Did the Yaqui Indian really try to take the horse away from you that day, or did you start loping him back toward the barn and let him take the bit and run away with you?"

Paula Mary jumped up and ran at her brother like a banshee. She kicked and hit him and screamed, "I'm not a liar!"

Mark was surprised by the onslaught, but he kept his face out of range and took it until she got tired and quit.

She stood back, narrowed her eyes, and said, "Take that, Mark Cowden, for calling me a liar."

"Of course I'll take it, Paula Mary. You're my little sister, and I love you, but you ought to be ashamed. I could never hit you like that, or even think of it, and neither would anyone else in this family."

That made Paula Mary feel so bad, she said she was sorry and then started crying.

Mark hugged her. "That's all right. I didn't mean to hurt your feelings. You can't hit hard enough to break an egg."

CHAPTER 8

Les met the train in Patagonia with a buggy. Jarboe stepped off looking fresh and spry, but Ben and Eileen were sorry sights. Their expressions were miserable, and they had little to say. Ben and Les carried the luggage to the buggy, and Jarboe stayed back to help Eileen.

"How did everything go in Hermosillo?" Les asked.

"*Todo para la chingada*, everything turned into a fornication," Ben said. He meant it figuratively but realized it was literally true. No, not a fornication—an adultery.

"How's that? Didn't you buy the ranch?"

"I paid for it, but I don't know if I'll be able to keep it."

"Why not?"

"I fell into a great big trap."

"Who set it?"

"Vincent. Somehow he got Don Juan Pedro to bait it with the Cibuta ranch to make me uncover the alazanas I took off the stage."

"No, Ben. Don Juan Pedro wouldn't throw in with Vincent, would he?"

"I heard him talking to Vincent and Kosterlinsky. He owes them a lot of money, and they've got something on him. He has to do anything they want him to do."

"What've they got on him?"

"I don't know everything, but he's been helping them smuggle Chinamen into Arizona."

"I haven't seen any Chinamen, or any Chinaman tracks."

"Neither have I, but where do Chinamen go?"

"I don't know—to work on the railroads, I guess."

"That's right, and Vincent's syndicate owns railroads. I'm going to find out how they're getting across. If we can catch Vincent and Odoms smuggling Chinamen, they might quit bothering us."

On the way home, Ben rode up front with Les, Jarboe in back with Eileen. Once, when Jarboe was talking loudly so Eileen could hear him over the noise of the team and buggy, Les quietly, carefully asked Ben, "Did you tell Jarboe about this? He's a U.S. marshal, isn't he? He's helped us before."

"No," Ben said. "He only got himself commissioned a U.S. marshal in Kansas so he could come out here and get his money. He's no lawman; he's a businessman. After I give him his gold, he won't need to be a marshal anymore, and I bet he turns into a businessman again and heads home. Tomorrow he might find another way to do business with Vincent. Let's not trust him."

"It seems to me he's worth more to us as a U.S. marshal than he is as a satisfied customer."

"He is. I just wish I could figure out a way to keep from giving him his money. We need him to stay here in case we get in another tight spot with Vincent's constables."

Ben and Les were practiced at making themselves understood to one another with little more than a whisper. They were sure Walter Jarboe could not hear what they were saying. He had not stopped talking to Eileen since they pulled away from the Patagonia station.

"How come you and Eileen are so down?" Les asked.

"Just tired from the trip and lack of sleep."

"That's not what I mean. You can't hide it from me when you're miserable."

"I feel bad that Juan Pedro Elias threw in with Vincent, Odoms, and Kosterlinsky."

He thought, I wish that was all that hurt me. I can see the very good possibility that Margarita *Odoms* set me up so Jack Odoms could knock me down. What better way could Vincent ruin me than catch me committing adultery? They already have me in pain, because I don't think I can stay away from her.

Well, maybe I'm just jealous. She sleeps with Odoms and takes his abuse when I can't be with her. She talks about going away with me but never about trying to be rid of him. She's staying with that marriage, no matter how I feel. She even encourages me to stay with Maudy. The farther I get away from her, the more I suspect that she does not give a real damn about me, yet I'll go back to her as soon as I can. I'll keep cowboying that side of the Buena Vista so I can be close to her.

On the other hand, she's her father's daughter. If Vincent has Don Juan Pedro in a trap, he has Margarita in a trap. She would do anything to help her father. I know she loves me. She'll come over to me openly when it comes time for her to choose between me and Odoms. I hope she'll tell me if she finds out what they plan to do to the Cowdens in this war. It hurts me to think that she might be manipulated by Vincent to bring me down, but I like being with her so much, I don't care.

Maudy was at El Durazno. She came out the front door with the rest of the Cowdens and waved as the buggy passed under the walnut trees, then again as it crossed the creek and pulled up in front of the barn.

She went with the family to the barn. Her face was so open, pretty, and full of goodness, her look so trusting, Ben felt a stab of guilt for not being happier to see her. Margarita had an awful hold on him, and that was all there was to it. Maybe being with Maudy could loosen it. If he could give all his attention to Maudy, maybe the pain of being away from Margarita would stop. Being with Maudy might do it someday, but not as long as he knew Margarita's rosy skin was waiting for him across the Buena Vista.

Ben kissed his mother and Paula Mary, shook hands with his papa and Mark, then turned to Maudy, his whole family beaming at him. He kissed her quickly, as though too modest to make it last in front of his family. She kissed him good-humoredly.

Maudy's love was happy and healthy because she was not addicted to Ben. She needed to know him better to be addicted. She would have to know his body and have it taken away. She would have to be with him in a forbidden way before she could start craving him. Because of that, she would never suffer for him the way he suffered for Margarita. She would wait to know his body until they were married, and then they would never be apart. Maudy would never know what it was like to turn hot and sweaty and have her legs and hands shake at the thought of him. She would never be jealous because her love was not marred by obsession. When he wasn't with her, she'd simply do without him and never suffer a craving for him. Maudy was a *good* girl, thank God.

Ben walked to the house with Paula Mary hugging him around the waist on one side and Maudy holding his hand on the other. Inside, his sister Betty came and kissed him. Betty had kept to herself a lot since Frank Marshall had tried to rape her and she had helped put him to death. After Marshall's carcass was carted away to the cemetery, Betty had taken to her bed for a month. Then one day, without a word to anyone, she rose, dressed, and helped Eileen clean the house. She stayed in the house though. She had not been outside since that night in September when Marshall had come raging into El Durazno and tried to kill the whole family.

During the evening, Ben could not stop thinking about Margarita. He was in the saddest, most depressed state of his entire life, and his family made him cranky. He wanted to be alone with his craving for her. He was so cranky that Viney finally came over and felt his forehead to see if he had a fever.

"Why are you so short with everyone, son? Are you coming down sick?"

"Just coming down, Mama. I had a lot too much to drink in Hermosillo."

"Lordy, I never saw it fail. Every time you boys come out of that Mexico, you're sick. What is it you fill up on down there that makes you so ill?"

"I don't know for sure, Mama, but I think it's the mixture of mesquite smoke and toilet water."

The family laughed at that.

"Or maybe you got hold of a spoilt tortilla," Les said.

Everybody except Mark and Betty laughed at that. They were so alike, they could have been twins, and they knew Ben's heart was changed. This puzzled them, and they watched him for a clue to the change.

Ben thought, When they get tired of trying to figure me out, they might notice Eileen is hurting as much as me from the same malady. Eileen was staying away from everybody as though she had a lot to do unpacking her clothes. A normal Eileen would have finished that chore and taken charge of the household quickly.

Johnny Bonner gave a whoop from the road to announce his arrival. That whoop he always gave was the most spirited act he ever demonstrated.

"Eileen," Paula Mary sang out. "It's Johnny Bonner, coming asparking."

Eileen kept sorting her clothes. Ben knew she was trying to keep her memories fresh. She had bought fine new clothes in Hermosillo and was comparing them to her old clothes to see which old ones could keep company with the new ones. That was a way she could remain tied to the good time she had enjoyed with Pancho. She sure was lucky she had not fallen in love with him.

But look at her—maybe she was in love with Pancho. Ben had been so intent on his own misery, he had not seen that Eileen was also smitten. Now that he looked at her, his poor sister seemed to be as mournful as she was before she visited Dr. Inukai.

Maudy was beginning to look puzzled too. Even though she must still trust that Ben could not have been unfaithful to her, she was sensitive to him and knew he'd come home a different Ben. He was rarely in any kind of a mood, but both of them knew he should have been happier to see her. Maudy was strong enough to be quiet and let him find his own way through the trouble. Knowing he could be with her now made Ben feel better.

On the other hand, Johnny Bonner would not know a heartsick girl from a keg of beer. Eileen did not have a soul to help her.

Ben followed her into the kitchen. She scooped a drink out of the water bucket with the old long-handled tin dipper the Cowden children had used all their lives. Ben put his arm around her, squeezed her, and looked into her face. Two spare little tears were drying in the corners of her eyes.

Eileen had only glanced at Ben to see what he wanted. She was the housekeeper again. She figured the vacation was over and Ben needed to be handed something or shown where it was. When she saw the look on his face, she put her arms around his neck and her head on his shoulder. "Brother, what am I going to do? Here comes Johnny Bonner."

That tickled Ben, because for the first time, he saw Johnny Bonner from Eileen's point of view. Eileen felt his sides shake, stepped back so she could see his face again, and started laughing too.

"Oh, God," she said. "I'm hurting so much. You too?"

"It's awful."

"What are *you* gonna do?"

"I've been wondering, and everything I can think of to do hurts too."

"Hell, I hoped you would help me get rid of this pain."

"Me? I'm *smitten*. Laid low."

"I've got no will, no hope. It's two hundred miles over a battleground to the man I love, and he ain't Johnny Bonner. He's a goddammed gentleman and feels he has to stay away from me. What am I going to do? You're my brother, and I need you this time for something more than finding me a good horse to ride. Tell me what to do."

Johnny came through the back door, glanced at Eileen's face, stepped up, and shook her hand. "Hello, Eileen, you look good, you sure do." He walked away to shake hands with all the other Cowdens.

Eileen turned to Ben. "See that? How in the world can I start up with that again? Did I reach the peak of my life in Hermosillo? Is it all downhill to Benson, Arizona, from here till I die? Do I have to give up?"

"Sister, go the way you want to, and I'll back you up."

"How can I? I'm needed. Why else would Johnny Bonner push himself like a lost dog to get here every third Thursday of the month for two years?"

"I thought it was every first Thursday."

Eileen did not answer. She went to the living room and said, "I'll have your supper in a minute, Johnny. Can I get anyone else anything?"

The family was sitting around a table. Walter Jarboe was in the rocker smoking one of A.B.'s cigars. A.B. gave one to Ben when he sat down. Ben wished Jarboe would go to bed. He wanted to talk to his family.

Tomorrow he would take Jarboe to the Mowry camp and give him his gold. From there he would go work the Buena Vista so he could be close to Margarita. He'd have to watch it. He craved seeing her so much, he might kill a horse getting back to her.

Ben wanted to move the Cowden stock from the Buena Vista to a place called Temporal Canyon to keep Odoms's men from shooting them. As wrong as Odoms would be in killing the cattle, Ben did not think he could stop him from doing it unless they were moved. He must move the cattle out of danger without getting his brothers caught or killed by Odoms. He would try to enlist his two wild and reckless cousins to help him.

"What are the Farley twins doing, Papa?" he asked.

"I think they're working the Mowry, son," A.B. said.

"That's good. I'm taking Mr. Jarboe up there tomorrow, and I need them."

"They went up there about ten days ago. Yesterday their dad told me they're overdue, but that often happens when they camp on the trail of stray cattle."

"Why hasn't someone gone to look for them? If they were up on the Temporal and overdue, we would already be looking for them. The Mowry country is three times more dangerous. It's on the Apache trail to Mexico, the border is only three or four miles away, and they have Mexican mutineers and bandits prowling the country. They're only seven or eight miles from the VO headquarters. The VO is worse than all the Apaches and bandits put together. How come nobody's worried about them?"

"Well, everybody relaxed when you stopped the old Yawner and his band."

"We'd better unrelax. Some of us think he might have played dead and slipped away after we ambushed him at Los Bultos."

"That's what your brothers told me."

"If he did, he'll be in the Huachucas, above Grandfather Porter's headquarters. If he decides to head west, his next watering place after the Santa Cruz River is Mowry Spring. The Mowry is not a safe place."

"Well, everybody figures the twins can take care of themselves."

The family stayed out of the kitchen so Eileen and Johnny Bonner could be alone while he ate supper. She sat across the table from him and watched him eat. He knew no accepted table manners. He handled his knife and fork and cup and saucer in the most awkward manner, but he was a clean and silent eater. He kept his eyes on his plate. He would never look Eileen in the eye when he was being scrutinized, as he was now. During the past year, Eileen had stopped looking at his face. Now that she looked at him, she found characteristics, lines, expression that she had never seen before and realized she knew little about him.

"John, when am I going home with you to meet your mother and family?"

"Someday, I guess."

"'Someday,' you guess?"

"I guess so."

"That's what you always say."

"I have to say that. How can I take you through the darned Apaches? Men run for their lives across that country, and more than one lady has been dragged off her rig and chopped to pieces."

"Then I can't really say you'll ever take me home with you, can I."

"Well, sure you can, but not for a while."

"Another 'while' can turn into a lifetime. I'm kind of glad it's lasted all this while because I don't really think I want to live over there with you anymore."

Johnny Bonner swallowed and looked squarely into Eileen's face. "Why not?"

"If I braved all the hazards you say exist between here and there and made it, I'd probably never get back. The way you operate, I'd be there for life, cut off from my family and everybody I love."

"I'd be there. I'd be . . . er . . . lovin' ya. I think my pa and ma would. You'd never be lonesome. I've got three brothers all older'n me. You'd be so busy, you wouldn't want to come home."

"Glory be, you finally told me about your family. Are your brothers the ones who'll keep me busy, or will the whole outfit have things for me to do so I won't get lonesome?"

"There's plenty to do. I know you like to have plenty to do."

"Sure, why else would I want to marry you, Johnny? I don't know a thing about your people. My papa told me your pa and your uncle Arnold are two of the finest men he's ever known and that's why he recommended you as a suitor. No one else came forward with such a good recommendation, so I might as well take you to wed, is that it?"

Johnny Bonner smiled. Eileen liked his smile, his clean breath in the brushy way he kissed her from time to time, and his honesty. "That's the way I figure it," he said. "Nobody else loves ya but me. I figure I'm lucky I found ya, lucky to get ya, and everybody else is unlucky as heck."

"You do?"

"Yeah."

"Well, let me tell you something. I'm taking a brother and sister with me, and I'm going over to Benson to meet your folks."

"You better not try to do that right now. It's—"

"John Bonner, it's now or never. I'm going home with you Sunday. If you insist on leaving without me this time, you can figure on never coming back to see me."

"Now, Eileen, I don't think that's right."

"What's not right? After two years, I insist on seeing your home and meeting your family. Have you been lying to me? Do you really have a mother and a father and brothers? Papa says you have a sister too. Isn't her name Louise? How come you've never mentioned her?"

"I've mentioned her."

"Never."

"You're gonna meet her, but now's not the right time."

"Why not?"

"My pa, and Uncle Arnold, and my brothers are out on roundup. Only my ma and little sister Louise are home."

"Let's get over there and trot 'em out."

"Now?"

"Now or never."

"You're not trying to back out on me, are you?"

"I'm not trying to back out, but I won't sit here and watch you ride home alone one more time. If you want to marry me, it will have to happen now, by the end of the month, or never."

The family headed for bed. Ben and A.B. walked down to the barn together. Joe and Jimmy Coyle were asleep in their quarters. Ben and A.B. sat down in his office with their cigars. A.B. brought a quart of his whiskey and two glasses out of his desk and poured them each a measure.

"Papa, Ducan Vincent and Kosterlinsky are smuggling Chinese into the country."

"Do you know where, son?"

"Somewhere on Don Juan Pedro's ranch."

"His border is one hundred fifty miles long. How did you find out about this?"

"I was in Don Juan Pedro's house one evening when I was not supposed to be, and I heard the three of them talking."

"Oh, then Don Juan Pedro knows about it?"

"He's in it with them, though I think against his will. He owes them a lot of money."

"I've heard about this smuggling Vincent and Kosterlinsky are suspected of doing, but nobody's been able to find out where they cross. The Salazar brothers told me they saw Chinese in Magdalena."

"That's lucky. Weren't they hiding?"

"I think they probably thought they were, but you know, everybody shows his face when a parade goes by. That's how the Salazars saw them. They were riding in a Guadalupe Day procession, and the Chinese showed themselves at the windows and doors where they were staying."

"How do they know Don Juan Pedro and Kosterlinsky are the ones doing the smuggling?"

"The Chinese were in a house that belongs to Don Juan Pedro, and a squad of Kosterlinsky's Rurales' horses were stabled in the back."

"We'll be working the Buena Vista. We'll see if we can find out where they're crossing."

"You won't catch Vincent or Kosterlinsky, or even Don Juan Pedro, smuggling Chinese. They hire it done."

"I bet Odoms will have something to do with it, though. I can move our cattle out of there and give him a lot of other trouble while he's busy smuggling Chinese."

"Don't get into any firefights, please."

"We won't. I'll take my brothers and the Farley twins,

if I can find them. We'll camp at Yerba Buena, Proto, Paloma, Providencia, and Sycamore canyons, in that order, for a while. We'll move every day, so if you need us, you'll know, more or less, how to find us."

CHAPTER 9

The next morning Ben and Les told their mother they would not have breakfast with the family. They wanted to stop in Harshaw and have *menudo*, a stew made from beef paunch, hooves, and bleached corn. Ben thought this drunkard's stew might help him come down from his trip to Hermosillo.

Ben and Les would be the only ones going with Jarboe to the Mowry. They saddled their horses, packed their beds and camp on another, then harnessed a team so A.B. could take Johnny Bonner, Eileen, Paula Mary, and Mark to the railway station in Patagonia. Eileen and her brother and sister would be a week visiting the Bonners.

Walter Jarboe, Ben, and Les rode to Harshaw in a light drizzling rain. Jarboe went into the Harshaw Hotel to check his mail and send telegrams. Ben and Les put their horses in a corral behind the hotel and went in their Uncle Vince's saloon for the *menudo*. Vince provided *menudo* every morning at seven as a special service, absolute cure, salve, balm, and consolation for hangovers.

As they walked through the back door, Ben met Dick Martin, the constable of Patagonia. Martin had joined the range war in the beginning on Vincent's side. Vincent arranged Martin's commission as constable so he could use him against the Cowdens. However, Vincent had not figured on Martin's fairness. Martin had objected to Vincent's bullying methods and was shot by Frank Marshall when he tried to stop Marshall from beating A.B. and killing Guilo Soto, the Cowden stableboy. The Cowdens carried Martin to the doctor and saved his life, but his recovery had been slow.

"How are you, Dick?" Ben asked.

"Coming along."

"Want to have menudo with us?"

"Well . . ."

"Come on, friend," Ben said. "We're at peace, aren't we?"

"All right."

The three men sat at a table by the saloon's kitchen. Uncle Vince brought them a pitcher of beer.

"Bring us guts, Uncle Vince," Les said.

"Coming up, coming up." Vince went in the kitchen, and after a while Lorrie Briggs came out, carrying a bowl of menudo in each hand.

Lorrie and Ben had almost become sweethearts, but she blamed Ben for the deaths of two of her brothers. Now every time Ben got close to her, she tried to smite him with something. In Tombstone, on September 16, she had shot his little toe off. His absent toe hurt all the time and reminded him the girl wanted to keep hurting him.

She sure was pretty though—fresh-faced and shiny of eye, with dark auburn hair, clear skin, wide-set, long-lashed eyes, and a profile and figure men would give their souls to keep all their own. That was her trouble. A man would have to give his soul away to mate with Lorrie. She required it. Duncan Vincent had tried to take her as his mistress but was not man enough or audacious enough to keep her.

When Ben saw the way Lorrie was carrying the menudo, he stood up and backed away from the table until she set the bowls in front of Dick and Les.

"What's the matter with Ben Cowden?" Lorrie asked.

"He thought you might hit him with a plate of menudo," Les said.

"Tell him he's right. I would like to smear it in his face."

"Can we have some corn tortillas?" Les asked. "And some *chile tepin?*"

Lorrie went back to the kitchen and came out with another bowl of menudo, a bundle of tortillas wrapped in a cotton dishcloth, a saucer full of chile tepin, and a dish of diced onion and cilantro. Ben sat down and stirred the menudo gently with a spoon, inspecting it.

"She wouldn't poison me, would she?" he said.

"Aw, eat it. She didn't have time to put poison in it," Les said.

Ben's mouth watered from the delicious smell of the steam that rose off the dish, but he did not eat the menudo. He drank a glass of beer and watched Les break up the seed pods of chile tepin and scatter the debris over his stew, then scrape onion and cilantro into it. Like a man working at a job he loved, Les began shoveling in the tasty chunks of paunch, sucking on the gelatinous hoofbones, and filling up with the white, puffy stewed corn and corn tortillas.

The smooth-textured soup and the paunch were the best part of it. The other was good but mostly took away the room that could better be filled by the meat of the cow's stomach.

Les's face began to sweat, but he did not stop to wipe it off or look up until he emptied the bowl. He pushed it away and looked at Ben's. "Aren't you going to eat your menudo?" he asked. "Think about it. The worst thing the girl ever did to you was shoot off your little toe. You can't lose a toe by eating a bowl of menudo. Besides, it was your idea to come here."

"She wishes me no good, and I didn't know she was here," Ben said.

"Let me have it, then. I'll taste it for you. If it don't kill me, it won't kill you."

Ben pushed the menudo over to his brother and

looked away from it. "Go ahead. You have it. It probably won't hurt you, but it's bound to have some special venom in it for me."

Les stirred it, inspected it, seasoned it, started eating it, warmed to the task, and finished it off. He sat back, washed the chile debris off the tips of his fingers in his beer so he would not forget and rub it in his eyes, drank the beer, and poured himself another glassful. "Ah, that was good. How long before any kind of poison takes effect?" He pushed the empty bowl back in front of Ben.

Ben shook his head. "You lead a charmed life, brother. I doubt anything could affect your health now. You ate enough menudo to block a dose of strychnine."

"Lorrie wouldn't do anything to you here," Dick Martin said. "She's too grateful to your uncle Vince for giving her the job."

"I bet Uncle Vince is happy to have her," Les said. "I bet the miners flock to Lorrie like bees to their hive."

"That's true."

"I bet Lorrie takes their money regular as a tollmaster. A saloon is the perfect place for that girl."

Martin's face colored, and he straightened in his chair. "Les, if we're to be friends, don't say anything bad about the girl."

Les was amused, but he took a close look at Martin. "What's your stake in her?"

"We've set up housekeeping, and we're to be married."

Les's look became respectful. "I didn't know that. I apologize, Dick. If you want to do that, I want it too."

"It turned out that I was the one who had to look after her after everyone else quit her. She'll only have to work here until I go back to work. She's going to have a baby in about six months."

"I sure admire you, Dick, but I hope you're not dumb enough to think the child is yours."

"No, but the child will be mine when it's born."

"Shhh," Ben said. "Here she comes again."

Lorrie came back and stopped across the table from Ben. "Well, did you like your menudo?"

"It sure smelled good," Ben said.

"Looks like you ate it all. Sucked all the stuff off the bones, did you?"

Ben looked at her face. She sure had a beautiful face. Tendrils of the chestnut hair, damp from the steam over the stove, curled against her cheeks, and she wore bold earrings of Mexican gold.

Les stared straight ahead with a smirk on his face, enjoying Lorrie's putting warts on his brother. He believed Ben should have married her. They looked so good together, everybody in the county except A.B. and Viney and Lorrie's brothers had wanted it. Instead of handling Lorrie right and giving her what she wanted when she begged him for it, Ben gave in to his parents and dropped her. No wonder she acted like a gutshot lioness every time she saw him coming.

"Filthy pig," Lorrie said softly. Every customer in the place perked up to listen. Everybody who came there watched her all the time and listened to every word she said. No other saloon girl in the Arizona Territory was as lovely as Lorrie Briggs. "You're so greedy, you don't even know when you've been slopped, do you?"

"It wasn't slop. It was good menudo, Lorrie. Thank you."

"It was slop, because I spit in it."

Ben looked to his brother, watched the awful change in his expression when he realized he had eaten it *all*, and nearly fell out of his chair laughing. Les's eyes widened as he examined the new workings of his innards for trouble, innards he thought he had made content by lining them with the soft and smooth and tasty innards of a cow. Les enjoyed the best appetite of the whole Cowden clan, but he was the most easily made sick by even the suggestion of tainted food. Ben collapsed in his chair with mirth.

"What's so funny?" Lorrie demanded. "I hocked up in your menudo, you stupid fool."

"Ben didn't eat his menudo," Dick said. "Les ate 'em both."

Everybody in the bar laughed at that, and Lorrie smiled and slapped Les on the back. "Be sure and come back, old boy."

"Tell me you didn't do that," Les said.

Lorrie turned to go back to the kitchen and saw Uncle Vince laughing at the end of the bar. She raised her head a bit higher, and her smile widened as she went out of the room.

Outside, the drizzle had stopped, and the sun was out. As he caught his horse, Les said, "I don't even believe that girl could *hock* up anything nasty enough to hurt a feller. She's too pretty to have boogers."

Ben tightened the cinches on his saddlehorse, haltered the packhorse, led both horses out of the corral, and could not stop laughing. His legs were shaky when he mounted his horse Star. The laughter had so relieved him of his worry and obsession over Margarita that it left him weak.

The brothers rode around to the front of the hotel, sat their horses in the sun, and waited for Walter Jarboe. After a while Lorrie came out of the saloon, carrying a basket of dirty linen. Several men were lined up on the boardwalk in front of the saloon and hotel, warming themselves in the sun. Now they basked in the girl's smile as she passed by. She gave even Ben and Les a good-humored glance, but it was an impersonal glance she gave men she did not really see, a glance that acknowledged the admiration of men.

"See there?" Les said as she disappeared into the hotel. "How could anything worse than crushed fruit come out a girl that shiny? Can't you see the change in her?"

"Oh, you like it 'cause she's spitting on us now instead of shooting us?" Ben was still laughing.

"Well, at least she's stopped trying to kill you. She could easily have laced your menudo with rat poison."

"You mean your menudo."

"Well, yes. And another thing, only a month or two ago, she was strutting around the hotel as Vincent's mistress. Now she's going into the same place to wash and iron the linen from the saloon. To me, that's a big change for the better."

"I hope she's a better washerwoman than she is a pistol shot," Ben said. "She emptied a forty-five at me in a crowd of people and only registered hits on my toe and a sack of flour fifty feet away. Maybe she's given up trying to shoot us, trap us, or poison us because she's just not good at it."

"Naw. I think she only wants to live and let live so she can hold her head up in public."

"Listen, she doesn't care what she does, in private or in public. She wants a lot more than the wages and tips she makes in that saloon, and she doesn't give a damn how she gets it. Sooner or later she'll bust loose again, just like Jesse James. Did you see those big solid gold earrings she's wearing? That's what she wants, a lot more old gold. If she can't have it by being somebody's mistress, she'll get it by robbing a bank or becoming everybody's madam."

"Brother, I think you're wrong. She might be a little wild, but I think she's good-hearted. She's a little tough, but she's honest, and I bet her word's good. If she ever finds a man she can love, she'll stick to him."

"No, Les, don't believe that. She hasn't changed. She's just gone back in training for the thing she's really good at—manipulating men and putting the hurt on people."

Les's faint smile showed he did not like hearing the truth about Lorrie Briggs. Ben understood her effect on him. She could spit on a man and make him like it.

Walter Jarboe joined them. The Cowdens left town and climbed toward American Pass in the rain. Five minutes after they started up the trail, they were alone. The effort of the steep climb that wound through catclaw, oak brush, and manzanita isolated them from the world. No one ever stopped on that slope unless it was to adjust the load of a pack quickly, or straighten a saddle, tighten cinches, and go on. The labor of the horses was immense and the trail dangerously steep and slick with wet rock that day.

Ben stopped to let the horses blow and to adjust the load on the packhorse when he reached the pass under American Peak.

"That's some climb," Jarboe said. He spoke in the same tone he had used in the lobby of the hotel, but out on the open plateau between American and Harshaw peaks, his voice sounded too loud.

Ben moved to the shoulder of Jarboe's horse and spoke quietly. "Mr. Jarboe, excuse me, but it's easy to hear even a soft voice out here in this quiet. You'll have to be silent now until we reach a place where it's safe to talk. We're headed into a country that belongs to the wolves. Almost everything out here will bite, claw, shoot, or trample you if you give it any chance at all. In order to stay alive, we have to see the hunters before they see us. We won't be able to see or hear them if our mouths are going. If they hear us first, the next sound heard by anybody will be the squawk we make when they slit our throats."

Jarboe gave Ben a grouchy look.

"Believe it, or go on back and wait for us in the hotel," Ben said. "Do you believe it? Because if you don't, you'll get us killed."

"All right, I'll be quiet."

"Good. No offense." Ben mounted and hurried across an open plateau on the trail to the Mowry Mine. *Bellota*, black oak, *encino*, white oak, piñon, and cedar trees gave the riders some concealment, and the horses made no dust because of the rain, but Ben always hurried when he used that trail. The plateau was exposed for a long stretch to any predator who might be watching from the Mexican border, the peaks above the trail, or the VO.

Ben breathed a sweet sigh when he was able to turn down a hidden trail for the three-mile *jornada*, journey, to the cow camp in Mowry Canyon the Cowdens shared with the Farley twins. The trail was hidden from above by an overhang of rock and along the bottom by another shelf of rock. The Cowdens and Farleys kept improving the trail so they could have swift and secret access to and from the camp.

Ben led the way into the camp at midafternoon. The refuse in the corral told him the Farley twins had not been there for a week. Their tracks were still plain though. Ben tracked them until he was almost sure they had gone to Santa Cruz.

The brothers unsaddled their horses and grained them in morrals, the burlap nosebags they carried on their saddle horns. They built a fire under a natural rock shelter at the base of a cliff. While coffee water heated, Ben took Les and Jarboe up to the entrance of a fissure that split the cliff's brow. He crawled down into the fissure.

The deep fine silt on the floor of the fissure was damp and fragrant from the rain. Ben crawled to the spot where he had buried the gold coins and found nothing but an empty hole. He clawed into the pile of dirt around the hole, stopped, and stared at it. Every single sorrel alazana was gone. The only other people in the world who knew about the fissure as a hiding place, as far as he knew, were the Farley twins. He hoped they were still in Santa Cruz. They could not have spent much of the money in that little pueblo. He'd better hurry and catch them before they decided to go find a place where it would be easier to spend.

Ben crawled out to face Walter Jarboe. "It's gone," he said quietly.

"What?"

"The gold's gone, Mr. Jarboe. Somebody dug it up."

"Let me see," Jarboe said. He went down on his knees to crawl into the fissure.

"It won't do you any good to crawl in there."

"I have to see for myself," Jarboe said.

"If Ben says its not there, it's not there," Les said.

"Let him go," Ben said.

Jarboe crawled tentatively into the hole. "How far do I have to go?"

"Just keep going until you find the hole they left digging out the money."

Ben could hear Jarboe moving through the fissure, and he followed him. "Right about there. Do you see the hole yet?"

"Yes, here's a hole."

"That's where I buried it."

"Damn me."

Ben could hear Jarboe digging with his fingers. He dug furiously through the moist earth until he reached the dry. Dust rose out of the hole.

"Come out, Mr. Jarboe. You'll choke on that dust."

"*Dammit.*" Jarboe crawled out an angry man. "Are you sure you buried it here?"

Ben did not answer him.

"My brother brought you to the right place," Les said. "He's not one to forget where he buried a certain fence post in a line of a thousand, let alone forty or fifty thousands dollars in gold.

"How do you explain it not being here, then?" Jarboe whined.

"Somebody got it, and I think I know who," Ben said.

"Who got it?"

"The Farley twins."

"Well, let's not stand here, let's get the law. They've stolen my money."

"No, we're not getting the law after them," Ben said. "They're probably in Santa Cruz. We'll just go get it back."

Rainclouds, thundershowers, and lightning hid the sunset that evening, and the trail to Santa Cruz was so dark, the Cowden horses could not follow it. Ben and Les were hours leading Jarboe down the Santa Cruz River to the town. When they arrived, the storm kept them from seeing even the lamplights in the houses until they were almost on top of them.

They rode around to the back of the Campana sisters' house and dismounted. Three horses were in the corral, but the Cowdens could not see well enough to identify them as the Farleys' mounts. Ben backed up and leaned against the trunk of a cottonwood on the edge of the corral. "The Campana's *loco* will start keening like a watchdog the minute he discovers us, so we'd better talk here," he said.

"What's the loco?" Jarboe asked.

"The people who live here keep a crazy brother in a cabin in the middle of their patio," Les said. Ben sensed his brother's grin. "He's a special friend of mine."

"They keep a crazy man?"

"Yes, but he's chained, and he can't do anything but announce our presence, unless you go in his cabin and crawl in bed with him," Les said.

"Shhh. Let's not wake him up," Ben said. "What I'm trying to do is make Mr. Jarboe aware that this is not a friendly place for us Cowdens. We're in Sonora, and I'm wanted for murder. By now, a warrant has probably been issued for Les for beating the hell out of Odoms. So, Mr. Jarboe, you're not in the safest of company. If we get the money back from the twins and then get dragged off by the law, you'll find yourself alone down here where you don't speak the language, and you won't have a good chance of getting home with your money.

"The only thing for us to do is find the twins, get the alazanas back, and hurry back across the line before daylight if we can. Let's stay together and try to remember that."

CHAPTER 10

Eileen and Paula Mary had never been east of Tucson.
Mark knew the Benson country because he had worked on
general roundups on the Empire, the Mescal, Chamiso,
and Lonesome Valley ranches along the San Pedro River.
He knew the Bonner ranch that lay in the Dragoon
Mountains. The Bonner men were capable hands who had
built their herd with wild cattle caught in the Dragoons.
They kept to themselves, as mountain people were wont
to do.

Now, as the train drew into the station at Benson,
Johnny pointed to his waiting family. Eileen saw two
young men sitting skinny horses beside a sturdy buckboard with a jaded team. The hats of the men were pulled
down low over their brows, and Eileen could see only half
their faces. A big woman sat in the driver's seat on the rig
holding the lines. Oh, Lord, she has those bleak eyes that
I don't like, Eileen thought.

"That's my ma on the rig," Johnny said.

The woman was bareheaded, with kinky blond hair
that was flattened in spots like a crop of trampled wheat.
Gusts of wind swiped and parted it, and showed her white
scalp at the temples, but the rest of it was too wiry to
bend. Women in that country who thought anything of

their looks wore hats, long sleeves, high collars, and gloves when they went out in the weather. This woman's face, neck, wrists, and hands were baked and wrinkled from sun and wind, but the sockets of her deep-set pale blue eyes were white, and her gaze was bleak as a drouthy flat that had long been overgrazed.

Eileen watched to see her expression when she spotted Johnny. Johnny did not make an effort to attract her attention. His brothers must have been searching the train from under their hats, because one's lips moved and the mother's eyes skimmed to Johnny, stopped an instant, then skimmed coldly over the Cowdens.

Johnny stepped off the train ahead of the Cowdens, and his backside was about the only side they saw of him for the rest of the day. He led the Cowdens to the buckboard and without addressing anyone in particular said, "This is Sybil Bonner, my ma. Ma, this is her." Mark loaded the suitcases and his rifle, and looked for a place to seat the girls.

"Just put the little one up here with me," Sybil said. "I need room to handle this team."

Mark and Eileen sat on their suitcases in the back. Johnny mounted a saddlehorse his brothers had led to the station for him, turned him toward home, and rode off ahead of the buckboard with his brothers.

Out of politeness, Eileen faced Sybil Bonner so she could pay attention to her, the most uncomfortable way to sit a suitcase in the back of a buckboard. She would have been able to keep her balance for the team's stops and starts better if she sat facing back toward Benson. She wished she was going back to Benson.

When she was under way, Sybil said, "What's that Porter-Cowden clan up to now? Are they shipping their females off to relations because the law is making it hot for them again, or what? It's always something with that outfit. You—what's your name?" she asked Paula Mary.

"Paula Mary Cowden."

"Why are *you* here? We're not going to let you stick any of us with a pitchfork."

Paula Mary smiled, hoping the woman had said it in good humor.

"No, ma'am, we're decent people," Sybil said. "Have to be. We don't wage war against our neighbors, and we don't like contention. How long you think you're going to stay?"

Eileen sighed and thought, We've already stayed too long. She almost laughed out loud when Paula Mary said, "I think we'll go home tomorrow, ma'am."

"Huh! You think we're gonna turn around and bring you all the way back to town tomorrow? You think your war in Harshaw's gonna be over tomorrow? We wouldn't make this trip two days in a row for anyone, especially not the Cowdens."

You can turn around right this minute and save yourself the whole trip, Eileen thought.

"You Cowdens been having it your own way too long. Anybody comes to visit us don't ever come all the way home from town with us one day and go right back the next. We don't go to town every day, and we don't go every week. We don't go to town, period."

Who asked you to? Eileen thought. Lordy, and coming here was my idea.

"You know, I went to school with that old ma of yours. She was always highfalutin. You three *look* like somebody Melvina Porter would raise."

Eileen thought, You old bitch, you couldn't wait to hold us prisoner like this and abuse us. Johnny Bonner doesn't look like a mule, but the rest of you do. Johnny's no racehorse, but he's at least a saddlehorse, and saddlehorses don't run with mules.

Eileen stared at the back of Johnny's head. He had assumed the same hunched-over position on his horse as his brothers, an attitude that said he disclaimed responsibility for anything that happened three feet behind him.

"Johnny tells me you Cowdens all take your bowel movements inside the house you live in, is that right?" Sybil said.

That tickled Paula Mary, but she knew better than to laugh out loud.

"Several different people told me that. Now if *that* ain't something. I'd like to know how you can eat and sleep in the same place you have your bowel movements. That's the nastiest thing I ever heard of."

She shut up for a while, then said, "Well, is it true?"

This surprised Eileen, for the woman had not required an answer before. "It sure is, missus," Eileen said. "We have an indoor bathroom that has a toilet with running water in it."

"What do you do with the waste matter?"

"The water washes it away."

"Where does it go, under the house?"

Eileen did not really know where it went. "I guess so," she said.

"Huh! Don't it stink?"

"No."

"No? Like fun it don't. You just been living on top of it so long, you cain't smell it. That's what's the matter with you Cowdens, you been wallerin' in your own filth so long, it don't bother you like it does decent people."

Paula Mary slowly turned her head to catch her sister's eye, rolled her eyes toward the woman, sniffed, and wrinkled her nose to let Eileen know the woman smelled bad herself.

Sybil Bonner raved about the "sorry Cowdens" all the way to the ranch. They arrived at dusk. The headquarters was located in a canyon without a flower or a tree to grace or shade the yard. A pack of hounds was chained under sycamore trees by a creek a hundred yards in front of the house. A great gaggle of buzzards perched in the trees above the hounds, and the ground underneath them where the hounds lived was whitewashed with their offal. They flapped insolently, sullenly, into the breeze when the Bonner party arrived home and then returned to their perches when the buckboard stopped at the barn.

The wind shifted, and the Cowdens caught the stench of a decaying carcass, looked for it, and saw the bloating, oozing hulk of a dead cow lying by the creek. More buzzards stumbled over it, tugged at it with their beaks, and scrambled and hunched for better leverage.

Eileen was astounded. Talk about filth. Any decent family would have taken a team and doubletree, and dragged the carcass away from the house the minute it fell dead.

The Bonner brothers dismounted to unsaddle their horses. Mark unloaded the rifle and suitcases, and waited to be told where to take them. The woman turned the team over to her sons and went into the house through the back door without even looking at the Cowdens. When she had been gone so long, they figured she must have forgotten them, they walked around the house and lined up at the outhouse. The winter darkness came on fast.

Mark went to the house and knocked on the back door. "Excuse me, Mrs. Bonner," he called.

She did not answer, so he went inside. A moment later, he came hurrying out, chased by the woman. She stopped at the back door, holding the front of her bathrobe.

"You can't come in here," she screeched. "Don't ever come in here again."

Mark rejoined his sisters without looking back. "Lord, I walked in and caught her wide open to the knees," he said.

"Enough of this," Eileen said. "Enough is just *a damned nuff*." She marched up to the door before the woman could retreat out of earshot again. "Mrs. Bonner, you apparently don't want us, and to tell you the truth, we don't want to be here, so we think we'll head home, even if we have to walk."

"Naw, you'll stay, by God. You just had to come and meet Johnny's family. Well, this is it. You can sleep on the front porch. I'll get the boys to put a cot out there, and you can come in the house when it's time to eat. That's all I'm gonna do for a bloodthirsty bunch like you who shit inside the house."

Johnny came around the corner. "Where you gonna put 'em, Ma?"

Sybil put on her sweetest smile. "Out in front, son. Go find the extra cot, if you will, please."

"Cots you mean."

"Well, son, I don't think we have more than one, if we still have one. You know my rules. No one comes in my house until mealtime, and nobody but my family sleeps inside. Anyway, they'll be warmer if they all sleep together on one cot.

"We Cowdens don't sleep together in a heap like a pride of cougars, Eileen said. "Give us two cots and some blankets so we can get through the night, and we'll go back to Benson in the morning."

"What's wrong, Eileen?" John asked.

"Your mother has made it damned plain—"

"Don't you use cursewords in my presence, you trollop," Sybil shrieked.

"—that we're not welcome here. So you can trot out your goddammed buckboard and take us back to Benson *right now*."

"They don't all sleep together like we do, Ma." Johnny said.

"Right now, goddammit," Eileen said, quietly. "We're not staying here another minute."

"I told them they could sleep on the front porch. Get 'em a cot and a blanket."

"Come on, Mark," Eileen said. "Let's hitch a team and get out of here."

"Naw, you can't do that," Johnny Bonner said. He turned back to his mother. "Hell, Ma, they'd be warmer in the hayloft. Let's put 'em up there."

"I don't care what you do with them. Just keep them out of my house."

Johnny shouldered past his mother and went inside.

Eileen wondered if this was a nightmare. She took Paula Mary's hand and followed Mark to the barn.

The other two Bonners were hunkered on their heels

against the closed double doors at the back of the barn, rolling cigarettes.

"We need a fresh team. We're going back to Benson," Mark said.

"Haven't got a team," the one Mark knew as Jake said. He was dark-haired. Josh, the other one, was sandy-haired. Both of them were stocky and stubby-legged with square jaws, bull necks, and small, deep-set colorless eyes.

Mark opened the back doors to look into the corrals. The horses were already leaving across the horse pasture, looking for something to eat. The country was drouthy, and all the grass close to the house had been cleaned up.

Mark turned back to the Bonners. "Don't you keep a wrangling horse?"

"You see one anyplace?" Josh Bonner said.

"How do you wrangle horses, afoot?"

"They'll come in by themselves in the morning."

"We're not waiting until morning. Me and my sisters are going back to Benson tonight. Where do you keep your morrals? I'll go catch one and drive them back in."

"What's a morral?"

"A nosebag."

"What's that?"

"A nosebag to grain a horse in."

"Never use 'em."

"Where's your grain barrel, then? I'll get a pan of grain and go catch them."

"Don't have any."

"Don't you grain your horses?"

"What's that?"

"Don't you feed them corn, or oats, or barley grain?"

"Who ever heard of doing a thing like that?"

Mark turned to his sisters. "Well, I guess we walk."

Johnny Bonner came into the barn. "Jake, where's the extra cot?"

Jake had begun carving a stick with his pocketknife. He took a sidelong look at Josh from under his hat brim. Mark read the look. Jake knew where the cot was but wanted to torment the Cowdens by keeping his information to himself. He was smart that way.

"Don't bother to look for your cot," Mark said. "We're leaving."

Eileen stepped in front of Johnny. "Johnny Bonner, you couldn't make us comfortable here if you gave us each a feather bed. Wrangle the horses so we can ride out of here."

Johnny sat down on the Bonner anvil. "Listen, I know your feelings are hurt, but now you can see the reason I've never asked you here. Our mother is dippy."

"To your everlasting disgrace, we found that out for ourselves."

"I want you to stay. In spite of everything, she's our mother. Once you get to know her and used to her rules, it won't be bad. After we're married, you'll have so much work to do, you'll learn not to listen to her. She never hurts anyone."

"No thanks. I want no part of any marriage to you now. Whose decision was it to leave that carcass to rot in the front yard? Don't tell me you haven't noticed it."

"Well, it's wintertime, you know, so we didn't think the weather was going to turn so warm. But anyway, there's no flies. The flies are what make it miserable near a carcass, not the smell."

"You didn't think the weather would turn warm? Do you stop smelling when you stop thinking?"

"Look, we'll drag the carcass off where you can't smell it."

"No thanks. Don't put yourself out for us because we're headed home."

Johnny bowed his head, stricken.

Mark felt sorry for him. He felt sorry about the prospect of having to walk fourteen miles in his boots, carrying suitcases, too. He could stand anything for one night, or at least until the horses came in. He took Paula Mary's hand. "Look, Eileen, you talk this over with Johnny. We'll wait outside."

Jake and Josh rose sulkily and moved themselves out the back doors.

On his way out of the barn, Mark sensed he was being watched. He heard a rustle in the hayloft overhead. He and Paula Mary looked up at the same time and caught a wild dirty face surrounded by tangled hair staring at them over the edge of the loft, and then it was gone.

"Who was *that*?" Paula Mary whispered.

Mark rolled his eyes. "Did you ever see such a spooky bunch of people?"

Eileen watched her brother and sister go out the door and saw the ragamuffin in the loft.

Johnny put his hand on her shoulder. "Eileen, I'm sure sorry you thought you had to come here. It seems to me we were doing good before you decided you had to meet my family. I let you have your way, and now you want to leave and probably don't want me to come see you anymore."

"You've sure got that right."

"Well, if you don't want to see me anymore, I want to know."

"I said you've got that right."

"Well, see, that *ain't* right. I didn't invite you here. You just made up your mind to come. I tried to tell you it wouldn't be right for you to come here before we married."

Eileen faced him. "*Damn*, Johnny. How ignorant can you be? Did you think I'd like coming here any better if we were married?"

"I figured you'd *have* to like it, is all. When a body *has* to like something, he finds a way."

"Is that what you do? Is that how you get along with your family? You find a way? It doesn't look that way to me. You're miserable as you can be. And that child hiding up in the loft is turning into a wild animal. If you can live like this, there's no telling what else you're capable of."

"Give me a chance. We've made promises to each other. I want us to keep them."

"I just want to go home."

"Well, you can't go afoot. It's too dangerous. You'll have to wait until the horses come in again. Believe me, that's a hard fourteen miles, all hills and rocks, Apaches, and who knows what else. Look, just stay the night. I'll take you back to Benson tomorrow. Give me a chance to explain a few things. You owe me that."

"Johnny Bonner, I don't owe you one thing. I thought I did before I made this trip, but now that I see what you've been hiding from me, I don't owe you a damned thing."

Johnny sat back down on the anvil. "I *knew* you'd turn out to be like this. Every single person that comes out here ends up leaving mad and never coming back. We live so far out and see so little of anybody else, we've never learned to get along with other people. I hoped you would be the one to make things different for us out here, as smart and as hard a worker as you are."

"Well, you're wrong about that. I never knew you before now. The isolation of these ranches makes people either real good or real bad. This outfit is real bad, and I wouldn't even try to make it good. I'd perish if I did, or turn bad myself."

"Will you let me do one good thing for you, then, to prove I'm not all bad?"

"What?"

"Let me talk you into staying the night. I promise I'll drive you back in the morning. You can't leave without giving me a chance to become your friend again."

"I'll never marry you now, Johnny Bonner. I demanded to come here because I wanted to start my own life, but now that I've seen what you've been planning for me, I thank God for my good family and home."

"I can change and be like you. I know I can. Just stay here tonight and listen to me. I'm worried about you walking back to Benson in the dark. You'll get lost or waylaid."

"I don't know. I'll talk to my brother and sister."

"Thank you."

"I'll tell you one thing. I won't stay unless you let me talk to everybody on this ranch, and that includes that poor little animal in the loft."

"Everybody'll be at the supper table."

When Eileen caught up with Mark and Paula Mary, they were looking for their suitcases. Eileen went to the screen door and asked Sybil if she knew where they were. She opened the door, dropped them on the veranda, and shut the door in Eileen's face.

The catch on one of the cases was unlatched, so Eileen opened it to see if anything was missing. Her clothes were in disarray, and two of the dresses and a pair of shoes she had bought in Hermosillo were gone. Two of Paula Mary's dresses were gone and two pairs of Mark's trousers and two shirts. That left the Cowdens with all their socks, stockings, handkerchiefs, and underwear, but only one change of clothes apiece. "The old thing must not have any use for socks and underwear," Eileen said. "And I'm pretty sure she's never even seen a handkerchief."

She heard the woman call her sons to supper, and after a while Johnny opened the front door. "Come and eat," he said.

The Cowdens were hungry and did not let pride hold them back. They had been taught a body needed to eat in order to make a hand. They knew they would have to be strong if they wanted to get home. They did not wash; they were not shown soap and water, a wash basin, or a towel.

The Bonners were seated at a table in the kitchen. Johnny found chairs for the Cowdens and sat them down. Besides the old lady and the three boys, a dirty little girl about nine or ten scuffed her bare feet under the table. Eileen figured she must be Johnny's sister Louise.

The Cowdens picked up the plates, knives, forks, and spoons that remained on the table. Sybil Bonner put a coffeepot, a platter of cold beef, a pot of cold beans, and a basket of cold biscuits on the table. The Bonners fell on the food like hunting dogs. All the Cowdens could do was sit back and watch them until their frenzy of grabbing and snatching had passed. When Johnny could get hold of a platter or pot, he passed it to them, but not until after he served himself.

When her brood had settled to its feeding, Sybil picked up a pan of cold baked potatoes from its place by her feet. She gave a potato to each of her brood and put the pan back by her feet. "Why, Miss Cowden," she said sweetly. "I guess I didn't count right. There don't seem to be any more spuds."

"Oh, that's all right. We didn't care for any," Eileen said as sweetly.

The Bonners devoured the potatoes, skins and all. The girl had not fared well in the grab for the meat and beans, and she cried to her mother for another potato. "Now, now, don't cry, Merle," Sybil said in her sweetest tone. "You can have another one." She reached down and brought up another potato for Merle.

Paula Mary, who never allowed her curiosity to go unsatisfied, stuck her head and shoulders under the table for a look in the pan, raised up, and said, "There's a whole *bunch* more potatoes down there."

"My children just love baked spuds," Sybil said. "I never worry they'll have enough to eat as long as we can grow a pile of spuds every year."

"I thought you said your sister's name was Louise," Eileen said to Johnny.

"Where did you get that idea?" Johnny said.

"From you. You told me your sister's name was Louise. Your mother called her Merle."

"How could he tell you that?" Sybil said. "His sister's name is Merle. This is her right here. What's your name, girl? Tell these Cowdens your name."

The girl stared at Eileen, took a big bite out of the potato with her side teeth, and chomped it into pulp with an open mouth. "Merle," she said.

"Who is Louise, then? Is that the girl we saw in the loft?"

"Oh, yeah, that's Louise," Johnny said. "I forgot about her."

"Why isn't she here at the supper table?"

"She has to stay away from the house."

"Why?"

"She's sick."

"What's the matter with her?"

"We don't know."

"What are her symptoms? Is her sickness contagious, for God's sake?"

The brothers grinned into their potatoes and giggled. Johnny looked at them and tried to keep a straight face, but a smile flitted across his face before he could stop it. "She has a bad swelling."

The brothers shook with silent laughter.

"Shut up! *Shut* up!" Sybil spat.

The table fell silent except for the sounds the Bonners made as they tore at the roast beef and potato skins.

The Cowdens took some biscuits and went out on the porch. Eileen had brought a jar of her mother's peach jam for the Bonners, but she intended to spread it on the biscuits. Viney had wrapped it in an old housedress so it would not spill on their clothes. The jam was gone. The woman had taken it along with the housedress and the other clothes.

Josh brought the Cowdens a wide burlap cot and an army blanket. The cot was too small for the three long-legged Cowdens.

"That's all right. I'll go to the loft and cover up with hay," Mark said. He picked up his rifle.

Eileen picked up the suitcases. "If that's where you're going, brother, me and Paula Mary are going with you." As they trooped through the dusk to the barn, an eerie wail issued from the house. "Listen, what was that?" Eileen said.

" . . . *hoooly night. Aaall is calm, aaall is bright. Round yon viiirgin, mooother and child. Holy infant so . . .*"

"My God, they're singing 'Silent Night,'" Eileen said.

"Will we ever get home for Christmas?" Paula Mary asked.

"Of course we will, honey."

"We, by God, better," Mark said. He carried one of the suitcases up the ladder to the loft. He stopped and stared at something in the loft before he stepped off the ladder. "My, my, there's somebody already up here."

"What?" Paula Mary asked.

"Looks like a little person, or a big mouse."

"Is it Louise?" Eileen asked.

"Are you Louise?" Mark asked. He looked down at Eileen and Paula Mary, and winked. "It can't talk, so it must not be Louise. I can't tell what it is. Come on up and see if you can."

"It won't bite us will it?" Eileen was laughing at Paula Mary's wide-eyed look.

Mark went out of sight in the loft. "I think it's only a little girl mouse. It's trying to hide under the hay, and its foot is shaking."

Eileen and Paula Mary climbed up. The loft was warm and fragrant with that summer's crop of sacaton hay. "Where is she?" Eileen asked.

Mark pointed to a pile of hay in the corner. Eileen gently uncovered a foot, and it scurried farther into the hay. Eileen uncovered the top of her head, and the girl showed a wild, frightened face, then broke out of the corner on her hands and knees. Eileen caught her by an ankle and stopped her, then held the foot and squatted down beside it. "We won't hurt you Louise," she said.

The child was not as active as Eileen had expected she would be. She moved ponderously. She tried to rise, then lay back, panting. Tears smeared the dirt on her cheeks. A hard varnish of smooth and polished dirt protected her feet, and she wore only the shreds of a petticoat. Her hair was like an old spider web, thick enough to catch everything the wind blew by.

"Are you Louise?" Eileen asked.

"Yes," the child said in a tiny voice.

"What's the matter, honey?"

"Nothing." She was seized by a spasm that wrenched a groan from her.

Eileen moved closer, shielded her from Mark and Paula Mary, and lifted the petticoat.

"What is it?" Mark asked.

"My God," Eileen said. "This child is having a baby."

CHAPTER 11

Ben and Les left Walter Jarboe with their horses and went to the house. The drizzle started up again, and lightning struck a tree on the river nearby. They paused by the loco's window and saw he was sound asleep. They went on and let themselves into the Campana girls' house.

The girls' other brother was one of Duncan Vincent's hired constables and an enemy of the Cowdens. He was sleeping fully dressed on a pallet in front of the fireplace in the living room. Les drew his pistol, stood over him, and cocked it to awaken him.

Campana opened his eyes and Les said, "*Crei que te había matado en Nogales.* I thought I killed you in Nogales." Campana stared at the pistol and did not blink. "Then I heard you didn't die, but that did not worry me. I don't mind killing you again."

"I don't want trouble anymore."

"Why did you stay in Sonora, then?"

"I've been too sick from my wounds."

"Leave him alone, Les," Ben said. "But make sure he's not armed."

Ben made a stir in the house but did not find the Farley twins. He went and looked in a cabaña in the patio, and they were not there either. When he came out of the cabaña, the loco awakened, saw him, and began to wail. Ben hurried into the house so he would shut up.

Campana's suffering had made him hollow-eyed and bony. Ben sat in a rocker by the fire and waited for the sisters to come out. The women had once been friends of the Cowden brothers. After the brothers flushed two of Vincent's constables out of the sisters' beds and shot them, the sisters told them they could not come back anymore.

Josefa Campana, the elder sister, came out in a long robe and stood by the fire, her face flushed and creased by sleep, her heavy curls flat against one side of her head, her bare toes peeking out from under the robe. "You here again?" she said quietly. She yawned, seeming only slightly perturbed. "Why? There's no one here for you to shoot. You've already shot my brother. A miracle saved him, so leave him alone."

"Where are the twins?"

"Why ask me? They're not *here*, Ben."

"Were they here?"

"Yes, a week ago, but they stayed one night and left for El Paso."

"El Paso? What day was that?"

"Today is Saturday, no? Maybe last Tuesday."

Ben went to the back door and called to Walter Jarboe. He could see well enough to identify the two horses in the corral now. They carried Vincent's VO brand on their hips.

Les found no pistol on Campana. Ben searched the blankets. "Are you armed, Campana? Where's your pistol?"

"I don't want pistols," Campana said. "No more."

"What have you been doing lately for your *patrón* Vincent?"

"Nothing."

"Yes you have. You still ride his horses."

"I ride from time to time to build my strength, but I haven't been working."

"*Aprovechado*," Josefa said mildly, accusing Ben.

"Bully. Don't you see how worthless you've made him? Leave him alone now."

Jarboe came in. "Did you find the twins?"

"These people say they left for El Paso a few days ago," Ben said.

"What if they're lying?"

"We can't do anything about that, I guess. I'm tired of shooting people every time they say something I don't like."

"Can I go out and throw the water?" Campana asked.

"Go on," Les said.

"Damn it to hell, this is awful," Jarboe said. "You better find them before they spend all that money, Ben."

"I'm not going after them."

"How will we get our money back if you don't?"

"I think you'll have to get yours from Vincent and Kosterlinsky. They're the ones who owe you."

"I thought you promised to pay me out of the gold coin."

"I would have, but I can't now, so I'm not going to worry about it."

"Well, then, maybe I won't be able to protect you anymore."

"I don't care about that. The money's gone. The twins'll spend it. I can't help you anymore, either, unless you join our side in the war and stop consorting with Vincent and playing tricks on me. Vincent and Kosterlinsky owe my family a whole lot more than they owe you, and that's why I took their money. I'm not obligated to you."

Jarboe turned cold. "Well, I'm glad I finally found out how you feel."

"That's how I feel. The twins won't come back until it's all gone, and I won't chase it. I have more important responsibilities."

Jarboe gazed distractedly around the room. Josefa offered him a chair. "Oh, thank you," he said, and sat down.

"Tell the poor gentleman to calm himself, and I'll bring him coffee," Josefa said.

"Thank you, Josefa," Ben said. "You're nice."

"Can we have some too, Josefa?" Les smirked, expecting her to cuss him out.

She sighed. "How can I not give you and Ben coffee?"

Jarboe watched her walk away. "Pretty girl. I thought you told me she was angry with you."

"She has been," Les said.

"My Spanish isn't very good, but didn't she say she was bringing us coffee?"

"She'll give us coffee because she knows we would invite her for coffee if she stopped at our house. If she hated us, she'd have told us to leave when we first came in. Since she doesn't, the rules of hospitality require that she make friends with us again."

"That's a different rule of hospitality than we know in Kansas. If you'd shot my customers in my house like you did theirs, I don't think I'd let you come back. If I gave you coffee, it'd have poison in it."

"These girls are old friends of ours. They won't hold it against us for shooting their customers if we won't hold it against them for consorting with our enemies."

"That's a helluva deal. What do you fellows plan to do now?"

"We have to leave you here and go on with our business, Mr. Jarboe," Ben said.

"Well, I won't ask you what that business is."

"We're still in a drouth and have to take care of our cattle."

"I daresay. What's the best way for me to get back to Harshaw?"

"Take the stage to Tombstone, then the train to Patagonia. That's about the safest way."

"I'll miss your protection, boys."

"You'll be all right. The Guaymas stage comes through on its way to Tombstone tomorrow, and Kosterlinsky provides it with a guard of Rurales."

"Well, he's good for something, isn't he?"

After they drank coffee with Josefa, the brothers left
Jarboe in conversation with her and went out to grain
their horses. They decided to pay the Campana sisters to
keep Jarboe's saddlehorse until they could come back for
him, and ride on to work the Buena Vista.

"We'll go tomorrow, then," Ben said. He knew Les
would want to spend the night with the Campana sisters.

Les surprised him and said, "Why wait until tomorrow? We ought to ride over there today, make camp, and
start work tomorrow."

"I want to ride out on the road to Nogales today."

Les looked puzzled a moment. "What for?" Then he
said, "Oh . . ."

"What do you mean, 'oh'?"

"Hell, you can't hide anything from me. Today's
Saturday. Margarita comes to Santa Cruz for provisions
today. It's a cinch she'll come on a Saturday before
Christmas."

"What else do you know?"

"Well, I don't really know anything, but anybody who's
seen the way you look at each other lately knows you'd
like the chance to be alone together."

"You rest and wait here. I'll ride out and meet
Margarita."

"No need of that. You'll come back here with her,
won't you?"

"Sure."

"I'll go with you, then, if it's all right. I'd worry about
you riding alone on that road."

The brothers registered for a room in the hotel,
carried in their blanket rolls and slept awhile, then rode
toward Nogales to meet Margarita.

They rode past the presidio of Santa Cruz, the fortress
and penitentiary that supplied Kosterlinsky with his black
hats. Every time Ben thought about being caught for an
offense against Mexican law, a picture of the presidio at
Santa Cruz showed itself to him. The place was run by a
platoon of ogres that devoured its inmates. People who

lived nearby complained about the screams of tortured prisoners.

The lawmen of Porfirio Díaz did not like to take prisoners. When they took a live criminal into the presidio, they inflicted intense punishment upon him for as long as he could stand it, and he died without mercy. Once in a while a felon who had proven himself particularly vicious and was known to be a good horseman was given the option of joining Kosterlinsky's Rurales.

"Maybe you ought to let Kosterlinsky put you in his jail," Les said quietly as the brothers rode by the presidio. "He'd give you a black hat and a tight suit, and put you in his Rurales. The way you're able to run him, you'd soon be a partner in all his schemes."

"Don't talk so big about what I ought to do," Ben said. "Odoms won't put you in the Rurales. He'll hang you up and dry you to jerky. Have you been watching for him?"

"No."

"Well, you better."

The brothers crossed the Santa Cruz. The river had come alive with the *equipata*, the long drizzly equinoxal rain. The water was not high, but it was muddy and swift.

The climb out of the San Rafael valley into the San Antonio Mountains was through black oak, white oak, juniper, and *tascale*, scrub fur. The horses made little sound on the wet, crushed granite. Ben was so nervous and impatient about meeting Margarita that he made his horse sweat.

The people who had been granted the Buena Vista by the Spanish Crown were named Tuvera, and a spring in the San Antonios where one of them had died was called Ojo de Tuvera. The Eliases kept a cow camp there. The brothers did not expect to see anyone because all the Elias vaqueros were down in the Santa Cruz valley working on the roundup. They were surprised when they heard mariachi music coming from the camp.

A sentry waved to them with a bottle of mescal in his hand from a high rock in Tuvera Pass before they rode into the camp. Ben recognized him as a young townsman from Santa Cruz.

"That's some lookout," Les said. "He's nothing but a target."

"The music will call bandits and Apaches from ten miles away," Ben said.

"There's nothing a bandit likes more than mariachi music. That's why Mexicans turn to crime, so they can afford the music."

When they came in sight of the camp, they could see the musicians were playing for a gang of drunks. "This might be Jacinto, the main bandit himself," Ben said.

"Well, if it is, we'll probably have to stay."

The brothers watered their horses in the clear spring and gave the revelers time to look them over. Saddled horses were tied under the trees close to the camp's house and ramada. The place was well populated. Ben counted fifteen men with the sentry, enough of a force to discourage enemies who had better things to do.

Jacinto Lopez came down to the spring to greet the Cowdens.

"By God, it *is* the main bandit," Les said.

"Look what we have here," Jacinto said. "Horsemen, how have you been?"

The brothers shook hands with him. Jacinto's chaps and jacket were smooth with brush and saddle wear. His big hat was pushed *a media cabeza*, to the back of his head, so the Cowdens would recognize him, and his long black hair hung in his eyes. The sun had baked his face and hands as dark as an Apache's, and his grin was a white slash underneath the trimmed bristle of his mustache. He showed the brothers where they could tie their horses in the shade.

"You're just in time," Jacinto said. "Your relatives are celebrating Christmas."

Danny and Donny Farley were sitting under the shade of the ramada with two pretty *teguecas*, Indian girls. Ben and Les shook hands with the Farleys and saw they were not drunk. They might have to ride like hell to escape all kinds of enemies now that they had brought the music to Jacinto Lopez.

Ben liked his cousins' faces. They had the same freckled open faces as his sisters. In their hearts they were as innocent as angels. They were always ready to throw in with the Cowdens for a job of work or a firefight. So as far as Ben was concerned, they could spend all the alazanas they wanted to.

"We thought you fellers went to El Paso," Les said.

"We started that way but ran into Jacinto, and he needed a fiesta," Danny said.

"You sure picked a fine place to have a party," Ben said. "Apaches will sure be glad to know you're here so they can kill you for your mescal, and if the Rurales catch you with Jacinto, they'll drag you through the cholla until you come apart in little pieces. Every wolf in the country will take that music as an invitation to come and eat you."

"We were forced to throw in with Jacinto," Donny said. "He's the only one who knows the way to El Paso."

Ben and Les doffed their hats and shook hands with the *teguequitas*, the pretty Indian girls with the twins. They were trim and brown, and if they had not been wearing rouge and powder on their faces, they would have been indistinguishable from the landscape of Tuvera Pass. They even smelled like the damp, crushed-granite earth.

"I guess you had to find sweethearts someday," Ben said.

"These teguequitas aren't ours. We only borrowed them," Donny said. "They're too expensive for anybody to own."

"You just ought to see how expensive they are," Danny said. "You wouldn't think anybody could possibly spend the money it's cost us to get a party going up here."

"What kind of money are you talking about?" Ben asked.

"Solid gold alazanas. I guess you've spent gold money, but we sure never have. Believe me, it don't go near as far as a common old paper banknote."

"Have you got the coin you found at the Mowry with you?"

"Naw, it was too heavy. We hid most of it down by the river."

Ben looked at the solid rain clouds that covered the sky. Another heavy rain might carry away the alazanas.

"Jacinto, do you know that Margarita Elias goes to Santa Cruz on this day every month?" he asked.

"Yes, I always let her pass."

"Odoms and his Texans will probably be with her today."

"No, Benjamin. We were on San Bernardino Peak and saw the Texans ride with Kosterlinsky and his Rurales toward Magdalena yesterday."

"I wonder what they're doing in Magdalena?"

"They have a livestock business there."

"Kosterlinsky has all kinds of livestock, doesn't he?"

"This livestock is as rare and precious as lotus seed."

"You mean Chinamen? What could they be worth?"

"These are not *chinos corrientes*, common Chinamen," Jacinto said. "These are very beautiful young and tender Chinese girls, the trained ones they call the *sonsonetes*, singsong girls."

"Where does he cross them, Jacinto?"

"I don't know, but he goes away to do it from time to time."

"I'd like to know where he crosses them and how he transports them. Does he cross men too?"

"Young men and boys."

"Those are probably being sent to the railroad gangs, but the girls?"

"They're valuable everywhere at three thousand dollars a head."

"How do you know this, Jacinto?"

"My compadre Luis Felix lives next door to the house in Magdalena where Kosterlinsky rests them. They come by boat from Baja California and land at Puerto Libertad."

"It's odd they would tell your compadre about it."

"But it's no secret, Benjamin. Kosterlinsky's been

doing it a long time. Everybody in Magdalena knows it. He did it when he was my commander in the cavalry."

"I knew he was a pimp, but I didn't know he was a slaver."

"It's good business, Benjamin. Singsong girls are resold several times, and the price goes up every time."

"Would you do it?"

"No, I'm a revolutionary, not a *padrote*, a pimp. I'm a horseman like you, not a slaver."

Ben took a swallow of mescal from a bottle Les was holding. The twins shouted for more music, and as the mariachis started up again, Ben walked to the spring for a drink of water. His friend Victor Roblez, another of the original mutineers, was kneeling at the edge of the pool as though to drink, but had paused to search for something in the boulders above him.

"I heard something up there, and now I don't see the sentry," Victor said.

"What do you think you heard?"

"Like a groan."

"Oh-oh."

"The boy was up there on the rock before I drank at the spring. Can you see him, Ben?"

A bird flushed out from under the sentry's rock and flew straight at Ben's eyes. Ben thought, That bird is so scared, he is looking behind him at the thing that scared him, and he's going to hit me headlong between the eyes. Ben dropped as it rushed close at his head.

"An arrow!" Roblez fired his pistol at the rocks. "Apache!" he shouted as a hail of arrows flew toward the camp. Ben fired once and sprinted for his horse. He and Les loosed their horses at the same time, jerked their latigos tight, and swung on. They spurred away from the camp, using boulders and trees for cover, and drew rifle fire and arrows away from the camp. They circled until they were on a flank above the Apache position.

They could not see Apaches, but they fired into the boulders below the sentry rock and made the Apaches move and show themselves to the camp. The weapons in the camp exploded with fire.

Ben and Les charged uphill and reached the pass as five Apaches broke away from the boulders and ran across an open space toward the other side of the mountain. The Apaches were intent on returning fire to keep the camp from pursuing them and did not expect to see Ben and Les come up on their flank. Three Apaches made it over the pass out of sight, but the last two stopped to fire at the camp and still had a long way to go. The brothers dismounted, knelt, and fixed them in their sights.

The Apache in Ben's sights saw him, wheeled, ducked his head, and ran. Ben's rifle ball struck him in midstride and crumpled him on the ground. The other Apache, as though he knew where Les's ball would strike, scattered back down the hill toward the camp. Les had led him up the hill, and the round missed by five yards. The Apache recovered, gathered himself into a short compact ball of muscle, and zigzagged across the pass after his brothers. Ben and Les emptied their magazines at him, but he evaded every round and disappeared over the skyline.

Ben and Les spurred their horses past the corpse of the young sentry. He was on his face, arms outstretched. The arrow had pierced his spine between the shoulder blades.

Ben and Les knew each other so well, they did not have to talk about strategy. When they reached the top of the pass, they veered toward the nearest high ground and ran up behind the Apaches. They fired from their horses as the four Apaches streamed out of sight again. The Cowdens turned back to Jacinto's camp. If they pursued any farther, they would be ambushed.

Ben and Les met Jacinto and two of his men on the way back to camp and did not have to discourage them from going after the Apaches. They laughed and talked about the fight but quieted when they heard one of the Indian girls crying in the camp.

A heavy rain began to fall. Ben and Les tied their horses and took shelter under the ramada with the twins.

An arrow had pierced the thigh of one of the teguequitas and severed the artery. Danny and Donny had broken off the arrowhead, pulled the shaft out of her leg, and stopped the bleeding with a tourniquet. They could not hope that she would survive. They had seen the first gush of blood from the artery.

"The sons of the fornication stole two horses," Roblez said. "They got our attention on the uphill side and stole the horses off the downhill side."

One of the townsmen was about to mount his horse.

"Where are you going?" Jacinto said.

"Those two horses were mine," the townsman said.

"Forget it. The Apaches are waiting on their tracks to kill you."

Ben mounted Star.

"Where are you going?" Les asked.

"I better see if I can hook up with Margarita," Ben said.

"She's all right. The savages weren't headed her way."

"They were headed any damned way they wanted to go. I better go find her."

"*Está bien*, wait for me."

"No, brother. You stay with the twins and get our stuff away from the river. This rain could wash away a whole herd of sorrel horses. I'll meet you at Yerba Buena Spring on the Buena Vista tomorrow evening."

Les waved and turned back to the camp.

CHAPTER 12

Ben rode all the way to the María Macarena ranch without meeting Margarita. When he topped out above the ranch, he began to worry that she might have decided to go somewhere else for provision that day. He hurried down to the corrals.

The Santa Cruz River ran south past the pueblo of Santa Cruz, then looped north again beside the María Macarena and on to Tucson. The washes were shedding fast water into the river. Ben did not worry that Les and the twins would not make it back to the river in time to pick up the alazanas before they washed away. They were in a hurry to take the wounded to the doctor in Santa Cruz. The twins were good-hearted young men.

The storm hid Ben's approach so well, no one on the ranch knew he was coming. The dogs did not discover him until he rode out from behind the corrals into the barnyard. He heard the blacksmith's hammer ring off the anvil in the barn. He called his greeting before he rode in sight of the open barn door. Chapito Cano, the mayordomo, was holding up a hind foot of his horse Lucero so the blacksmith could fit it with a hot shoe. His expression did not change when he recognized Ben. Margarita's carriage was missing from its place in the barn.

Lucero and Ben's horse Star were half brothers, both named for the star on their foreheads. They had been sired by the same Cowden stud. Don Juan Pedro Elias had intended to keep Lucero for himself. He entrusted Chapito with the task of breaking and training the colt, but Chapito had become attached to him. Now Don Juan Pedro would never get him back or be able to sell him without doing away with his mayordomo.

"Get off your horse and put him in the stable out of the rain," Chapito said.

The rainwater was accumulating in deep manurey puddles around the barn and stables. Ben led Star into a dry stall, gave him clean straw bedding, unsaddled him, and fed him corn and cornstalk *tasol*. He put away his saddle and went back to the barn.

Chapito and Cuco the blacksmith did not look up at him this time.

"Who is here, Chapito?" Ben asked. "Is Don Juan Pedro home?" He only wanted to know only about Margarita. He was afraid she had gone away.

"The old man doesn't come home anymore," Chapito said. "He has too much business in Hermosillo."

"A bunch of Apaches jumped Les, the twins, and me up at Tuvera today."

"Imagine that," Chapito said. "Was anyone hurt?"

"The twins were camped up there, making a scandal with music and girls. One of the girls, the little Rosita Davila from Santa Cruz, was pierced through the leg by an arrow, and the sentry, that young grandson of Moises Cano's, was killed."

"Imagine it."

"Who is in the house?"

"Margarita is alone."

That news was as bad as it would have been if she were gone. He could not go in the house if she was there alone unless she came out and asked him in. At most ranches he would not go in, even if the lady asked him in. Putting yourself alone with a woman in the frontier was bad manners.

"Go and knock, Benjamin. I'm sure she wants to see you," Chapito said. That meant he knew of the new intimacy between Ben and Margarita. The way they had been looking at each other was not lost on anyone at Macarena.

Margarita went to the back door to see why the dogs were barking and saw Ben when he first rode into the yard. She left the door open and stood back in the shadows so she could watch him. People already suspected her of being too intimate with Ben. They were angry about Ben's part in it and hurt about her part. They could not stand it that their Margarita might be committing adultery. She had always been their guardian angel, their protector, their living patron saint who baptized their children and taught them catechism, reading, writing, and arithmetic.

The people had seen the way Ben and Margarita looked at each other at the same time Ben's brother's saw it, the look lovers could not hide. Then Colorado, the driver, came back from Hermosillo and told everyone about the long hours Ben and Margarita had spent alone together in Don Juan Pedro's house and in Ben's room in the hotel when Odoms was away with Kosterlinsky.

The people kept track of their *patrona* the way they kept track of their mothers. Being unhappy in a marriage was a state that most of them learned to live with. Her sinful coupling with a man who was respected and admired by the people doubled the offense in their eyes.

The people respected Ben Cowden. They knew him to be reckless in his dealings with horses, cattle, men, and women, but always a gentleman. In order to do a thorough job of catching the wild bovine and bringing him to market, a man had to be wild as the cattle and reckless as the devil. But now his recklessness had made him commit a vicious sin.

Before he became intimate with Margarita, Ben had been more welcome at the María Macarena than Odoms.

Now, even though they did not like him, Odoms was their Margarita's husband, Don Juan Pedro's son-in-law, one of the María Macarena ranch family, and he was being insulted, betrayed, and made to look a fool.

It now seemed to the people of Macarena that the war Ben waged against Duncan Vincent, Kosterlinsky, and Odoms must be a selfish one. He must be the cowthief Vincent and Kosterlinsky said he was. It seemed he was bringing the pall of his war to settle on the Macarena, too, as he had done to the Romero family. Had not the Romeros seen their son Hector hanged when he sided with the Cowdens in that war?

Margarita knew what they were thinking, and she did not care. Ben Cowden was *bello*. She loved him and he loved her. She had always loved him. Before she married, she had been too shy to approach him. She first noticed him when she was twenty-one and he fifteen. He had come to the María Macarena with her father and uncles after a fight in which he liberated a Mexican woman from the Apaches. She had known him all his life, but that day she was astounded by the length of his legs, the blueness of his eyes, the black, black hair. At that age his limbs seemed more graceful because of his young awkwardness. He had moved slowly toward her, looked directly into her eyes, and smiled at her in a way that she never forgot.

Since that day, he had always treated her the same. She knew from that first day that he was ready to serve her in any way she wished, as a friend, as a man, and as a lover. Through the years she found that he offered himself that way to everyone when he first met them. She wondered how anyone could become his enemy.

Margarita was happy she had chosen Ben for a lover. She had been watching his desire grow, watching him rein it in so he would not offend her. In a way, it was a good thing Odoms had abused her. That made her desperate for kindness and forced her to turn to Ben. She thanked God he had not been too timid to respond when she decided she wanted him. If he had waited one day, one hour, she would have turned to someone else, maybe Bouvet.

Les and Mark Cowden were too slow, too gringo, to be anyone's lovers. Ben was the passionate one. His eyes could show the snap of ice shining in the winter sun or the warmth of a stove lid at suppertime.

He was one man who never coasted through a passive moment. He gambled the moments of his life like chips in roulette. The risk of being Margarita's lover was tonic to him, and maybe it was too strong. She knew that he was becoming obsessed with her. She wanted that. She liked it. If she gave him all the love he wanted, he might become satiated and tired of her. He might get too comfortable, too familiar with her.

If she kept him occupied with their affair, he might be safe. He might forget his war. However, he must remain a bit unsure of her. He must believe that he needed to keep wooing her. She wanted him to think he could not go off and fight wars or gather wild cattle for long, because she might not be available for him when he came back.

Margarita could have shown herself outside the back door and been open about inviting him in, but she wanted him to be shameless about being with her. She wanted him to come in the house even though she did not answer his knock. She wanted everyone to think he was the one who pushed to be alone with her and would take every chance to be with her.

Ben knew Chapito and Cuco did not approve of his going to the house, but he did not care. He'd waited too long to see Margarita. He felt he risked more by putting himself alone with her than he would if he stalked Odoms's whole gang of Texans and did not give a damn. Odoms would feel wronged enough to kill him for it if he found out, but Odoms wanted to kill him anyway.

He tried not to hurry on his way to the main house. He went through the gate of a picket fence that protected Margarita's flower bed and closed it carefully and deliberately to keep from trotting to the back door.

The door was open, and Margarita was standing back in the shadows, watching him with a smile on her face. He knocked for the benefit of Chapito and Cuco, pretended to hear an answer, and went in. He shut the door and pushed the smiling Margarita deeper into the passageway. He kissed her as a man drinks from a stream of clear cold water when he is near perishing from thirst.

"Come on, I have coffee," Margarita said.

"Have you a swallow of mescal too?" Ben said.

"That's a better idea for a day like this. We'll have a trago while I warm you a broth of melted cheese and green chile peppers." She kissed him again. "I love you and missed you."

"Me too." Ben was so happy, he could barely talk.

Margarita sat him at a table under the veranda that sheltered the line of Don Juan Pedro's saddles and poured mescal into small clay cups. "This ought to loosen your horseman's joints," she said. She went away to put the soup on the stove to warm, then came back and sat across the corner of the table to be near him and be touched by his knee.

He watched her sip the tiny measure of mescal, and she stopped and looked up at him self-consciously.

"Are you thinking it is nice to be alone like this?" she asked.

"I wonder how we can ever be together as long as you are married."

"But I'm not married, Ben. I don't share my bed with the man. I tried to be a wife to him, and he did not want me. I am not married in the eyes of God, only in the eyes of Kosterlinsky."

Ben watched Margarita pour them more mescal. She was already greatly affected by it. He showed his concern.

"A strong drink helps me forget how long you were away," she said. "I need to celebrate your return. I think of you all the time. You came in time to save me from a death of neglect."

"I'm worse than you. I feel as trapped as an opium

fiend. I crave you so much, I don't care about anything else."

"Good. That makes me happy."

"It's not good."

"I'm happy you love me."

"It's forbidden. People know about us, though they can't be completely sure. They know, though, and they blame us."

"They forgot about my cheerless marriage and the shock they felt when I brought that great pale hulk of cold gringo home and introduced him as my husband. They were astonished and did not like me for doing it."

"Why are they angry with me, then? I was always a favorite around here, like you."

"In their eyes, we were too honorable to commit adultery. You could chase all the unmarried girls and drink mescal with both hands and sleep with prostitutes all you wanted, and I could discard my widow's weeds six months too soon, marry a gringo, and go out and sing and dance at a tardeada because that was what they admired in us. But when we fell in love with each other, they disapproved because that's adultery."

"That makes me feel bad, to be called an adulterer."

"Nevertheless that's what you will be called. You also must know that you did other things to me that needed to be hidden. You don't rub me in the same way you do a horse. . . . Come on, this kind of talk will make us feel bad."

Margarita led him to the kitchen and set the large bowl of *caldo con queso* in front of him. "Be consoled by this," she said.

The soup was hot and thick with melted cheese, and the green chile made Ben's scalp tingle. Margarita sat across the table from him. "I like to watch you eat. I'd like to be with you all the time so I could watch you shave and bathe."

"That's going too far." He thought, Those eyes are so dark, I can't distinguish the pupils. "Can you say 'I love you honey' in English?"

Margarita laughed. "No."

"Try it."

"What does it mean?"

"'Honey' means *miel*, a nickname for a sweetheart. 'I love you' means *te quiero*."

"I loff jou hawny," Margarita said and laughed. "I loooff jou haaawny. How is that?"

"Very, very good. Remember everything I teach you. Remember you are beautiful, capable, and you love me. Nobody will ever be able to ridicule you or put you down again."

"Yes."

"We are alone on a beautiful rainy evening."

"And you believe I am a capable and confident woman, don't you?"

"Yes, and I love your rosy fingers and cool, rosy ears."

"And you love my business sense."

"Yes, and I remember the way your knees and toes and the soles of your feet turn rosy at certain times when I am the only one watching."

"I told Jack I was going to start a horse business. I told him he could not beat me, humiliate me, or bully me anymore. I told him I was going to start making my own way."

Ben wanted to talk about rosy knees, but he said, "How did he take that?"

"He laughed at me. He said the only kind of business a woman could do well was whoring. He said he doubted if I could be a good whore because I probably would like that line of work too much and give away my wares."

"Well, you are a good lover. It's too bad he thinks it's nasty. I don't. Don't you think we ought to stop wasting time and do this talking lying beside each other?"

Margarita pushed her face forward as though to kiss him, closed her eyes dreamily, and said, "Ah, no, Ben, I'm sorry, but I'm expecting my father and his guest."

"When?"

"Anytime now. I have to light the lamps and get the house ready."

"I thought we had finally been given an evening alone with each other."

"No, but I'll come to your room when I'm sure everyone is asleep."

"No, I'll come to yours. It's in the back of the house."

"How will we ever be together, Ben?"

"We have to find someplace where we can meet, that's all. You're never alone. Today was a miracle."

"You know what I would like, the dream I dream?"

"Tell me."

"I would like to have a private railroad car. You and I could go aboard, lock the doors, and go away and never stop. We would have no destination, and no one would ever see us. We would not be tied to land, people, or obligations. No one could come to us and ask us for anything. We would serve only one another, until we decided to come home again."

"I'll buy one right away, by God." He thought, If I can get my gold alazanas back.

"Will you?"

"As sure as God is a saint, I will."

"That would be so good."

"It's the best idea I ever heard. We could disappear. Everybody would have to learn to fight their own wars while we were gone."

"We'll always have to come back."

"You can decorate and furnish the car. I'll put it on the siding at Cibuta."

"No, I'll find a secret siding to keep it in Hermosillo. Nobody will know about it. A good dream, no?"

"It won't be a dream much longer. I'm going to buy us a railroad car."

The dogs barked. The back door opened, and Pepe came in. "Mamá, my grandfather is at the pasture gate."

Dusk had fallen, and Ben and Margarita finally became aware they were sitting in the dark. She left him to light candles and lamps. Ben went out on the patio to shake Pepe's hand. The boy looked worried.

"Why don't you come and work for me, Pepe?"

"When—now?"

"Tomorrow, after you've had your breakfast."

Ben expected he and Margarita would find a way to be together late that night when everyone else was asleep, as they had in Hermosillo. They were accustomed to the risk. Stealing into each other's room seemed to Ben even more audacious than sneaking up on the Yawner in his camp and scalping him.

"I will, Benjamin," Pepe said.

"Get your horse and bed ready. We'll sleep at Yerba Buena tomorrow night."

"I'll be ready."

Ben heard Don Juan Pedro's buggy pull up behind the house, heard the leather springs creak as the passengers stepped down. A moment later, Don Juan Pedro was seating Martín Bouvet at the table where Ben and Margarita had sipped their mescal.

Bouvet paid no attention to anything around him while he waited to be served a refreshment. He had not removed his hat and cloak. He wore a full-length cloak with a high collar, a straight-brimmed hat with a string pulled snug under his billy-goat chin whiskers, a pair of delicate boots that would have fallen apart with one mile of walking. His eyes were cold and dim as smoked glass. He kept his cloak wrapped closely around him, and his expression showed he was sure he could not possibly like anything he saw on the María Macarena.

Before he addressed Ben, Don Juan Pedro drank a tiny measure of mescal from Margarita's cup, then rid himself of the cup and drank a fat swallow straight out of the pitcher. "So, I encounter you in my home, Benjamin?" he said.

"I arrived about an hour ago," Ben said.

"Where is Margarita?"

"I don't know. She was here a moment ago."

"She went to your room, Tata," Pepe said. He stepped up and shook his grandfather's hand. The man's eye softened, and he ruffled Pepe's hair. "Are you getting along well with everyone now?"

"Sí, Tatita. Benjamin asked me to work for him."

Don Juan Pedro would not look at Ben. "And what have you decided? Will you go with him?"

"With your permission, Tata."

"I feel bad about it, but I can't allow you to go."

"Why not? He'll be doing honest work," Ben said.

"Cowden, I can't lie to you. I've been pressured from all sides to stop giving you sanctuary. The governor himself ordered me to stop protecting you. If I were you, I'd go back to the American side and stay there."

"I guess that's clear enough," Ben said.

Margarita came in with a dusty bottle of brandy and two fine crystal snifters. She kissed her father, pulled the cork, and poured him a healthy snort. Bouvet stopped her when she had poured him the same measure Ben's mother would have given one of her girls as a remedy for a bad cold. She did not ask Ben if he wanted any. She smiled into Bouvet's face exactly as she had smiled into Ben's when they were alone.

Bouvet's hat was dove-gray, the string on his chin dove-gray, his cape dove-gray. His hands emerged from the cloak, and he removed his dove-gray gloves one finger at a time. When he had placed them carefully together on the table, he picked up the snifter and held it close against his chest in the palms of both hands. His eyes focused on it briefly as he swirled it, then he touched it to his lips enough to wet a bristle or two of his thin straight mustache.

"It's your brand," Margarita said. "It's Courvoisier."

Ben wondered why the Eliases were coddling Bouvet all of a sudden. He knew Don Juan Pedro did not like him because he took graft. He was probably taking a mountain of it in the business of smuggling Chinese. Now, her lips still warm from Ben's kisses, Margarita was fawning all over the son-of-a-bitch.

Ben sat at the ranch's leatherworker's bench and lit his pipe.

Bouvet raised his dead eyes to look at Ben. "Is it not awfully late for you to ride home in this rain?" he asked.

Now he was deciding who was to stay the night on the María Macarena and who was not. Margarita looked at Ben as though she would like an answer to that question herself.

"Never too late for me to ride," Ben said.

"Ben has work to do at the Yerba Buena," Margarita said.

"I've been wondering when the Cowdens would find time to do their share of work in that country," Don Juan Pedro said.

"We've been waiting for some help from our neighbors," Ben said. "Today, Les and the Farley twins and I were attacked by Apaches at Tuvera."

"Ah well, you see. Other matters keep all of us from working the Yerba Buena, don't they?"

"Cowden, I suggest you return to your own side of the border as soon as possible," Bouvet said. "The governor is about to put a price on your head. Were it not for Señor Elias, you would probably already have been administered ley de fuga."

"For what? For defending myself and my property?"

"For the murder of gringos. Those are very serious offenses against Mexican law, regardless of the reasons for which you justify them. In fact, I myself have the authority to deliver you to the nearest post of Rurales, if I want to."

"I'm sure you want to, Bouvet, but you're certainly not man enough to accomplish it."

"Ah, Martín, let's not talk about arrests. Instead, let's discuss the horse-buying trip I plan to make to Cuernavaca," Margarita said.

"Young lady, I am at your service," Bouvet said.

"Then tell me, can I find twenty Andalusian mares and one good stallion in Cuernavaca?"

"Maybe not all in one place, but probably they can be found in the region between Cuernavaca and Mexico, the capital."

"How long would it take me to buy and ship that many horses?"

"Ah, that would depend on how much you enjoyed your visit to that region."

"I have a perfect means for enjoying the trip. I'm going to buy myself a private railroad car."

"*Ah, caray!*" Don Juan Pedro said. "That would cost a lot."

"Not so much, Papá. Anyway, I have the money from the sale of my late husband's livestock."

"You don't need to buy a railroad car just for a trip to Cuernavaca."

"But it will not be used only for that trip. I'm going in the horse business. I want to go to California too. My first trip will be to Cuernavaca because Martín has graciously offered to accompany me, advise me, and even recommend me to the horse breeders there."

"Ah," said Don Juan Pedro.

Ben felt he was down and Margarita had just kicked him. As nonchalantly as he could, hoping he could get out without a fuss, he picked up his Saltillo, spurs, and leggings. "I'm going now. Thanks for the soup," he said.

"Adios," Margarita said. She waved and smiled, but turned back to listen to something Bouvet was saying.

"I hope everything goes well for you," Don Juan Pedro said.

Outside, Pepe asked Ben if he could still go to the Yerba Buena with him. Ben told him he could not, but he would appreciate it if he would keep Ben informed on Odoms's comings and goings. Pepe promised to leave messages for Ben in the hollow of a certain giant alamo tree at the edge of the river a half mile from the house.

CHAPTER 13

A strong wind swept a sheet of rain into Eileen's face as she stepped out of the barn. She thought she heard crazy laughter mixed in with the Bonners' singing. She ran in the darkness to the Bonner house and slammed through the door. The Christmas-caroling stopped. Sybil and her brood were sitting at the kitchen table.

Eileen saw Johnny's brothers for the first time without their hats. Their bright red hair was slicked down and dark with water. They had bathed and changed into clean clothes. Their shirts were buttoned right up through the top button and made them look stiff-necked. Their big knobby hands rested on the table in front of them like bathed children who did not want to get dirty while they waited to be carried to bed. Their heads swiveled around to look at Eileen.

"Missus, your daughter's about to give birth to her child," Eileen said.

"So what? That's no reason for you to disrupt our singing," Sybil said. "Do you know your Christmas carols? If you do, sit right down here and sing with us awhile."

"No, I won't sit down and sing with you. I'm trying to tell you that you have a child in labor out there."

"Well, it's not the first time, and it won't be the last. If you'll sit down, we'll talk about it and see what we can do."

"How can my sitting with you help her?"

"I can't talk to you with you standing over me like that."

Johnny offered Eileen a chair. "Sit, lady."

Eileen slid reluctantly into the chair.

"That's better," Sybil said. She hunched over the table, her face jutting toward Eileen. "I think it's time you and me discussed the dowry."

"What dowry?" Eileen said.

"The loot you're bringing to this marriage. We have to know what you're worth before we Bonners enter into this marriage. In other words, how are you going to make it worth our while if we let our son marry you?"

"Ma'am, I'm not marrying Johnny Bonner, and when I get back home, I'm going to make sure the whole country knows what a damned bunch of savages you are."

"Now see, you've always got a mouthful of cursewords. That's the first thing we'll have to remedy, your use of cursewords."

"I told you, Ma," Johnny said. "She has thirty-eight head of mother cows and two bulls under her own brand."

"And how many will Viney and old man Cowden add to that? Then there's the wedding gifts. I need to know who is being invited so I'll know what to expect in the way of goods and presents.

"You can see we don't own much in the way of worldly goods, missy. So we'll be sacrificing a considerable lot when we take you to feed and clothe. So what we need here tonight is honesty. How much cash do you have, and how much will you be given when you marry? How much livestock have you really got? What kind of rolling stock? Do you own a carriage, or a wagon, a buggy, or a surrey? I'm sure old Cowden don't expect you to carry your dowry all the way over here riding sidesaddle like some great dame from the boulevards.

"In a way, it's a good thing you decided to come over and stick your nose in our business before the wedding.

Now we can find out just what we're getting when our Johnny marries you. When you come over here, that's gonna be it. You won't be seeing no Cowdens no more, or puttin' on airs like you been. With us, a marriage is sacred and final. You're becoming a Bonner for good and forever."

Mark and Paula Mary came in and stood by the back door.

Sybil said, "I've decided the best thing for us to do is keep you here until you satisfy us about the dowry. You're not going home until we're satisfied it's big enough."

"You can't make me stay here. If me and my brother and sister decide to leave, we'll walk to Benson in this rainstorm tonight."

"Now ain't that admirable? How you gonna do that with no shoes?"

Eileen jumped to her feet. "No shoes? I have good shoes on and good legs to walk with, and so do my brother and sister."

"You think so, missy? Then I'll get my boys to take their hoof knives and trim the bottoms of your feet. How far will your good legs take you after they do that?"

"Why, you cold-blooded old bat." Eileen whirled, looked for something to hit the Bonners with, and found an old worn-out broom. Johnny Bonner stood up between Eileen and his mother. Eileen yelled, "Dammit, I came here to tell you your little daughter's in labor. Get off your sour old tail and help me clean her up so she can have her baby."

Sybil Bonner stood up, marched up behind Johnny, pushed him aside, and clawed Eileen's face with both hands. Eileen recovered and rocked her back on her heels with the broom.

"Out, you *trollop*," Sybil squalled. "Get out of my house. Get to the barn with the rest of the livestock."

Johnny pushed Eileen, and she brought the broom down on his head too. He caught it, wrenched it from her, and calmly slapped her with forehand and backhand. "I knew I would have to slap you down someday," he said quietly. "Now go on back to the barn." He pushed Eileen toward the door. "Go on."

Foolishly, he ignored Mark. Mark waited in the corner, and when Johnny came in range, he poleaxed him with a right fist to the jaw. Johnny did not see the blow coming, never knew what hit him. He skidded under the table on the side of his face.

Jake and Josh quickly jumped up and tripped away from their brother's carcass as though it might dirty their feet.

Eileen took a full teapot of hot water off the stove, a bar of soap and a lamp, and went back to the barn with Mark and Paula Mary. Mark drew a bucket of water from a well by the corrals, and Paula Mary found an old beaten enamel pan. With those tools and clean linen from their suitcases, the Cowden girls washed Louise Bonner and helped her have her baby. The birthing was an easy one, for this baby girl was not Louise's first child.

Mark threw some hay down out of the loft and rested at the foot of the ladder during the birthing. When he heard the child cry, he asked Eileen to come down as soon as she could. Paula Mary came to the edge of the loft and showed him the baby wrapped in one of his shirts.

Eileen came down the ladder. One of her eyes was puffy from Johnny Bonner's slap, and both sides of her face were scratched from eyebrow to cheek, but the new Bonner and her mother had survived. Mark was ready to take the next step.

"Better have Paula Mary wash those scratches," Mark said. "That old hag's claws are bound to be as filthy as a stinking old badger's."

"I will. I don't like the look on your face though. What are you going to do now?"

"I'm going up there and kill those goddam Bonners."

"No you're not. That won't help us. I think you'd better go to Benson and telegraph Papa so he can send Ben and Les to help you, then come back and get us."

"Why don't you and Paula Mary come with me?"

"You think they'd let us go? They'd worry us and shoot at us all the way to Benson. Me and Paula Mary aren't strong enough to fight them off all that way."

"They'd only be a worry until I shot the sonsabitches."

"I don't think they'll be easy to shoot, so you better be careful. You'll have a lot easier time of it if you don't have me and Paula Mary to worry about."

"I ought to just shoot 'em now."

"Get going, Mark. The rain's in your favor. They won't even know you're gone until tomorrow morning."

"This is a damned shame. That poor little girl. Who do you think fathered the baby?"

"Who fathers anybody in a family?"

"You mean the *father*?"

"The one Papa says is the finest man he ever knew, or one of his whelps."

"The brothers?"

"Maybe the uncle too. I think they all had a hand in it. I bet this child has been fair game for any of these damned Bonners who could run her down."

"A helluva family for anyone to marry into."

"You better get moving. Me and Paula Mary are going to take all the pitchforks, hammers, and horseshoes we can find and defend the loft until you get back."

Mark handed Eileen his pistol and cartridge belt. "My rifle's enough for me," he said.

Mark walked out into the rain. He stopped once to look in the window at the Bonners, then started down the road. The wind pelted him with heavy rain. He stopped once to catch his breath, wondering how much headway he could make before he wore out. A bolt of lighting struck a sycamore in the wash, and he saw a man standing stock still facing him fifty feet away. The man wore an old pair of faded bib overalls and no shirt, no hat, no shoes. The sight of him with his staring eyes gone blank in the white flare of the lightning made Mark's blood run cold. Mark fired once in the man's direction as thunder clapped overhead. The man was gone before the next lightning flash. Mark started trotting down the road.

He pulled up soon and began alternating fifty steps trotting with fifty walking. He could keep going at that pace until he reached Benson. Benson was downhill from the Bonner headquarters, but he left the road and headed for Sybil siding on the railroad to see if he could catch a train or a handcar, or borrow a horse. Sybil siding was only about eight miles away. The maniac he'd seen in the lightning flash would have to pick 'em up and lay 'em down in a hurry if he wanted to catch Mark.

In the morning, Johnny Bonner came early to the barn. Eileen and Paula Mary sat on each side of the ladder, their long black-stockinged legs hanging over the edge of the loft, pitchforks in their hands. Johnny smiled up at Eileen. "If this rain keeps up, we'll be able to kill a fat cow at our wedding," he said.

The Cowden girls stared at him.

"You better come on down and get ready for breakfast. As soon as me and my brothers do the chores, Ma'll be ready with biscuits and gravy. I know all the fuss musta made you hungry. Where's Mark?"

The girls stared at him.

"Where's your brother?"

Johnny searched the stalls and saddle room in the barn, went outside, made a circle, and came back. "Is Mark up there with you?"

The girls stared.

"I see I'm gonna have to come up there and see for myself." He climbed up the ladder quickly, smilingly. When he came in range, Eileen jabbed him through the hat once, and when he howled and ducked his head, she jabbed him in the ear and detached him from the ladder. He thumped the back of his head against the ground and lay very still.

Paula Mary said, "I was afraid to poke him. Then you poked him, and I didn't even get a chance to."

"Looks like my pokes were enough," Eileen said.

"Do you think he's dead?"

"No, but I don't think he liked getting poked very much, do you?"

Paula Mary was wide-eyed again. "He sure hit hard."

"That's some howl he's got. I wonder if they all howl like that."

Jake and Josh came into the barn and stood over Johnny, saw the top of his head was bleeding, then looked up at the Cowden girls. Josh knelt and lifted his brother's head, and got blood on his hands. He saw blood seeping from Johnny's ear and the side of his head. He put his ear against Johnny's chest. This scared Eileen. She did not want to kill anyone. Jake and Josh carried their brother's carcass outside.

"What shall we do now, Eileen?" Paula Mary asked.

"Hope they don't come back and shoot us, I guess."

"Gosh, will they do that?"

"Fair is fair, I guess. We just cowkilled their god-dammed brother."

After a while, Jake and Josh came back with rifles. Josh stopped at the door and aimed at the girls. The girls backed into the loft in a hurry. Jake set his rifle aside, drew his pistol, and climbed the ladder. He stopped at the top of the ladder when he saw Paula Mary in the corner with Louise and the baby.

"You sorry thing," Paula Mary said. "You just get on back down that ladder and leave us alone."

Jake waved his pistol at Paula Mary and grinned. Eileen rushed out from under the hay at his feet, screamed at him, forked the pistol out of his hand, followed through, and poked him howling off the ladder. Josh fired his rifle at Eileen and splintered the top of the ladder as she scampered back out of sight. The back of Jake's head whipped against the ground and addled him, but he got up.

Eileen cocked Jake's pistol with both hands, walked up to the edge of the loft, and sent a round past Josh's head.

Both Bonners scurried into a stall under the loft. Eileen went to the water bucket and took a drink in the palm of her hand, feeling like a soldier under siege.

"Let's get a pitch torch and burn 'em out," Jake said.

"Hell, no. We ain't gonna burn our barn down," Josh said.

"Well, what're we gonna do?"

"We're gonna get Ma."

Eileen went to the edge of the loft again, and when Josh made a dash for the door, she sent another round after him that skimmed at his head and made him stumble and fall out of sight.

After a while, Sybil Bonner came to the barn. "Ladies," she said. "Come down, ladies."

"They won't come down, and we can't make 'em, Ma," Josh said.

"What do you want 'em down for, anyway? I'd rather they stayed up there and got hungry. Get your rifles, and if they show themselves, shoot 'em. They'll come down or starve, or the cedar man'll flush 'em out."

Eileen and Paula Mary felt they could stay up there without anything to eat for as long as it took Mark to come back. They weren't sure Louise and the baby could though. Louise had left the baby untended and was cowering in a corner of the loft.

Paula Mary picked up the baby.

"She needs some milk," Eileen said.

Paula Mary went over and tried to hand the baby into Louise's lap. The girl rolled on her side but kept her eyes on Eileen. "Your baby has to nurse, Louise," Paula Mary said.

"No."

"You've got her breakfast in your titty."

"No."

"Why not?"

"She'll die."

Eileen took a shawl from her suitcase, draped it over Louise's shoulders, and sat by her side.

"Why will she die, Louise?"

"I'm dirty."

"No you're not, and neither is your milk. You're bursting with milk, so just do what comes natural and let your baby suck. You'll feel better."

"You'll look at me."

Eileen made Louise take the baby to her breast, then covered the baby with the ends of the shawl. "Now let her suck, and we won't look," Eileen said. The baby took her breakfast then.

Paula Mary stationed herself at a crack to watch the house. Eileen watched through a knothole in the rear. "The horses are coming in," she said.

A remuda of eleven skinny sore-backed horses came in and waited outside the gate to the water trough. Eileen could see she and Paula Mary would never get away on horseback. The Bonners would catch them before they were even out of sight of the house. She did not want to go away and leave Louise and the baby to the Bonners either. She wondered what had happened to the other babies.

The man Mark had seen in the lightning flash was called the cedar man by the Bonners. He was the oldest brother. He had gone mad and lived in the cedars. He scavenged for his food at night. He went anyplace he wanted to go, and the Bonners stayed out of his way.

Sybil Bonner left food on the front porch for him when the weather was good and on the kitchen table when it stormed. She had forgotten to put out his food only once since he had grown to manhood. That time, he went into her bedroom when she was asleep, lifted her over his head, and dropped her on the floor. Her own arm and fist had broken her ribs when she landed on top of them, and she almost never got her breath back. Now all the Bonners slept with one eye open every night until the cedar man had eaten his supper and gone back to the cedars.

Tonight he would come in the house because it was

raining. Tonight he would be especially fearsome because of Louise's baby. He had gone mad when Louise's first baby was thrown away like trash. Now he prowled around the barn to make sure the Bonners did not go near Louise and the baby.

CHAPTER 14

Ben felt sick at heart as he walked away from Don Juan Pedro's house. Pepe sensed it and was as attentive to him as he would have been to someone who was old, decrepit, and finished with life. Ben was happy the storm hid him as he left the María Macarena with his tail between his legs. He forgot about the confessions of love Margarita had made him when they were alone and remembered the look she had given Bouvet. He was baffled by the way she had acted after Bouvet and her father arrived. Margarita had made it plain that she could give herself away to anyone anytime she pleased.

He rode slowly and blindly through the darkness, thinking of Margarita. Near La Acequia, the trail passed through a dense mesquite thicket. He could not see the way unless a lightning flash helped him, so he kept his eyes wide open and his arm in front of his face to protect himself from the thorny branches.

He looked toward the gate at La Acequia so he could find it in the next lightning strike. The next flash showed him five riders in yellow slickers on tall horses coming through the gate. This was Odoms and his Texans, or Ben was a bank teller.

Ben pushed Star out the other side of the thicket so it

was between him and the Texans. He was about to make a dash across an open flat to hide in the less spiny brush along the river when another flash of lightning showed him a rider running headlong toward him from the María Macarena. The rider was Margarita.

Ben rode back to the trail, and she saw him in the next flash of lightning. She sat her horse down hard and slid to a stop in front of him. He touched her lips, told her to be silent, and hurried her into the thicket on the river. They dismounted and held their horses' muzzles to keep them from nickering as Odoms's horses went by.

The storm increased, and a wall of rain separated Ben and Margarita from the Texans. When they were gone, Ben said, "Thank God they were too lazy to cook for themselves tonight."

Margarita laughed. "Now why did you say that?"

"They're headed to your house to beg for their supper. If not for you, they would have stopped at La Acequia to dry out and cook their jerky gravy." Ben hugged Margarita around the waist and kissed her. "I'm sure glad they're going to your house."

"Why?"

"Because, by God, I'm gonna sleep here tonight."

"Me too," Margarita said.

Margarita said she had not called to him when she first saw him in the lightning because she was bent on surprising him. In the next flash she saw the Texans and thanked God she had not yelled.

They rode to the camp and stabled their horses under the ramada by the house. Ben stretched his reata across the open side to hold them and gave them corn and tasol while Margarita went inside to build a fire. When he went in the house with their saddles and his blanket roll, he found her stripped to her wet underwear, her clothes drying on a bench in front of the fireplace. Her face, arms, and shoulders were wet and shiny, and her calves and feet were bare under the knee-length pantalets. Her black curls were plastered against her head from wind and rain and the wild, headlong run through the dark.

She took Ben's amphora of mescal out of his morral, uncorked it, drank from the bottle, and began to cry. Ben took off his Saltillo and put his arms around her.

"You almost got away from me," she said. "I was so afraid I wouldn't catch you. I don't want to lose you."

"I have to admit, the farther I came, the dimmer your kisses got."

"I lost a husband here at La Acequia. I can't lose you too. If I lose my man again, I'll die."

"Don't worry about it now. You caught up to me with one kiss."

"I know I was cold to you in front of Bouvet and my father. I could not show them I wanted you. I also wanted you to think I can always turn to someone else if you get yourself killed in your war, or by your horse or your livestock, or put in jail."

"You played that game with me?"

"Yes."

"Don't lie to me like that again. I don't like that game."

"I know, but I was sweet to run you down in the storm, wasn't I?"

"Yes."

"Will you promise to stop warring and taking risks if I show you how much nicer a gentle life can be?"

"Yes."

"See that you do, and I'll always be sweet to you."

Ben sat her down on a cot, took off his shirt, dried her legs with it, then threw it over her head and tried to dry her hair.

Ben and Margarita rode away from one another two hours before dawn. The same rain that had soothed the lovers in their bed continued to soak the country. Margarita had made up a song for him, *La Llovisnita*, "The Little Rain." His heart swelled now as he remembered how she had sung it to him in a soft, husky whisper. He made himself remember the song word for word, and the rain drummed down on his hat and gave him no discomfort.

He worried that Margarita would be wet to the skin by the time she reached home. The results of their carrying-on were harsh. That was what it was, carrying-on. They carried a big load when they tried to be together, making long wild rides through the rain, risking discovery, shame, death. They made themselves fair game for killers. He was glad he had no one to answer to, but Margarita would surely have to tell a big lie when she got home. Sooner or later he would have to start lying, too.

He decided he'd better not think about it. He knew he would not stay alive in the war with Vincent if he rode around worrying about Margarita and all the consequences of their love affair. He had always thought a "love affair" happened only to self-indulgent people. He would never fall for anything like that, let alone allow it to cause his death. Only womanish men got themselves caught in love affairs. Weak men and women looked for lo-o-ove when they shouldn't, got their tails caught in the same crack, and then couldn't get away from one another, and that was a "love affair."

He decided he'd better forget it now. And instead looked for signs that would help him start working cattle around the Yerba Buena. Plenty of livestock might still die from the drouth. This part of southern Arizona and Sonora was great grass country in spring, summer, and fall when it rained, but rain did not much help it in the winter. The runoff from this rain would swell the river and fill the tanks so cattle would not have far to go for a drink, but it would not help the grass grow. Right now, rain only made everything wet. If the weather turned cold and froze, drouth-weakened stock would die.

Ben wanted to move the Cowden cattle to the Baca Grant. The Salazars had promised to help him. The Baca was a million-acre Spanish grant that joined the Buena Vista on the west, and it still had some feed. Ben would ride to Nogales and talk to the Salazars again. He had promised to start earlier but stayed in Hermosillo and took care of his love affair instead.

The Porters, Cowdens, Salazars, Gandaras, and Noons

shared the Baca. The Gandaras had once owned title to it when it was part of Mexico but let it go in the Gadsden Purchase when the American government bought it from Mexico. The Salazars, Porters, Noons, and Cowdens had been using it under the nose of the Apaches ever since the Union Army abandoned Arizona to fight in the War of Northern Aggression.

Ben decided to follow the Santa Cruz all the way to the Yerba Buena. The Cowdens maintained a good camp, a good set of corrals, and a forge there. Freighters who worked for A. B. Cowden used it for a stopover when they hauled to Nogales. Ben hoped he would find somebody to keep him company there.

Cattle scattered and looked for shelter a long way from one another in a storm. Ben did not expect to see any along the river, but he could ride to the Yerba Buena through the river brush without being seen. The storm would help him in another way. Cattle were so scattered, Odoms would not find many to shoot.

Ben found himself on the tracks Odoms's men and the Rurales had made the day before when Jacinto saw them ride toward Magdalena. The tracks were rain-washed, but that many horses were easy to follow. At an abandoned homestead called Dove Springs he saw that two riders had left the main body. He followed those tracks up Dove Canyon.

He rode fifteen minutes up the canyon and saw the tracks of a cow dragging her hind end. He followed the swath she made and found her in a thicket. She was a three-year-old bearing the Cowden AB-Bar brand, and she had a six-month-old calf.

Ben figured Odoms and his men must have found the cow when they heard her bawl for her calf and shot her before the calf answered. She might have hidden the calf in the thicket and gone back to him after the men shot her.

The Texans had shot to maim her, make her suffer, and make the cowman who owned her go mad with anger. They shot her through the hipbones. He knew the cow.

She had always been gentle and easy to work. This calf was her first.

The cow was slobbering from the pain and effort of her ordeal. She kept turning her head and looking at Ben over her shoulder, then turning back to her calf and lowing to him, more worried about him than herself. The calf seemed unconcerned. He could not fathom what had happened to his mother. He nuzzled her, threw his head up comically, playfully, looking for a game, then turned back to nuzzle her again. He was too young to be afraid. He could not see that his mother was afraid. She was not running.

Ben built a loop in his reata, caught the calf, dragged him out of the thicket, and tied him down. Then he went in the thicket and shot the cow. He did not feel the loss of property. He felt he had lost an ally in the survival of cattle and cattlemen. He wondered if it would do any good if he skinned her to have the hide for evidence and decided it was not worth the effort, not worth even the thought. A thousand hides of dead cows would not decide this war or make one bit of difference in the way Ben felt. The hides of the Odoms gang and Duncan Vincent would though.

Ben lifted the calf into his lap on Star and headed for the Yerba Buena. The sonsabitches had told him they hated cattle and would shoot his cows, but he had not been able to imagine that anyone could really do it.

The calf rode along comfortably, trustingly, seeming not a bit afraid that something bad could happen to him in the hands of a man. His head bobbed along in rhythm with old Star. Star's ears kept turning back to investigate him. The calf's clean, spare, sweet-smelling little hide kept Ben's hands warm.

Ben did not stop at the Yerba Buena but rode on to the Salazar ranch outside Nogales. He shouted a greeting when he came in sight of the house to tell the family he was there. Then he heard a new surge in the river and saw a fresh wall of water widen and deepen the flood.

The whole Salazar family was home. The three brothers put on their slickers and came to the corral to help Ben unsaddle, feed his horse, and turn the calf loose with other calves in the milk pen.

Margarita reached home an hour before sunup. The rain kept everyone indoors, so she did not know if anyone saw her return. She put her mare away and went to the house. The house was quiet. She started a fire in the kitchen stove, put water on to boil for the coffee, and placed a kettle of milk on the back of the stove to warm. She went to her room to change clothes.

She had stripped to her underwear when Odoms came in. He made straight for her. She backed up and covered herself with a housecoat. "Yes, Odoms?"

"Where have you been?"

"What do you want in here?"

"I want to know where you've been."

"Out to the stable." Margarita backed into her dressing table and sat down on its stool.

"Where?" Odoms took a handful of her hair and pushed her head back.

"To the stable."

He slapped her face so hard her neck cracked. She covered her face. He forced her to her knees. "I can see you need another haircut," he said. He unsheathed a big skinning knife and in a few deft strokes cut off Margarita's hair.

He stood back a step and kicked her with the point of his toe until she stood up and backed away. He sheathed the knife, loosed a quirt he carried on his belt, grabbed her, and raised the quirt. His face showed no more expression than it did when he sat down to his supper. Without a sound, he began lashing Margarita's back. When she twisted away from the quirt, he lashed her legs. She kicked at him, and he lashed the soles of her feet. She did not scream or beg for help, but the pain made her weep.

When he was through with the whipping, Odoms dragged her out of the room and down the veranda. Pepe came in the back door and heard his mother crying. He jumped on Odoms's back and beat on his head. Odoms took the back of Pepe's head in his big hand and slammed him to the floor.

Bouvet opened his door, saw Margarita being dragged past Pepe's body, and quickly closed the door. Don Juan Pedro came out of his room, and Odoms threw Margarita at his feet.

"I knew this woman was a whore and a slut," he said quietly. "I needed a slut when I came to you, but I told you I didn't want it to show. Her showing it off so everybody knows it defeats my purpose. This time I just gave her a good licking and cut off her hair so she'd be ashamed to show her face outside this house.

"If I ever come back from a patrol with my Texans again and she's not here to feed them and tend to my needs, or I find out she spent the night away from this house like she did last night, I swear by my holy Lord, I'll cut off her nose."

Odoms stalked out of the room. Margarita and Don Juan Pedro carried Pepe in and laid him on Don Juan Pedro's bed. She pulled on a dress and ran to ask Luz Cano, Chapito's wife, to help her. When she returned to Don Juan Pedro's room, Pepe had revived. She examined him and found he might suffer only a stiff neck.

Odoms came back and stood at the door. "And another thing," he said. "Get rid of that damned whelp of yours. If he ever touches me again, or even so much as picks up my bridle, I'll kill him."

"Rabid dog," Margarita said. "Woman beater. Child beater. You don't fight men, do you? You think you can get away with beating me? You think you can cut off my nose? Before I'm through with you, I'll have every man in Sonora in love with me, and they'll be fighting among themselves for the right to kill you."

She walked up to Odoms. The top of her head reached only his shirt pocket. "You and your big knife and your whip. You think you can keep me down by cutting off my hair and whipping me, or even by cutting off my nose?

You are already at my feet and don't know it. Your 'holy Lord' is going to push your face down in the mud of my pee for abusing my family."

Margarita struck Odoms's chest with both hands. He raised the quirt again, but her show of antagonism had plainly shaken him. He did not want every Mexican in the state of Sonora crying for his blood. Don Juan Pedro embraced her from behind and carried her out of range of the quirt, and Odoms left.

Margarita did not sit down and weep. She ordered her son to his feet and went out and packed their suitcases.

That evening, Ben rode to La Acequia and waited for Margarita. Pepe came instead and told him his mother could not come. Her message to Ben was brief and clear, and he knew her handwriting: *Ben, don't try to see me anymore. I must go on as Jack's wife. I'm sure someday we will be together, but we must not see each other now with so much life and property at stake. I love you, M.*

By the time Ben returned to the Yerba Buena, he hated Margarita. Now all she wanted to do was live with Odoms, but she would find time to go on that trip with Bouvet. Why did she choose this time when he felt so close to her to tell him she preferred to live with his enemy? How could she smile into Bouvet's cold eyes, give him brandy, and take him away in their railroad car to Cuernavaca?

Ben could hear the little common laugh she used when she entertained admiring salamanders like Bouvet. Now it hurt him to remember the way she had sung softly to him with the rain when they were close in each other's arms at La Acequia.

CHAPTER 15

Les and the twins were holed up with the Campana sisters, spending the last handful of the golden alazanas. The girl who had taken the arrow through her leg died before they could get her to Santa Cruz. Les made the twins take him to the river to dig up the alazanas, but a flash flood from a cloudburst up Porter Canyon had washed away the riverbank where the cache was buried.

Les felt so miserable about the death of the girl and the loss of the gold that he got drunk. Gabriel Kosterlinsky carried a message to him there the next morning. Jesús Romero, the telegraph operator, knew Les was in the house with the Campana girls, but he did not like to go in there with messages. Drunks who received bad news were inclined to shoot the messenger, and those who received good news were apt to take the messenger captive and make him join the party. He took the telegram to Kosterlinsky and let him deliver it. Kosterlinsky liked to know the content of any message that came to Santa Cruz.

The twins were lying out on the cold bricks on the edge of the patio, asleep. Kosterlinsky searched until he uncovered Josefa Campana. She gave him directions, and he found Les asleep alone in a room.

Les awakened before Kosterlinsky was halfway between the door and the bed. "What the hell do you want, Gabriel?"

Kosterlinsky unfolded the telegram and read: "Urgent Cowden brothers proceed Benson meet with brother Mark immediately. Confirm message received. Signed, A. B. Cowden, Undersheriff, Harshaw, Arizona."

Les sat up and read the telegram, then pulled on his boots. "Thank you, Gabriel," he said.

"What does this mean?" Kosterlinsky asked.

"Mark took Eileen and my little sister to Benson to meet with Eileen's fiancé's people, and now he needs me and Ben. That's all I get out of it."

"Is there anything I can do to help you?" Kosterlinsky asked.

"It's decent of you to ask, but I don't think so. I do wish you would forgo any warrants or orders for my arrest until after I find my brother and see about this."

"I've received no complaints against you, Les. I'm Vincent's partner in various endeavors, but I'm not your enemy."

"Have you seen the Farleys?"

"They're on the patio."

"I'd better gather them and get going."

Les picked up his pistol belt and hat, and tucked in his shirttail on his way out the door. Josefa called him for coffee in the kitchen, and he roused the twins. He and the twins drank their coffee standing up, then caught their horses and left town at a high trot. Les figured to look for Ben at the María Macarena first. He knew Ben had said to meet him at the Yerba Buena, but he did not trust his brother to be there. Ben was too sweet on Margarita to go off and leave her if he was offered any excuse to stay. Somebody there would know where he was.

Les and the twins topped out and let their horses blow before midmorning on the pass above the ranch. They watched people load a carriage in the yard behind the main house.

Margarita was dressed to go somewhere, supervising

the loading. Odoms was down by the stables talking to a man who was saddling a horse. "Well, Odoms is there, and it looks to me like Margarita's leaving," Les said. "So it's a cinch my brother's not down there."

Don Juan Pedro followed Margarita around as she gave him instructions about running the house. When she was ready to leave and she had to say good-bye to him, her face went white. She kissed him and patted him harshly. She knew the Indian-fighter vaquero was still somewhere inside the man. The real statesman was there, but the statesman, fighter, and doer had given way to a politician. Politics had not been inside this man. He caught it like a pox after his good qualities were defeated.

Margarita said, "Papá, you're doing these things with Odoms and Vincent because you want to, not because you have to."

Tears started in Don Juan Pedro's eyes. "Stay with me, daughter. I'll protect you."

"You can't protect me and fight Odoms. Find a way to protect yourself. My responsibility now is to protect myself and my son."

The last thing Margarita did before she left the house was go into her father's bedroom and unearth the Colt .45 her mother had kept by the bed. She saw that it was loaded and put it in her handbag.

Colorado was on the carriage with Cuco waiting for her. Cuco was armed with a pistol, shotgun, and rifle. Chapito and his son Chico were sitting their horses in front of the team. Odoms stalked up to the carriage as Margarita and Pepe climbed in.

"Where do you think you're going?" Odoms demanded.

Margarita produced the pistol and aimed at Odoms's eye. "I'm free of you, dog."

"Maybe we better talk about it."

Margarita cocked the pistol. Odoms turned to Chapito. "You and these other *pelados* are fired."

"You can't fire anybody," Margarita said. "Dogs don't give orders on this ranch."

"I give orders by the strength of my legal right as your husband. If these men go with you, they might as well take their women and children too. I'll house my Texans in their quarters before nightfall."

"What about it, Chapito?" Margarita asked.

"My family can sleep under the mesquites until I come back," Chapito said.

"That's where they'll sleep, then." Odoms raised his quirt, lashed the off horse in the team, and made him lunge against his harness. Colorado gathered him in line with the near horse and went on.

Les and the twins watched the carriage go down the road toward La Acequia. When it was out of sight, the man who had been with Odoms at the stable mounted his horse and followed.

Les said, "That's one of Odoms's Texans with orders to see where Margarita goes and who she meets. That's just fine. Let's watch Odoms and see what he does now."

Odoms went to the corrals and flashed a mirror toward the camp of his Texans in the San Bernardino peaks.

"He'll meet with his Texans at La Acequia, and the one who's following Margarita will see Ben and come back and tell him, don't you think, boys?" Les said.

"I bet that's right," Donny Farley said.

"He's using Margarita as bait to catch Ben."

"How could that be?" Donny asked.

"Ben loves her."

"Aw, everybody knows Ben's crazy about Maudy."

"Not now. These sonsabitches couldn't keep him in jail, shoot him, or ruin him any other way, so they got Margarita to give him the sweetass."

"How could they get Margarita to do a thing like that, or get Don Juan Pedro to go for it?"

"Our war is changing all the time, cousins. Who could have believed Margarita would marry a son-of-a-bitch like Odoms? But she did."

Ben and the twins skirted the ranch and crossed the

river so they could use its cover to hide their progress. The rain had stopped, and the sun came out, but a strong wind came up to chill the riders. Their trail led them through the cottonwood, willow, mesquite, ash, and sycamore trees along the river. The trail furnished easy going because cattle had been hanging close to the river in the drouth and most of the foliage was gone with winter. The Cowden and Farley brothers had tracked and chased wild cattle down every foot of this river trail and flushed them out of this brush. The cattle had shown them how to hide on the river and taught them ingenious ways to escape in the brush.

The river paralleled the road Margarita was taking. The tree bark smelled good from the rain. The smell of the wet cottonwoods always reminded Les of the good times he and his brothers and sisters enjoyed when they played on the banks of this river at picnics. The river forest was a friend of the Cowdens, always cool and shady in the summer, sheltered against the wind in the winter.

Les and the twins passed Margarita, then rode out into the open and waited for her on the road.

Chapito stopped the carriage when he saw Les and the twins. He and Chico came down the road until they recognized them, then waved for the carriage to come on. They all came on, but nobody smiled. Les and the twins did not act friendly either. Les asked Margarita where she was going, and she told him Nogales. He asked if it was all right to ride along with her, and she said yes. He rode beside the carriage so Margarita could talk to him if she wanted to, but he kept his eyes straight ahead and did not offer conversation. Neither did she. She did not show him her swollen face either.

Every once in a while when he could do it without giving away that he knew they were being followed, he tried to see if Odoms's man was still coming. He never saw him. He did not think he would turn back until he saw Ben though.

At the Yerba Buena, Margarita told Colorado to stop underneath some big cottonwoods in a parklike clearing beside the river. Colorado and Cuco got down, unharnessed the team, and watered the horses. Chico went out to find some mesquite wood, and the twins built a fire. Margarita invited Les and the twins to share her lunch. She put coffee water on to boil and unpacked a lunch of lean sirloin strips, potatoes that were already boiled, and whole cooked beans that she mashed in a skillet. She added cheese to the beans and put the skillet on the edge of the fire to warm.

Pepe took down a sack of corn from the buggy, measured rations of corn into morrals, and Les and the twins hung them on the horses. While everyone waited for the lunch to warm, Les mounted his horse and rode away to hide himself on a high point where he could watch for enemies. He was sorry the wind was blowing. A predator could sneak up on the picnic without being heard. The day was crisp, bright, and wintry, and the wind made it cold for a lookout who was forced to hide and keep still.

After a while Les saw Odoms's man come up and stop. The man could not see Margarita's carriage through the river forest. Les thought he deserved to be potshot for being Odoms's man. He would not shoot him though. He'd had enough of shooting people.

Chico came up and found Les on the hill. This time he smiled. "Your brother is down there," he said. "Go eat, and I'll watch."

Les showed Chico where the Texan was hiding.

"Ah, sí? You think he's following us?" Chico said.

"You knew it, didn't you?" Les smiled at him.

"No, as God is a saint, I didn't."

"As soon as he finds out Ben is down there, he'll head back to tell Odoms."

"Shall I kill him?"

"No. Keep him in sight, and be sure and tell me if he heads back."

"I will."

Ben was leaning against the carriage eating a strip of broiled beef in a tortilla. He started and turned when Les rode into the clearing. The look of misery on his face shocked Les.

Ben looked like an orphan. His work kept him lean, and he could not spare any flesh at all, but he looked as though he had lost ten pounds. His eye sockets were cavernous, and the deep blue eyes looked feverish.

Les shook hands with Ben and told him that Odoms's spy was tailing them. He said it to put the Cowdens on an even footing with Margarita in case Margarita thought she was the bait in an Odoms trap. Les knew Ben did not suspect he was being brought down by his love for Margarita. Ben would never believe Vincent could defeat him that way or that Margarita and Don Juan Pedro would betray him.

He told Ben about the telegram their father had sent, ordering them to Benson. They had to throw Odoms off their track so they could be free to do what had to be done in Benson. Les picked a hot tortilla out of a bundle wrapped in linen dishcloths, placed a long strip of broiled sirloin on it, painted the meat with red chile sauce, and rolled the meat up in the tortilla. He poured himself coffee, sugared it, and stepped over to the carriage beside his brother. Ben was watching Margarita tend the fire. Neither Ben nor Margarita had said a word since Les's return to the clearing.

"What do you think we ought to do, brother?" Les asked him. He added the "brother" to remind him the Cowdens were engaged in a blood feud and every clearing in the country was a dangerous place for them. He wanted to remind him they needed to get moving. They had a long way to go, and almost everybody else who carried a gun in the country was against them.

"I don't know," Ben said, his eyes still on Margarita. Margarita looked back at him pitifully, as though she did not know what to do with a desperate love such as Ben's. She looked to Les for help.

"I think I do," Les said. "We go to the Salazars with Margarita and stay there until dark. Then we let the

Salazars put on our Saltillos and impersonate us like we did before, and go on to Nogales with Margarita."

"It won't work again."

"It won't matter. We have fresh horses with the Salazars, and it'll be dark. We can still get away. Some of them will have to follow the Salazars. The others can only try to look for us. They can't chase or track us in the dark."

Ben looked at Margarita.

"Don't you think I'm right?"

"I know you're right, but I sure am getting tired of doing this," said Ben.

"Don't be tired, brother, get mad. Something's gone bad with our sister's trip to visit her future in-laws, and we've got to get amoving."

Ben went loosely, almost languidly, to the edge of the stream where Pepe had dug a hole so clean water would seep in, and washed his hands and face. He mounted Star and started up the river forest trail.

"Where are you going?" Les asked.

Ben stopped and turned back to his brother for a long moment. Finally he said, "I've got too many things on my mind to be able to concentrate. I have to keep what I do simple."

"But where are you going?"

"I'm going to find our spy and tie him to a tree so he can't tell anyone what we're doing."

"Wait a minute. Let me help you."

"Come on, then, if you're coming."

Odoms's man was Lige Rote. His job was to spy on Margarita and tell Odoms when she met with the Cowdens. The Texans knew what the Cowdens looked like, because Teddy Briggs, Lorrie Briggs's brother, had taken them over to spy on the ranch at El Durazno when they first came to the country.

Lige did not like this job. A bronc rider, he wished he could ride broncs for a living. He guaranteed his customers that he could give any bronc his fill of bucking after two or three saddles. He couldn't teach one anything, but he could sure make him hate that bucking worse than death.

He did not consider himself a good spy though. He did not like to hide in the brush and watch a woman go down the road. But he did not complain about being given the task because he hoped the woman would lead him to Ben Cowden. He wanted to be the one who let all the blood out of Ben Cowden and carried his head back to Duncan Vincent for the $5,000 bounty.

He'd seen Les Cowden come to the road to meet the woman, so he reckoned Ben Cowden would be along pretty soon. Lige wondered if he could get any money for Les Cowden's head. He would have to take it. If he was to believe the stories, he would have to kill Les Cowden if he killed Ben Cowden, or be killed.

Lige Rote admired brotherly love. He was an orphan and had no brothers and sisters. That was how he knew he had to kill both brothers if he was to live to enjoy spending the $5,000. He would have fought to the death for a brother or sister if he had one. In the time he had been given to watch the Cowdens, he came to know that he would like them a lot if they were his brothers and sisters. He would have liked to have A.B. and Viney for his father and mother too. He'd envied Joe Coyle his job with the Cowdens.

Now Lige had snuck up on the Cowdens in time to hear Les Cowden's plan to have the Mexicans imperson- ate them so they could get away. Then Ben Cowden mounted his horse and said he was going to tie Odoms's man to a tree, and Lige guessed that meant him. He would wait until the Cowdens went up the trail, and then he would slip up behind them. He couldn't go yet though. Margarita's kid was in a place where he could see him if he moved.

The kid finally moved, and Lige raised up to hurry after the Cowdens. He wanted to jump the Cowdens when they found his horse and stopped to talk about it, while they were away from the twins and the Mexicans. He raised himself to his knees, drew his pistol, and looked down at the loads. If he was to believe everything that was said about the Cowdens, he needed to be careful.

Ben had seen Odoms's man out of the corner of his eye when he went to the seep to wash his hands. He did not see all of him, only the heel of his boot and his spur jutting up out of a brushy ditch. That would have been a helluva hiding place if it could have been four inches deeper. Ben stopped out of sight of the clearing, motioned for Les to go on, built a loop in his reata, circled back, and rode up behind the Texan.

Lige's drawing his pistol to check the loads cost him his life. Ben did not know that Lige was an orphan or would have liked to belong to a family like the Cowdens or even that his name was Lige, but he did not want to kill him. Instead of drawing his pistol, he had taken down his *lazo*. He did not know Lige was hard of hearing either, but he rode boldly up behind him in the wind, wondering why the man did not hear him.

Ben tossed a small loop to catch the man around the arms and jerk him down, but while the loop was sailing to the target, the man drew, looked down at his pistol, and changed his attitude enough so the loop settled on top his shoulders. When Ben saw the man draw his pistol, he jerked his slack and tightened the loop around his neck. To keep from getting shot, Ben spun Star, dallied the tail of his reata around the saddle horn and spurred away. Kneeling as he was, with his back to Ben and his head turned slightly and bent toward his pistol, the weight of the horse snapped Lige's neck like a reed, and he died instantly.

CHAPTER 16

Early in the night, the rain stopped, and Eileen and Paula Mary were less confused by sounds. Wind and rain covered the sounds the Bonners made, and several times they had been able to get close to the girls. The Bonners seemed to enjoy having the Cowden girls treed in their barn. The girls wondered if every visitor to that ranch got run up a tree. They did not wonder what the Bonners wanted to do with them when they got them down. The girls knew they would not like it.

Eileen and Paula Mary lay down and covered themselves with hay near the top of the ladder. Louise and the baby were in the corner farthest from the ladder. The baby was a Bonner through and through, and helped her relatives by bawling. The Cowdens could not hear a thing that went on outside the loft when that baby tuned up.

The girls decided fretting only made them feel bad, so they discussed the kinds of punishment the Bonners should suffer when their brothers came to even the score. They agreed trimming the bottoms of their feet would be a good one, since the Bonners seemed to want to do that to other people.

Mark had been gone two or three days, maybe more. They had lost track of time, but he'd been gone long enough to telegraph Harshaw. Ben and Les might already be on their way. The quickest way for them to come was horseback. Their uncle Billy Porter headquartered at the Baboquivari ranch halfway between El Durazno and Benson, and they could change horses there. The Bonner ranch was fifty miles from El Durazno. If they left at that moment, they could meet Mark in Benson and be at the Bonners' by midmorning tomorrow. Their brothers could make tracks at night almost as well as by day.

The girls hoped they would have to endure only one more night under siege. They were tired, but both of them could not rest at once, so Eileen said she would take the first watch and let Paula Mary sleep.

The Bonners started singing Christmas carols again, and they opened their windows so the girls could hear. Eileen observed they were awful damned proud of their singing, but to her, bands of coyotes singing after an August rain sounded more like Christmas carolers. Then she realized Paula Mary had gone away to sleep.

Eileen sank into the hay, relaxed her bones, and felt her muscles mend. She held the heavy pistol on her stomach. She was thankful when the baby started crying again. That would keep Louise awake, and she would certainly let out a howl if her brothers tried to get into the loft again. They would have to use the ladder. Eileen hooked the heel of her hand in the corner between the side of the ladder and a rung so she would feel it if anyone started up. Then she fell asleep.

She woke to tiny regular snores coming through Paula Mary's nose inches from her ear. The baby and the caroling had subsided. Someone was afoot in the loft. She could not hear any movement, but she knew someone was standing near the center of the loft. She carefully moved her hand so she would not rustle the hay and stuck a finger into Paula Mary to stop her snoring. She felt a stealthy movement, and the floor of the loft creaked. Paula Mary was between Eileen and the sound, and Eileen knew her sister was about to start snoring again.

Eileen fought the urge to brush the hay off her face so

she could see. She knew it was too dark to see anything in the loft, but she desperately needed to try. She forced herself to listen and hoped the baby would not cry again or Paula Mary snore. She did not want to cock the pistol because it would give away her position. The stealthy one crept toward her across the loft. He must have come in through the trapdoor in the roof.

Eileen was lying on her back and had felt as still and settled as a boulder when she awakened, but now her every muscle and nerve wanted to jump up and run. Paula Mary was lying on her side, her back toward the creeper, her nose still puffing in Eileen's ear. Eileen knew Paula Mary was hugging herself in her sleep and feeling cozy and safe because she was protected by her big sister. Eileen had always thought a person needed to be lying on her back to snore, but that sure was a lie. She dug her finger into Paula Mary's belly again to prevent her snoring.

The creeper took three quick steps toward the ladder and stepped on Paula Mary. Paula Mary let out a squashed yelp, and the creeper let out a Bonner howl. Eileen swiped the hay off her face, cocked and raised the pistol, and popped the cap. A flame burst from the muzzle of Mark's .45 and licked at the hair above a long white face floating overhead. Strands of the hair stood up and waved as though charged by electricity and seemed to catch fire in the pistol's muzzle blast. The eyes in the face were wide open, surprised in the effort of looking for the girls in the dark. The face kept howling as it was caught in the wind of the pistol blast.

Eileen cocked the pistol, sat up, and fired again. The creeper lunged over the top of the girls toward the ladder, missed it, sailed out into space, and howled all the way to the ground. Eileen sent another round after him, and the flame of the charge lit up his flight as he ran out the door.

Eileen jumped up and lit the lamp she had brought from Sybil Bonner's kitchen. "Louise," she said. The Bonner girl was not in sight. Eileen handed the lamp to Paula Mary and felt in the hay with her feet. Her heel touched flesh. She stepped away, dropped to her knees, and uncovered the baby. She picked her up quickly and brushed hay off her face.

The baby's eyes were open and glazed, and she was not breathing. "Oh, poor little thing," Eileen said, and looked at Paula Mary. She rolled the child from side to side on the palms of her hands. "She's dead."

Eileen was about to wonder aloud how such a noisy, strong child could have died so suddenly, but the absence of the mother explained it for her.

"How could she be dead?" Paula Mary asked. "She was squalling like a banshee, and she'd had regular meals."

"I think her neck's broken," Eileen said.

"How could that happen?"

"Either Louise is just another goddammed Bonner, or that big thing did it before we put him to flight."

"Louise wouldn't do that to her own baby, would she?"

"I didn't think she would, but she sure kept quiet when she slipped out of this loft."

Paula Mary looked through the crack toward the house. "They must be used to hearing shots in the night. They aren't showing a light."

Eileen shone the lamp on the ground below the ladder to see if the creeper had left any debris or if Louise might be down there but saw no sign of them. "Paula Mary, did that big thing step on you?"

"Yes, and it was heavy."

"Did it kick you, or just step on you?"

"It stumbled on me, then stepped down hard on me, but it was barefooted."

"It was a Bonner man, wasn't it?"

"Yeah, the howl sounded like a Bonner, but the thing's foot was big as a bear's."

The girls sat by the ladder and counted their ammunition. Mark's cartridge belt was full, and the pistol had two bullets left in it. Eileen knew the Bonner pistol had four bullets left in it. She loaded Mark's pistol to capacity and put it on the half-cock safety. She did not know where the Bonner pistol was. She blew out the lamp. "I'm not a

very good shot. I've shot at the Bonners four times and
haven't hit a thing," she said.

"Can I shoot the Bonner gun next time?" Paula Mary
asked.

"Do you know how to shoot it?"

"I just pull the trigger, don't I?"

Eileen could not demonstrate because the loft was too
dark. "Cock it first; then *point* it, and pull the trigger. Ben
says if you're in a hurry to shoot a person, just point the
pistol the way you would your finger at the middle button
on his shirt, or his belt buckle, or his shirt pocket. Try to
pick some detail in the middle of him to point at."

"I'm not taking any chance on being too late to shoot.
I've already got it cocked."

Eileen gasped. "Don't move, sister." She felt for Paula
Mary's face. When she found it, she said, "Now put my
first finger on the handle of the gun. Be real careful I don't
touch the trigger."

"What's the matter?"

"Never mind, just take my finger to the handle,
gently."

Paula Mary took her hand to the pistol, and Eileen
picked it up and put it on half cock. "Paula Mary, you
scared me to death. You could have shot yourself. This
pistol has a hair trigger. Don't *ever* carry a cocked pistol
around."

"You oughtta throw all your guns down and come
down and get something to eat anyway," a voice said.

The girls went to the edge of the loft and looked down
but did not see anyone.

"How about it?" The voice came from outside the
barn.

The girls did not answer. The first light of dawn
showed through the doorway.

"It's Johnny, girls. If Mark will tell you not to shoot me
on sight, I'd like to show myself. Can I come in?"

"Sure, come right on in," Eileen said, "so I can shoot
you right between the slats."

"All right for you," Johnny Bonner said. "You know,

this is no good. You gave me a hell of a headache. I'm not right sure I didn't crack my skull when I fell off that ladder. You ought to listen to me while I can still talk. You won't get along very well if anything happens to me. My ma and brothers don't like you as much as I do. Let me talk to Mark, will you? Mark?"

"We don't like you any more than we do the rest of the tribe," Paula Mary said.

The girls heard the sound of a wagon and team coming. A deep, masculine voice hailed the house.

"Don't go to the barn," Sybil Bonner called. "Come in the house."

After a while, the girls heard footsteps with the ringing spurs coming to the barn. A tall man stopped in the doorway. He was wearing a big dark hat and a mackinaw coat. His trousers were tucked inside elegant custom boots. The big rowels on his heavy silver-mounted spurs rang like bells, and heavy silver conchos adorned the straps. The character of his dress made it plain to the girls that he was a cowman, and he looked as if he could be trusted. They could not distinguish his features in the dim light. Another man, like the first, came through the doorway leading two saddlehorses and a team of horses with the harness still in place.

"Misses Cowden," the man in the doorway said in his deep melodious voice, "I'm John Bonner, father of this passel of coons that's been pestering you, husband of that cranky old lady in the house, and good friend of A. B. Cowden, your father."

The girls showed him only the tops of their heads, their eyes, and the muzzles of the pistols.

"Oh, I see you're armed. Now, I want an honorable truce. We won't shoot if you won't. Give me a chance to explain about my family." He walked into the barn and stood below the girls. He had straight, even features and a strong, kindly face.

Eileen had already tried to shoot the Bonners from only an arm's length away and was unable to hit any of them, so she figured she did not have anything to lose by letting him talk.

"Now if you'll listen a minute, I'll satisfy you that no one wants to hurt you," Bonner said. "These wild children of mine had been having a little fun trying to scare you, but they'd never hurt you. You have to understand, they've had very little schooling. Johnny is the only one who's been given formal education, and his whole charm comes from the time he spent in school in Tombstone. These others never liked school and were too ornery to be bothered with it. The boys are good cowboys. The girls—well, they're just girls, still too young to do anything right but carry water.

"Try to understand, Sybil is crazy, but the children are only wild. I know they've been giving you fits, but believe me, none of them would harm you.

"By the way, is your brother Mark up there? I know Mark. We've been good friends since he came over here for the general roundup in eighty-three. Mark, show yourself. Let's talk."

When Mark did not show himself, Bonner said, "Is he up there?"

Eileen whispered, "Watch him." She crawled to the crack in the wall so she could see the house. Louise was standing with Merle by the back door, eating a potato. Against the barn's outside wall below her she could see Johnny Bonner's hat and the toes of his boots. Beside him stood a giant of a man with a tousled head of blond hair and the biggest dirty bare feet she had ever seen in her life.

Sybil, Jake, and Josh came from the house and stopped at the barn door. Sybil said, "If you ask me, Bonner, Johnny's way too good for the likes of the Cowdens, but if you can get 'em down, I'll feed 'em and be good to 'em for the rest of the time they're here."

"Now, then, you hear that, girls?" John Bonner said. "The game's over. My outfit won't pester you anymore. If you ask me, you've taught them some manners. They'll know better than to hooraw the next people who come out to visit them."

"Come on, girls, we give up," Sybil Bonner said. "We were only playing."

Paula Mary joined Eileen at the crack in the wall. Eileen pointed to Louise standing with her sister and feeding her face, innocent as she could be.

"I'm hungry," Paula Mary said. "What can they do to us now that their papa is home?"

Eileen pointed down and showed Paula Mary the barefoot man. Paula Mary gasped. "Will you look at those feet? You think that's the one stepped on me?"

"Yes, and there he is, rubbing elbows big as you please with Johnny. Somebody murdered that baby, and none of them care a damn."

Eileen looked around in time to see the face of the uncle at the top of the ladder. Her first thought was, Well he's up here and hasn't hurt us, so we might as well climb down and see how they treat us. We need something to eat. Then she read the sly expression on the man's face—the look of an Apache who has moved out ahead of his band to commit some depredation to show off; the look of a coyote when he first gains entrance to a chicken coop. Eileen brought up the pistol, pointed at the expression, and blew the man off the ladder. His hat sailed away, spinning from the bullet.

Eileen peeked over the edge of the loft. Bonner was bending over the uncle, and the uncle's toes were quivering toward each other. Sybil shouted, "You'll burn in hell for this, you trollops. Now you see, Bonner? I tried to tell you these Cowdens were bloodthirsty. How could you let our Johnny marry into a family like that?"

"Them Cowdens get a lot of work done," Bonner said. "Like I told you, we need new blood in this family. I think the Bonners and the Cowdens will make a good cross, if these two don't kill us before we get 'em bred."

"The devil you 'think.'"

"Girls, I tell you what," Bonner coaxed. "If you come

down right now, we'll only keep one of you and let the other one go."

Johnny called from outside, "Well now, which one you want to keep, Pa?"

"We'll keep the big one and send the little one back on the train."

"Pa, we gotta keep 'em both," Jake Bonner yelled. "The littleun's big enough. She's ever bit as fit as the other'n."

Paula Mary's mouth fell open, and she stared, shocked, at Eileen. She heard laughter and looked through the crack and watched as Johnny Bonner and the barefoot man, in a fit of giggling, began slapping each other on the back.

Then, the barefoot man screamed with laughter and slapped Johnny on both sides of the head. Johnny tried to cover up. The barefoot man was bigger. He rose above Johnny and pounded down on the back of his neck with a wallop that drove Johnny's head in the dirt, then he ran and danced through the doorway of the barn. He jumped high, whirled in the air, and slapped his butt with both hands as though inviting Eileen to shoot it, laughed maniacally, and ran back outside. Eileen saw blood on the bib of his overalls, smudged across his mouth, and on both cheeks—probably the result of missing a ladder, falling off a dark loft, and landing on his face.

Bonner straightened over the uncle and said, "He'll have to sleep awhile. The little lady creased him like a mustang."

The top of the uncle's head was bloody. The bullet had creased the top of his head, plowed through his scalp, and parted his hair.

"What do you mean, Bonner?" Sybil said. "His head looks like it's been split open with a cleaver."

"How do you like that, you old blister?" Eileen said. "You're next."

"Now, you just come down from there and stop making trouble," Sybil yelled, waving her finger at Eileen.

"This is serious, now," Bonner said. "This man tried to help you, and you practically murdered him."

"Listen, we defended ourselves against that man and all four of your other maniacs, and we'll continue to defend ourselves."

"The cedar man almost got you, didn't he?" Sybil yelled.

"Is that what you call him? Who's he, your herd sire? He does show a bit finer breeding than the rest of you."

"Yeah? Well it's a wonder he didn't break all your bones," Bonner said. "We can't control him, and he ain't fooling. He'll be more careful when he comes to get you next time. You're probably doomed."

"Is he the father of Louise's child?"

"Little lady, you don't know the half of it," Bonner said.

"I know Louise gave birth to a child up here night before last and one of you Bonners is the father. Was it you, her uncle, one of her brothers, or that other maniac?"

"Jason the cedar man does as he pleases around here. Louise is the only one who has any control over him. If it wasn't for her, there's no telling what kind of tricks he'd pull on this family."

"So you give him Louise so he won't bother you, is that it?"

"You have to understand, little lady. We live the best way we can out here. We have our own ways of keeping the peace."

"Well, you're a bunch of animals, because you keep the peace with incest and murder. That's against the law, and my papa will hear about it as soon as I get home."

"What do you mean 'murder'? Who's been murdered?"

"One of you killed Louise's baby, and there's no telling how many more babies you've killed."

"That ain't murder any more'n drowning a litter of pups is murder."

"I bet the judge in Tucson won't see it that way."

Bonner laughed crazily, recklessly, and his lips flopped

loose, the first sign the girls had seen that he was as crazy as the rest of them. "Well, you're not going to tell anything to a judge or your papa from up there in that loft," he said.

Eileen shut up. She did not want the Bonners to guess her hole card. The Bonners were not watching their backs for the Cowden brothers because they still did not know Mark had gone to Benson.

Then Paula Mary blurted, "We won't be up here much longer. Our brothers are coming."

Eileen pinched her to shut her up, but the secret was out.

Bonner's face took on the look of a weasel who suddenly needs a hole to hide in. "Where's your brothers? What do you mean? Where's Mark?"

"Mark's in Benson by now. He's coming back with Ben and Les," Paula Mary blabbed. "When they find out what you've been doing, there's no telling how many more Porters and Farleys will come down on you. It won't be long now, mister."

John Bonner ordered Jake and Josh to take positions as lookouts away from the house. "Johnny! Johnny Bonner!" he shouted.

"The cedar man near broke his neck, I think," Merle said.

Bonner went outside. Eileen watched him through the crack. Johnny was stretched out on his face, his arms under his body, out cold.

"What did he hit him with?" Bonner asked.

"His big old paw," Merle said.

Bonner went to the well and came back to the front of the barn. "Where's the bucket we keep by the well?"

Paula Mary thought a minute. She had his bucket, by God. She sang out, "Over here it is."

"Can we have it? This boy's bad hurt."

"Oh, all right, I guess so," Paula Mary said. She looked in the bucket. It was a quarter full of water.

"Drop it on the ground."

"All right."

"Can I come in?"

"You been in, haven't you?"

Bonner came through the door, looking up at Paula Mary.

"It's already down there," Paula Mary sang.

Bonner stood beneath her, looking up. "Where?"

"Right in front of you."

"No, no, Bonner! Get back!" Sybil shouted.

Bonner looked down, and Paula Mary dropped the bucket on the back of his head, water and all. He kissed his boots under the bucket and collapsed. Paula Mary sang with laughter.

"My Lord, girl." Eileen laughed. "You threw away our water."

"Yeah, but that was their best thinker. Who said maniacs are smarter than anybody else? I think that one's the smartest one they had. He knew I couldn't hit him with a bullet, so he thought he didn't have to watch me."

CHAPTER 17

Ben and Les Cowden rode into Benson and found Mark at the train station the same morning Paula Mary dropped the water bucket on John Bonner's head. They were leading a saddled horse they had borrowed for Mark from their uncle Billy Porter at Baboquivari. They found out that a freight train was leaving for El Paso in one hour, so they went in to talk to the stationmaster, who was also the telegraph operator. They wanted to see if they could arrange for the train to carry their horses to the Dragoon ranch's shipping pens. The pens were at the base of the Dragoon Mountains, only three miles from the Bonner ranch.

The brothers walked into the office and stood at the counter. The stationmaster was sitting at his desk with his back to them, receiving a message over the wire. He kept his head down and one hand on the telegraph key while he copied the message with pencil and paper. Ben was mesmerized watching him tap a message with one hand and write the answer with the other.

Ben was impatient to keep moving, but he was also so tired, he wobbled where he stood and saw everything overly clear with heavy edges on it. He allowed himself to be entertained and rested by watching the deliberate movements of the stationmaster.

The man was heavy-shouldered and heavy-faced, with thick, iron-gray hair that stuck out from under the visor of his black hat, cocked as though to allow a spot on the side of his head to air out. The hair on the spot was plastered down with sweat from the man's toil, and he seemed cocky about it.

Ben was almost sorry when the man tapped out the tail end of his message and signed off. The man glanced sideways at the Cowden brothers and methodically rearranged papers on his desk. Then, without turning to ask the brothers' business, he pulled his pipe out of his pocket, packed it with tobacco, and struck a match to it. He held the bowl in his palm to feel its warmth and looked way off out the window.

To Ben, this was typical railroader behavior. A railroader who became a stationmaster was just another twenty-year incompetent who had managed to keep from being fired by other incompetents as he climbed to the position of stationmaster. He was the man who for twenty years had survived the wrath of cattlemen whose livestock he lost at sidings for weeks at a time or failed to feed and water or shipped to the wrong destination because he was lazy, mulish, or indifferent. He was the one who carried a watch that kept impeccable time but did not believe anyone else in the world needed to be on time unless he said they could be on time. He was the one who kept a store of excuses for being late but would not wait one minute over the scheduled time of departure for any customer.

Les could not stand one more minute of this. "Excuse me," he said.

The man looked out the window a moment longer, then slowly swiveled around in his chair to face Les. His legs were spread to make room for the tight paunch with the vest and gold watch chain spread across it. His gray mustache was full, well cultivated, and trimmed to a short bristle. His cheeks were ruddy and well fed, his eyes clear. Here was a man who kept his hands and face clean all day, and that made him superior to the dusty customers now present in his office. "What do you want?" he said.

"Just be a stationmaster for a minute, will you?" Les was being as civil as he could, but he was frowning. "We need to load our horses and get on the next train headed east."

The stationmaster pulled his watch out by the chain. "It'll be here in an hour and ten minutes, and you need to have your stock ready on the siding one hour ahead of time."

"All right, we want to order a cattle car, one *furgón*, to carry our horses to the pens at Dragoon."

"Can't do that. The train don't stop at Dragoon."

"What do you mean it don't stop? What're the cattle pens and *embarcadero* there for if not to load and unload livestock off the trains?"

"That's for scheduled trainloads of cattle. I can't schedule a stop for one carload of stock. What're you loading?"

"Three saddlehorses and ourselves."

"Can't do that either."

"Why not?"

"You'd have to pay the same money you'd pay for forty horses."

Ben put his hand on Les's arm. "We'll pay it," he said. "Just show us the car."

"I told you, I can't do that. I won't stop the train in Dragoon just to let off three horses."

"Where is the next scheduled stop?"

"Willcox Playa."

"We'll pay for a car to Willcox Playa."

"That's a long way from Dragoon. You might as well ride horseback from here to Dragoon as ride back to Dragoon from Willcox Playa."

Ben's brothers looked at him with that same problem on their minds.

"Nevertheless, we'll pay the freight to Willcox," Ben said.

"All right, but you'll have to be ready in five minutes."

"We're ready. If you're waiting on us, you're backing up."

"Don't hang around here, then. Get your horses to the pens, and if you're back here in five minutes with the pen foreman's papers, I'll take your money for the car and your fares for the caboose." The man took a sheaf of forms out of a basket and carried them to the counter.

"Go on, brothers," Ben said. He was so wobbly, he thought he might keel over. His normal strength had not returned after his wound healed because he'd been pushing himself.

Ben watched Les and Mark through the window as they led the horses to the pens. They did not look tired. He turned to the counter. The stationmaster was back in his swivel chair. He pointed to some papers on the counter. "Sign those papers for your car and pay the amount specified in the upper right-hand corner."

Ben read the contract, signed it in triplicate, and laid the money down. "Which copy is mine?"

"I'll give you yours." The man stood up, walked to the counter, turned the papers around, and read Ben's signature. "So you're Ben Cowden." He picked up the papers and turned away before Ben could answer. He dropped the papers on the desk, sat in the swivel chair, and lit his pipe. "What're you doing here, Cowden?"

"We have business with the Bonners."

"That doesn't surprise me."

"Why is that?"

"I heard you were intermarrying with the Bonners. Them Bonners are another bunch of outlaws."

Ben looked at him.

"Yeah, it's no surprise to me the only visitors they've had in about seven years turns out to be you Cowdens."

Ben was about to lose his temper. "What's your reason for saying a thing like that?"

The stationmaster was an old hand at needling people. It came with the authority he held over their time. When people were impatient to be gone, they would take almost any abuse from the man who controlled their passage. "No reason. Both families seem to come from the same kind of stock, though anybody can see, you and your brothers ain't as simple-looking as the Bonners. The Bonners look and act downright idiotic."

"If you think you can offend me by calling the Bonners idiots, you're wrong. This is not a friendly visit."

"Ah, not friendly, huh? I should have known. From what I hear, you Cowdens aren't too good at having friends. But isn't one of the Cowden girls engaged to marry Johnny Bonner?"

"That's off."

"Yeah, I heard they took two Cowden girls out to the ranch the other day. That'll make a *helluva* cross. The get from a union like that could really be called a bearcat, with the Bonners supplying the bear and the Cowdens supplying the cat. You better take a preacher with you. Knowing the Bonners the way I do, they'll already have those girls knocked up."

"Now, by God, you're going too far with your mouth, mister."

"Hell, Cowden, don't get mad at me. I'm giving you good advice. The damned Bonners jump on every female that comes in range, even their own sisters, probably their own mother. They're loonier'n a bunch of coons. The very best advice anybody could give you would be for you to take a preacher with you and make them do the legal thing by your girls."

Ben was mollified, even though the advice was no good at all. The Bonners deserved killing for their behaviour, not marrying.

"I thought you knew they were a bunch of inbred simpletons. Johnny Bonner isn't quite as crazy as the rest, but I sure am surprised he was able to hide his idiocy from that Cowden girl he's been courting. Listen, those Bonners are so crazy, not even the Apaches'll go near 'em. If they were decent, sane Christian people, their scalps would be hanging on some Apache's pony's mane. The Apaches still use the Dragoons as a refuge, but they avoid the Bonners like the smallpox."

The train pulled in, and Ben went out with his brothers to load their horses. As they were walking toward the pens, Ben asked, "Do I look like a village idiot or something?"

Mark laughed. "Well, sometimes I look at you and wonder if my mother and father adopted you."

"Why ask us a question like that?" Les said.

"That stationmaster says the Bonners are all insane and he's not surprised to hear they're intermarrying with the Cowdens. Did either of you ever hear anyone say the Bonners were insane?"

"Hell, no, but sometimes I thought Johnny was soft in the head for riding a hundred miles through Apache country every month to see our sister," Les said.

"I thought you were crazy when you paid for a cattle car all the way to Willcox, brother," Mark said. "That's as far from the Bonners as Benson is."

"Never mind how far Willcox is," Ben said.

The brothers learned the train would take an hour to reach Dragoon. The car the Cowden horses were riding in was right behind the coal car. Ben told the railroaders that he and his brothers would ride in the car with their horses. The brothers climbed in the car, laid their blankets and tarps down on the deck, and went to sleep. Fifteen minutes before the train reached Dragoon, Ben climbed out the trapdoor in the top of the car and went up to the engine. He could see the shipping pens at Dragoon. He dropped down into the cabin with the engineer and the stoker.

Both men turned and smiled at him, ready for conversation. "Those your horses back there in the first car?" the engineer asked.

"Yes, sir," Ben said.

"Going to Willcox, eh?"

"No, we have to stop at Dragoon."

"I thought we was taking you all the way to Willcox. We ain't supposed to stop at Dragoon."

"I know, I paid that stationmaster to ship us to Willcox, but we have an emergency at the Bonner ranch and have to get to get there quick. I'd be obliged if you'd let us off at Dragoon."

"You're the Cowden boys, aren't you?"

"Yessir."

"I've hauled many a trainload of your cattle."

"I know you have. I recognize you now."

"I've always been up in the engine, and you've always been down in the pens or on horseback, and I never got to talk to you before. I've heard a lot about you though."

"I hope you've heard a good thing or two."

"It's all been good. You bet I'll let you off at Dragoon."

"What's your name? I'll get you a couple quarts of whiskey someday soon."

"I'm Don Getzweiler, and my partner here is old Knagge."

Ben shook hands with them.

When the train stopped and Ben went back to open the door of the car, his brothers were still asleep. He shouted to wake them up.

The brothers mounted their horses and headed south. The engineer gave them three short toots on his whistle as he pulled away, and the brothers waved without looking back.

They rode to the first highpoint on the foothills of the Dragoons where they could see the Bonner headquarters. They did not see the place again until they stopped on the north rim of Bonner Canyon at noon.

Their place on the rim was a hundred yards from the barn. Chickens pecked and scratched in the yard between the barn and the house. The Bonners' horses were waiting for someone to open the gate so they could water. None of the people could be seen, but Mark told his brothers that one more rig was parked in the yard than before.

Les climbed to the top of a knobby hill higher on the rim. Mark scouted below the ranch. They came back to Ben at the same time.

"They've posted two sentries on the road to town," Mark said. "One is on each side of a narrow notch a half mile down the canyon."

"Are they Bonners, or hired hands?"

"It's the two stiff-necked brothers."

"How many people were here when you left for Benson, Mark?"

"Those two brothers, Johnny, old Sybil, the two girls. I saw a real funny-looking man in a lightning flash when I was leaving."

"What was funny about him?"

"He was out in the rain—crazy-looking. The wagon you see there in the yard tells me old John and the uncle must have come back."

"No sentries on the Dragoons side of the place, Les?"

"I couldn't see any. They must not expect anybody to hit them from the high side."

"Don't bet on it. They've got somebody over here. They haven't survived all these years with the Dragoons at their back without watching them."

"What shall we do?"

"Hell, we might as well go in the barn and see if our sisters are all right."

The brothers rode to the corrals through the horse pasture. They let the Bonner horses into a pen so they could water, tied the gate closed, put their horses in a pen out of sight of the house, and walked up behind the barn.

John Bonner began shouting at the girls from outside the barn's front door. He gave the girls orders to come down, then pleaded with them, but they did not answer. Bonner's yelling told the Cowden brothers their sisters were still there.

Les drew a bucket of water out of the well, and the brothers had a drink. Ben looked up, saw the eaves were strong, signed for Les to help him, and they lifted Mark up to the eaves, then gave him an extra boost to the roof. Les cut the well rope and threw it up to Mark so he could pull up the bucket and take the girls a drink.

Mark quietly disappeared. After a while, Ben and Les heard a girl's tiny squeak and knew Mark was in the loft with his sisters.

"I guess you know, ladies, we can let you stay up there until you starve," John Bonner shouted. "I know you'd like a drink. You can't stay up there without water."

Ben motioned for Les to go along the side of the barn to the front, then he walked into the barn. John Bonner could not see him because he was staying out of sight of the girls.

Johnny Bonner was stooped over, his back to Ben, lighting a pile of oily rags on the floor of a stall under the loft. Ben walked up behind him, and he did not turn around.

Johnny said, "Damn this outfit! Can't get two little old girls out of a hayloft. Can't even light a pile of rags." He straightened up and stretched a hand back to Ben, but kept his eyes on a tiny flame that licked at the rags. "Gimme another match, and we'll get some smoke going."

Ben took out a match, wet it with spit, and handed it to him.

When Johnny couldn't light it with his fingernail, he looked at it and said, "Damn, it's *wet*. What did you do, spit on it?" He turned angrily, his face a foot from Ben's, and said, "Ohhh, *shit!*"

Ben spat in his eye. "Yes," he said. He swung his pistol from the hip and stunned Johnny to his knees. He found rope and tied Johnny's hands and feet behind his back. He walked to the front of the barn and stood in the door, holding his pistol at his side.

John Bonner was sitting in a chair in the yard between the house and the barn, whittling. His head was down, watching his sharp knife plane long thin, curly shavings off a mesquite limb. The limb was the size and heft of a club for a big man. The uncle was seated on the ground beside him, watching him whittle.

The uncle saw Ben first and scrambled to get his butt off the ground. Bonner looked down at him, then saw Ben out of the corner of his eye, sighting a pistol at his face. He dropped the knife and club, and called to the house, "Ma!" He struck both thighs with his fists. "Now, if this just don't beat all. We dammit fooled around until the whole damned Cowden outfit showed up."

Sybil charged out the back door of her house. "Who is he, a sheriff?"

"Ben Cowden, Ma," Bonner said.

"*Kill* him, then! *Kill* him, by Gawd."

"Yes," Ben said. "Draw your pistols, you sonsabitches, so I can blow your heads off."

"No," the uncle said, shaking his head and raising his hands. "Don't shoot."

"By gosh, John Bonner, if you don't kill him, I will," Sybil raved. She ran up to her husband and clawed for his pistol, then clawed at his eyes. He closed his eyes and slapped at her with both hands to protect himself. When she jerked the pistol out of its holster, he slapped it out of her hands.

The cedar man came howling around a corner of the barn like a dervish gone wild, charged past Ben as though he was not there, stampeded over the top of Sybil Bonner, then knocked John and the uncle down and trampled them. He stayed on top, stomping and felling them with blows when they tried to rise, then ran away and left them crawling distractedly on the ground.

The girls had come down out of the loft with Mark. Les was walking across the yard ahead of them. The cedar man bounded toward the girls. His hands clawed the air above him, his hair stood on end, his mouth opened wide in a banshee screech, his big feet pounded the ground.

Mark and the girls were shocked in place by the awful

sight of the lunatic bearing down on them. Les was not impressed at all. He stepped in front of the maniac, swung his rifle barrel into his teeth, and knocked him to the ground. He could not have stopped him better by shooting him through the heart, except he did not kill him. One instant the maniac was a giant dervish in full momentum; the next, he was not even quivering.

Eileen Cowden's face was white as she walked toward Sybil Bonner.

"Well, the little whores are out in the open at last," Sybil said. Her head and wide-open mouth were bloody. She took hold of the chair and stood up. Ben surveyed the damage the cedar man had done to the kin. The uncle was sitting on the ground, holding his head, and John Bonner was on his hands and knees, retching.

"Whore, get off this place," Sybil Bonner said. Her tone had turned fearful because Eileen was making a beeline for her.

Eileen picked up John Bonner's whittled mesquite club without breaking stride and began to whale Sybil Bonner with it. She whacked Sybil left and right until she fell to her hands and knees, then methodically followed her along and bounced the club off her head and tailbone as she tried to crawl away.

Ben stopped Eileen before she killed the woman, but not before the woman shut her mouth for the day.

The brothers herded and dragged the Bonners into the stall with Johnny Bonner and took their boots and shoes. They searched the house, picked up all the weapons, shoes, and boots they could find, and dropped them through the holes inside the outhouse. The Bonner girls had last been seen running toward a thicket of mesquite brush up the canyon, so the Cowdens did not worry about them.

Les and Mark caught and saddled horses for their sisters while the girls found bread to eat. Ben packed the suitcases on another Bonner horse and mounted his horse, ready to go.

"What about the two Bonners down the canyon?" Mark asked.

"Let 'em alone. We'll ride to Benson another way so they won't see us. They probably won't know we're gone until they come in looking for their supper."

The Cowdens reached Benson an hour after sundown and two hours before the westbound freight arrived. They went to the office to hire a car. The stationmaster was operating the telegraph when they walked in. The Cowdens waited patiently around the stove until he finished, turned to the window, and struck a match to his pipe.

"We need to contract a furgón to Patagonia this time," Ben said.

"Can't do it until tomorrow. This office is closed." The man did not even turn toward the Cowdens. Ben drew and cocked his pistol. The man turned toward Ben with a mulish look on his face, his upper lip drooping over his lower lip. Ben launched a bullet through the telegraph box. The man fell off his chair as though he had taken the bullet through the heart. His round hat rolled and thumped over its visor across the floor.

"Get up from there and tend to us so we can go home," Ben said.

The man crawled over to pick up his hat. Ben went behind the counter, found the form he needed, and put it on the desk. He swiveled the man's chair around so he could sit and handed him a pencil.

The man sat in his chair and filled out the contract. Ben signed it. The man said, "The switchman's gone home."

"Hell, you can be our switchman," Ben said.

When the train arrived, Ben climbed up into the cabin and found the same engineer who had taken the brothers to Dragoon that morning. He stayed with the engineer and stoker until the Cowden horses were loaded and Mark and Les and the girls were in the caboose. As he stepped down off the engine to go back to the caboose, the stationmaster walked by.

"Those horses we left in the pens belong to the

Bonners," Ben said. "You will see that they're fed and watered and the Bonners find out where they are, won't you?"

"Yes," the stationmaster said sullenly.

"Mighty decent of you." As Ben walked back to the caboose, he breathed a sigh of accomplishment. He had not thought of Margarita Elias all day.

CHAPTER 18

That same night, Jack Odoms and his three Texans rode into the yard at the VO ranch headquarters to the sounds of "God Rest Ye Merry Gentlemen," sung by Duncan Vincent and his guests with Doris Vincent on the piano. The Texans unsaddled their tired horses and went to the bunkhouse. The VO cowboys were not back from working cattle, so the cook was still up, keeping their supper warm.

Odoms went up to Vincent's house. The Texans knew the cook required that everybody who came to the bunkhouse from the corrals stop and wash at the hand pump by the door. If the cook fed them, this would be the first good meal the Texans had eaten in a week, and they did not want to walk in on the wrong side of him. The cook was a cranky man.

While the Texans waited their turn to wash, they took off their chaps, hats, and spurs. The cook did not allow those articles to be worn in the bunkhouse. The VO hands were not even allowed to put them on in the morning until they went outside. The Texans would ordinarily not have given a damn, but on this night they dearly wanted to feel at home. They had been sleeping on rocks and eating jerky gravy too long.

The three Texans were quiet men and not prone to bold laughter, but because they were cold-blooded murderers, they always tried to stay in a good humor. They were serious about being killers, prided themselves in their imaginative ability to take human life. They were all capable of killing any person with no qualms, so they tried to get along without committing murder carelessly, enjoying it too much, or making people angry enough to challenge them. They had learned that when a killer starts killing randomly just because he is good at it and enjoys it, his career is over, and so is his life.

Leroy Ford was the hottest-tempered man of Odoms's three remaining Rangers, but he killed in a detached manner because he was a contemptuous man. His expertise with weaponry and his fearlessness were legendary in the three Texas counties where he had served Jack Odoms. His ability to make people hate him in the first three minutes of their acquaintance was also legendary, so when he really wanted something, he tried to keep his mouth shut and his eyes turned away. Ford had received three official commendations for valor in his service for the Texas Rangers, but the Texas Rangers did not want him around when he was not fighting. They hired him when they needed a smart killer and let him go when the killing was done.

The other two Rangers, Blocky and Dallas Hardin, were brothers. Blocky, the older, was short, quick-moving, and solidly built. Dallas was tall, slow-talking, and quick to smile. They were orphans who had been raised in the streets of New Orleans by the transient ladies who came and went in a bordello. They were good-humored young men, expert in the quiet, quick, humane ways of killing other men, and they were never troubled by doing it. They did not love any human being and cheerfully did not give a damn about themselves either.

The Hardin brothers smiled at the VO cook, whose name was Charley Capp. Charley stirred the beans. "Howdy, Mr. Cook," they said.

"You'll have to sleep in the barn," Charley said. "The crew's at full strength, and there's no empty bunks."

"How's chances of you giving us something to eat?" Ford asked.

"No chance of me giving you a damned thing," Charley said. He lowered the oven lid, pulled out a platter of roast beef, and laid a butcher knife and fork beside it so the Texans could cut their own. "Get it yourselves. It's hot."

Ford took a warm plate out of the compartment on top of the stove and filled his plate with beef, beans, potatoes, gravy, and biscuits. He filled a tin cup with hot black coffee. He was so hungry, his hand shook.

The hands of the twins did not shake. When they took meat they were as sure of themselves as wolves. They sat down with their plates, and Charley Capp looked at the remnant of his roast.

"Put it all back," he ordered. "You can have two slices, even three, but you can't have the whole goddam roast. You can fill up with biscuits and gravy and beans, but you can't have all my roast. I've got eleven more hungry men to feed tonight."

The brothers looked at each other, grinned, and attacked the meat first. Ford's face went white, and he lost his appetite. He had taken a chunk of roast that would have made a half-dozen good slices, but only half as much as each brother took.

"I'll be goddammed if I'll let you cutthroats come in here and finish off a meal that would be plenty for a dozen good hardworking men," Charley said.

Ford started to get up and put some of the meat back.

Charley picked up his meat cleaver and waved it. "Now, do it, or I'll show you a handy way to split a skull."

Ford sat back down and grinned at Charley. "I was going to, but to hell with it. I'd rather watch you try to split my skull with that cleaver."

"You think I won't?"

"You might try, but you'll die. You'd do better to get started frying some steaks for your crew. They'll want to kill you if you don't have something for them to eat."

Charley turned white. He was all bluff and knew he would be lucky to hold his ground, so he shut up and turned his back to make sure Ford knew he was not in the market for a real battle.

Ford winked at the Hardins and ate his supper. Charley kept mumbling about Rangers and gangsters and syndicate thugs, but he never turned his face to the Texans. His mouth never stopped running. When they finished the meal, the Hardins stood up, thanked Charley, and went out. Ford sat awhile, picked his teeth, and listened to Charley mumble.

When Ford was ready to go to bed, he carried his plate to the wash pan and stopped behind Charley. He drew his skinning knife, reached around and grabbed Charley's upper lip as he would a horse he was about to twitch, and sliced off the lip. When he turned Charley loose, Charley could not close his lips. An inch and a half of his smile would show for the rest of his life.

"There, old feller. Now you can smile without even trying, and you won't have to look so cranky all the time," Ford said, and went to bed.

Odoms had entered the main house through the kitchen. The place was rich with the smell of good food. Odoms walked across polished emory-oak floors to the great drawing room where the Christmas-caroling was going on. He stopped in the door, watching the people sing, and was not discovered until they finished the carol. Doris Vincent left the piano and walked across the room to invite him in. Vincent gave him an eggnog-and-brandy drink and introduced him to the guests, five executives of the railroad, mining, and meat-packing syndicate, and their wives.

Odoms was well acquainted with these kind of people, who used him so they would not have to get dirty themselves. He enjoyed sipping brandy with them and answering their questions. He was usually feted by them when he turned up unexpectedly and caught them at their holiday parties. At Christmas they liked to be especially kind to him.

He would be rich himself one day. While he was making a good name as a peace officer, he had learned he would never earn big money that way. From now on, he would make war. Killing was profitable.

As an arm of these syndicate bosses, he would acquire land, cattle, and money by killing, but still remain respectable. He was in a position he had always coveted. He would someday become as powerful as these people because they needed him.

After a while, Duncan Vincent asked that he be excused, took Odoms into his study, and closed the door. He gave Odoms a cigar and lit one himself.

"I didn't mean to take you away from your party, Mr. Vincent," Odoms said. "I could have waited until morning to talk to you, or stayed with the party until it was over, for that matter." He smiled.

"I wanted to get out of there and smoke a cigar with you."

"That's a good party you're athrowin', and this is a good place to smoke a cigar. I think you've got it every way you want it, Mr. Vincent. I congratulate you. Mrs. Vincent is finer-looking and more gracious every time I see her. She's a good hostess and helps you keep these people in the palm of your hand. You're having a party right on a centuries-old Apache trail, and it don't bother you a bit. Those people will never know the danger and fighting you and I have known."

"I haven't known any fighting, Odoms. I'm not a fighter. That's what I have you for. That's also what I want to talk to you about."

"That suits me, Mr. Vincent. I'm a Ranger, and I like to talk about it. I eat and sleep fighting."

"When are you going to start fighting, then?"

"What do you mean? I've already lost two of my Rangers."

"That's being a victim, not a fighter. I hired you to regulate the removal of a family of cowthieves who have made it impossible for me to bring progress to this country."

"We haven't been able to make them mad enough to turn and fight. They keep running. I'm sure I'll tree them this week. In the last few days, we maimed a dozen of their cattle."

"How will that make them turn and fight?"

"We didn't kill the cattle outright. They'll stay alive and crawl around awhile and attract attention. Don't worry, I know what I'm doing."

"Excuse me, you apparently *don't* know what you're doing. As far as I'm concerned, you're not doing a damned thing for a fighter who loves fighting so damned much. You can maim and kill cattle, but they don't fight back, do they?"

"It's not something everybody can do."

"No, only cuckolds like you can do that kind of work. Maybe I ought to let you handle the cattle killing and the wife beating, and hire somebody else to do the fighting."

"'Cuckold'?"

"Yes, you're a cabrón, Odoms. A cuckold. Someone whose wife is making a fool of him by taking other men into her bed."

"How can you call me that? I married real well, and I've got it the way I want it. I have a good hold on the Macarena ranch and the Elias family. That's what you wanted, wasn't it?"

"I arranged that marriage to give you prestige, Odoms. Instead of that, you've become a laughingstock. Every Mexican in Sonora knows by now that Ben Cowden's been performing in your bed for you. Hell, he climbs in your bed from one side as soon as you go out the other. On this side of the border, you might find someone who would be outraged about this, might even think you've been unjustly wronged, might even pity you. In Sonora you've just made a damned fool of yourself by beating up a good woman and driving her into your enemy's arms. Evidently, she's made damned sure everybody but you knew about it."

"Listen, Mr. Vincent, I've got Cowden where I want him. The slut's got him moon-eyed, and to me that's the only thing that's important about my matrimony. The damned Arizonan is so pussy-whipped, all he can think about when he gets up in the morning is when will he get a chance to lay down with that woman again. I had to be sure the slut was convincing, so I drove her right to him. He's, by God, so convinced she loves him, he's ready to do anything she wants and to hell with his family and neighbors and everything he's been fighting for. If I don't kill him before Christmas, the sentimental fool will take the woman and leave the country and be out of your hair for good anyway."

Vincent shook his head. "I send you out to resolve the most vital problems in my business, and you come back to me with a cockamamy story. I'm telling you, Ben Cowden won't fall for it. I tried the same thing on him with Lorrie Briggs, and it didn't work."

Doris Vincent heard that. She was next door in her dayroom, looking for a sample of Jesusita Romero's needlework that she wanted to show to her guests, and the door between the dayroom and the study was not closed all the way. When she heard Lorrie Briggs's name mentioned, she stopped and listened.

"You gotta get 'em in the habit of sleeping with each other," Odoms said. "Once that happens and at least one of them is married, they feel guilty about it being illegal and immoral and unpopular. It don't work so well when two single people do it."

"Odoms, you can't convince me of that. If you don't get on with the projects I've assigned you, including the singsong project, and show me positive results within the next seven days, you're out. I'll not only fire you, but I'll join with the Eliases and the Cowdens and run you all the way back to the goddam swamps you came from."

Doris went back to her guests. So that was the new way Duncan was trying to beat Ben, by tempting him into Margarita Elias's bed and ruining his reputation. If he loved the woman and they were able to use her, they could chop away his manhood as surely as if they castrated him. She wondered if Margarita knew what they were trying to do. That was not a bad project for any woman, taking Ben Cowden to bed.

Doris had promised Vincent she would try to help make her marriage endure, and part of that was to mind her own business. All she needed to do was attend to her husband, house, and guests. She put on her smile and went back to the guests. That was where she belonged, helping Duncan move a million trains, supply millions of pounds of beef, acquire millions of acres of land, and become a millionaire frontier builder.

The Texans were slow getting started the next morning. The cook was not able to cook without an upper lip. Odoms closeted himself with Vincent again while the Texans caught fresh horses. It was midmorning when Odoms finally came out, saddled his horse, and mounted.

Doris and her guests were sitting out on the veranda, waiting for Vincent to join them. The guests were having gin fizzes and brandies to counteract their champagne hangovers. All of them were relaxed in their prosperity and enjoying what they believed was a well-deserved outing away from the grind of big business.

The guests watched the Texans ride by with the same detachment they watched cattle go out to graze, ore cars emerge from a mine, or oil pour out of a can; knowing full well they had been hired to commit murder. Odoms only glanced at their faces, and even though he and his riders passed within fifty feet of them, he gave no greeting. He knew when he'd been put in his place.

Odoms led his Texans south on the Santa Cruz River. At breakfast, the VO cowboys had told him about seeing Mexicans moving cattle east of La Noria, a homestead owned by the Pendletons on the Arizona side of the border. The public land in that part of the San Rafael valley was shared by the Cowdens, the Pendletons, the VO, the Porters, and the Romeros. Odoms figured he ought to be able to catch those Mexicans doing something wrong. He didn't care if they thought they had a right to be over there. In a cattle war, they'd better not be doing anything more offensive than gathering firewood. As far as Odoms was concerned, since they had lost the Mexican War, no Mexican had any right to be on the American side anyway.

The Odoms Rangers rode across the open San Rafael valley as the morning sun melted the frost. They rode into the brush on the Santa Cruz River and headed downstream on the tracks of two men driving cattle toward La Noria. They followed the tracks south past La Noria. The Texans had stopped there once, and Maudy Jane Pendleton had given them jam and butter on fresh baking-powder biscuits. They were each privately disappointed when the tracks did not turn toward the La Noria pens. They had been hoping for another visit with Maudy and her biscuits and jam.

South of La Noria was Sonora. Halfway between La Noria and the town of Santa Cruz, Odoms and his Rangers smelled smoke, saw it hanging over the river, and heard cattle bawling. The Rangers stopped in the brush, and Odoms rode to the fire by himself.

Odoms stopped at a set of pens. A saddled horse stood tied outside a corral, and another was tied inside the corral opposite him. The horses became aware of Odoms and raised their heads, rolling their eyes at him.

Two men were working on a calf tied down in the corral. They had already earmarked and castrated him. A young man stood on the calf's neck and wiped the blade of his stock knife on his leggings. An old man went to a fire to pick up a hot branding iron. Two other calves had already been branded and earmarked, and returned to their mothers' sides in the corral. A brindle cow lowed near the tied calf, indignant over the treatment her calf was receiving. She wore an old flowery brand on her left hip. She was so old, the scar of the brand was welted with hard crusty tissue. Odoms drew his pistol and held it down by his side so the corral fence hid it.

The branding iron burned through the hair on the calf's ribs, and the smoke boiled thickly around the men.

The brand on the calf was different from the one on the cow.

To Odoms, an old hand at putting an end to cattle rustlers, the fresh tracks across a border, the branding smoke, the bawling cows, and the different brands on the cow and calf were all characteristic of cattle theft and criminals caught dead to rights. These two unfortunate men could not avoid his justice now. It was his duty to prosecute them on the spot.

He knew the men. They were Tomás Romero and his son Edmundo. They were the ones who had helped throw his Texans off the track when the Cowdens got away from them in the rain at La Acequia. This was real justice, to catch these two confederates of the Cowdens in the act of branding stolen cattle.

The Romeros had seen Odoms when he first came in sight, recognized their enemy, and kept their backs to him.

"Good day," Odoms said.

"Good day," the Romeros said as they let the calf up. "One more," Tomás Romero said. He mounted his horse and built a loop in his reata. The cattle streamed down the fence away from him.

"Whose brand did you put on the calf?" Odoms asked Edmundo, who remained afoot by the fire.

"My brand."

"Whose brand is on the cow?"

"My grandmother's."

Odoms waved the Texans in. When they stopped beside him, he said in English. "This Meskin just admitted to me he put his brand on another person's calf."

"He's a cowthief, then," Ford said in Spanish. "*Manos arriba*, hands up, Romero. I knew you were crooked when you lied to us about the Cowdens at La Acequia."

"Crooked? You and your compañeros are the crooked ones, Meestair."

Ford went into the corral and disarmed Edmundo. Don Tomás sat his horse, the reata draped over his saddle horn.

"Get over here, Romero," Odoms ordered.

As he rode back to the branding fire, Don Tomás Romero regretted not exacting vengeance against Duncan Vincent for the hanging of his son Hector. He was sixty-one years old and carried the scars of two arrow wounds and one bullet wound. One of his legs bowed abnormally because of a bad break sustained in a horse fall. His shoulders and knees ached all the time from various other injuries and the results of fights against Apaches, bandits, livestock, and other enemies and friends, but he had never in his life fought against the law.

The Hardins rode in through the gate of the corral and took Don Tomás's pistol. They left the gate open, and Don Tomás watched the cattle stream out of the corral. One more calf, and the Romeros would have finished branding. "We weren't finished," he said quietly.

"No matter. You were not supposed to brand cattle today," Odoms said. "You weren't entitled to the ones you branded, but I'll let your family have them because you are going to pay for them with your lives."

"No!" Edmundo shouted, and he threw himself on Leroy Ford. Ford's pistol fell out of his belt. Edmundo dove for it, gathered it up, cocked it, and turned to shoot the Texans. To the Texans, the time he took to prepare for battle was laughable, and they were laughing when he faced them. Their bullets struck him down and killed him before he could even point the pistol.

They led Don Tomás's horse out of the corral, draped him headdown over his saddle. They clove-hitched the middle of the reata around his neck, passed one end between the horse's hind legs, and tied it to the saddle horn. They tied his feet to the stirrup and his hands behind his back with the other end of the reata.

The tall Hardin smiled at Don Tomás and said, "*Adios, viejo.*"

Don Tomás made him stop smiling by spitting in his eye. Hardin stepped back and quirted the horse across the hindquarters before he wiped his eye.

The horse jumped away, the rope tight between his legs. Don Tomás stayed on the horse five jumps. When he fell off, he was jerked under the horse by the neck, and the horse kicked him in the head with every jump in the stampede toward his home corral.

CHAPTER 19

In Tombstone, Ben sent a messenger from the station to Sheriff Rutledge reporting the death of the Bonner baby, then telegraphed his father that he and his brothers and sisters were coming home. Joe Coyle and Jimmy met the train in Patagonia with a carriage, and the Cowdens slept all the way home.

A.B. called the brothers to the back porch and poured them generous measures of his whiskey. Ben was often invited to join his father for whiskey, but his brothers were not. A.B. considered Les too wild to drink and Mark too young, but that evening all his children were home unscathed and had shown the heart and bottom of mature Cowdens, so he gave the boys whiskey.

A.B. told his sons that a new wave of public opinion was spreading against the depredations of the territorial and county politicians and the eastern syndicate bosses, especially Duncan Vincent. Vincent was now claiming 1,750,000 acres of public land as his own. His brother Royal was heading a Washington, D.C., lobby to acquire legal title to that land. He claimed that when he bought land from the Romeros and Eliases of Santa Cruz, he had acquired legal title to most of the San Rafael de la Zanja and Buena Vista Spanish land grants. A.B. knew Vincent had paid for only 17,500 acres in the San Rafael valley where the VO headquarters stood. The Buena Vista was entirely public land except for a few camps of patented land. One of those camps, the Yerba Buena, belonged to the Cowdens.

The VO hands, who had all been made constables of the county, were dispossessing miners, homesteaders, and ranchers, and fencing the water so other people could not have it. Newspapers in Tombstone, Nogales, Patagonia, and Harshaw labeled the VO faction "rapacious" and "ruthless." The constables demanded "royalties" from miners who refused to give up their claims. They arrested them when they came in town to ship ore or sell metal. Woe to the miner they caught eating beef.

All the politicians, lawmakers, and law enforcers in the county seat, Tucson, had been bought and installed in office by Duncan and Royal Vincent. The newspapers called Duncan Vincent "would-be King Vincent."

Ben Cowden was not the only rancher who had found maimed cattle. The Porters, Romeros, Gandaras, and Salazars had also reported Odoms for killing and maiming their cattle. The Pendletons at La Noria were Vincent's only neighbors who were not affected by the war. Will Pendleton was steadfastly neutral and seemed to disapprove of the Cowden faction more than the VO.

Viney called the family to a supper of sourdough biscuits, pan-fried sirloin steaks, mashed potatoes and gravy, fried beans with white Sonora cheese, tomato preserves, and peach cobbler with whipped cream. Halfway through supper Ben fell into a fog. He awakened in his own bed ten hours later and was unable to remember eating supper or going to bed.

Only Betty, Viney, and A.B. were up when Ben went into the kitchen the next morning. He and A.B. drank their coffee out on the south side of the house where they could take the morning sun. Ben smoked his pipe with his coffee, and A.B. smoked a Mexican cigarillo of dark tobacco.

Ben told A.B. that Vincent was using Jack Odoms to

grab land in Sonora and enforce false charges against the Cowdens. He also told about the beating Les gave Odoms and his own fight with Bud Hawkins at Cibuta. He told him about the killing of Lige Rote.

"You see what they're doing, don't you, son?" A.B. said. "Vincent's desperate to eliminate you. He's keeping our family split up, and that reward he's offering for your head is rich enough so people will risk their lives for it. That will bring strangers into the fight, so you won't be able to tell who will try to kill you next."

"I wish we could stay home for a while, but we have to go back to the Buena Vista and move those cattle," Ben said. "If winter doesn't finish them off, Odoms's Texans will."

"No, son, you can't do cow work and watch your back for Odoms at the same time. Gather Odoms first and get rid of him. The weather and lack of feed will kill only your cattle. Odoms will kill your cattle and you too."

After breakfast, the Cowden sisters began decorating the house for Christmas. Mark rode out to cut a piñon tree for the front room. When the activity overran him, Ben went to the barn, saddled a horse, and rode to Harshaw. He tied his horse behind the hotel and went in the back door of Vince Farley's saloon.

He was standing at the bar with a glass of whiskey when he remembered that Lorrie Briggs worked there. He decided to leave, but before he could drink his whiskey, she came out of the kitchen and made a beeline toward him. He groaned.

"Well, well, well," Lorrie jeered. "Don't you know Duncan Vincent's offered everybody five thousand dollars for your head?"

"I wouldn't trust him to pay it. He'll find a way to welsh."

"Now I've got two reasons to want your head. You killed my brothers, and Duncan'll give me five thousand dollars for taking revenge."

"Aw, Lorrie, I didn't kill your brothers, so you'd be making a mistake, and you'd probably hang for it. That wouldn't be any good. You couldn't gloat if Vincent gypped you out of the five thousand dollars and his judges in Tucson hung you to boot."

"You're right. Duncan Vincent would love it when I handed him your head, then love to gyp me out of the reward. Trying to kill you and gypping me are the pastimes he likes best. I'll have to settle for the revenge and cut your throat when nobody's looking. I don't need to be paid for that. I'd do it for the fun of it."

Les came in and headed for the table where Lorrie served menudo, stumbled with surprise when he saw Ben, then reluctantly joined him. Ben knew his brother could not be hungry enough to eat a bowl of menudo after Viney's big breakfast. Les kept looking toward the kitchen. He had come to see Lorrie, sure as hell.

This was wonderful. If Les could keep the creature from pestering him, Ben could drink whiskey and think sad, lonesome thoughts about Margarita Elias.

After a while, Les went to the table, called Lorrie over, and ordered a bowl of menudo. Lorrie stopped across the table from him, leaned over, and looked him in the eye. "You sure you want menudo?"

"Yes, Lorrie, I do."

"You found those other two bowls you ate good and tasty, did you?"

"They were fine, Lorrie."

"Well, my Lord, what's it gonna take to keep you Cowdens out of here, a dose of strychnine?"

"Gosh, Lorrie, you wouldn't poison a feller, would you? You're too pretty to be that mean. That's what I've been telling Ben."

"I'd poison a Cowden. That's one of my heart's ambitions."

Ben shook his head. She was pretty as an angel and damned shapely. The look of her eyes was warm and good-humored, the color on her cheeks high, and the swing of her hips quick and graceful. If looks could make a person good, Lorrie Briggs would be a saint. Her only trouble was that her heart was as black and empty as the forty days and forty nights before the creation of the world. Ben shook his head, drank the last of his whiskey, and left the place. Poor Les—he was probably smitten. Ben knew how hopeless that could be.

He went to the hotel veranda and sat in a rocker. He was not used to being idle. He had been putting out so much effort and seeing so much country lately that he should have been happy to sit still and do nothing for a while, but he was nervous and agitated. He had work to do in every direction, but no gumption for working. He'd slept well last night, eaten a good breakfast, and was riding a fresh horse. He ought to go find Margarita.

Ben had about decided to ride south when he saw Maudy Pendleton and her father coming toward him in a buckboard. His first thought was to hide his lying, cheating face from the girl, but she had already seen him.

Will Pendleton drove around to the back of the hotel to park the rig and put the horses away. Ben went back to help them. He watched Maudy jump down off the front wheel and skip to the front of the horses without seeming to touch the ground.

Lorrie Briggs and Margarita Elias both enjoyed a lazy voluptuous grace. They were confident that men liked to watch them move, so they moved languidly to give them time. Maudy was quick and light and chaste as a butterfly. She moved unselfconsciously, innocently, and was fun to watch because movement made her happy.

Will Pendleton gave Ben a hard look. Ben walked up to him and shook hands, then went to the front of the team to give Maudy a hug. Hugging Maudy was like putting on a clean shirt that had been washed and dried on a clear, sunny summer day. The breath of her kiss was sweeter than any other in the world.

Maudy had just turned sixteen, and she still dressed like a young girl, showing some ankle, a supple little figure with a straight back and waist, and a pert little butt. She moved on long dainty legs like a deer, and she had a redhead's clear, delicate complexion, but she took hold of the team like a teamster when it was time to lead the horses away.

Ben helped her put the horses in a stall of the hotel's livery barn and unharness them. He decided he ought to be happy about the women he loved, to enjoy them both, and stop being so chickenhearted. Both of them always seemed happy to see him coming, showed him a lot of love, and took hold of him with sure hands and happy hearts. Maudy would never do anything to make Ben suspect her of deceit though. She did not play love games with him as Margarita did.

Will excused himself to attend to his business. He no longer approved of his daughter's engagement to Ben, and he did not mind showing it. Ben had long ago stopped trying to placate Will Pendleton. Will did not fight Indians or the VO. He was not the only one who let the VO do as it pleased. Several other families had done nothing when Vincent fenced them off their pastures and water, and jumped their land or mining claims. Those families were still Ben's friends though. Will Pendleton seemed to think the Cowdens wronged him personally when they broke Duncan Vincent's rules.

"You look awful, Ben," Maudy said. He woke up out of his daydream sitting with her on the sunny side of the barn. She had taken his tobacco pouch out of his pocket and was packing his pipe.

"What are you doing?" Ben asked.

"I want you to smoke your pipe."

"How come?"

"You know I like it." She handed it back to him.

"You can light it and puff it for me, then, if you like it so much."

"Oh, no. I'm not puffing on that nasty thing. I just like the smell."

Ben lit the pipe and dropped the match on the ground. He did not even have the strength to shake out the flame.

"Haven't you been getting any rest at all?" Maudy asked. "I've nursed you through two serious wounds in the last six months, and I know you still need a lot of rest.

Will I have to put you to bed again to keep you out of trouble?"

"No."

"I know you've been through an awful time lately, Ben, but you have to rest. A person can put up with a lot of trouble if he can make himself lie down from time to time."

Ben wondered what Maudy knew about his trouble, wondered if his face showed his real turmoil. He felt sicker now than he had ever felt from fatigue or wounds. He could survive wounds. He did not know how he would get over his addiction to Margarita Elias.

"What else is wrong with you? You're thin as a rail," Maudy said.

"I have a disease." Ben laughed. "It's called ladino. The disease of being a bad, antisocial outlaw."

"Oh, you're not so bad. I've heard about all the bad things you're supposed to be doing, and I don't think they're near as wrong as the things I know about the VO. After all, we only live three miles from the VO headquarters. The VO hands are so lazy, they do most of their dirty work within a half day's ride of headquarters so they can be home in the bunkhouse before dark.

"Yesterday our cowboys, Juan and Alfredo Heredia, were in Santa Cruz when Tomás Romero's horse drug him home almost dead. He'd been tied to the horse. They backtracked Don Tomás's horse and found Edmundo Romero murdered in the Santa Cruz cow pens."

"That's awful. Who did it?"

"Jack Odoms and his three Texans rode by Don Tomás's house after his horse drug him in. Their tracks were around Edmundo's body. The Heredias have no doubt that Odoms and his men committed the murder."

"Was Don Tomás able to tell anyone what happened?"

"He's been unconscious." Maudy put her arm around Ben's shoulder and looked into his face. "What's the matter with you?" she said gently. "You're not yourself. You *are* sick, aren't you. Listen, I don't want to tell you what to do, but maybe you ought to stay out of Mexico for a while. Every time you go down there, you get in a fight, or shot, or some kind of blood poisoning."

"Aw, it isn't Mexico. A lot of things are bad on both sides of the border."

"Something real good must make you keep going back, then. No man would stay down in the middle of all that trouble unless something real good was holding him."

"Maudy, you know we have business down there. We've always had as much to do in Sonora as we have in Arizona."

"Yes, but you've never been in as much trouble down there. What if they arrest you, or shoot you?"

"They won't."

"How can you be sure?"

"I'm sure."

"It seems to me you're taking an awful lot of risk when you go to Sonora. They say Vincent has a price on your head and you're wanted down there for shooting one of his Rangers."

"That's what they say."

"Then why do you stay down there? Do you have another woman? Margarita Elias?"

"What makes you think that?"

"Margarita has always liked you. I know her real well, Ben. How has she been doing since she married Odoms?"

"She's not doing so well. She left the María Macarena."

"Listen, I can't compete with someone like Margarita. You've been by our place lately on your way down there, and you haven't even come in to say hello, so somebody must be giving you something I'm not."

"No, Maudy, I rode by with Walter Jarboe not long ago, trying to catch up with the twins, but it was late at night. Your father would not have made me very welcome if I'd tapped on your window again at two in the morning."

"Uh-huh. Odoms is spreading the word that you're having an affair with Margarita so he can have an excuse to kill you. I have friends in Santa Cruz, too, Ben. Everybody down there is laughing about the way you and

Margarita have been carrying on right under Odoms's nose."

"Margarita's been my friend a long time, Maudy. She confides in me. Odoms has been mean to her."

"That's fine. I believe you. I don't care how much anybody talks as long as you tell me you love me. I know I won't be able to keep you if you ever decide you would rather have a woman of Margarita's experience. I can't compete with her until you marry me."

"You don't have to compete with anybody, Maudy. Nobody's trying to take me away from you."

"You know what? I expect you to be tempted by other women from time to time, but I don't believe you can be trapped by one. If a married woman was after you, she'd have to trap you by making you do something you're ashamed of. I think you're too good a man to do anything that bad."

"Don't worry, Maudy."

"Ben, I'll be here for you or come to you any time you need me, unless you tell me you don't want me anymore. But please be careful with Margarita, especially if you're doing something you're ashamed of. A woman who will lead you on and give you everything you want might not have as much to lose as you think she does and might not be as generous as you think she is. You don't seem to respect anything anymore, but I know you'll get over it. I love you anyway. Come on, I have to buy some material, and you can carry my packages. Do you still love me?"

"Yes." Ben stood up and walked with her.

CHAPTER 20

Ben ambled around town with Maudy and said hello to townspeople he had not spoken to in months. People respected him enough to stop and talk a moment but got away as soon as they could. The caution he saw in the eyes of the townspeople showed Ben how Vincent had separated the Cowden family from friends and community.

Ben was able to suspend his thoughts of the war awhile when Maudy brought her purse into play. He liked to watch the girl use her purse. She did not use it only to carry money. She carried other small but essential and private things that Ben got to see when she opened the purse to take her money out.

He could only call the things she carried in her purse "things." This day Ben caught sight of a small pink miniature pencil with a brass knob to protect the sharp end; a tiny pink hardbound book that was like a diary with lined pages; lemon drops that made the clean satin innards of the purse smell good; a tortoise-shell compact and other shiny and perfumy mirrors and porcelain boxes with rouge and powder for Maudy's face.

When Maudy rummaged in her purse, satiny whispers issued forth, and exotic, valuable, gemlike things moved into sight. These articles had important uses only for her, and they were secret, small, new, shiny, clean things, the likes of which Ben was hardly ever privileged to see.

While Maudy was in Goldwater's Mercantile choosing bolts of material, Ben went next door to the barbershop for a haircut. Two barbers ran the place, and Ben sat in Joe Gerwitz's chair. Joe was a veteran of the Mexican War and had been running his barbershop since the Harshaw mine opened in 1870. Joe ran his business and his life with no concern for Apaches or land and cattle wars. He would not pick up a rifle unless he went hunting. He was able to take any game he wanted within shouting distance of Harshaw.

Ben tried to find out if the townspeople were un-friendly to him because of the war. Everybody was nervous, but no one showed antagonism. Joe was friendly, as always, but he seemed quicker and more businesslike than usual.

"Well, Joe, tell me what's new," Ben said. Joe was so quick at combing his hair down flat to trim it that he bit into Ben's scalp with the teeth of the comb. Ben had known Joe so long and sat so close and still for him that he seemed like family. Joe had watched him grow to a man in this same barber's chair and had never poked him in the scalp with a comb before.

"I was hoping you'd come in here and tell *us* some news, Ben. I haven't cut your hair in a long time, have I?"

"I can't remember when I came in here last. My sis Eileen's been trimming it from time to time."

"We've heard about you and seen you go by, but you're always in too big a hurry to stop and say hello."

"Our cattle have been dying in the drouth. Now it's raining, and we're still losing cattle. Cattle are facing the winter with wet backs and empty stomachs."

"Duncan Vincent was in here a while ago . . . said he's got plenty of feed."

"Oh, he does? I'm glad for him. Everybody else is short."

"He went to the hotel from here . . . had two New Yorkers with him . . . visitors for Christmas."

"Oh?"

"I'm from New York, though I left for good when I went off to war. They didn't know anybody I did." Joe laughed. "They're the same age as me, but we missed each other in the social whirl."

Ben smiled, almost.

"How's your social life been lately, Ben?"

"Seldom have any. We'll probably just have Cowdens for Christmas."

"Will people be able to travel anywhere without getting their throats cut?"

"Depends on who you are, I guess. Apaches can. The Gerwitzes probably can, and the Cowdens usually manage. Apaches killed two and wounded two more at Tuvera the other day. You never know. Geronimo's still loose."

"Vincent's loose, too. The newspapers are giving him hell, aren't they?"

"I haven't seen the papers. I'll go over to the hotel after a while and buy one."

"Go over to the hotel, and Vincent himself can tell you about the trouble he's having, Ben."

Big flakes of snow began to settle in a blanket on the town. The town pond was across the street from the barbershop, and Margarita Elias's carriage swung around the end of the pond, turned into the street, and passed the barbershop. Colorado was driving, and two of the Salazar brothers were acting as outriders. The top was up, but Ben saw Pepe's face in the window.

Ben went to the door and watched Margarita, her face hidden under a *rebozo*, go into the hotel with Pepe and the Salazars. He sat back down and tried to relax. He knew he ought to be patient now that he knew he would see her, but his hands shook under the barber's sheet.

He paid for his haircut and went outside. Maudy came out of Goldwater's looking for him, and he walked down to the grocery store with her. The place was so small and crowded with people, Ben found it easy to break away from her again.

As he stepped outside, the Salazars rode by, headed for Mrs. Soto's dinner table. They stopped their horses to shake hands with Ben. They were hungry and kept looking up the canyon toward Mrs. Soto's house by the jail. Ben felt guilty for stopping them. He knew he should not detain them only a hundred yards from their dinner and expect them to be civil, but he did not want to let them go until they told him what he needed to know about Margarita. She had hired them to serve as her bodyguard from Nogales to Harshaw. She was sick with a bad sore throat and had gone to bed in room 330 of the hotel.

Rafael Salazar stared down from his horse at Ben and said, "I told Margarita I saw you in the barber shop when we rode by. She made me leave word at the desk that she did not want to have visitors."

Ben let them go. They rode away a few steps, and Rafael turned back. "Another thing. Odoms jailed the twins in the presidio at Santa Cruz. I think Kosterlinsky wants to talk to you about that."

"Where is he?" Ben asked.

"He said he was going to Frank Wong's for his *sopa*."

Ben told Maudy to join him at Wong's when she was through in the grocer's. A bay horse Ben had given Kosterlinsky a month before was tied up and resting shot-hipped behind Wong's. Ben had broken and trained him, and ridden him in his string for a year. He gave him to Kosterlinsky for treating Ben decently after a gunfight with Vincent's thugs at the Nogales, Sonora cattle pens.

Ben put his hand on the bay's hip. "Hello, Joker," he said. "How's my Joker?" The horse rolled an eye at Ben and did not know him. He was sleek and in good shape. His cinch was tight, so Ben loosened it. "Tell Kosterlinsky your old boss came along and left his card."

Ben went in Wong's back door. Kosterlinsky was sitting in a corner booth, his big sombrero hanging by the chin strap on the back of his chair. A henchman wearing a black hat was at the table with him. Ben was surprised when he recognized the henchman. He sat down at the table.

"Benjamin, where have you been?" Kosterlinsky said.

"Will you join us? We have more than enough food. Here, I'll have them bring another plate. No? Will you have a cup of tea? It's wonderful tea."

Kosterlinsky introduced the black hat. "You know Roblez, do you not?" he said.

Roblez had been standing beside Ben at Tuvera when the Apaches' first arrow flew at Ben's eyes. Ben did not think he'd better remind Roblez that they had been in Jacinto Lopez's camp together.

"Yes, we've even been in jail together, haven't we, Benjamin," Roblez said.

"The last time I saw you, Victor, your chief here was cussing you out in Frank Marshall's jail in Tucson," Ben said. "He promised to send you to hell for joining the mutiny against him."

"True." Roblez grinned.

"Then I heard you escaped ley de fuga. Now he's fattening you with Frank Wong's pussycat meat. How come?"

"I surrendered to him, and he relented."

"I had to take him back," Kosterlinsky said. "His father is my friend. I need him. He has absolutely no conscience."

"What brings you to our town, Gabriel?"

"Chinese." Kosterlinsky did not look at him.

"Chinese food?"

"Yes, Chinese food."

Ben thought, I know other Chinese things you're interested in, you brigand. He said, "Gabriel, thank you for taking my father's telegram to Les in Santa Cruz."

"I could say it was nothing, but it was really a very great favor I did the Cowdens that day, Benjamin. I could have arrested him for breaking Odoms's nose. He shed Odoms's blood, you know. That makes it a serious offense. He should spend time in the presidio for it. Odoms had already lodged formal demands against him. My duty was to arrest him."

"I know, Gabriel. Thank you for letting him go. We needed to attend to a family emergency."

"It was nothing, Benjamin. Forget it."

"I owe you a favor."

"No, we're about even, but please don't come back to Sonora for a while. The population is being depleted enough by Apaches and Jack Odoms." He finished eating and wiped his mouth with a napkin. "There is one thing you can do for me."

"Name it."

"Please stop committing illegal and immoral acts in Mexico. You're driving me crazy trying to keep you and your relatives out of jail, and your activities are threatening important business I'm trying to conduct with my partners."

"I don't know, Gabriel. I have to defend myself."

"Every time you shoot someone in Mexico, you say that. If you could only imagine a barbed wire fence between Sonora and Arizona and *ladinear*, go wild, only on the Arizona side, I would be so grateful. Commit your rampages and take your gold and women only on the Arizona side for a while. Surely, Benjamin, Arizona is large enough for you."

Kosterlinsky told Ben that Walter Jarboe had set Odoms on the Farley twins. Odoms was doubly angry at them for diverting the Texans away from the Cowdens in Nogales. Kosterlinsky said that he did not want the Farley twins in his jail. Public opinion on both sides of the border was against his jailing anyone from the Cowden faction. He was tired of being unpopular. Unpopularity killed like leprosy, slowly but surely, and a man was made to feel hideous to his neighbors. He asked Ben to please not try to break his cousins out of the presidio. Rumors were about that Jacinto Lopez might try to break them out. Kosterlinsky begged Ben to stay away from the presidio so he could catch Jacinto. Ben thought, Yeah, you'd catch Jacinto like I would catch a full-grown jaguar bare-handed.

Kosterlinsky said the governor of Sonora had issued a warrant for the arrest of Duncan Vincent for the murder of Hector Romero. "Ben, all your enemies are here in

Arizona now, or soon will be. You don't have to go back to Sonora to get them. Settle with them, make peace, while they are here."

Ben smiled.

"Why do you smile? You must be happy. I'm happy too. For once, maybe you'll shoot your enemies in a place where I will not have to bury the bodies."

"Why don't you turn the twins loose if you're so unhappy to have them in your jail?"

"I don't want to contend with Odoms's disapproval right now."

"Why did Margarita come here?" Ben asked.

"I don't know. You'll have to ask her . . . No, don't ask her. Stay away from her. She's your enemy's wife. Don't you know she's your enemy's wife, Benjamin?"

"Why are you telling me all this? You're my enemy's partner, aren't you, Gabriel?"

"But, Benjamin, I'm your friend and I'm Vincent's friend, and I just don't want you to fight in Mexico anymore. Look, here I am, too, if you want me, if you consider me an enemy. Attack me here in Harshaw, but please, please don't do it in Mexico anymore."

"Why do you say all my enemies are here, Gabriel? Odoms isn't here, is he? The Yawner isn't here."

"You can be sure Odoms is not far away."

Kosterlinsky told Ben that Vincent was holding a meeting that day of the cattlemen who represented the syndicates. Kosterlinsky suggested Ben might be able to resolve all his differences with Vincent if he went to the hotel and talked to the syndicate bosses. When those problems were resolved, Kosterlinsky would be happy to let Ben come back to Mexico. He would arrange complete amnesty for Ben and his brothers and cousins if they would help him find and kill or capture the Yawner.

"The Yawner? Has he been seen?" Ben asked.

"He and three others caught some travelers outside San Lazaro and killed them the day after they attacked the twins at Tuvera Pass."

"Somebody saw the Yawner? How does anyone know the Yawner did that killing if he killed everybody?"

"They didn't kill everybody. Doña Elena Machuca, the woman you and Don Juan Pedro recaptured from the Yawner when you were a boy, was in the party, and the Yawner spared her."

"Imagine that. Who would have thought he would even know her, let alone spare her life."

"They recognized each other instantly. His companions began to strip her so they would not ruin her clothes when they lanced her, and he said, 'Not that one,' and spared her."

"Maybe because she is Che Che's mother."

"Che Che?"

"The one who used to spy for the Yawner and was killed by Frank Marshall at my father's house."

"Ah, yes, the Apache who liked *la reyezuelita,* your youngest sister, Paula Mary, the little wren. I know the story. They are telling a lot of stories about the Cowdens these days."

"What are you going to do next, Gabriel?"

"What do you mean?"

"If it comes to a fight, will you join in or stay out?"

"Ben, of one thing you can be sure. You won't ever have to count me on the side of your enemies in a fight. I only do business with your enemies." He offered his hand.

Ben shook hands with him. "All right, Gabriel. Just stay out of the line of fire."

Ben went to Dr. Tucker's house looking for medicine for Margarita's sore throat, but Tucker was not in. He went to Mrs. Soto's, and she told him to tell the patient to gargle with warm salt water, then to do the same with mescal, and then to dip hoarhound candy in mescal and suck on it. He went back to the grocer's to buy the candy and finally remembered that he had left Maudy there, but she was gone. He bought the candy and went down the alley to the back room of his uncle Vince's saloon. He washed out an empty quart bottle and dippered it full of mescal from the saloon's fifty-gallon barrel.

Les was still at the menudo table. Lorrie was too busy to pester anybody, so Ben was able to take him out the back door. He told Les to go home and get Mark and A.B. so they could go to Vincent's meeting.

Ben watched his brother go to his horse and ride away. Alone in the alley behind Uncle Vince's saloon, all of a sudden he felt a sense of danger and doom, as though his enemies were upon him. He knew he should be afraid to go to Margarita's room. Something about the hotel bothered him, as though his death was waiting for him there, death for being dishonorable. His enemies had never been able to say that honor was on their side, until now. He did not want to be shot by Odoms for being in Margarita's room.

As he climbed the back stairs of the hotel, he explained to God that he was going to Margarita only because she was sick. He knew her being alone in a hotel room was the perfect bait for a trap his enemies could use as an honorable reason for shooting him. He asked God to keep in mind that he was willing to risk death and dishonor so he could talk to Margarita and help cure her sore throat, not so he could get in bed with her.

Margarita's door was unlocked, and he went in. She was in bed asleep. Ben sat on the bed and put his hand on her hip. That did not wake her, so he shook the hip slightly and watched her eyes until they opened.

The dark coffee-luster eyes did not look at him until he shook her hip gently again, and then she did not turn her head, only moved her eyes to his face. "What are you doing here? How could you come here like this?"

"I brought medicine for your sore throat."

Margarita closed her eyes. Nothing but her eyes and lips had moved, and now she was profoundly motionless again.

"Come on, little pichoncita, sit up so I can give you medicine."

"I have medicine. Just go."

Ben sat and watched her awhile, then said, "Let me help you get well."

She opened her eyes. This time he thought he saw a red glare in the depth of her eyes, a glare of hate. He looked again to be sure, and it was still there, staring at him with the meanness and arrogance of a beast. He was not mistaken about the red glare. He was so disappointed at recognizing the look that it must have shown on his face.

She closed her eyes to protect herself. "Go," she said.

Ben left, again feeling like a dog with his tail between his legs, expecting to run into his enemies at every turn.

CHAPTER 21

After he saw Vincent's syndicate bosses at leisure with their wives, Jack Odoms decided he was sure he wanted money. He had never admitted he liked money and thought he was content with the wages he made as a peace officer, but Vincent's abuse made him realize he was not being paid enough.

He'd been handling himself in a completely righteous manner for twenty-five years, and now the only people who would help him in his work were murderers like Leroy Ford and the Hardins. The syndicate bosses kept their precious skins in the background, safe with their money, and felt they had the right to abuse and ridicule him.

He had always suspected he should pursue money instead of righteousness, and now he was sure of it. He would make war for money. He cast about. Where could he find a sufficient amount of money that would merit his attention? He would kill for it.

The only decent quantity of money he knew about that would warrant taking it by force was the gold Ben Cowden had taken from Kosterlinsky's shipment in September. The Farley twins were said to have appropriated that money. After he savaged the Romeros, he decided to head

for the presidio at Santa Cruz for an interview with the
Farleys.

Odoms and the Texans passed the Romero home in
time to see Tomás's horse drag him into the yard. The
horse had run out his initial panic and was only walking.
He could not get used to the burden of Tomás's body
beside him, and he sidled so he could keep his eye on it
and not step on it. The Odoms gang rode along and
watched, anticipating the excitement the horse was about
to cause among the Mexicans.

A pair of children playing on the swept ground in front
of the house stood up and stared as the horse nickered and
hurried around the house toward the corral. One of the
children trotted into the house. An old woman came out,
followed the child around to the back, and let out a shriek
that brought out more women and children. Shrieks
turned into moans and weeping, and that chased the horse
back around to the front. The women followed him in
great excitement and surrounded him. The old woman
calmed everybody down then, and they swarmed in
gently and freed Tomás.

As soon as they took the horse away, the old woman
looked around to see if she could find more help. She
turned her face to Odoms and his Rangers two hundred
yards away, and they turned their backs to her. She called
to them and waved her arms. The Texans looked at each
other out of the corners of their eyes, grinned, and rode
on to Santa Cruz.

As they passed the house of the Campana women,
Leroy Ford said, "When are we going to take a rest,
Captain Jack? I know a hot woman in that house who
would die if she knew I came this close and didn't go in to
see her. Right there inside that house lies a case of true
love for Leroy Ford."

"Yeah, a whole dollar's worth," Blocky Hardin said.

"I'm serious, Captain Jack. Let's stop here. You fellers
can have dinner. Them women serves a good meal at
noon."

Odoms kept going. "It's early. We'll come back tonight. I'll let you waller in all the whorin' you want after we get some work done. We're *behind*."

Inside the presidio Odoms gave orders that the Farley twins be brought to him. The guard who went to get them smiled when he received the order, as though he enjoyed the prospect. Odoms and his Texans sat in the office and waited. They heard the Farleys joking with the guards as they came through the building. The guard who brought them was resting his hand on Donny Farley's shoulder when they came in the office, and both twins were laughing. Odoms sat on the front of the desk and waved the guard out of the room.

"Be nice to them; they're friends," the guard said.

"We'll see you later, Hilario," Danny Farley said.

"That's a nice jailer you gave us, Odoms," Donny said.

"I'm Captain Odoms." He did not raise his voice. His eyes seemed almost as colorless as his hair. "Come here and stand one pace in front of me."

"Me?" Donny pointed at his own breast.

Odoms pointed to a spot on the floor in front of him. Donny ambled up and stood his rumpled, smiling, happy self in front of Odoms.

"Closer."

Donny took the next step warily, feeling ahead with his toe, and did not change his attitude. Odoms leaned with a straight right hand and hit him in the mouth, stood on his feet, and followed him to get in range again. Donny held his mouth with both hands. Odoms hit him in the ears with a left and right. Danny flew at Odoms, and the Texans took him to the floor. Odoms was not distracted by Danny. He beat Donny on the head with the leaded handle of his quirt, and the boy went down on his knees. The Texans took turns holding Danny down and striding over Donny with their boots and spurs, stomping him the way they would a stubborn steer that was down in a chute. They raked their spurs down his back and hooked them in his ribs. When he was senseless, they let Danny up.

"Which Farley are you?" Odoms said.

"I'm Danny, you son-of-a-bitch."

"Well, Danny, you can't make me mad, and your brother can't make me tired. You don't bother me, so we're not going to put any knots on your carcass. You can be the audience."

"Why did you beat up my brother?"

"So you'd tell us where that gold coin is."

"We don't have it anymore. It washed away in the flood."

"No, it didn't, but I'll find out what happened to it. Money is the root of all evil, and golden money is most evil. I'd rather whip a thief than have money. I'm going to whip your brother until nobody will believe he's your twin or you tell me where that money is."

"That gold washed away in the flood."

Odoms whacked him across the bridge of the nose with the quirt handle. "Aw, I'm sorry. I know I said I wasn't going to hit you, but I always go back on my word with a liar."

Odoms sat on the front of the desk again, unperturbed by the nature of his chore. The Texans advanced on Danny, but Odoms told them not to beat him. He wanted Danny to be able to watch with a clear eye as they changed Donny's looks.

Donny regained his senses, and the Texans beat and kicked him methodically. They did not hit him hard enough to knock him out or even stun him, only enough to hurt him. They were adept at administering glancing blows that hurt a lot, and every once in a while they caught him by surprise and knocked his wind out. They did not want him to bleed. They bruised him so he would swell. They let him keep his feet so he could recoil from a blow; that way, each waited his turn for Donny to bounce his way. Donny began stumbling around the room like a blind man. If he went down, the three Texans stood over him and kicked him incessantly with the toes of their boots until he got up. While he was on his feet, at least he could have respite while he bounced from one man to another. Odoms never let him come in range without landing a blow himself.

After a while, they left him in a heap in a corner of the room, his eyes so swollen he could not see. They sat Danny down, tied his hands together behind the chair, tied a long rope to his hands, and looped it over a rafter in the high ceiling. Without a word, the three Texans hoisted Danny's hands a foot toward the ceiling. They stopped when his weight bore down on his shoulder sockets and he groaned.

"Have you ever dislocated a shoulder, Farley?" Odoms asked.

"No," Danny answered innocently, almost crying, trying to show that he was brave without being antagonistic. Trying to show he could take the pain. He did not know how he would be able to stand another eighth-inch lift on his hands though.

"I bet you always thought you could endure pain so well that you would never give up if you were tortured, didn't you? You've heard of Apache torture?"

"Yes."

"Well this one is called Comanche Persuasion." Odoms nodded to the Texans, and they lifted Danny's hands another quarter inch. He screamed and kept screaming because they did not slacken the rope. He screamed so much he could not hear or talk when Odoms asked him again to tell him where the golden alazanas were.

The whole town of Santa Cruz could hear the screams. After a while, Walter Jarboe left the Campana sisters' house and walked the block to the presidio. Jarboe was still in Santa Cruz because he had become fond of Josefa Campana. He was the one most responsible for the Farleys' being in the presidio because he had filed the demand for their arrest. Jarboe wanted only to find out for sure if the gold coin could be recovered. Kosterlinsky had believed the boys would be safe in his jail, besides being put out of the way of trouble. He never figured Odoms would become greedy for the money himself and return to try to torture the boys into telling him where it was.

Jarboe had visited the boys two or three times since they had been jailed, so the guards knew him as Kosterlinsky's friend, the U.S. marshal. He had seen Odoms and the Texans go by on the way to the presidio. He was not sure the screams were coming from a Farley, but he suspected they were. At any rate, the screams were too disturbing to be allowed to go on, no matter whose they were.

The guards seemed glad to see him and opened the doors and gates quickly. He did not have to ask where the screams were coming from. The guard friend of the Farleys was standing outside the office, and the door was locked.

Odoms and the Texans were only about an eighth of an inch from popping Danny Farley's shoulderbones out of their sockets. Donny Farley said he would tell Odoms where they had hidden the alazanas.

Odoms went over and prodded Donny to his feet with the toe of his boot. "Where is it?"

"*Da Probdencia bine.*"

"Say it again."

"*'dencia bine.*"

Odoms took a notebook and pencil out of his shirt pocket and told Donny to write it. When Donny handed the notebook back, Odoms read *La Providencia bine*. "Where the hell is that? Never mind, I'll find it. Where is it hidden at the mine?" He handed the notebook and pencil back. Donny wrote, *In the south side of the ore heap*.

"Good." Odoms stepped back. "Get down on your hands and knees in front of me." When Donny complied, Odoms stomped down on one of his hands with the heel of his boot. When Donny screamed and lifted the hand off the floor, Odoms stomped the other hand and turned to the Texans. "You fellers were negligent. You missed his hands. Lift a little more on that one's shoulders."

The Texans tightened the rope, and Danny shrieked. Odoms sat on the desk in front of Danny. "Now give him slack." The Texans let Danny's hands down, and he screeched again. "My, my, which way do you like it, up or down? Can you talk now?" Danny nodded. "Where's La Providencia mine?"

"East of Washington Camp." Danny started weeping. He was only seventeen.

"How far?"

"Twenty-five miles from here and an hour's ride across the mountain from Washington Camp."

"Do you want to be hoisted again?"

"No."

"Then don't tell anybody else where you hid that money. You got it?"

"Yes."

Odoms opened the door for Jarboe, then nodded for the Texans to hoist Danny again. When Jarboe went into the room, it was full of screams, but the torturers and the tortured were absolutely motionless. Odoms was leaning forward in Danny's face as though he felt he needed to be inside the very fullness of the screams, poised like a stalking cougar, as though his prey's violent reaction to pain had made him pause in the killing.

The Texans were also still. The end of the rope was looped on one Texan's foot to keep it in place, and the other two were applying only enough pressure to keep the rope from slipping and giving slack.

Walter Jarboe was not a warrior, only a businessman and father, but he knew when to take command of a situation. "Enough!" he shouted. He buffeted Blocky Hardin on the side of the head to make him step off the rope and release the pressure on Danny's shoulders.

Odoms lit a stogie.

"What in the world are you *doing* in here, Odoms? This is the most shameless, the most depraved sight I've ever seen in my life. My God, you've been *torturing* these boys."

"Just seeing how high a note this one can reach," Odoms said. "Want to hear it? Hoist him again, boys."

Jarboe snatched the rope. "No, by God. I'll send you all back to the States in irons if you do. Stand away from that rope."

The Texans looked to Odoms for their orders, but they did not try to hoist Danny again. Jarboe untied him. He looked around for help, and three Mexican guards came into the room. Jarboe could not speak Spanish, but he did not have any trouble conveying to them that he wanted the twins taken out of there. The guard who had brought the twins to the room took them away, but the other two stayed at the door.

"Well, you messed that up, Jarboe," Odoms said. "Another minute, and I would have found your gold for you."

"I know where the gold is. Somewhere in the bottom of the Santa Cruz River."

"Naw. They've got it hidden somewhere; I know it. It's probably good you came in though. They'll be easier to crack if we let 'em sore up. We'll give the hurt a few hours to settle in good, then take hold of them again. They'll talk before nightfall."

"You're taking hold of nobody, Odoms. You're a damned disgrace to the human race, and so are these other cutthroats of yours."

"Well, Mr. Jarboe, that gold is evidence in a crime, and I think we oughta try and find it."

"Odoms, you ought to be locked up and the twins released." Jarboe stood with the guards at the door.

Odoms saw how easy it would be for Jarboe to lock him in, so before the man could think of doing it, he trooped out of the office with the Texans. Jarboe signed to the guards. The guards shouted ahead of Odoms, and he was given liberty to leave.

Outside the jail Odoms said, "We should have gagged that screaming bastard. I'm sure sorry we didn't at least get to finish dislocating his little shoulders. I kind of enjoyed listening to him."

Odoms and his Rangers reached the María Macarena ranch an hour after dark, and Don Juan Pedro came out with a lamp to meet them. When he saw Odoms, he blew out the light.

"Here, light that lamp again, *Suegro*, Father-in-law," Odoms said. "We need it. What do you have for supper? Did the cook come back?"

"What cook?" Don Juan Pedro asked.

"What cook? My *wife*."

"No, she's not back, and I'm not sure she'll ever be back until you're gone for good."

"Well, you and I know I'll be here from now on, so I guess you'd better go get her."

"I will never bring my daughter back to you, Odoms."

"What's that? What's that you say?"

"I say you're not welcome here. Take your killers and get out."

"That's right. They are killers, and they like to kill Mexicans more than anything else. Now what's that you said?"

"I won't be the only one to die, Odoms. You're in Mexico. Hurt me, and you also die."

"Oh, well, nobody's going to kill anybody, Suegrito. You and I have a deal." He put his arm around Don Juan Pedro's shoulders. "If anything happened to you, I'd have hell making it in Mexico, so I'm going to be your bodyguard."

Odoms walked Don Juan Pedro around to the stables where Margarita's mare and Odoms's Arab stud were kept. "How's my stud doing, good?"

"Good enough for the office his worthless balls hold. All he's good for is to *cultivar huevos*, cultivate his own eggs."

"And this mare, what is she good for?" The mare's head was sticking out of the open upper half of the door to her stall. "For carrying that woman to her love nest? For starting a 'horse business'?"

Don Juan Pedro struck a match to the wick of the lamp so he could see Odoms. Odoms had taken the mare's upper lip in his big hand and was holding her head down with that hand. He raised the other hand above her head, and Don Juan Pedro saw that it held a skinning knife.

"No!" he shouted, but Odoms plunged the knife into the mare's spine below the poll knot. She dropped dead, and all her weight fell into the door so completely and so suddenly that she broke off the latch, the door flew open,

and her head flopped against the ground in front of the
stall. The door knocked Odoms back against Don Juan
Pedro, Don Juan Pedro sprawled on his back, and the
lamp smashed and went out. "No!" he shouted again.

Odoms walked away and laughed. "She's not worth a
damn now."

Don Juan Pedro struck a match. The force of the
stabbing had driven the mare's tongue out of her mouth,
and it was lying in the dirt. She had not even quivered.
"You cabrón. How could you blame the animal? Cabrón."

Odoms turned back. "Are those people gone yet?"

"What people?"

"Your mayordomo's people. The wives and spawn of
that bunch of peons who live here with you? Didn't I tell
you I wanted them out of here? No? Well, I do. I want
them gone."

"They're here until they die. You're going, Odoms.
Only Mexicans live here."

"They're here until they die? Suegrito, I can make that
happen very soon. You want them to live? You better stay
with them tonight so you can help them get an early start
in the morning. There won't be any room for you in the
main house tonight, Suegrito. My men and I will be using
it. Maybe I'll see you in the morning."

The next morning when Odoms came out of the house
picking his teeth, Don Juan Pedro was standing by while
Chapito Cano hitched a mule and singletree to the dead
mare to drag her away. Odoms stopped beside Don Juan
Pedro and watched Chapito drag the carcass into the
brush out of sight. "Nice mare. I understand she was a
good mare too—well schooled, quiet. She was fast, too,
wasn't she?"

Don Juan Pedro was wearing his thick suede brush
jacket. Odoms picked his teeth and looked him over. Don
Juan Pedro was armed, wearing a bandanna sweat band on
his brow under his sombrero and spurs. "Going to work
for a change, Suegrito?"

Don Juan Pedro did not turn toward him or answer.

"That's good. It's time you did some work. I want you

to get this ranch to producing better. You'll have to ride harder than you have in twenty years if you are to put this place in the black for me. After that, you can ride away for good."

"We'll see."

"Yes, you'll see what I mean when I get back. If you don't want to see a lot of killing, you'll do as I say. I'm taking this place over in a peaceable manner, as is my wont, or you can count on your family coming to your funeral before another month goes by. But we can talk about all that when I come back in a few days. For right now, I won't keep you from your work. Hop to it."

That day, Odoms sent his Texans on to Harshaw, telling them to take a room in the hotel and wait for him. They had heard from the twins that the gold was at La Providencia, but they did not know where that mine was. Odoms had been supplied a good map by Duncan Vincent. He rode alone to La Providencia and found the gold buried in pack panniers inside the ore heap. He carried the panniers into the miner's shack and poured the coins out on the table. He counted $23,625 of golden coins in $5, $10, $20, and $50 peso denominations.

He put $5,000 of the alazanas in his saddlebags. He loaded the panniers on his horse, picked up a shovel, rode over a ridge to Sycamore Canyon, and buried the panniers high on the side of a hill. He hid the shovel in the brush and rode away, gloating. It sure had not taken him long to own a fortune in gold after he decided he wanted one.

Winds began to gust in front of a storm forming in the east as Odoms rode back down the steep rocky trail into La Providencia Canyon. He wanted to water his horse before he went on, so he followed the trail to a deep pool of clear water in the canyon below the shack.

Two big ladinos, a bull and a steer, looked up at him in surprise when he came around the shack. They usually made sure people did not see them. No one had been around La Providencia for a long time. The ladinos had watched Odoms when he went in the shack to count the money, watched him ride away, waited a long time after he went out of sight over the ridge, and thought he was gone forever. The wind had hidden his scent and sound when he came back. They discovered him and threw their heads up only a few seconds before he came in sight. He surprised them from so close a distance that they stayed a moment to see what he would turn out to be.

They moved unhurriedly up the side of the canyon, away from Odoms. They did not need to hurry on that steep rock. They knew what a horse and rider could do. An unencumbered ladino could not be overtaken and caught on terrain of the ladino's choosing.

The younger animal was the brown-and-white three-year-old that Ben had branded and left a bull early that month. The older was a ten-year-old steer that carried the spur brand of the Salazars. He was spotted with a red-and-white motley face and red circles around both eyes. He carried the widest, most twisted set of horns Odoms had ever seen.

Odoms went to the ground with his rifle. The big steer paused a moment and looked back at him, confident he could not be hurt or caught. In a moment he would be out of sight, and the man would not even be a lasting memory. Odoms put a bullet through his heart. His four legs stiffened, and he slid down to the creek.

The explosion of the cartridge and its echo in the canyon sent the brown-and-white spotted ladino running in panic back toward the man. He came to his senses when he saw that he had almost run all the way back to the man. He shied away and ran for a thicket of willow brush. Odoms had time for only one shot from the rear. He waited until the ladino was headed straight away and fired. The bullet grazed the middle of the animal's tail and thigh, and stung him enough to make him double his speed. He ran through the thicket until he put a solid rock promontory between himself and the man, and then he climbed out of the canyon and was gone.

Odoms rode around the pond to look at the old steer's horns, the biggest warbonnet he had ever seen on a bovine. He dismounted, skinned the animal's cape off shoulders and neck, separated the head from the neck, and set about loading head, cape, and horns on his horse.

His horse did not like all that dripping blood and glazed eye coming at him on a cooling carcass, and he had never, never liked horns since an old milk cow had blown snot on his flank and pinked him with her horns. He snorted and ran backwards, fell, and dunked Odoms's saddle in the pond.

Odoms dropped the head so he could keep hold of his reins. He led the horse back up on the bank, hoisted his head up high, and tied it in a tree with his rope. He blindfolded him with his coat and hobbled his front feet. He draped the cape over the horse's hips and tied the head to his saddle strings behind the cantle. He did not worry about blood on his saddle. Blood was good for the leather.

That evening, he rode down saloon street in Harshaw, the big horns bracketing him on both sides. He stopped and left the head with the taxidermist next to the barbershop, then went to the hotel, happy.

CHAPTER 22

Ben, Maudy, and A.B. went out to catch the morning sun at El Durazno the next morning. Will Pendleton had left Maudy with the Cowdens and gone home alone. The Apache attacks at San Lázaro and Tuvera and the killing at the Santa Cruz pens had made him afraid to keep Maudy at La Noria.

Maudy had begun sitting with Ben and his pipe in the morning sun when she nursed him through an infected stab wound at La Noria that year. The smell of his pipe made her happy because it helped her remember how deeply they had fallen in love.

A.B. told his son he did not want him to go back to Mexico for a while. The brothers' cattle work was enough to keep them home for several months. He wanted Ben and his brothers to avoid confrontation with Vincent, Odoms, and the VO hands. If Ben had to fight, he did not want him to go far afield.

Ben would dearly have loved to be able to work cattle and horses again, raise fine animals and sell them for a good price, saddle a fresh horse every morning, change horses at noon. He was near the end of his stamina. He knew he would endure, but he felt used-up. He was not a shipwreck yet, but he might be about to spring a leak.

As A.B. talked, Maudy moved in close to Ben and leaned against his side, held his hand in both of hers, and pressed her elbow into his thigh. She seemed to want to impose her person upon his. Ben liked that. He loved her touch and felt that she could be making him well of all kinds of ailments that bothered him.

A.B. told Ben his brothers and sisters were under orders not to let him out of their sight. The trouble with Vincent was coming to a head like a big boil, and all the principals that could cause it to burst were in Harshaw.

Ben thought, Well, that boil hurts and itches so much, the only thing a man can do is squeeze it. He wanted to take his brothers into town and do it. He did not think this was a time to stay in the front room at home. He did not tell A.B. what he intended to do though. A.B. knew they would soon have to fight. He was only wishing they could avoid it.

Ben was happy all his enemies were finally bunched together. He understood that Royal Vincent, Duncan's brother, would be in Harshaw too. Ben wanted to smash his face, but Doris Vincent would be somewhere nearby if he was there. It anyone could keep the meeting from turning into a shooting match, it was the presence of A.B. and Doris, the two most level heads on the opposing sides of the conflict.

When Ben announced that he was going to town, the whole family followed him to the barn. A.B. harnessed his bay team, Jack and Mack, to a surrey and loaded all the Cowden women. The brothers saddled horses, and the Cowdens went to town. Joe Coyle was the only person left on the place. He had sent Jimmy to town with a wagon early to bring back scrap iron from the Harshaw mine.

Ben tied his horse behind the hotel and went in with his brothers. A.B. tied up beside the Cowden saddle-horses and took his ladies in. Ben had to wait for them. The family went in the dining room and ordered café con leche.

Margarita was at a table close to the Cowdens' having

breakfast with Odoms. Odoms's back was to the Cowdens, and Margarita was profiled to them. (A white mantilla framed her dark eyes and brows.) She gave the Cowdens a slight nod of recognition, then turned back to Odoms. He was showing off, telling her a story, and Ben was surprised at his cordiality. Margarita seemed entranced by him. Odoms was not talking loud, but his deep voice filled the room.

Garbie Burr was waiting on the Odomses and Margarita was soft-spoken, sweet, and gracious to her, as though she were content with the whole world. For about the fortieth time Ben found himself confused by Margarita's behavior.

The Odomses got up to leave, and Margarita stepped over to Viney, took her hand, kissed her on the cheek to say hello, nodded to each Cowden, even Ben, and Maudy. Odoms stood by and smiled indulgently until she finished, and then they went out. That was the first time Ben noticed the bruise on the side of her face. That side had been on her pillow when he visited her room in the hotel.

Ben was grateful to Margarita for not sending him one of her hot looks, but he would have liked one small one. She had not given his brothers even a hint of her famous Margarita look either. She must have reformed, by God.

Vincent and his five syndicate bosses came in. Also with him were Jack Akin and John McClintock, ranchers like Vincent who represented syndicates from the States. Akin and McClintock were honest men, though Akin was cold-blooded in his dealings with his neighbors. McClintock got along well with the Cowdens, but his business interests were all on the side of the syndicates.

Vincent ushered the bosses to a long table. After a while, Jack Odoms and Gabriel Kosterlinsky joined them. They talked in low voices for a while. Each man took a turn at examining the Cowdens. The syndicate men were forced to turn clear around in their chairs to do it, but they took their time so they could have a good look. Then Kosterlinsky walked over to the Cowdens' table and asked if Ben and A.B. would join them.

Ben and A.B. saw that Les and Mark took the ladies out before they left their table. Kosterlinsky introduced them and asked them to take the two empty chairs that put their backs to the door.

Vincent opened by explaining that A.B. was there as undersheriff of the county and head of the Cowden family. So far, the VO faction could say little against A.B. as an undersheriff. His dealings seemed fair to everybody, except that he had taken it on himself to break his son Ben out of Frank Marshall's jail in Tucson that fall. Vincent conceded that not a man there could blame him for breaking a son out of any jail run by the late Frank Marshall, and the syndicate men smiled at that.

He said that the differences between the VO and the Cowdens had deteriorated into open war. Both sides were suffering casualties, and the differences seemed irreparable. He said he was glad the Cowdens had happened upon the meeting, though he did not have any hopes they would be convinced to stop fighting. No, it was up to the syndicate leaders, as major investors and employers in southern Arizona, to take the war in hand and stop it. He did not believe the Cowdens were representative of the other small ranchers of the region. His dealings with all the other ranchers and miners were amicable. It was up to the leaders of the syndicates to serve notice on the Cowdens here and now that they were to surrender their claims to grazing rights on land the syndicates claimed. To enforce this, Vincent had asked the Arizona Live Stock Association to send him fifty men. They were on their way from Tucson with his brother Royal and would arrive in Patagonia on the evening train.

"That show of force is illegal and immoral," A.B. said. "To whom do you answer legally for recruiting fifty more gunners from Tucson, Mr. Vincent?"

"The Pima County Live Stock Association is legally authorized to recruit constables of its own choosing in the war against cattle theft. These fifty men have been duly sworn by the sheriff in Tucson. They will be met at the train by the fifteen-man VO crew."

Odoms turned and stared at Ben. "Now, you listen to me, Cowden. This is your last chance. I give you one month to take your cattle off the Buena Vista, the American Boy, the Temporal, and the Canelo Hills ranges. I give you five minutes to give up the fight."

"We won't," Ben said.

"Are you listening to me? If you stand up from this table without coming to terms with us, I'll kill you."

"Fine. Now is a good time to finish it."

"Mister, you killed two of my constables in Mexico. You might not have to answer for it to your old man the undersheriff, but you have to answer to me . . . not only for those killings but for the terrible wrong you've done my family."

"Your family? What family?"

"The Elias family, for which I am now responsible."

"That's a joke. You might make your bosses believe that, but you and I know you are in this to take the Elias's property. No decent family in the world would have you, Odoms."

Kosterlinsky spoke up and accused both sides of depredations. He figured the state of Sonora and its people were the biggest victims in the war. He said he did not think a table in the Harshaw Hotel dining room was the place for anybody to threaten anybody else with force. This table was a place to look for a solution to the fighting. Kosterlinsky would take the first step toward peace. He would have all charges dropped against the Cowden brothers in Sonora if they would serve as scouts and advisors in a new campaign against the Apache *El Bostezador*, the Yawner.

"Like hell you will, Kosterlinsky," Odoms said. "The charges against the Cowdens in Sonora are legitimate. I made them and will enforce them, here or anywhere."

"The deaths of your two constables in Sonora were caused by Duncan Vincent's advertising a five-thousand-dollar bounty on Ben Cowden's head," Kosterlinsky said. "Ben defended himself against those men, and they died. On the other hand, Odoms, your killing of Edmundo

Romero and the brutal attempted murder and crippling of Tomás Romero can in no way be construed as self-defense."

"My men and I had nothing to do with that," Odoms said. "I'll kill the next man who accuses me of it."

Kosterlinsky looked to the syndicate bosses for appreciation of his situation. "There you are, gentlemen. I leave it to you."

"What do you expect from these city-bred salamanders, Gabriel?" Ben said. "You expect them to come up with a reasonable solution? They are the cause of our trouble."

Ben addressed the bosses. "Everybody knows you won't be satisfied until you have a stranglehold on all the pasture, mineral rights, and waterholes in the country. It doesn't bother you that the territorial government has given Vincent a license to turn his cutthroats and thugs loose on the country. Doesn't good business sense take into consideration that the families who pioneer this country and fight Apaches for it make better allies than enemies? To you, the Cowdens are 'squatters' and 'nesters.' To us, you are worse enemies than the Apaches, yet we're all Americans in pursuit of a good way of life and a peaceful place to work."

Ben turned to Vincent. "Let me tell you something, Mr. Vincent. It's a good thing you're importing fifty men. That shows it hasn't bothered you to lose the relatively small number of men you've lost. Maybe sending us fifty more to hurt will make you and your hotshot bosses stop and realize that we Cowdens, Porters, Farleys, Salazars, Delaossas, Romeros, Heredias, Canos, Eliases, and other pioneer families are here to stay. My family has been fighting predators like you in this country for three generations and has not been dislodged. We'll fight others long after you're gone. You could have been our friend. We helped you and gave you our hospitality when you first came here. Now, you're giving us a chance to scatter fifty more of your cutthroats. Thank you. That will make you look bad to your bosses, and they'll fire you and send you back home to New York where you belong. I don't know what kind of lies you've been telling them to justify the way you handle their business, but they're about to find out the truth."

Ben turned to his father and asked him if he wanted to say anything more. A.B. stood up. "Gentlemen, your money is at stake in this war. My son has given you good advice. You will lose money if this war continues. Weigh that against any other reason you might have to back Duncan Vincent. Mr. McClintock and Mr. Akin have been more or less neutral in this, and I'm sure they would like to see it end. Everybody loses in a war, even the bystanders."

Ben stood up.

"Cowden, I told you I'd kill you if you stood up to leave this table without surrendering to me," Odoms said.

"Mr. Vincent, how can you hope to win the war if your best man is a jackass like Odoms who makes threats he can't back up?" Ben said. "I'm leaving this table—now."

Odoms made a big show of noise and motion by scraping his chair backwards with all his weight and clawing his jacket aside so he could pull his gun and point it at Ben. He knew better than to commit cold-blooded murder in front of a bunch of rich eastern dudes though. He had been hired so they would not ever have to see murder.

Ben drew his pistol, aimed it at Odoms's nose, and cocked it.

The bosses froze.

Ben was never quick to shoot. He shut his left eye, sighted the pistol on Odoms with his right, and was absolutely confident Odoms would find something to say.

Odoms backed down and growled, "Go on, get out, Cowden. But you're going to your death."

McClintock stood up between Ben and Odoms, endangering himself so neither man would shoot. The bosses got out of their chairs and backed away from the table.

"Know this, Cowden," Vincent said. "You don't have a month to move your cattle off the Buena Vista anymore. I'm taking my force of constables through there tomorrow, and I'm killing every animal not branded with the VO. You and the rest of the Mexicans who've been using the Buena Vista are finished."

Ben and A.B. walked out into the hotel lobby. The rest of the Cowdens were gone.

Garbie Burr had taken the rest of the day off and gone for a walk with Mark and Paula Mary. They met Jimmy Coyle on the street and took him with them into Frank Wong's where Garbie also worked as a waitress part-time.

Wong's was empty of customers. The visitors sat in a booth by the kitchen door, and Garbie brought them cookies and tea. Garbie and Mark had been friends since she had come to a dance in the schoolhouse her first evening in Harshaw a few months before.

Paula Mary had been watching Mark and Garbie get more and more stuck on each other every time they met. She enjoyed chaperoning them. Paula Mary was hard to subdue. She held up well during the Bonner ordeal, but she'd been having nightmares about it since she came home, and now the war was upon them again. Being with Jimmy, Mark, and Garbie Burr made her feel happy again. Then two of Odoms's Texans came in.

Mark's and Jimmy's faces showed they did not like the two men who shouldered their way through the shell curtain on the door to Frank Wong's quarters. Paula Mary did not know who they were, but she wondered what they were doing in Frank's back room. The men smiled at the Cowdens as they walked by, as though they were friends. One was short and stocky, the other tall. They opened the door to the kitchen and hollered at Frank, then took a table in the center of the room.

Frank came out, smiling subserviently, nodding, nodding at the men. The men ordered food loudly as though Frank were hard of hearing.

Garbie went into the kitchen to help Frank and soon came out with tea for the men. The stocky one grinned admiringly at her. "Garbie, have you been thinking about my proposition?"

"Your noodle soup will be ready in about five minutes," Garbie said. "Isn't that what you ordered, noodle soup?"

"That wasn't what I proposed to you the other day," the stocky young man said.

Garbie went back in the kitchen, and the man turned to Mark. "Women!" he said. "Who can figure them?"

Mark studied one of the cookies.

"We're the Hardin brothers. I'm Blocky, and he's Dallas. You're Mark Cowden, aren't you?"

"Yes, I'm Mark Cowden."

"Well, you and your brothers are supposed to be our enemies. Did you know that?"

Mark did not answer him.

"What's the matter, can't you hear me?"

Mark sighed. "What do you want to hear?"

"I want to hear you tell me and my brother that you're a cowthief, you're sorry you're our enemy, and you know you're about to die."

The Hardins did not see Les appear in the kitchen door with his pistol drawn. Jimmy took Paula Mary by the hand and pulled her out of the booth. Paula Mary did not want to go, but Jimmy hurt her fingers so much, she hurried to catch up. "Ow, Jimmy!" she said as Jimmy hurried her toward the seashell curtain.

Paula Mary tried to balk, but the room erupted with explosions of gunpowder that propelled her through the curtain with Jimmy. They tumbled across the dirt floor inside Frank's room, and Paula Mary tried to dig deeper as more shots were fired. The pine building was so small and the explosions so big that Paula Mary was afraid the place would catch fire. Smoke from the pistols boiled through the curtain, and she heard a man holler with pain. Another voice said, "Oh God, no." Paula Mary knew the voices did not belong to her brothers.

She became aware that Jimmy's body was pressing against her on one side and another body was pushing her from the other. The new body, in soft and dark silk clothing, was whimpering and rooting to get underneath Paula Mary—a tiny Chinese girl.

Les stood in the curtained doorway. "You kids all right?" The Chinese girl moaned in terror at the sight of Les, big as a house with a pistol in his hand.

Paula Mary and Jimmy stood up. Frank Wong hurried in, took the girl by the hand, and scolded her in Chinese.

"Frank, is that your little girl?" Paula Mary asked.

"Yeh, yeh, my girl." Frank grinned.

"Your daughter? Where's her mother?"

"Yeh, yeh, dotta."

They heard cries in the restaurant.

"Is Mark all right?" Paula Mary asked. "Mark!"

Les pushed Paula Mary and Jimmy out the back door. "Mark's gone for Dr. Tucker," he said. "The Texans are the ones that got hurt."

CHAPTER 23

Ben had gone to the telegraph office and wired his neighbors in Nogales and Santa Cruz, informing them that Vincent planned to make a cattle-killing drive and asking them to move cattle from their various ranches to La Acequia. The telegraph offices in those towns were accustomed to sending messengers to the ranchers. He was sitting in the lobby with A.B. when they heard the shots fired between the Cowdens and the Hardins. Gunsmoke still clouded the room when they went inside Frank Wong's. Mark was holding Garbie Burr in his arms.

Blocky Hardin was down on his face in a big odorous pool of blood with his toes turned in. His brother, Dallas, was sitting next to him with his face in his hands, crying.

A.B. examined the corpse, and when he straightened and turned away, he wore a stricken look. "What happened?" he asked.

"Papa, I had to shoot the man." Les said. "It wasn't my fault though."

"I didn't ask you whose fault it was. A man lost his life. What happened?"

"I was at the blacksmith's and saw their horses tied in back. I knew the horses weren't from this country. When I finally realized they belonged to the Texans, it was almost too late. I came in through the kitchen, and Garbie told me they were badgering Mark. When I opened the door and saw they were about to jump him, I shot the short one."

"Were he and Mark fighting?"

"No, Papa, but they were having words."

"What kind of words?"

"The stocky one asked Mark if he knew they were going to kill him, and I could tell he was getting ready to do it. Mark was in a poor position to defend himself."

"So what happened?"

"Paula Mary and Jimmy were in the booth with Mark. Jimmy could see they were getting ready to shoot. He jumped up and pulled Paula Mary out of the booth, and I shot the bastard before he had a chance to draw his pistol."

"Did he draw his pistol?"

"He had his hand on it, and he had that look in his eye, but he never got it out."

"What did the other boy do?"

"Nothing. When he saw I'd shot his brother, he lost all his fight. It was pitiful, Papa. I'm sorry his brother tried to kill my brother, but he was ready to do it, and Paula Mary or Jimmy could have been shot."

A.B. went over and put his hand on Dallas Hardin's shoulder. "Come on, son. We have to hold an inquest. Sit down over here."

A.B. poured Dallas a shot from his silver flask. Dallas let it sit. He looked at his brother and wept. "Blocky," he kept saying. "Blocky." Ben felt sorry for him. His face was wet with tears and slobbers, his voice thick.

"What made you think you had to shoot the boy, son?" A.B. asked.

"Papa, I didn't have time to think. The way Mark was sitting, he was nothing but a target. The Texans were both turned toward him, and they were behind him. All they had to do was point their pistols at him. It was impossible for him to draw and shoot back at them."

"All right, both of you get out of here. Les, stay at the

blacksmith's so I can call you when the judge comes. Ben, get clear out of sight. Find your mama and the girls, and take them home. I don't want you near the inquest."

Ben watched for his family as he walked toward the back entrance of the hotel. He had to talk to Margarita. He knew he might be making himself and Margarita trouble, but unless his family came out into the alley and took hold of him, nothing could stop him from taking the shortest, most concealed route to room 330.

As he walked down the alley toward the hotel, he came upon the taxidermist skinning the hide off a steer's skull, the head graced by an enormous set of twisted horns. The man looked up at Ben and grinned. "Some trophy to have mounted, isn't it, Ben?"

Ben came out of his haze and looked clearly at the head. "I think I know that steer." He tilted the head around by the tip of one horn. "Looks like old Hirey himself. Who you mounting him for?"

"Your friend Odoms."

"Oh?"

"That's a great set of old ladino horns, ain't it?"

The man said something else, but Ben went on, too preoccupied to understand or answer him. He went up the noisy lumber stairs to the top floor of the hotel and down the hall toward Margarita's room. He did not try to be quiet. He heard the voices of people in their rooms.

Kosterlinsky was in Margarita's room. "How can you do this if you love me?" Kosterlinsky said.

Margarita laughed. "Hah, you think it's so hard?"

"Don't say that. You hurt me."

"I don't care. I'm going."

"No, Margarita, you love me. You're attracted to him and you may even care for him, but you love me."

"All right, then, I love you, but I'm going to Los Angeles with Martín Bouvet."

"You can't go now. Odoms is going against your father, against me. We'll have to be on the Cowdens' side in this. We can't let Vincent and Odoms do what they plan to do."

"That's between you men. I've done my part."

"No, you haven't. You didn't get Ben out of the way like you promised. You only made him unhappy."

"That's what you and Odoms and my father wanted, wasn't it, for me to make him unhappy, bring him down so Odoms could shoot him for adultery? I did my part and was paid in beatings."

"Benjamin looks like a madman, but I think he's only angry."

"So, Benjamin's mad. Benjamin's a fool. I made a complete fool out of him, and you couldn't capitalize on it. It's not my fault, not my problem. Listen, I had him on his knees by my bed begging to help me any way he could. How much more helpless could he be? You promised to have someone at hand when he came to my room. You had me up here playing helpless and sick. What better bait could you have?"

"That wasn't my idea, it was Duncan's. I was out of it by then. I've been out of it since Odoms killed Edmundo Romero and tied Tomás to his horse to be dragged."

"The seduction was your idea, not Vincent's. I did my part. Ben, true man that he is, was enough of a fool to do his part, and you still couldn't trap him. Now you'll have to face him in another fight."

"There's a lot you can still do."

"No, I'm sick of this. As soon as Odoms turns his back, I'm going to catch the train to California with Bouvet to buy Andalusian horses."

"How did you get Bouvet to do that?"

"Ah, he likes women like you do. He likes money. He's in Patagonia, waiting for me. We arranged it before I left the ranch."

"You've become *muy lista*, very smart and ready, haven't you, Margarita?"

"If I don't look out for myself, nobody will do it for me."

"Let me take care of you. Benjamin couldn't do it. Bouvet won't do it. Odoms will be the death of you. I'm your real love."

"Yes, my love. You are my love, my *great* love, but I *love* that tall black-headed horseman."

Ben knocked and walked in on them. Margarita was seated on the edge of the bed, Kosterlinsky in a chair across the room. They saw he might have heard their conversation, and their smiles of greeting were uncertain.

"And here he is," Margarita said.

"Hello, my friends," Ben said. "I caught myself listening outside the door, so I thought I'd better come on in. Congratulations. You managed to lay a winter kill on me that almost finished me."

"Tell me what you're talking about, Ben," Margarita said.

"You know. You did a good job of humiliating me. You discredited me with myself, my family, my friends. If I had not been standing outside the door just now, I might never have found out. I certainly was fooled when you begged me to make love to you. I fell into every trap you laid for me. I was on my way to becoming a drunk and a whiner."

"Don't believe it, Ben. You would never let yourself hit bottom like that. I've always been confident of that."

"Oh, I'm plenty down, Margarita. You did a good job."

"I did it because I love you, Ben. When they told me to seduce you for them, I was happy to do it. I had the consent and approval of my father to woo you, take you to bed, fall in love with you if necessary. I didn't care about the consequences. What did I have to lose? Face it, I did you no harm. On the contrary, we've vented a lifetime of passion in three short weeks. I'd love to do it again."

"I didn't see your hand in this, Gabriel," Ben said. "Vincent couldn't beat me in a war or control me by law, so you almost brought me down with a woman. You struck a painful weakness in me. Nice try. I should have shot you a long time ago."

"Ben, you told me in the Chinaman's the other day that you owed me a favor for taking your father's message to Les. Consider us even now. You can't shoot me. I'd rather see you lose your heart to Margarita any day than allow Vincent to assassinate you, as he planned. You should take her now and leave the country. It will put an end to the war. You are the only force that stands in Vincent's way."

"You would have shown me more respect by having me killed, Gabriel."

"I couldn't risk that. You would have beaten the assassin, as usual. Then you would have found out who ordered it, and I would have fallen into your disfavor again. You have warned me repeatedly to stop bothering you. You might have decided to make good your threat to shoot me."

Ben shook his head in disgust and turned to Margarita. "It doesn't seem that your gamble to stop me from fighting Vincent was a good enough reason for marrying Odoms. That was the reason you married Odoms, wasn't it, so you could help your father settle his obligations to Vincent?"

"Of course I did it for my father, but I also did it for myself. How could you go back to Maudy after being exposed as an adulterer? I almost got you for myself."

"I still can't see it was a good enough reason to make you marry a naked-tailed rat like Odoms."

"It was good enough for me."

"I can't love you now. You've cheapened my feeling for you. The worst of it is, you insist on staying with Odoms."

Margarita's eyes filled with tears, but she did not surrender. "Jack Odoms is not so bad. We get along now, sometimes beautifully. He's assured me he will try to be a good husband. He wants to forget what I've done and make something of the marriage.

"Let me tell you, Ben. I am able to endure his abuse and live with him because I know I will always be able to turn to you. I believe you'll always love me. A good man like you doesn't lie when he tells a woman he loves her."

"Don't believe it anymore." Ben started for the door.

"How can you turn your back on me now, Ben? I know you still love me."

"How? For the love of God," Ben said, and went out. He did not know how he reached the hotel veranda.

He did not remember his feet touching the floor. He remembered the tears in the woman's dark eyes and the little wet mouth turned down in the corners like a child's.

Ben looked up the street and saw a crowd in front of Frank Wong's. Catastrophes were happening so fast that day, the killing at Wong's already seemed like ancient history.

He went to his uncle Vince's saloon and asked him for a glass of A.B.'s whiskey. He stood at the bar and did not care that he was finally allowing himself to be a tall stationary target. He knew he was asking to be killed, and could not bring himself to move. He did not look around for adversaries until he had taken two big swallows of whiskey. He was standing at the corner of the bar near the kitchen.

Lorrie Briggs stopped across the bar from Ben, saw that his mind was far away, and posed with her hands on her hips to make the customers pay attention to her. She announced, "Well, here's that five-thousand-dollar head again, still on its shoulders, but a million miles away. This'd be a good time to take it off and give it to Duncan Vincent. Mr. Cowden, just hold that pose, keep your eyes glassy, and I guarantee you won't feel a thing."

Lorrie picked up a butcher knife the bartender used to slice lemons and brandished it in front of Ben. It never took Lorrie long to attract an audience. When she brandished the knife, everybody in the bar laughed.

A short wiry man stopped at Ben's elbow. "Is he bothering you, Lorrie?"

"Yes, Lee-roy, he darned sure is," Lorrie said. "I want his head, and I can't reach it from here. Will you do me a favor and cut it off even with his shoulders?"

Leroy Ford took the butcher knife. Ben looked into the man's face and saw nothing but friendliness. He did not know him. The only time he had ever been close to him was the night Odoms brought his gang through the gate at La Acequia in the storm. No faces had been distinguishable in the lightning flashes that night.

Ford was on Ben's right. He switched the knife to his

left hand. Ben was several inches taller than he. Ford moved the knife toward Ben's back, and Ben turned to face him. Ford brought the knife back to the top of the bar.

"Keep the knife to yourself, if you please, mister," Ben said.

"Aw, Cowden, don't you know me? I'm an admirer of yours. I've heard great things about you."

Uncle Vince Farley came and stood across the bar from Ford. "What's going on?" he asked good-naturedly.

"Lorrie's trying to recruit another assassin to take my head," Ben said. "They're juggling the butcher knife to see who'll get to do it."

"That's *right*," Ford hissed. He casually sliced the top of Ben's wrist with the knife. Ben hooked at his head with the heavy whiskey glass, but Ford stepped back and he missed. Ben lost his balance. Ford raised the knife over Ben's neck. Vince Farley bludgeoned Ford on the back of the neck with a sawed-off black baseball bat he kept behind the bar.

Ford stumbled forward, fell on his face, and knocked Ben's legs out from under him. He recovered and raised the knife again. Vince came around the corner of the bar and dispassionately thudded the heavy bat left and right against Ford's temples. Ford collapsed but still held the butcher knife. Uncle Vince kicked it out of his hand and it skidded past the corner of the bar. Lorrie picked it up.

Lorrie looked to see what she could do with the knife. Ben was looking down, wrapping his handkerchief on his wrist. Vince put himself between the knife and Ben, and tapped Lorrie on the wrist with the bat. "Give me the knife, Lorrie," he said.

"Just a minute, Uncle Vince."

"Give it to me."

"I want to wash it in Ben Cowden's blood," she growled. She slashed at Vince's face to get by him. Vince caught the sharp blade in his hand, knocking it free with the bat, and Lorrie staggered away. Vince slumped over his wounded hand. Lorrie kicked and pummeled Ben with so much hate that spit flew with her growls. She was not big enough to hurt Ben, but she kept screaming in his face as he tried to turn away from her. Vince recovered, wrapped an arm around her waist, and carried her out of the room.

Ben staggered with exhaustion as he walked up the alley toward Wong's. He intended to find his brothers and leave town. He saw Jack Odoms go in the blacksmith's where Les was waiting. He heard a loud bang, the sound of something heavy smashing into the tin side of the shop. He hurried inside and found Odoms and Les in bare-handed combat.

Both men had big hands. Les was heavily muscled, Odoms sinewy as a whip. Odoms's advantage was in his height and experience, Les's in his youth, weight, and natural ruthlessness.

Both men had landed a half-dozen solid blows to great visual effect, but neither seemed to have felt them, and neither man faltered. Now they knew respect for each other as they circled to fall on one another again.

Odoms feinted, caught Les by the hair, and slammed the heel of his hand into his nose. Les rammed him between the eyes with the top of his head and shovel-hooked him with both hands in the softest part of the belly below the belt.

Neither man could see well now. Ben caught Les around the neck, pulled him out of range, and tried to start him toward the door. Les jerked away. "No, by God, I'm going to finish it this time."

"Here, you son-of-a-bitch." Odoms found the side of Les's head with a right hand that bounced Les on his tailbone off the floor. Les charged and rammed the top of his head under Odoms's chin, bowled him over, and walked on him with his boot-heels. Odoms caught a boot, regained his feet, and used the leg to ram Les into the wall. He pulled Les down, kept his hold on the leg, and stomped on his groin.

Les caught a boot-heel, regained his feet, and rammed

Odoms into the forge, but he was tiring and he could not keep hold of the foot, and could not keep his arms up.

Odoms rested by the forge a moment. Les charged him and took two blows on the way in, but he grabbed Odoms's thick hair in both hands and butted him in the face all the way to the floor. He kept butting Odoms, though his face was taking as much punishment as Odoms's. Blood ran off the faces of both men and splattered their shirts, hands, and hair. Odoms pounded Les's ears bloody with both his fists, but those blows began to weaken, and Les's butting weakened. Finally Les was so tired, he could only raise his upper body, aim his head at Odoms's face, and let it fall. He kept that up, and Odoms kept pounding weakly on his ears.

Ben pried Les loose and led him outside, but he did not turn his back on Odoms until he saw the man relax and lie flat on his back.

CHAPTER 24

Ben escorted the Cowden ladies home, then went back to the inquest in time to hear Judge Dunn, the coroner, proclaim his ruling on the shooting of Wesley "Blocky" Hardin. Paula Mary and Jimmy had been brought back to tell their version of the shooting, but they were kept in the kitchen and not allowed to be in the room with the corpse. John Porter, Viney's brother, acted as secretary and wrote down the ruling.

"In my judgment," Judge Dunn said, "Mark Cowden was in Frank Wong's restaurant with his sister and two friends for the purpose of spending a quiet time together. Soon after they sat down, the Hardin brothers arrived and took a table toward the rear of Mark Cowden and almost immediately began to badger and insult him.

"At that time Mark Cowden was helpless to defend himself because of the position the Harden brothers had taken in the room. The two children, Paula Mary Cowden and Jimmy Coyle, would have been in the line of fire from the Hardins.

"A critical point that has influenced my decision is this: The child Jimmy Coyle saw the danger of the situation and hurried to take himself and Paula Mary Cowden out of the way. In my judgment, if Jimmy Coyle was able to foresee that the Hardins were about to shoot Mark Cowden, a man of Les Cowden's experience was able to judge Hardin's intent even more surely.

"Les Cowden did indeed appear in the kitchen door of Wong's and hear Wesley "Blocky" Hardin state his intention to kill Mark Cowden. Hardin's hand was on the handle of his pistol, and Les Cowden fired his own pistol to prevent Hardin from shooting his brother. Les Cowden fired three bullets into Wesley "Blocky" Hardin. One struck him in the very center of the sternum, one in the heart, and one behind the ear, each a killing shot. No shots were fired at Dallas Hardin, further evidence that Les Cowden fired at Blocky Hardin for no other reason than to prevent him from hurting Mark Cowden.

"It is my judgment that Les Cowden fired his pistol only to prevent a crime. Dallas Hardin evidently posed no threat to Mark Cowden, so he was not fired upon. Les Cowden did not know either one of the Hardins, entertained no preconceived ideas about an enmity between the Hardins and the Cowdens. He only fired at the one who was threatening his brother. I therefore rule that Les Cowden fired his pistol with lawful intent to prevent the progress of a crime that was completely unprovoked."

Ben, his brothers, and A.B. were on the way home that evening when they met Royal Vincent's cavalcade of constables coming from Patagonia. Ben had put away his horse at El Durazno when he took his mother and sisters home, and he drove the surrey back to Harshaw for his father. Ben was driving the surrey because A.B. did not feel well after the inquest.

Dick Martin was at the head of the cavalcade. He must have been watching for the Cowdens because he recognized them a quarter mile away, stopped the cavalcade, and ordered it down into Harshaw Creek to water the horses. While the constables were seeing to that chore, Martin rode on to talk to the Cowdens.

"I was in Patagonia when the train arrived," Martin said. "Three VO cowboys brought the posse's horses and headed back to the ranch. Royal Vincent asked me to come to Harshaw with them and help them get settled. I don't want you to think I'm leading them against you."

"Don't worry, Dick," A.B. said. "You did right."

"I know I did, now. I got them off the road before they could recognize you and start something. They've been told they're here to fight the Cowden gang, but I don't think any of them know you by sight. You ought to be able to get by without them knowing it's you."

Ben caught himself surrendering to Dick Martin's fear that the constables would recognize the Cowdens and felt disgusted. "What the hell do we care if they recognize us?" he said.

"Well, I'd rather you didn't have a fight with them. There's fifty of them and only four of you." Martin was sneaking looks at Les's bloody shirt and ravaged face. "You don't want a fight at close quarters on this road, do you?"

"If they're looking for one, it might as well be on this road as another," Ben said. "We'll have to fight sooner or later."

"No, you won't," A.B. said. "Not here, or anywhere. Thank you, Dick. We'll just see if we can slip by and go on home."

Ben started Jack and Mack, and drove on. He watched the constables to see if he knew any of them. He saw a gang of youngsters who had probably been recruited because they did not have anything better to do around town. These boys were only a blanket, a campfire and a borrowed horse away from vagrancy.

One of them was not a youth though. A tall man in a big hat stood apart from the rest. Ben recognized Senator Royal Vincent, Duncan Vincent's brother. He was a politician, lobbyist, and influence peddler, thickly, dirtily involved with Arizona's other graft-ridden politicians. He knew the Cowdens well enough, but at that moment he was too busy acting important and he did not look up when the Cowdens went by. He took that moment to address the constables with a speech about The Care and

Handling of the Horse. The Cowden brothers examined each horse and each man so they would remember them. When the Cowdens were safely past the constables, Dick Martin rejoined them.

The brothers rested with their family that evening and left with the appearance of the *guia* star at two A.M. They rode through Harshaw and saw the constables' horses tied in front of the saloons. Mark dismounted and saw the constables having a good time inside.

The Cowdens rode out of Harshaw confident of their strategy. Slick Dicks who stayed up all night in saloons were prone to look for places to lie down in the day, were liable to have headaches that hurt their eyes when they tried to move them from side to side to see their enemies. Royal Vincent would be lucky if his force did not perish from a hangover. The Tucson Constables was certainly not the sort of expeditionary force the Cowdens would have worry about.

The Cowden brothers rode down Harshaw Creek and around American Peak to Providencia Canyon. They reached the Providencia mine at dawn and stopped to make coffee. Buzzards came to the carcass of the big steer Odoms had killed. Ben told his brothers about Odoms's leaving the steer's head with the taxidermist in Harshaw. The brothers all remembered the red-and-white motley-faced steer with the extra twist in his horns. They called him Old Hiry, after their father, whose first name was Ahira.

"Old Hiry was a real smart ladino," Ben said. "Odoms had to be damned stealthy to surprise him on the water that way. We ought to try and remember that."

The brothers worked Providencia Canyon toward the María Macarena. Mark led the packhorse down the bottom of the canyon and drove the cattle Ben and Les pushed down to him. Les took the ridge on the right so he could see into Paloma Canyon. Ben took the ridge on the left so he could see into Sycamore Canyon. After a while, Ben ran onto the same tracks he had seen around Old

Hiry's carcass, Odoms's tracks. This saddlehorse had left his hoofprints plainly when he floundered on the edge of the pool. Ben could see Odoms had ridden in and out of Sycamore Canyon from Providencia.

He went on, found cattle tracks on the next trail, and followed them down into Sycamore. The cattle were sunning themselves on the south side of the ridge above Sycamore Creek. He started them, and they ran down to the creek and tried to double back on him. He got ahead of them, stopped them, and held them awhile. He saw where Odoms had crossed the creek. He looked around and tried to figure why Odoms had ridden straight across Sycamore Canyon and then straight back to the mine.

He started the cattle walking toward Mark, then went back and followed Odoms's track up the side of the canyon. He found the place where he had buried something, followed his boot tracks to the thicket, and found the shovel. He took the shovel and dug up the twins' panniers with the alazana gold. He started laughing. He laughed so hard at first, he ran out of breath and scared himself. He tied the panniers behind his saddle and laughed and gloated all the way down the canyon. He was not able to contain himself until he threw the cattle in with the bunch Mark was pushing and lashed the panniers on the packhorse.

That evening, the brothers threw more than three hundred head of cattle in with the weaned calves in the pasture at La Acequia. They unsaddled their packhorse and left him there, and rode back out on the Buena Vista. They saw Odoms's campfire at a spring where the Cañon de la Paloma widened into a big flat. The constables had not come far.

The brothers waited until the constables had been asleep an hour, then Mark stood watch over them with his rifle in case someone woke up while Les and Ben went about their mischief. The constables' horses were tied to a picket line along the bottom of Paloma Creek. Les stayed by the sentry and let him sleep while Ben found the saddles, cut every cinch in half, and sliced through the leather that held the D cinch rings to the rigging on the saddles. He did not bother the Texans' saddles. He wanted Odoms to separate from the posse and come on after the Cowdens.

The brothers camped at La Acequia at midnight. The next day, they made another drive in the Mowry and Mount Washington country, turned the cattle into the pasture at La Acequia at dark, and rode on to the María Macarena.

Their uncle Billy Porter's saddlehorses were in the corral with the Romeros' horses. While the Cowden brothers were unsaddling and unpacking, the Salazars rode in from the Yerba Buena with another 125 head of the cattle of all the Buena Vista faction's brands.

The Porters and Romeros were roasting beef over mesquite coals and drinking mescal in the courtyard of Don Juan Pedro's main house when the Cowdens and Salazars walked in. Chapito Cano's wife and daughters were serving the vaqueros, and everybody seemed happy.

Uncle Billy's sons, Jim and Bud, were with him. The telegraph operator in Santa Cruz had sent messengers with Ben's telegram to Porter Canyon and the María Macarena.

Ben was surprised to see Bouvet come out of his room and call Don Juan Pedro to the ramada outside. He remembered hearing Margarita tell Kosterlinsky that Bouvet was waiting for her in Patagonia. Ben was sitting in a good place to hear their conversation.

"Señor Elias, I must insist that I be taken to Nogales in the morning."

"I told you, Bouvet, I can't spare any men right now, and I won't send you to Nogales without an armed guard."

"I can go without a guard. I insist! You've held me much longer than I intended to stay. I assume responsibility for my own safety."

"And who will drive you? I won't send a driver without an armed guard."

"In that case, give me a horse to ride."

"Helpless as you would be out on the road by yourself, you might as well walk. You'll lose my horse."

"I'll buy the horse."

Don Juan Pedro thought a moment. "*Basta*, enough, I'll loan you a horse, then. You can ride as far as La Acequia with us; then you can go on with vaqueros who will work the Baca ranch tomorrow. They'll take you to the outskirts of Nogales."

The twins read Kosterlinsky's telegram ordering their release from the presidio with suspicion. His reputation for releasing prisoners was bad. He often opened the doors to his jails with great generosity and then said, "Run for your life." His Rurales would be lined up with their rifles, ready to take target practice, while the prisoner ran to get over the nearest hill.

The twins' horses were brought to them, and they were handed their belongings. They saw no Rurales outside the presidio as they headed for Santa Cruz. They were not surprised no one shot at them, the presidio guards were their friends now.

They had spent the last of their alazanas in the jail, buying food and mescal for themselves and their guards, but they had some change, and they stopped at a cantina and bought a gallon jug of mescal. They went on to the house of the Campana sisters to get more alazanas. They unsaddled their horses in the sisters' corral and went in through the back gate to the loco's den in the center of the courtyard.

The loco brother of the Campana sisters was their friend. During the many hours the twins had spent with the sisters, they gave him mescal and broiled beef, took him mariachi serenades, and talked to him, though he could not speak or hear. When the twins were drinking and happy, their friendship knew no bounds. They had often passed out for whole nights in his den, staying out of the way so the sisters could go on about the business of receiving men in their house.

Donny shoved the jug through the door ahead of him so the loco would not be frightened, then held it up so he could take a swallow. Danny stopped at the well and drew a bucket of water. He rolled up his sleeves, knelt down in a corner of the den, lifted the lid of the one-holer toilet installed over a pit, dug down to his elbows, came up with two handfuls of alazanas, and dropped them in the loco's washbasin. Donny applied soap and water to the money and washed it shiny. The two handfuls amounted to $1,800.

The twins drank a few swallows of mescal with the loco, went in the house and took a bath, then joined a party Walter Jarboe was having with the Campana sisters. Danny's shoulders were still so sore he could not raise his arms, and Donny was covered with bruises from head to toe, but the mescal soon made them feel good enough to laugh again.

They could see Jarboe had certainly taken a liking to Mexico and the Campana sisters. He told them his stay at the Campanas was the first time in his life he'd had a good time. Then one of the Romeros came in and told them the Cowdens and Porters had all been called to the María Macarena ranch, and they took that as an excuse to leave.

They went back to the cantina where they had bought their jug and ordered supper. They were waiting at a corner table for the food with only one candle for light when Jacinto Lopez came in.

"I was hiding and waiting for my supper when they told me you were here too," Jacinto said. "Good luck for me. We can eat together."

After supper, the twins went with Jacinto to see the teguequita who had survived the Apache raid at Tuvera. They ended up sleeping in Jacinto's camp that night. The next morning, he asked them to help him move some cattle, so they rode with him to a hill overlooking Kosterlinsky's hacienda and garrison outside Santa Cruz. Jacinto knew about a telegram Kosterlinsky had sent that ordered the garrison to the María Macarena that day. After the colors were hoisted and the mounted troop left the hacienda, Jacinto, his men, and the twins rode into the pasture and cut out thirty-five head of Vincent's and Kosterlinsky's steers. The twins saw that six head were big S-dot steers belonging to the Cowdens and three were MO cattle that the Farleys owned in partnership with the Cowdens. When the cattle were a good way out on the trail, the twins cut the S-dot and MO cattle out, and Jacinto and another man helped them drive the cattle toward the María Macarena.

"Where are your men going with the other cattle?" Danny asked Jacinto.

"Those go for sale to the miners in Cananea," Jacinto said.

"How long have you been doing this with Vincent's and Kosterlinsky's cattle?"

"Since last fall when they started using this pasture to hold cattle they took off the Buena Vista."

"How many Cowden and Farley cattle have you sold in Cananea?"

"Ah, only a few."

"About how many?"

"Maybe a half dozen each trip."

"How many trips have you made?"

"Maybe ten."

"You've taken sixty of our cattle, Jacinto?"

"Yes, about sixty."

"Well, that's for the chingada—you've been giving us a terrible *screwing*."

Jacinto smiled. "Haven't I? It's awful. But we have to live."

"Doesn't Kosterlinsky ever miss the cattle?"

"No, up to now, nobody's been *campeando*, riding and checking the cattle, and the VO cowboys keep bringing more."

"And now somebody's campeando for Kosterlinsky? Who?"

"Victor Roblez." Jacinto laughed.

"Roblez the mutineer?"

"Kosterlinsky gave my partner Roblez a black hat and put him in charge of his herd."

Jacinto and the twins reached the María Macarena with the cattle two hours after dark. They turned the cattle into the pens and rode on to sleep at La Acequia. They were at La Acequia when the entire Buena Vista crew rode in with Bouvet the next morning.

Ben was happy to see the twins and to find out from them that they had hidden $25,000 of the alazanas at La Providencia and been forced by Odoms to tell where it was. He was surprised to find out that they still had nearly $55,000 hidden. He had never thought he took more than $40,000 from Kosterlinsky's stage.

Bouvet had ridden only one hour, but he was almost finished. He complained that he was not accustomed to the seat of the vaquero saddle. He said he was an accomplished rider, but he used the more traditional seat of English equestrian style.

He did not know Jacinto Lopez. Jacinto was the only one of the vaqueros who could not keep from laughing when Bouvet bragged about his classic English style of riding. "Your style is different, all right," he said. "When you first came through the thicket, I thought you were a tax collector named Bouvet. Do you know him? He's a *fantoche*, phony, who's been putting the bite on Don Juan Pedro. Don Juan Pedro has been saying he would love to get Bouvet on a horse to watch him suffer. You looked so full of pain, I was sure you were Bouvet."

"I am Martín Bouvet, at your service."

"Ah, it *was* you." Jacinto's expression was serious as he walked away to the twins. They stopped laughing when they saw his face.

"What's the matter, Jacinto?" Danny asked. "We thought you were joking. Didn't you know Bouvet?"

"No, I did not. I swore to kill that son of a bad act. He confiscated my father's farm after the mutiny." Jacinto said it loud enough for Bouvet to hear him.

Bouvet heard it, all right. Everybody in the vicinity heard it and stared at Bouvet. Bouvet's eyes went out of focus, as was their habit when he found himself lacking in comforts and amenities.

"Jacinto, will you help us today?" Ben asked quietly.

"Of course, Benjamin."

"Will you and the twins escort Bouvet to Nogales?"

"Ah, maybe the twins will help you with that. I'm headed the other way."

"I want the twins to go beyond Nogales, work Comoro Canyon on the Baca, and drive the river from that end."

"Do you know what you're asking me to do?"

"Yes. You don't have to·kill him today, do you?"

"I won't be responsible for him."

"Take him to the train station."

"No, Benjamin. I guess I can't help you, after all. I'll just go on and attend to my own business." Jacinto mounted his horse and rode away.

Bouvet grunted and moaned all the way to the Yerba Buena, but he did not ask for sympathy. The twins found it hard to hold their horses to his pace. They had to keep looking back at him but did not talk to him. They did not mind going all the way to Nogales with him because that would give them a chance to get a drink, but they sure did not want to take all day.

Bouvet dismounted at the Yerba Buena campground. He was so afraid for his bulk that he clawed the saddle with his gloved fingernails all the way to the ground. He was sweating, so he took off his cloak, laid it over a tree trunk, sat down, and began removing his gloves one finger at a time.

The twins squirmed. Danny said, "We don't have time to wait here, Señor Bouvet. We still have a lot of work to do."

"How far is Nogales, boys?"

"From here, only about five miles."

"How do we go?"

"We just stay on this trail, bear left around that hill, and ride up Proto Canyon from the river."

"Can I get lost if you let me go alone?"

"No." The twins spoke together.

"I just stay on the trail?"

"Yes."

"Good-bye, then, and thank you."

"Are you sure, Señor Bouvet?"

"Of course. I've been enough trouble for you. Go on."

"Adios," the twins said.

"Adios."

The twins had been gone a half hour before Bouvet lifted himself off the log, put his gloves on, folded his cape, and tied it on the back of the saddle. He dreaded mounting the horse again, so he took his time. He led him up and mounted from atop the log. The horse turned toward sounds coming through the river forest, and Bouvet was surprised when Jack Odoms, Dallas Hardin, and Leroy Ford rode into the clearing.

"Ah, my friend Captain Odoms," Bouvet said, and he smiled for the first time since he left Hermosillo.

Odoms did not smile. He knocked Bouvet off his horse with his fist. He used one of his hurting blows, not a stunning blow. Bouvet's English equestrian seat was so round that he toppled easily, but he splattered when he hit the ground. The María Macarena horse was gentle, though, and did not step on him.

Odoms turned to Ford. "What kind of luck is this? There isn't another son-of-a-bitch in the world I'd rather see today. There's some I'd like to see as much, but none more than this bastard."

Bouvet started crawling, gained a small amount of momentum, regained his feet, and started walking away.

"Come back here, Bouvet. That's the wrong way," Odoms said.

Bouvet stopped and looked around uncertainly. He half turned to Odoms. "Which way, Captain Odoms? I wish to go to Nogales. I don't mind walking."

"Come back here."

Bouvet came back, his eyes trying to focus on everything. He made a particular study of Odoms's face to find understanding and compassion.

Odoms pointed to the ground under his stirrup. "Stand right there."

Bouvet stopped by Odoms's foot.

"Now, I want you to tell me, what's so good about the Andalusian horse business?"

"I am sure I don't know, Captain Odoms," Bouvet whispered.

"I've been told you plan to advise my wife about Andalusian stud horses, brood mares, and breeding methods while you accompany her on a comfortable trip by rail to California. Is that true?"

"Preposterous. Who told you that lie?"

"Bouvet, my wife tells me everything." Odoms turned to Hardin and Ford. "Hoist the son-of-a-bitch."

The Texans grabbed Bouvet, sat him on his horse, tied his hands behind his back with a lariat, threw the rope over a limb above him, tied it to the trunk, and whipped the horse out from under him. When Bouvet's bulk came off the horse, it popped both his shoulders out of joint, and the stretch of the rope allowed only the tips of his toes to touch the ground. The pain of the double dislocation brought a shrill squeal out of him, but his delicate system had mercy on him, and he lost consciousness.

Odoms led the Texans away, as though he were leaving, then turned back and watched Bouvet from behind the brush. He was disappointed when the man did not revive.

Dallas Hardin had been in tears continually since his brother was killed. Now he began to cry quietly again. Ford sighed and looked way off toward Texas. Disgusted that Bouvet could not have endured more pain for him, Odoms rode up in front of him and stung his face with his quirt until he revived and began to weep.

"It's awful, isn't it, Bouvet?" Odoms said. "Don't you think you deserve this?"

Bouvet shook his head slightly.

"Well, I believe you do. You know, I'm kind of

ashamed you had to go through this over a whore. If I believed you'd slept with the slut, I'd castrate you too. Since I don't think you did that, I'm going to be merciful with you. I'm going to cut you down. Hold still, now." Odoms drew his sharp skinning knife through Bouvet's throat from ear to ear so gently and swiftly the man barely felt it.

CHAPTER 25

Ben felt his biggest worry was over. The Buena Vista cattlemen were bringing in all their cattle. Vincent would no longer be able to kill the stock without facing the owners.

During the work, some of the cattlemen had seen the Tucson posse straggling bareback or afoot toward Harshaw. Ben and his brothers circled the posse's last campsite and found the tracks of Odoms and his Texans headed toward Nogales. Content to have him out of the way for a while, the Cowdens did not go after him.

Ben knew he and his brothers did not have to look for Odoms. The Texans would come and find the Cowdens. If they still wanted to kill cattle, they would have to come to La Acequila.

Ben rested well during the cattle work. He settled down and enjoyed the warmth of the sun on his back and the performance of the good horse he rode. He was riding Toots. Toots and Ben trusted each other and knew what to expect from each other.

Ben's work healed his ailments. His heart didn't hurt all the time anymore. His effort, intuition, good judgment, humor, and compassion were appreciated again. The only females he saw were old cows. The frosty mornings did not put the deep chill on his bones that the absence of Margarita had done. His body heated and sweated with honest effort and nothing else.

The twins had not come back, so the Salazars had gone to gather the Baca ranch and make a drive to their own pens at Nogales the day before. They were expected at La Acequia with the Baca cattle that evening, and theirs was the only crew not in camp.

The Cowdens had put away their horses and were headed to the cook's fire when eighteen of Kosterlinsky's Rurales rode in. The sergeant in charge was Moises Cano, brother of Chapito. The Buena Vista cattlemen all knew him. Ben went over to invite the Rurales to coffee by the fire and to tell them a quarter of beef would be provided for their supper. Moises told Ben they had been on patrol to San Lázaro and were supposed to meet Kosterlinsky at La Acequia that evening. Kosterlinsky was traveling horseback from Harshaw.

While Ben was talking to the Rurales, the Salazars drove in their cattle and turned them into the San Bernardino pasture. A few moments later, Kosterlinsky and Roblez emerged from the river forest on the road from Washington Camp. Margarita's carriage came out right behind them.

Colorado was driving the carriage, and Pepe was sitting beside him armed with a rifle. When Colorado stopped in front of the house, Margarita dismounted and went inside without looking to the right or to the left.

Kosterlinsky dismounted at the Rurales'. camp, and Roblez took their horses to unsaddle and feed.

The Salazars stopped by the camp before they put away their horses. Rafael, the oldest, turned a serious face to Ben. "Bad news," he said.

"What happened?" Ben asked. He had left Les and Mark at the fire only a few minutes before, but he looked for them quickly and was relieved to see they were still there feeding on broiled beef.

"Señor Bouvet was found hanging dead from a tree at

the Yerba Buena. Somebody tied his hands behind his back, hung him up, and cut his throat."

"When?"

"The Valenzuelas found him night before last when they came down from San Lázaro. They loaded him in their wagon and took him to Nogales."

"What happened to the twins?"

"Nobody's seen them, but the law came by our ranch last night looking for them."

"What law?"

"Odoms and the Texans. They told us to spread the word that the twins were wanted for questioning. He said he heard in Nogales the twins were the last ones seen with Bouvet."

"Who could have known that? Only we here at La Acequia knew the twins were with Bouvet, and nobody from here has been to town. Somebody else carried that news to town. Was it Jacinto?"

"I don't know, Benjamin."

"I don't believe the twins killed the old featherweight. Maybe the one who killed him saw the twins with him."

"How did he come to harm if the twins were protecting him?"

"Ah, there you have me."

Ben mounted a fresh horse and rode out with the vaqueros who were to relieve the six sentries posted around the camp to keep cattle from straying into the mountains and to keep the VO faction from bothering them. Epifanio Romero, the patriarch of the clan, rode beside Ben. He had lost two grandsons, Hector and Edmundo, in this war. His son Tomás was alive, but his injuries were so many, no one could tell how long he would be laid up. Some people on the edges of the war blamed the Cowdens for those casualties.

"How is Don Tomás?" Ben asked.

"Better," Epifanio said. "His horse almost kicked and choked him to death. The damage to his neck was terrible. We could see the bone where the reata wore through the muscle."

"*Lástima*. What a shame."

"He'll get well though. He has feeling in his limbs. We thought he was paralyzed at first because he was too sore to move. Tell me, Benjamin, what is the purpose of our standing watch on these cattle? We already have a barbed-wire fence around them, and they are in Mexico now. They're not on disputed land."

"Now that we have them all together, what better opportunity for Odoms to kill them?"

"But you scattered the posse. Where is the danger?"

"The danger is with Odoms, Epifanio. A killer will look for a way. While you're on guard, don't let him steal in and kill the cattle, or kill you. Keep the cattle in front of you and turn them back from the mountains. Watch your front for stray cattle, but watch the mountains at your back for the murderers. The Texans camped up there, and they probably know every trail and hiding place as well as we do.

"I haven't done us any great service by bunching the cattle here, Epi, but I've made the fight simple. If Vincent and Odoms come here, they'll be legally wrong for starting a fight in Mexico, and they'll be forced to fight on our terrain. All we have to do is hold the stock together and wait for them."

"How do you know they'll come, Benjamin?"

"They can't put us out of business unless they come. You've stood this watch before, haven't you, Epi?"

"Of course. Every night since we started."

"Remember, you can't have a fire, can't show a light, so you can't even have a smoke while you're on watch."

"No, I won't ever be so cold up here that I can't stand it. This isn't cold. I can do without my *cigarros* too. For me, smoking is not a large vice."

Ben posted the sentries and rode back to the fire with the men who had been relieved. He put his horse in a corral without unsaddling him. Pepe caught up to him outside the corral, as he expected. He squatted with his back against the fence and lit his pipe. "How are you, Pepe, and how is your mother?"

"My mother says, *'Que ya ni la chinges.* Enough with your anger.' She surrenders, and needs very much to talk to you."

Ben thought, Now ain't that just dandy. I'm supposed to walk right in there, our private place, in front of the whole crew, and cozy up to her again. He said, "Her health is good?"

"Yes. What is your answer, Benjamin?"

"Tell her I'll visit her as soon as I can." Ben did not want to lie, but as far as he knew, that was the best way to stay away from her. He'd come down from the withdrawal but still feared the addiction. He had too much to do. He would always have too much to do. He did not want to get lost in that woman's eyes again.

When he went back to the fire, Kosterlinsky came over to talk. "I see you've made the cattle and yourselves the bait, Benjamin. I hope it doesn't get you shot."

"Gabriel, this is their chance to catch us standing still. They need to make targets of us if they want to win the war. I hope Duncan Vincent comes."

"I was in Harshaw when the posse straggled in. Some of them quit, but not all of them. Most of Vincent's VO cowboys were in town also. I warned him that he would be entirely in the wrong if he brought his force to Sonora."

"Well, if he comes, you'll have to arrest him and put him in the presidio, won't you? Then he'll have to pay you to go free. That's how you deal with each other, isn't it?"

"I will arrest him. I might have to jail people from both sides. Do you expect the twins to come back? What were their orders?"

"They were to escort Bouvet to the train station in Nogales, then make a drive back here from the Baca."

"It looks like they killed Bouvet."

"No, they're not killers, and they had no reason to kill him. They were respectful of the man, and they were his bodyguard, not his killers. But you'll probably have to say they did it if you don't want to accuse Odoms of it. I think Odoms did it. He knew the twins were with Bouvet at the Yerba Buena."

"I say it *looks* like they did it. I have to investigate the matter and talk to the twins."

"Jacinto told everyone here that he intended to kill the man for confiscating his father's farm."

"Jacinto Lopez could also have done it. I should have finished him a long time ago. Every time I think of him, I gnash my teeth. However, I am inclined to see it your way. Odoms did not tell the Salazars that Jacinto or anyone else was suspect. He blamed the twins."

Ben called Rafael Salazar over and asked him to tell Kosterlinsky how Bouvet had been killed.

"His hands were tied behind him, and he was dropped off his horse to break his shoulders. That's what the Valenzuelas said. They brought in his horse. They said the tracks showed the horse had been whipped out from under Bouvet. Then his throat was cut. The blood was on the ground underneath him, not on his saddle."

"Odoms tortured Danny Farley by tying his hands behind him and threatening to dislocate his shoulders." Ben said. He asked his uncle Billy Porter to come over. "Do you remember how you used to tell us those stories about the Comanches when we were little, Uncle Billy?"

"Yes."

"Remember you told us they did something to their captives' shoulders before they killed them?"

"Yeah, they liked to dislocate their shoulders, hang them on them."

"Have you ever known the Apaches to do that? I sure haven't."

"No, Ben, I never have. I knew the Comanches did it from stories my cousin Tom Parker told me. Tom was a famous scout and Indian fighter in the Texas army."

"That makes me sure that Odoms killed Bouvet. He and his Texans learned that shoulder business from the Comanches. That man I shot at Cibuta said he'd learned his trade as a killer from Comanches."

"We've had two very unusual killings and attempted killings in this region lately," Kosterlinsky said. "I've

never seen such imaginative and sadistic assaults as these.
Odoms and his Texans were the only enemies of the
victims who were in the vicinity of those crimes."

"Then you can leave the twins alone?"

"I want to talk to them."

"You need the twins and Jacinto so you can blame
them when you make a new deal with Vincent and
Odoms. You'll turn the twins into outlaws, Gabriel."

"If they come in and talk to me, I'll help them. If they
don't come in, they probably committed the crime."

Ben went to the fire for mescal and carne asada. He
wondered how Margarita could ever think he would go in
for a private talk with her with all these men watching.
The men were already scandalized by the stories they'd
heard about Ben and Margarita. He did not even look
toward the house.

At ten, Mark took off his hat, said good night, and
wandered away from the fire as though headed for bed.
When he was out of sight in the darkness, he went to the
corral and caught the Cowden horses. Les followed him a
few minutes later. When Ben left the fire, he knocked on
the door of the house, and Don Juan Pedro let him in. He
nodded to Margarita on his way through and went out the
back door, staying out of the light of the fire as he made his
way to the corral.

When he was with his brothers, Ben said, "Bring
Moose too."

"What do we need a packhorse for?" Les asked.

"I don't know, but we better take him. Just put his
packsaddle on him and tie on the *manta*."

Les reached inside the Cowdens' pack beside the
corral fence and pulled out a double-barreled shotgun. He
broke it in two and dropped two shells in the chambers,
the barrel tubes making slight burping sounds of recognition as the shells dropped into place.

The Cowdens rode east in the darkness. They did not
look back at the fire. The moon was on the rise, and they
did not look at it either, not wanting to blind themselves

to the trail ahead. They followed a wide trail up the south fence of the San Bernardino pasture. The only sounds between them and their quarry were their breathing and hoofbeats.

After a short, steep, winding climb, they stopped to let their horses blow on a divide. They stood on the line between brilliant moonglow on the east side of the mountain and the shade of night on the west. They followed a trail north along a *cordón*, a spine of jutting rocks toward San Bernardino Peak. The horsemen were grateful to be on the moonglow side of the mountain so they could see the trail and the edge of a precipice below them. The ridge narrowed as they climbed and finally leveled off to a ledge on the brow of an escarpment hundreds of feet above a slope of talus rock.

The horsemen descended from there to a narrow saddle where their trail intersected an old east–west trail from Santa Cruz. They were now directly above their own sentries. Ben and Les dismounted, and Mark took the horses a stone's throw off the trail and hobbled them and tied them in the brush.

The brothers expected their enemies might want to come through that saddle to do them harm. Odoms could do a lot of damage from this high ground. Gunfire and rocks rolling down in the middle of the night would cause the two thousand cattle in the pasture to stampede through the camp at La Acequia. That would kill and scatter a lot of cattle with little risk to Odoms.

After the sounds of their horses subsided, Ben went down to the dark side of the trail in the saddle and struck flint sparks off his knife to an oak punk, held the glowing punk close to the trail, and examined it for tracks. No one had used it since the last rain.

Ben went back to his brothers and patted them to let them know he would stand first watch. Les and Mark lay down on their sides with their heads in their hats, hugged themselves inside the Saltillos, and were asleep in an instant.

The sky was clear. The San Antonio Mountains east of Ben were close and still in the moonlight. If he did not miss his bet, death would try to come to him and his brothers from that direction.

Death came afoot. When Ben became aware of the three men, they looked like rocks moving. The short shadows they cast on the high side of the trail distorted their shapes. They came bareheaded in a file directly toward Ben, moving swiftly and quietly.

Les and Mark awoke to Ben's touch instantly, and the brothers moved away from one another. The men on the trail slowed. Ben was closest to them. He let them go past until they were in front of his brothers, then stepped across their trail and stood in the shadow of a crag behind a waist-high boulder. Odoms was the last man in the file.

"Stand fast," Ben said. Now they would fight, or surrender, but there would be no more talk.

Odoms whirled, pointed his rifle at Ben, and went down on one knee. Ford was second in line, and he turned, sighted along his shoulder, and fired over Odoms's head toward Ben. Ben fired at Odoms's head. Odoms's bullet glanced off the boulder and sprayed Ben's face with rock fragments. Ben's bullet missed Odoms and struck through Ford's belt buckle.

The spray of rock and the flashes from the firearms blinded Ben. His brothers' pistol and shotgun went off in the echoes of the first three shots, and Dallas Hardin fell. Ford bent over in the middle, staggered backwards, and tripped over Hardin. As he fell, he threw up his hands, and his pistol went off close enough to light up his face. The brothers' next shots struck Ford again. Ben fell behind the rock, sighted along the ground at Odoms, and fired, and fired again, then saw he was shooting at a rock. He straightened behind his pistol. Odoms was gone.

"Ben?" Les called.

"Quiet!" Ben shouted, but his echo went on. When all the sounds went away, he heard Odoms plunging down through manzanita brush in the dark shadow of the mountain. No one would be able to touch him or see him until daylight.

"Are you all right, brothers?" Ben asked.

Les and Mark were standing over Hardin and Ford. "We are, but these two are dead," Les said. "It's a good thing you thought to bring old Moose."

CHAPTER 26

Jack Odoms's worst worry had been realized. He'd lost all his allies. Duncan Vincent could never be counted on now. The man had made it clear—either Odoms won the fight and eliminated the Cowdens, or Vincent would give Odoms up to the law to pacify his neighbors.

The Cowdens' ambush had forced Odoms to make a hard run over rough, dangerous ground, and now they had him cut off from his horse. He decided if the sun ever came up for him again and he could get off that mountain, he would head for Texas. He could get Blocky Hardin's horse and saddle in Harshaw.

Being on the dark side of that mountain forced him to pull up and take stock. He was alone in the world now, and he might not survive the next hour stumbling in the dark. He slowed down. He was sensible enough to know that his situation would improve when the sun came up, but the darkness would continue forever for him if he took one wrong step that found a chasm deep enough to kill him. The dark mountain had him so scared, he might even change his ways if he ever got down and the sun came up again.

While his brothers were lashing the Texans' bodies on

Moose, Ben went back and found their horses, tied them together head to tail, and led them back to the saddle.

"Maybe we should have left those horses where they were," Les said. "Odoms might be dumb enough to come back for them."

"He's not that dumb," Ben said. "But I want him to stagger around afoot on this mountain in the dark. I hope he comes back up here looking for his horse and finds him gone. That'll make him lonesome, for a change. The cold-blooded son-of-a-bitch might think he doesn't need anything or anybody in the whole world, but sometime tonight he'll miss his horse."

The brothers rode back to camp and gave the Texans' bodies to Kosterlinsky's Rurales for burial, then gave their sworn statements to Kosterlinsky. Hardin and Ford were buried beside their partner Lige Rote in La Acequia's old cemetery.

The brothers went to the fire for coffee at dawn. Each man in the crew had stayed alert during his turn at watch and rested well afterward. The knowledge that Odoms was in flight and afoot relaxed them more. Some were even wondering if they could go home.

A pack of wolves were killing Epifanio Romero's cattle. He had tracked them to their den in the Chivato Mountains. The meeting at La Acequia gave him the chance to ask Kosterlinsky for the loan of a squad of Rurales to help exterminate them.

Margarita came out with a bundle of fresh tortillas. To her credit, she gave Ben the same smile she gave his brothers and did not flirt with the crew. She belonged to everybody again. She had known these men all her life, and each man entertained a special feeling for her. If she had flirted with Ben or his brothers or some other poor son-of-a-gun, she would have made the whole crew miserable.

Ben decided to see if he could make contact with his enemies. He had taken away most of Vincent's ability to surprise him, but he needed to find out what the man was doing. He told his brothers to stay in camp, changed horses, and rode out at a high trot.

The country was empty now. The feed was so short, even the game was gone. Winged predators flew high so they could search afar for prey. The coyotes traveled at a long trot, their tongues hanging out. Odoms was on the run but not gone yet. Vincent was not gone either.

Ben found Odoms's tracks where he expected them to be. The man's stride was long, his footprints light. He was probably hoping to do the same thing Ben wanted to do—make contact with Vincent. Ben rode behind a ridge that paralleled the tracks so Odoms would not look back and see him.

He saw the dust of Vincent's cavalcade gust over the ridge a half hour later. He rode up the side of the ridge, took off his hat and looked over the top. Seventy men sat their horses behind Vincent while he reprimanded Odoms and preached diligence. Anybody who trusted in that bunch of vagrants *better* preach diligence. Ben could see that most of the Tucson youngsters had borrowed saddles and mounted for the posse again, and the VO cowboy crew was in full strength behind the boss. Vincent became so excited with his speech that his face swelled and turned red. Odoms was bareheaded but seemed unperturbed. He'd lost his hat but saved his life. He was taking one of the constables' horses away from him when Ben headed back to La Acequia to prepare his stand against Vincent.

The herd was quickly moved up La Capilla Creek, and six men were left with it to hold it out of sight. Three groups of men were staggered along both sides of the road, so Vincent's constables would have to pass through a cross fire of sharpshooters to reach the pasture gate and the cattle.

Ben wanted to be sure they came all the way into the camp. Les rode out to the Sonora-Arizona border, to watch for Vincent, and came in when he drew near. The Buena Vista cattlemen hid themselves. Duncan Vincent, Royal Vincent, and Odoms paraded the seventy-man cavalcade up the road. Ben, Kosterlinsky, and Don Juan Pedro Elias sat their horses in front of the house and waited for them. Margarita stayed by the fire under the ramada, making a pot of coffee.

Vincent wore riding breeches, polished jodhpurs, and a straight-brimmed campaign hat. He carried his pistol in a holster on his belly. Sometime on his way to La Acequia, his face had turned pale and skinny.

Odoms could have chosen a better horse. This one was limber-necked and head-shy.

Senator Royal Vincent was dressed like his brother, except that he wore a big floppy hat, long military jacket with epaulets.

The cavalcade stopped in front of Ben. Vincent said, "Cowden, we're here, finally, to settle accounts. I see you've removed the cattle from the Buena Vista. You have taken my cattle off my land. I give you five minutes to show how you will pay me restitution in the amount of one hundred thousand dollars for cattle trespass on the Buena Vista and the San Rafael. Also, you will turn over all VO cattle in your possession."

"You're in no position to demand anything this morning, Mr. Vincent," Ben said.

"Are you blind? I have seventy armed Pima County deputies here, authorized to enforce my orders."

"I warned you against this, Duncan," Kosterlinsky said. "What you are doing amounts to a filibuster. You've been doing business to your heart's content in Mexico, but you can't run roughshod over me and the laws I am sworn to uphold. If you do not turn your men around and leave this minute, I will put you all under arrest."

"Anyone who gets in our way will be killed," Vincent said. "We're here with Senator Vincent on an official mission for the Pima County Sheriff to reclaim my property."

"Mr. Vincent, you can talk, but don't make one aggressive move because you're standing in the middle of an ambush," Ben said.

Vincent was a lot more confident in the men behind him than the men were. The posse unconsciously moved its horses closer together.

"Enough talk," Odoms said. "These greasers'll never pay you, Duncan. We've come for the cattle. Let's just ride in and take them." He spurred his horse ahead of the cavalcade and rode threateningly toward Ben. "Get out of my way!" he shouted.

Odoms was accustomed to having fighting men behind him. He should have looked back. Vincent and company sat back, watched him, and bunched closer together.

Odoms came too close, and Ben waved his rifle at the head-shy horse. The horse ducked away and bolted as though a gun had gone off in his ear, then balked on his front feet. Odoms dug in with every fingernail and spur to stay on. When he finally sat up straight again, he raised his rifle to his shoulder. A rifle bullet from Ben's left drilled through Odoms's horse's head and dropped him. Les and Mark rode into sight out of the river forest, Les's rifle smoking. Odoms scrambled to get his leg out from under his horse. Les and Mark rode up and brought their rifles to bear on the two Vincents. Not one of the VO posse touched a weapon.

The Vincents backed their horses toward the protection of the constables. The constables backed away from them and gave them room. The shots had made the posse horses easy to back up.

Odoms freed himself, stood up, located Les, and raised his rifle. Ben spurred his horse into his side, cut him off from the posse, and knocked him down. He regained his feet, and Ben ran Toots's shoulder into him again, driving him toward the house like a balky steer. Kosterlinsky shouted an order, and three Rurales rushed out from behind both sides of the house to seize Odoms.

Odoms fired the rifle from his hip as the Rurales reached the front of the ramada. He fired only one bullet. It struck Margarita as she stood by the fire keeping the coffee hot. The young woman closed her eyes, crumpled against the mud wall, and settled to the ground. She wilted and smeared the wall with her blood before the eyes of the startled men.

Odoms dropped the rifle. The Rurales recovered and tied his hands behind his back.

Ben carried Margarita into the house and laid her on a cot. She had been hit above the heart. He tore off her pantaloons to use as a compress for the wound and thought to himself, Well, you must be the best man for this job. You know how to find her underwear well enough. He turned her on her side, and the sight of the shattered wound in her back made him look at his hands and see all the blood. His anxiety almost stopped his heart. His hat would not have plugged that wound. He laid her down gently.

Margarita's eyes had that same red animal glare in them he'd seen when she was sick in the hotel. It was not a hateful look. It was a wild mean look an animal used just before it bolted to get away. She had gone absolutely limp except for that look.

"Pichoncita," he said. "Little pigeon."

"I was watching you and stumbled like the pichoncita."

"I know."

"I would have begged you."

"No. I wouldn't have let you beg me."

The red glare faded, and she died.

The room filled with men. Ben became aware of Don Juan Pedro and Pepe weeping and holding Margarita's hands beside him, the room full of men. Each man took a turn to say, *"Lástima. Pobrecita.* What a shame. The poor little thing." Someone handed Ben a tin cup full of mescal, and he took a fat swallow of it.

He closed Margarita's eyes for her, moved away, and sat against the wall. He did not know how long he stayed in the house, but when he finally went outside, Koster-linsky had turned Vincent's posse around, heading him toward Arizona.

Ben walked over and stared into Vincent's craven face.

The face was not angry, red, or pale anymore. It was sick with bald cowardice.

"You love bringing the fight to the women, don't you, you son-of-a-bitch."

"It's regrettable . . . er . . . uh, Cowden, but you're the one who said for me not to expect mercy from your women."

"You've had mercy from the women from the start, you bastard. The women hoped our differences could be settled in a decent manner. Regard for our women has held us in check, but there'll be no more gentlemanliness in this fight, Vincent. From now on, we'll settle for nothing less than scattering your hide, hair, and life's blood all over this country."

Ben stepped back and addressed Royal Vincent and the rest of the posse. "Before you ever show up in this fight again, tell your mothers and sweethearts good-bye, because they'll never hear from you again. We'll take you alive one by one and drag you with horses and scatter your parts so thin there won't be enough left of you to bury. Don't fool yourselves by thinking we won't remember who you are. We won't ever be able to forget your cowardly faces."

"Listen, Cowden. These men didn't have anything to do with the woman's killing. Odoms did that, and it looked like an accident."

"You caused the accident by forcing your way here, Vincent. You ought to hang for it."

"No. Talk to Odoms about that. If you have to hang somebody, hang Odoms, or shoot him, or drag him, but don't blame me or these constables." Vincent moved his horse away.

"You want justice? Get down off that horse and fight me," Ben said. "Let's you and I settle this right now. Nobody else has to suffer anymore."

"I'm not armed."

"Arm yourself, then."

"I won't. I'm not a fighter, and I don't know anything

about firearms, so I never carry one. Nobody in this country would shoot an unarmed man, not even you. You hurt me, you hang."

"That rule is getting awful flimsy with me, Vincent. It won't protect you forever."

"No, but it'll do for today."

Kosterlinsky's Rurales escorted Vincent and his posse back to the border. Kosterlinsky and three Rurales stayed close to Odoms to protect him. Ben followed when Kosterlinsky took Odoms behind the house to chain him. Odoms relaxed on a long bench, his back against the wall.

"Where will you take this son-of-a-bitch?" Ben asked Kosterlinsky in English. He did not want the Sonorans to understand this conversation.

"To the presidio, Ben. And then probably to Hermosillo for safekeeping."

"No," Ben said.

"I think that is the best course."

"No. Ley de fuga is indicated."

"No, Benjamin. You know I'm no good at that."

Ben thought, I'm counting on that. He said, "For once in your life, do something right. Fix it so the rotten bastard doesn't see the sun go down."

"No, Ben." But Kosterlinsky's look said "Yes, Ben."

Ben felt better after that. He and his brothers joined their companions and dug Margarita's grave. They wrapped her in a clean tarp and covered her with the rocky loam of the Buena Vista.

After that, Kosterlinsky and his Rurales left with Odoms for Santa Cruz. Ben helped turn the cattle out of the pasture so they could scatter to their favorite haunts. After Colorado, Pepe, Chapito, and Don Juan Pedro drove away to get the priest in Nogales, Ben and his brothers cleaned up Margarita's blood. Then he went and sat by her grave and smoked his pipe. At sundown, he and his brothers headed home.

*   *   *

Kosterlinsky and his Rurales took Odoms out on the old trail through the saddle where Ben and his brothers had ambushed the Texans. At sundown, he placed his men along the trail at a place where the northeast slope of the San Antonios stretched away toward the flats of the Buena Vista range.

He led Odoms's horse out in front of the troop and untied his hands. "Get off the horse, Jack," he said.

Odoms looked Kosterlinsky in the eye. "What for?"

"This is where you get off."

"You letting me go, Gabriel?"

"Yes, letting you go, Jack."

"Duncan tell you to do it?"

"Yes, Jack. Duncan told me to do it."

"I'll keep the horse, then."

"No, Jack. You go afoot."

"Why?"

"That's ley de fuga, Jack."

"You think you're giving me ley de fuga? How you going to explain that to Duncan?"

"It's Duncan's orders."

"Come on, Gabriel."

Kosterlinsky smiled into Odoms's eyes. "Don't beg, Jack. I'm angry enough to kill you, so you'll just have to take your chances like every other fortunate son-of-a-screw does when he is granted ley de fuga."

"You mean it, Gabriel?"

Kosterlinsky took out a cigar, put the tip in his jaw teeth, and struck a match to it. "Run for your life, Jack."

Odoms turned and started walking down the slope. Kosterlinsky led the horse away. Odoms manifested his normal insolence for the first few steps. Kosterlinsky let him go ten yards like that, then drew his saber.

"*Prepáren!* Ready!" he barked.

Odoms's right leg jerked involuntarily to take flight, but he controlled it and strolled on.

"*Aaapúnten!* Aim!"

Odoms started running smoothly, effortlessly, straight downhill.

Kosterlinsky watched him with great interest, and this time he really shouted the order. "*Fuego!* Fire!"

Odoms waggled his tail, zigzagged, and cut sharply to the right. The Rurales' bullets struck the ground in a close group five yards behind him.

Kosterlinsky's slanted Indian eyes narrowed with humor. "Fuego!" he shouted again.

Odoms zagged to his left, and the Rurales' bullets struck the ground three feet behind him.

Kosterlinsky waited until Odoms was about to duck into an oak thicket. "Fuego!"

The group struck the ground ten yards to the right of target. Odoms looked back over his shoulder once and disappeared into the thicket. Kosterlinsky smiled, barely. "*Lástima*, a shame!" he said.

Odoms headed for Texas. He knew the way. He had already spent most of that day traveling the same ground. It did not seem so far to go this time. He did not find Sycamore Canyon right away though. He crossed it, went up La Providencia Canyon, and did not know he was mistaken until he saw the miner's cabin. He found the trail and walked back over the ridge to Sycamore. He stopped at the creek, lay down on his belly, and drank sparingly. He would come back and drink more after he'd dug up the alazanas.

He found his shovel on the north slope, went to the bush where he had buried the panniers, started digging, and found nothing. He straightened, wiped sweat off his brow, looked around, saw the right bush, and dug for nothing again. He looked around again, went back to the first bush, and dug for nothing all around it. This time, he started cussing before he stopped digging. He looked around and saw no other likely bushes. He threw back his head and wailed to the sky like a wolf.

"It's not there, Odoms," Ben said. He stepped out of the night shadow into the moonlight so Odoms could see him. "For you, it's not anywhere."

"I'm not armed, Cowden."

"I don't believe you."

Ben's first bullet sent him staggering down the hill. Ben followed him and hit him with every shot until he emptied his rifle.

The last bullet landed Odoms dead on his face in the creek.

J.P.S. Brown

has been one of the most respected writers of the American Southwest for the past two decades. If you enjoyed **THE ARIZONA SAGA** Book 3: **LADINO**, you will want to read his acclaimed first novel

JIM KANE

Turn the page for an exciting preview from JIM KANE, on sale in August 1991 wherever Bantam Books are sold.

An arriero is a driver of animals. A drover. If a man herds a bunch of cattle or a remuda of horses or drives a packtrain of mules or one burro loaded with firewood, he is an arriero. Arrieros usually are horseback. A person who drives a car is not called an arriero but a good saying has been passed down from the time when there were no cars. With this phrase a man might answer politely, with meaning, a lady who thanks him for fixing her flat tire: "Arrieros somos. En el camino andamos. Algun día nos encontramos." "We are drovers. We travel the road. Someday we are bound to meet."

Guadalajara, Jalisco, is one thousand miles from Frontera, Sonora, on the U.S. border. Jim Kane hoped that he wasn't going to be rained on every mile of the way. He loved rain the way any man who had been raised on a droughty ranch in Arizona loved rain. But Jim Kane was on this road to Frontera in the rainy season of September with five truckloads, fifty head, of Mexican Appaloosa horses he had bought in Guadalajara. The trucks had been under continuous cloudburst for ten hours from Guadalajara to Acaponeta and now, at 3 A.M., were stalled in Acaponeta because none of the town's gas stations were open.

Kane climbed into the back of a truck and tried once again to help the old mare to her feet. She was down in six inches of mud, manure, urine, and rainwater with her head wedged in a forward corner. She was on her side with her legs doubled against the rack of the truck. Kane pushed against the mass of horseflesh around her to make room so he could drag the old mare out of the corner by the tail. The black rain redoubled and the whole storm seemed to Kane to be funneled into the truck onto his bare head and bare back. The horses hunched their backs against the storm and bowed their heads under each other's bellies and would not budge for Kane. He gave up and climbed over the rack and jumped to the ground. He washed manure and mud off himself from a deep puddle of rainwater on the ground by the truck. He opened the door of the cab and got his dry shirt and leather jacket from under the head of the sleeping driver. He got his hat from the top of the seat and walked over to the shelter of the gas station the trucks were parked by. He sopped the water off himself with a handkerchief already wet from being in his hip pocket. He put on his shirt, jacket, and hat and lit a cigarette.

A goddam gully-washer, he thought. Just what we need. A toad-chokin', horse-drownin', frog-stranglin', snake-floatin' gully-washer. Cowboys in the dry country would be happy to call a rain like this names like that. We went years on the ranch where I grew up when it didn't seem to rain as much as it has rained on me in the last hour. I only weighed a hundred pounds when I was fifteen years old I was so dried out. When we finally starved out completely my dad traded one hundred and eighty square miles of drought country for a thirty-room auto court in the cool pines near streams and lakes of cold water so he could live out the rest of his life in a place where he could have a sweet drink of water any time he wanted one. Now I'm thirty years old, weigh two hundred pounds, and a gully-washer is putting me out of business.

One of the drivers of the five stock trucks, a tall, energetic young man with mussed hair and eyes that were trying to come awake too soon, said "Buenos días" to start his day and came over and began pacing around the station. He stopped by the window of the office and cursed.

"Someone is in there," he told Kane. He pounded

loudly on the door. "He's alive! Wake up!" he shouted, and pounded again.

The master of the nightwatch of the Acaponeta station came to the door buttoning his pants.

"What do you want?" he asked.

"Gasoline, what else?" the tall driver said.

"We are closed," the master of the station said.

"Well, open us," the tall driver said.

"How much gasoline do you want?"

"The five tanks of the trucks. You sell gasoline, don't you?"

The master of the station finished displaying his act of buttoning his pants before the customers he might or might not serve and turned back into the office and switched on the lights of the station. Kane went to the truck he rode in and roused his driver, a short, solemn little man. The driver drove the truck up beside the pumps. The station-master came out stuffing a huge .45 automatic pistol into his belt. He shuffled around the truck to the pumps, stopped, looked at the pumps, and turned to Kane.

"Do you want that of a *peso* or that of eighty *centavos*?" he asked.

"*Peso* gas," Jim Kane said.

The attendant turned back, shifted the pistol to a more comfortable position between the belt and the large belly, cranked the pump, and filled the truck's tank with gas. He kept squirting the nozzle after the tank was full and gas belched onto the pavement. He squirted the nozzle again for good measure. This last squirt also ran out onto the pavement. Now he was sure the tank was full. He screwed the cap back on the tank and hung the hose on the pump.

Kane was in the dry cab of the truck and the caravan was headed up the road again when he felt that he might, possibly, be a fool. He thought, no one rides horses anymore and here I am with all my stake invested on this road in fifty head of scraggy, stunted studs, mares, and colts that will look so bad when I get them to the U.S. that no one but me will want them. I am their husband and I'd better be in love with them because I'm probably going to be stuck with them for quite a while until someone else can see how a buck can be made on them. By that time I will be broke again. I will be a day late and a dollar short again.

This had been the suspicion eating at him since he had turned loose the money for the old mare and now it took a big bite out of him. He did not state this suspicion to himself often but it was an empty-pockets feeling he got when he thought of his future with the horses. Not the feeling of being broke a man had when he had a job and was earning only a little money but the feeling of physical loss a man kept after he had lost a full pocket of money. Kane had brought $5,000 with him to Mexico to buy these horses. Now he had the horses and only $80 in his pocket and the freight paid to Frontera. His dad had once told him because he loved him, "Stay out of the horse business, Jim Kane."

No, Jim Kane said to himself. I also heard my dad swear once that he would never trade another horse, buy another Brahma steer, run another horse race, or marry again and within six months of that oath he had committed all four of those mistakes again. I am going to find a big demand for fifty-inch-tall Appaloosa horses instantly on arriving with them on the border. I am going to sell for a profit so big I will be able to come back down this road again and buy twice as many of these colorful little horses. These little horses will make me independent in my pursuit of happiness and give me extra money for singing and dancing along the way. After all, who else has ever done this? I am the first. No one in the horse business knows that central Mexico is full of little Appaloosas. The ponies are just the right size for twelve- to sixteen-year-old kids. They have the greatest variety of color of any Appaloosas I have ever seen. How about that blue and white polkadotted stud riding in the third truck up there ahead of us? They are not dwarfy like the Shetland or the Welch ponies. They have full manes and tails, not ratty ones like the U.S. Appaloosas. Just let's look at it this way, have faith in the way these little horses will charm the Western riders club members and their twelve- to sixteen-year-old kids.

Yes, and faith is what Don Quixote had when he was battling giants as he tilted with the windmill. And he promised Sancho Panza that after the battle he would be rich enough so that he would be able to give Sancho a dukedom or at least an earldom.

No. Keep faith. You have to now. You married these horses so now stay with them. The trouble with you is you are tired.

The rain was misty now in the daylight under the solid clouds as the trucks went on up the road. A slender man in his loose white garments and stiff-brimmed straw hat stepped out of the broad-leafed jungle by the road to walk out of the mud onto the pavement. He carried a machete and he walked in his tire-soled huaraches looking straight ahead and not looking at the trucks as they streamed by him spraying a coarse mist with their tires. He was going to work early. Kane envied the man because he was walking freely and unpreoccupied in a simpler pursuit of his happiness than Kane. After the trucks had passed the man, Kane thought, maybe soon I'll have myself a little place down here to raise these little horses and I'll have a man like that to help me.

In the morning the man will go one way walking in that free, graceful placing of his huaraches and I'll go another way horseback. I'll look over my mares and see if that fine sorrel mare has foaled yet. I'll fix some fence and make a circle looking for jaguar tracks to see if any have been around the mares in the night. In the evening I'll ride back to the house through a forest of *nopal* so thick I won't be able to see the house until I am in the clearing. At the corral

I'll take a dusty foot out of the stirrup and get down off my horse and call my son, when and if I have one, to me to help me unsaddle. He'll tell me in fine Spanish how he and the dog captured an iguana but the dog had fatally wounded the iguana and it had only just finished dying. The man who helps me will return at about that time and discuss the capture of the iguana with me and the boy and give a quiet observation about the habits of iguana which I will remember the rest of my life. The boy will remember it longer because he will have a longer life and I will have learned about the iguana much later in life than he did.

The sun was out on the road and an iguana, an ancestor of the animal Jim Kane's boy would one day capture, speared his way across the road in front of the truck Kane was riding in. He was a long, emerald streak. His long tail, held high at the base, seemed to lift him and rudder him as he flew an inch above the dark, water-shiny pavement. Many other iguanas, not as wise or as fast as Kane's boy's iguana's ancestor, had been caught by the tires of machines on the road and were no longer jewel-like living spears but were now muddy grease spots.

The man, the boy, and I will go to the house and sit down at a table under the porch. My wife, when and if I ever have one, will bring us hot coffee while we talk over what became of the day. The boy will drink one-third coffee and two-thirds hot milk and plenty of sugar. The man will have half and half and plenty of sugar. I will have mine black with no sugar and I won't have to tell my wife how to brew it as I will love just the way she does it. I will love her more each time she does it because she loves to do it so much.

Maybe she will have a dogied horse colt she is raising on a bottle because a jaguar got his mother. This colt might be living by the kitchen door, still weak and too timid to fight the many flies around his eyes, while the man and I discuss how we are going to get the *tigre* that killed the colt's mother. The boy and his mother, together, will put salve on the colt's eyes.

We will not use poison on the *tigre*, we say, we want more vengeance than that. We'll let the blood out of him and have him killed close to us so we can get his hide to hang on the wall. That is the only honorable way to kill a *tigre* on his way to putting us out of business. A *tigre* like that, a killer of the gentle, an *acebado*, would be the only kind of *tigre* I would ever kill. The man will excuse himself after this discussion and say he wants to go home a different way to cut for the jaguar's tracks before dark. Inside, while I'm lighting the lamps and getting ready for supper, I'll consider that a man like the one who is helping me is surely a fine man.

Jim Kane slept for more than a hundred miles and woke up to another heavy rain. The road was deeper under water and the trucks had slowed. They came to Culiacan in the night. The city was dark, probably from a power failure caused by the storm. At the edge of town, the authorities directed the trucks across the river through the water because they were not confident of the strength of the bridge. In the dark town in the black rain the people waded in a foot of water on the sidewalks in the lights of the trucks going by. When the trucks stopped for gas, Kane undressed in the cab and climbed into the back of the truck in his shorts and boots to see if he could help the old mare back to her feet. She was still down in the corner in the muck. The other mares around her had not done her much damage by stepping on her since horses naturally hate stepping on any living thing. But her own efforts had hurt her. She had banged her head so much against the corner of the rack in her efforts to get up that both her eyes were grotesquely swollen. Kane worked with her while the trucks were serviced and the drivers ate their supper, but he failed to help her.

Anyone would say she would be no great loss. She was

an old *canela*, cinnamon-colored, mare. She was parrot-mouthed and dead of hair but she had a fine filly colt. The filly was a wide-chested, straight-legged colt and she had a clean, white blanket over her rear with purple spots on the blanket. The mama had come along only because the filly was too young to wean.

Kane had six mares like the old *canela*. All were making this trip because they had that one, saving grace; they had given birth to fine offspring that needed them. Kane was sure the old mares wouldn't bring four bits when their colts were weaned. Anyone could tell him that. But Kane liked them. They would be called a bad investment but he wasn't sorry to be husbanding them. They looked like Don Quixote's Rocinante. They were peak-hipped, fork-legged, cow-hocked, calf-kneed, slack-lipped, and sparse of hair. Yes, but look how far and with how willing a heart Rocinante carried Don Quixote. It wasn't Rocinante's concern that Don Quixote was a madman. If Rocinante had been well fed and nicely groomed for it he might very well have served Richard the Lionhearted. He certainly had the heart for it. So how does jousting with grown men require any finer or more noble an effort than jousting with windmills to a horse like Rocinante? The old cinnamon mare was still trying her best to get up onto her own feet and make a living after thirty hours of being down in the muck. Kane still felt she might get up if he had some help and a dry, sunny day.

"Pheeootah!" the little driver said when he got back to the truck. "How you stink, man!" He found a clean cloth and wiped the manure and water off the seat covers in the cab. "These are my new seat covers, man," he said, folding the cloth carefully and putting it back in its place under the seat.

"They clean easily, don't they?" Kane said, laughing at him. The driver didn't answer but started the motor and let the truck idle and stared at his lights through the rain while the other trucks started up and pulled away from the station.

By noon the next day they were in Guaymas. The sun was out and the temperature was close to one hundred and ten degrees with not a breath of air moving when the trucks stopped in Guaymas for gas.

Kane got his driver and the tall driver to help him with the old mare. He climbed into the slop with all his clothes on because it was Sunday and the station was crowded with people. He tied a rope around the old mare's girth and threw it over a beam that ran across the center of the truck above the rack. He pulled on the rope and the two men on the ground held the slack over the beam. When he and the two men had lifted the mare three feet off the deck, Kane got under her with his back against her belly and lifted her to her feet. He stepped out from under her. The old mare swayed on her own feet. Her eyes were swollen as big as softballs. The hair on her side and hips had been scalded off by the hot, briny muck. She looked like an old, abused praying mantis but she was standing again. She had been down in that corner for forty hours. She breathed a deep sigh.

Kane climbed down off the rack, proud of the old mare. He didn't care that he was covered with the hot slime she had been lying in.

"You are not riding in my truck on my new seat covers as nauseating as you are now," the little driver said to Jim Kane. Kane smiled at him, not believing him, and reached for the door handle.

"No," the driver said and when Kane looked at him he saw the man was unhappy. He did not share Kane's sense of accomplishment. He did not consider Kane fit company on the road anymore. He was not going to be a Christian about Kane's filthiness.

"What is your problem?" the tall driver asked the little

driver. "I suppose you think you are going to leave the man here?"

"It is not my problem what happens to him," the little driver said solemnly. "Not even his own mother would ride with him."

"Stupid! It is only a little manure of a horse. Horses have clean manure. You act as though you never saw a little manure before."

"Only a little manure? Look in the back of my truck. A ton of *mierda* and urines of a horse. I won't stand for any of it inside my cabin. We have been fifty hours on the road now with very little sleep because we have not been able to stop long enough because we are hauling those ghosts and they might die on the road. And now this man wants to deposit more slop inside my cabin. No. I'm sorry. If he likes it so much he can ride in the back with his beasts. He is not riding with me. I am not a beast."

"Of course you're not. I can't stand it any longer myself," Kane said. "Pardon me, I have been in too much of a hurry. Wait a few minutes and I'll clean up." He got his suitcase and went to the men's room and washed and changed. When he got back to the truck the little driver had spread rags over the seat to make sure Kane didn't dirty his seatcovers anymore.

The old cinnamon mare stayed on her feet to Hermosillo, where Kane unloaded the horses and fed and rested them in the stockyards of the Cattleman's Union for a night and a day. She stayed on her feet all through the next night to Frontera. She walked off the truck under her own power at the Cattleman's Union corrals in Frontera and Kane's investment in her and the other forty-nine head was still intact.

The next day the American veterinarians took blood samples of the horses. Kane caught them one by one and held them while the vets bled them. The samples would be sent to Washington, D.C., to be tested for infectious diseases of horses.

The temperature was one hundred and five degrees, heavy clouds were building up, and the humidity was high. The vets chose the hottest time of the day to work the horses, the time of Mexican siesta between noon and 3 P.M.

After Kane had roped and eared down the thirty-sixth of his fifty horses for the vets, he began seeing everything in the corral from the end of a long, dark tunnel. He caught the thirty-seventh horse, a five-year-old bronc stud. He was leading the stud through a gate when the stud spooked and ran over the top of Kane. Kane had a trick knee, a knee that had been operated on but had not been remedied by the operation. The stud ran into that knee and knocked Kane down. The knee responded by going numb and then catching fire, a white fire that matched the white suffocation of the day in the corral.

The vets and their helpers stood in the shade of the *ramadas* and watched Kane pick himself up and catch the stud again. He led the stud to the shade. He hung on to the stud's ear as though they were handlebars and got hold of one of the ears with his jaw teeth.

He was watching the vet, an old man with a very unsteady hand, trying to find the vein in the throat with the needle. The tunnel he had been seeing everything through for the past thirty minutes began to lengthen and narrow. All he could see now was the man's hand, the syringe, and the place in the horse's neck where he was trying to jab the needle. Then all Kane could see was the needle and the dirty thumb punching and probing the neck for the vein. The poor little stud was so thin that not much blood was coursing there. Then all that was left to see was the old, trembling thumb of the vet. Kane forgot about the corral and left it and went sailing far away from the tight hold he had on the stud. He passed out and the vets hauled him to the hospital with heat exhaustion.

Before he recovered in the hospital, Will Ore, the broker, came to visit him with the results of the blood test of his horses. Will Ore specialized in the import and export of livestock. He had corrals on the Arizona side of the border. He was from Oklahoma and like most dark-complexioned men from that state did not deny his Indian blood. He had a tendency to get fat but running the corrals and chasing cattlemen and Mexican politicians kept him worn down to a frazzle. His good humor kept the frazzle from tearing off at the ends.

He told Jim Kane that all the old mares like the cinnamon mare had tested out clean and healthy but four of the best mares were suffering from durine, a venereal disease of horses. That is, they had been suffering before Will had shot and burned them by order of the American vets. He had also removed and burned all the manure in the corral the horses had occupied. Kane was going to have to pay Will for the removal of the manure and the complete disinfecting of all the fences and troughs. A padlock had been snapped on the corral and the horses had been put under quarantine for thirty days. They would be bled again in fifteen days and again when their quarantine was over. If the two tests showed that the remaining horses were healthy, they would be free to cross the border into the U.S. after the thirty-day quarantine.

"Boy, you have been catastrophed," Will Ore said, laughing at Kane, who up to that moment had been having a good time resting in the hospital.

"I should take on a relapse and stay in bed. You shouldn't come here with news like that," Kane said.

"Don't relapse until you cross your horses and pay me for burning the mares and disinfecting the corrals. Boy, how did you get into this kind of mess?"

"Bad luck," Kane said.

"I only hope you aren't in for twenty years of bad luck

like a Chinaman. They say a Chinaman's real bad luck lasts for twenty years," Will Ore said.

"Don't worry. I'll have plenty of buyers looking at the horses in these thirty days. They are too poor to sell now anyway. This will give me a chance to put a little meat on their bones. I'll probably have them sold to someone by the time they cross the border. A lot can happen in thirty days."

"Yeah, and a lot of bad can happen to you in *three* days. I've seen that," Will Ore said. "Your banker came to my office. He had heard of your bad luck. I didn't tell him anything, though."

"Hell, I don't care. Tell him the truth if he asks you again. He has a right to know. We're partners."

"It looks like you and I are partners too. I've spent a lot of money myself on your horses and I'll have more in them when they cross. How much do you owe the banker?"

"Only my left eyeball but the note isn't due for six weeks," Kane said.

The author of **In the Season of the Sun** and **Scalpdancers** begins a multigenerational saga that will span the history of America, as seen through the lives of one family.

THE MEDAL

From a nation born of strife and christened with patriots' blood, there arose a dynasty of soldiers. They were the McQueens of America -- a clan hungry for adventure; a family whose fiery spirit would kindle the flame of a country's freedom. Keeping that flame from blazing into tyranny through the generations would take more than merely courage and determination. It would take a sacred secret: the proud legacy they called THE MEDAL.

Look for the first two books in this series,

THE MEDAL BOOK ONE: GUNS OF LIBERTY
THE MEDAL BOOK TWO: SWORD OF VENGEANCE

on sale wherever Bantam Domain Books are sold.

AN239 -- 2/91

TERRY C. JOHNSTON

Winner of the prestigious Western Writer's award, Terry C. Johnston brings you his award-winning saga of mountain men Josiah Paddock and Titus Bass who strive together to meet the challenges of the western wilderness in the 1830's.

☐ 25572 **CARRY THE WIND–Vol. I** $4.95

☐ 26224 **BORDERLORDS–Vol. II** $4.95

☐ 28139 **ONE-EYED DREAM–Vol. III** $4.95

The final volume in the trilogy begun with *Carry the Wind* and *Borderlords*, ONE-EYED DREAM is a rich, textured tale of an 1830's trapper and his protegé, told at the height of the American fur trade.

Following a harrowing pursuit by vengeful Arapaho warriors, mountain man Titus "Scratch" Bass and his apprentice Josiah Paddock must travel south to old Taos. But their journey is cut short when they learn they must return to St. Louis...and old enemies.

Look for these books wherever Bantam books are sold, or use this handy coupon for ordering:

In The Tradition of *Wagons West* and *The Spanish Bit Saga* Comes:

RIVERS WEST